KING PENGUIN

THE VACILLATIONS OF
POPPY CAREW

Mary Wesley was born near Windsor, England. Her education took her to the London School of Economics, and during the war she worked in The War Office. She has also worked part-time in the antique trade. Mary Wesley has lived in London, France, Italy, Germany, and several places in the West Country. She now lives "rather a hermit's existence" in Devon, England, where she has written five novels. She has previously written for children and claims that her "chief claim to fame is arrested development, getting my first novel published at the age of seventy."

The Vacillations of Poppy Carew

Mary Wesley

A KING PENGUIN
PUBLISHED BY PENGUIN BOOKS

PENGUIN BOOKS
Published by the Penguin Group
Viking Penguin Inc., 40 West 23rd Street,
New York, New York 10010, U.S.A.
Penguin Books Ltd, 27 Wrights Lane, London W8 5TZ, England
Penguin Books Australia Ltd, Ringwood,
Victoria, Australia
Penguin Books Canada Limited, 2801 John Street,
Markham, Ontario, Canada L3R 1B4
Penguin Books (N.Z.) Ltd, 182–190 Wairau Road,
Auckland 10, New Zealand

Penguin Books Ltd, Registered Offices: Harmondsworth,
Middlesex, England

First published in Great Britain by
Macmillan London Limited 1986
Published in Penguin Books 1988

LIBRARY OF CONGRESS CATALOGING IN PUBLICATION DATA
Wesley, Mary.
The vacillations of Poppy Carew/Mary Wesley.
p. cm.
ISBN 0 14 01.0828 9
I. Title.
PR6073.E753V3   1988
823'.914—dc 19   87-30838
CIP

Printed in the United States of America by
R. R. Donnelley & Sons Company, Harrisonburg, Virginia
Set in Bembo

THE VACILLATIONS OF POPPY CAREW

I

On parting with Edmund, Poppy Carew sank into a state of mind where physical need and emotion ceased as though she had been pole-axed. Instinct made her put foot before foot, directed the walk back to her flat, the insertion of key in lock, the closing of the door. Then she lay face-down on the bed, numb, tearless, cold; she did not even kick off her shoes.

Outside, lights came on in the street. London's Saturday night expended itself and, later, the dilatory quiet of Sunday morning expanded into a foggy dawn.

Pride, that ambivalent quality, roused her at her usual hour. She changed into tracksuit and trainers, let herself out of the house and trotted, zombie-like, towards the park. As she ran she felt light-headed from lack of sleep, lack of food and surfeit of emotion. Pride forced her to lope, through the streets of Paddington, across the Bayswater Road into the park. Habit led her padding feet towards the Serpentine, to turn right under the bridge as she usually did. It had not occurred to her that Edmund, also a creature of habit, would tryst his new girl exactly as he had trysted her years before, to meet and kiss in the shadow of the bridge, standing locked, their reflections wavering in the water a few feet away, broken by a passing duck, re-forming as they stood welded together by their fresh and enjoyable desire.

Poppy knew exactly what her successor felt like, knew the allure of the word 'tryst' as used by Edmund. She was tempted as she ran past to catch them off balance, with a vigorous push to join their watery reflection. She resisted the impulse, knowing she would

1

stop, reach out her hand, heave them spluttering out, be forced to find something apt to say. I look silly enough as it is, she thought as they stood oblivious of her brief presence. She noticed the wind lift the sweep of hair Edmund combed across his thin patch, remembered suddenly the voice in the night telling her that her father was in hospital. The message thrust swiftly out of mind.

Her father was critically ill, shorthand for dying.

No longer jogging, she raced through the park, forgetting Edmund, knowing herself guilty of purposeful delay in case her father should enquire after Edmund, say 'I told you so'. But I must allow him the last word, the pleasure of being right, it is the least I can do, she thought as she changed her clothes, checked whether she had money for the fare and took the tube to Paddington. The least, and I have never done much. Mixed feelings of resentment and love for her only parent superimposed themselves over grief and anger. She was in the unusual position, for her, of giving her father pleasure. It would make him well, cheer him up, put him in the mood to recover.

She bought a ticket.

But if I can get through this visit without telling him, I can think up something plausible later, she persuaded herself as the train drew out of the station: she felt she might be too raw and sensitive to aprise her parent of the parting.

Parting, she thought disgustedly as the train ran through the suburbs. To her mind, the act of parting was something that was mutual; there was nothing mutual about the parting with Edmund. He had left her.

2

The ward was a large one. Poppy had the impression of beds stretching to infinity, dwindling like the occupants' lives. In each bed lay an old man, grey-faced, white-haired, merging with the white sheets, grey blankets, cream curtains. Some had limbs encased in plaster hoisted by pulleys at improbable angles. Some lay turned away like sad children. Some eyed her with watchful, hostile eyes. Many slept, open-mouthed, oblivious, showing pinkish-grey tongues, putty-coloured teeth. At the foot of a number of beds, a notice clipped to the rail, 'NIL BY MOUTH'.

They had put her father in the geriatric ward.

'Here's your daughter to see you, Mr Carew. Isn't that nice? Wake up, Mr Carew,' said the nurse, bosomy in her white apron over grey dress, strong calves, useful shoes. 'He sleeps a lot,' she said to Poppy.

'I was not asleep.' Poppy's father swivelled eyes which had been fixed on the ceiling. 'Hullo, pet.' His voice grey, shadowy, faded, matching the environment.

'Dad.' She bent to kiss his stubbled cheek, rough and dry. Why hadn't they shaved him?

'You may stay as long as you like,' said the nurse, moving away, smoothing the sheet with a habitual hand as she did so.

'I'll get a chair.' Poppy fetched an orange plastic chair from a stack by the ward door. She averted her gaze from the old men who followed her with their eyes. She felt embarrassed in her bright sweater and trousers. She put the chair by the bed, sat, took her father's hand, cleared her throat, tried to speak.

'What's all this Nil by Mouth then?' She mustered false cheer.

'They are for the chop. Going to be carved up, patched up for a few months, sent home until next time.'

'Dad.' Tears pricked behind her eyes.

'They stop you dying. It's against the rules. No use carving me up.' Speaking tired him.

'Dad.' Her nose hurt from suppressed tears.

'I never cared much for rules.' He was, he implied, beating the system.

'Darling Dad.' She held his hand, feeling it dry and illusive as it lay between hers. It was useless to deny the proximity of that which he had once jeeringly referred to as 'The Great Combine Harvester'.

'So, if there is anything you want to know or say,' her father murmured, 'now is the time. Now or . . .' A new nurse appeared, held his wrist, popped a thermometer into his mouth, chopped off the word 'never'.

Father and daughter's eyes met, gleaming with shared amusement. The nurse shook the thermometer, made a note on the pad at the foot of the bed, moved to the next patient who burst, on her arrival, into a lament of condensed acrimony. The nurse popped the thermometer into his mouth. 'Now then, Mr Prule.' The lament ceased abruptly.

'There's one small thing I've never asked you.' Poppy watched her father, how thin his face had become.

'Yes?'

'Why did you call me Poppy?' A belated question; surely at a time like this there was something more pertinent.

'Poppaea.' He breathed the name.

'I know, but you and everyone call me Poppy it's so—' Why worry about her stupid name now? She could not stop herself.

'She bathed in asses' milk; I was into the Romans just before you were born. I liked the idea. Then there was this horse. I bet on a double, The King of Love and Poppaea. Look them up in the stud book. Poppaea won the Oaks at twenty-five to one and The King of Love romped home at thirty to one. Bit of luck, eh? Then you came and we thought you beautiful, so Poppaea it was. All seemed to tie up. I was working as a milkman at that time. Your mother said nobody would ever spell it right and shortened it to Poppy which reminded her of a wallpaper she'd liked.' He smiled faintly, pausing to catch his breath. 'The other, The King of Love, if you'd been a boy she might have taken a bit more persuading, but she was content with the wallpaper. Not all that keen on horses your mother.' He smiled remembering his wife.

Poppy watched her father. 'I never knew you drove a milk float.' She would resent her mother's frivolity later. To be named for a glorious racehorse was acceptable but wallpaper took some swallowing.

'A *lot* you don't know about me.' There was satisfaction in his faint voice. He rested eyes closed, his breathing an effort.

Watching him, she tried to visualise him young, vigorous, driving a United Dairies van, clinking bottles on to doorsteps in the early morning while fellow citizens lay still asleep or drowsing in their lovers' arms as she and Edmund— Was her father asleep? His eyes were closed.

'I'm awake.'

She tried again.

'And you, Dad. Is there anything you want to tell me?'

'Yes.' His voice was weaker now.

She waited while he mustered his strength, his breath faintly whistling. Suddenly, the fingers, lying lax in her hand, clenched

4

urgently.

'Poppy?'

'I'm here, darling.' She leaned close holding his hand.

'Something I never told you. Didn't want it to influence you. Didn't want that bastard chasing after you because of it. . . .'

'What?' He was tiring, he was a horrible dark grey under the eyes. What sad secret did he feel he should tell her?

'There's a lot of money for you.'

'Oh Dad, please.' His savings would cover funeral expenses, and there was always her holiday money. 'You mustn't worry about. . . .' Her father frowned, tried to pull her closer as she leant towards him.

'We mustn't tire ourselves.' The nurse was back, standing watchfully.

'We'd like a cup of tea, wouldn't we, Mr Carew?'

'Bugger off.' His voice suddenly came out strongly. The nurse moved away, unruffled.

'How is that fellow Edmund, still nosing after you? Done a bit more than nose, hasn't he?' He was bitter now.

'I . . . er . . . we. . . .' Surely Dad had not forgotten they lived together.

'He'll marry you for your money. Live off you, a sponger, a leech.'

'But I have no money.' Where was all that shredded pride?

'Wait until you see my will.'

Poppy grinned at him. If that was her father's idea of a joke, okay, she would string along with him. 'Did you win the pools then?' She tried to laugh, felt banal.

'You could call it that.' There was an expression on his face she had never seen.

'You did not answer me about Edmund.' Tenaciously he returned to his question, desperately his eyes pleaded. 'Platt,' he sneered at Edmund's surname.

If I tell him I shall break down, she thought. If I cry I will upset him. Oh God, this is horrible. Why did I come? I could have pretended not to get the message, caught the later train.

Effortfully, her father was speaking again. 'Get that fiend to prop me up.'

'The nurse?'

'Who else?'

Poppy signalled. Two nurses came, heaved her father up. Punched pillows, propped him up like some dreadful baby. One of them smoothed his hair with a possessive but offhand gesture. All about the ward, nurses tidied patients whose relatives and friends came bustling in with flowers, sweets, fruit, letters, books, get-well cards. Visiting hour, with its bonhomie, had begun, time to hide the bedpans.

'There's a fellow advertising in the *Field*.'

She leant close to hear. 'Yes?' This position was making her back ache.

'Furnival's Fun Funerals. You'll see, I've marked it.'

'Furnival's Fun Funerals?'

'Yes.' Her father's voice was fainter now. 'I want one. Horse hearse, plumes, mutes, the lot, I want one. Something to look forward to. Think you could organise that?'

'I'll have a bash.' Why have I never given him what he wanted while he was alive? she mourned.

'Pricey.'

'That won't matter if you are so rich.' Her voice sounded jocose.

'So what's happened to Edmund?' He was back on the track, remorseless. 'Platt.' His voice a hoarse whisper.

'He's found a rich divorcée. Very pretty. He's chucked me, Dad. He's going to marry her.' There it is, out, like a bad tooth: I am giving him all he wants. Giving him my unbearable hurt and pain. Giving him something he wants while he's alive to enjoy it. Her eyes swam with angry tears, she hated her father.

'Oh, ho, ho, *ho*! How *lovely*! Ouch!' Bob Carew let out a rattling shout. His head fell to one side and his hand lay, lifeless, in Poppy's. He dribbled.

A nurse came up with a rustle and a swish, rattled the curtain round the bed with one hand, felt for the non-existent pulse with the other, frowned at Poppy. 'Look what you've done,' she hissed. 'He should have lasted until after visiting hour.'

'That will do, nurse.' The ward sister stood now beside Poppy, who looked at her father with wonder.

'Is he dead?' He died laughing, she thought with satisfaction, at least I gave him that.

'Yes, dear.'

'Don't you dare call me dear,' Poppy shouted at the ward sister. 'I

6

am not your dear. I will not be called dear by you.' She began to cry loudly, messily, unrestrainedly, her breath coming in angry hiccups. She bent to kiss the dead face, her tears dripping into its open mouth. 'He wanted me to have this.' She snatched at a copy of the *Field* topping a stack of magazines on the locker by the bed. 'Wasn't it wonderful that he died laughing?' She shouted, 'Wasn't it marvellous? I made him die laughing.' She stood by her father's bed, staring at the ward sister until tears blinded her.

'You'll upset my other patients.' Sister had Poppy by the arm, was leading her towards the door.

'They are not upset. They are loving it. They are still *alive*,' Poppy shouted.

An old man, destined for the operating theatre (Nil by Mouth) made a thumbs-up sign as the sister pushed Poppy towards the swing doors into the corridor.

'Nurse, bring Miss Carew a cup of tea in my office.'

'I don't want your fucking tea,' Poppy yelled.

'Good on you,' croaked another old man.

The sister pushed Poppy into her office, forced her down on to a chair.

'Shut up,' she said. 'Be quiet.'

Poppy sat. 'I think I'm going to be sick,' she said in her normal voice.

3

At about the time Bob Carew was dying, Willy Guthrie was crossing the Park to lunch with an old cousin who had offered to buy from him a house he had inherited from his mother who had died the previous year. The capital realised would enormously help the expansion of his present enterprise, relieve him of worry.

As he walked Willy compared the faded London grass with the sweet-smelling turf on his farm and looked forward to the day's end which would find him back home breathing country smells instead of petrol fumes, hearing country sounds instead of London's roar.

He was a contented man, free – here Willy crossed his fingers – of emotional entanglements, happy with the life he had chosen to lead. Looking down his long Scottish nose at the citizens of London taking their lunchtime break in the park, Willy pitied them and marvelled that he had endured several years of city slog before opting for self-employment and the challenge of running a farm. He felt no regret for the large salary and safe prospects he had chucked in favour of agriculture and was even glad that his present profession was more robust and risky than the lyrical idyll he had falsely imagined it to be when he started. Even his ulcers, should he get them, would be, he felt, of a healthier sort than those of Lombard Street aficionadoes.

His cousin was waiting for him in the bar of his club, a double gin at his elbow.

'You look very well,' he said resentfully, eyeing Willy's sun-browned face, taking Willy's hard, brown hand in his pale city paw.

'What will you drink?'

'Vodka.' Willy subsided into a chair beside the old man who thought Willy horribly tall and healthy and that his dark eyes and springy hair made him look a gypsy in this discreet rather academic environment.

'This is rather an academic club,' said the cousin hoping to make Willy feel bucolic. It was important to assume the upper hand, he lived in London and was of the opinion that people who lived in the country were less sharp than those in the capital.

'I wouldn't have guessed,' said Willy grinning at his cousin who remembered rather belatedly that Willy's degree at university had been rather good whereas he in his day had gone down before taking his finals.

'You have your mother's eyes,' said the old man uneasily. 'Shall we go in to lunch and discuss her house, yours now of course. I had a soft spot for your mother.'

First I've heard of it, thought Willy following his host into the dining room and it certainly was not reciprocated. Too late he wondered why he had let himself in for this meeting.

An old waitress handed him the menu.

'The Irish stew is good today,' she said persuasively.

To please her – she looked weary – Willy agreed to the stew.

'The food in this club is disgusting,' said the cousin, 'but it's cheap.'

Willy, who during his banking period had had occasion to learn his cousin's income and assets, stiffened at this parsimonious remark.

'Why do you want to buy my mother's house?' he asked, leaping to the point of the meeting without preamble.

His cousin flushed. He had prepared what he thought of as his orderly mind for other tactics, a long build up to confuse, ending with an astute offer the country bumpkin Willy would be grateful to accept.

Willy looked round the room while awaiting the Irish stew, listening with half an ear to his cousin who, deciding to ignore Willy's verbal jolt, set off along the route he had plotted.

The stew arrived.

To please the waitress Willy ate but asked for extra bread to sop up the watery gravy, refused wine, asked for lager. He did not wish to linger longer than the minimum time to register tolerable manners. There was an earlier train than the one he had planned to take. If he was nippy he could catch it.

Meanwhile the old cousin droned on (he was not all that old, years younger than Willy's mother). He had, Willy knew, a perfectly good house already. Through the verbal screen it became clear from what was left unsaid that the cousin would benefit greatly by moving into Willy's mother's house. It was nearer his club, nearer Harrods, nearer the favourite bus routes and the tube, it was SW1 rather than SW14, it would be cheaper to heat (cheap, Willy noticed was a recurring word) needed no money spending on heavy repairs. If he sold his present house (there was an offer in the offing, he hinted) he would make a respectable profit.

As the old man rambled along his chosen course Willy plotted the future of his farm. He would expand, build more piggeries, fence more land eastward under the sheltered lee of the woods, he would pipe more water, increase the number of drinking troughs, build an annexe to the smoke-house, increase the insurance.

'How are your cows?' The cousin had noticed Willy's silence.

'I keep pigs.'

'So you do, so you do, I forgot.' He returned to his dissertation.

Now I come to think of it, Mother couldn't stand this man, thought Willy buttering his bread, she would hate him to have her house. I should have thought of that before. This stew is really revolting, all water, no dumplings, only one carrot and potatoes I wouldn't insult my pigs with.

'Of course the whole house needs redecorating,' said the cousin brazenly. 'One must take into account your mother has not touched it for years and Lord knows what I'll find when I take the carpets up.'

'Rugs, parquet.'

'What?'

'I said parquet.'

'Oh really, I thought—'

'Never mind. I wonder, could I have some cheese?'

'Of course, of course.' The cousin snapped his fingers towards the waitress.

'Bring the cheese board. I rather doubt the roof, you know, and the gutters and down pipes are, let's say, suspect.'

Didn't he say earlier there was no fear of spending on heavy repairs? Willy helped himself to cheese, a surprisingly beautiful Stilton wrapped as it should be in a damask napkin. 'What do you suspect the gutters of?' he asked.

'Dear boy! Your jokes, ha, ha, ha.'

'They were all renewed when Mother had a new roof put on three years ago.'

Willy was enjoying the cheese, its bite took away the flaccid taste of stew. There would be no time for coffee if he was to catch the earlier train. He let his eyes rest on the cousin's face. What an old fraud.

Catching Willy's thoughtful eye the cousin felt uneasy. Those dark eyes in the boy's mother had concealed a pretty sharp . . .

Behind the dark eyes Willy was now calculating just how much he could risk borrowing from the bank, how to spread the improvements to the farm over a longer period – no need to rush. 'The Stilton's good,' he said.

'Good, good, what about coffee? A brandy?'

'No, thank you.'

'Are you in a hurry?'

'I have a train to catch.'

'Of course you have. Back to the cows.'

'Pigs.'

'Pigs of course, how stupid. Now about the price, I was going to suggest—'

'I think there is a misunderstanding,' said Willy. 'I have not decided to sell.'

10

Leaping into a taxi, speeding towards Paddington Willy hoped he had not been too rude, hoped on the other hand that he had. Then he thought I can use Mother's house as collateral on the loan, she would far rather I did that than sell to the old cousin. The taxi driver, who enjoyed a joke, slid back the glass partition asking Willy why he was laughing.

'A near miss,' said Willy getting his money ready and thrusting it through the partition into the man's hand. 'Thanks. If I run I can catch my train – bye.'

Saying goodbye on the steps of the club, crafty enlightenment had lit the old cousin's eyes.

'I *see*, the penny's dropped. You are getting married, want to keep the house. Very wise to have a London base.' Cousin had looked wonderfully cunning.

'No.'

'But you want to keep the house for – er – girls. Of course! There aren't many who'd want to dally on a pig farm. You did say pigs?'

'No girls.'

'Ha, ha, no girls?' The rather pleased disbelieving expression on cousin's face had delighted Willy. 'Boys?' he suggested, lowering his voice.

'No boys either. I am free, free, free.' Willy had laughed as he said goodbye.

'Famous last words!' shouted the old cousin as the taxi left the kerb.

4

'Yes,' said the voice, 'Saturday's okay, can do.'

'Thanks,' said Poppy.

'Do you want four horses or two?' asked the voice. 'One could make do with two.'

'Oh no, he wants, I mean I want, the lot.'

'That's the spirit,' said the voice. 'Black and gold, or silver and black? Mutes? What coffin do you fancy? Oak? Black lacquer or red, tricked out in brass or plate? Loops?'

'Loops?' There was nothing about loops in the advertisement.

'Silk ropes, nylon actually. We do a good line in a sort of frogging round the box – the coffin I should say. You can choose from the catalogue when it reaches you: it suits military gents.'

'He is not – was not – military. I gave you my London address, but I'm in the country in my father's house.'

'Ah, not so easy then. Shall I send another?'

'I could come and choose for myself, then I would know he was getting what he asked for. You are not very far away.'

'Fine. You do that. Pass the time until Saturday. Any particular flowers?'

'I will decide when I see you.'

'We do a good line in laurel wreaths.'

'He is not – was not. . . .' was not the stuff of laurel leaves. 'I'll come tomorrow.' She put the receiver down and looked dubiously at the advertisement her father had ringed in red biro. (Get me this) 'Furnival's Fun Rococo Funerals.' Dad, what have you let me in for? Why rococo in death when, in life, his taste had run to restrained eighteenth century?

Time to get ready for Anthony Green, her father's solicitor, hers now, she supposed. She must change her clothes, have a reviving bath. She had not slept since leaving the hospital, had not slept the night before. She felt light, as though levitating, as she went up the stairs.

The house was full of her father's presence: she related to him in a way she had never managed in life.

Avoiding her old bedroom, she took her bag into a room reserved for visitors, which held no special associations of childhood. She ran a bath, found clean clothes, laid out black shirt and sweater, sensible skirt, clean tights. She must impress Anthony Green as sober and responsible. They had not met for years, although he was one of her father's oldest friends, had known her mother.

The visitors' bathroom was equipped with large towels, expensive soaps. Who had been her father's visitors during the last years when they had met only in London, in restaurants, agreeing not to quarrel, not to cause an irreparable breech? The breech, she thought as she soaked in the bath, wedged open by Edmund.

Enough of that. She left the bath, dried herself and went to dress. Picking up her discarded clothes, she looked for a laundry basket.

One of her father's foibles had been that unwashed clothes should be out of sight until whisked into the washing machine. Seeing no basket, she braved her father's room, dumping her clothes into his basket.

There were signs of hasty packing for the departure to the hospital, drawers half shut, cupboard doors ajar. Illness had come like a thief. Moving to shut a cupboard, Poppy saw a parcel in festive wrapping labelled, 'Happy Birthday, Poppy'. My birthday, Saturday, on Saturday. . . . She untied the ribbon, held up a dress, put it on, viewed her reflection in the glass, wondering where he bought this marvellous garment, composed of a multitude of triangles in bright colours. She brushed her hair, saw that the dress suited her, felt elation.

Outside the house a car crunched on the gravel, stopped, the door clunked shut. She ran down to meet Anthony Green as he let himself into the house.

'I see you found your father's present.' He bent to peck her check. 'He bought it in Milan. It suits you.'

When had he been to Milan? She had not known her father's movements, nor he hers, carefully kept secret.

'Come in. Would you like tea or a drink?'

'Tea, please.' Anthony followed her to the kitchen. 'Feels odd,' he said in his pleasant voice, 'without your father.'

'I feel closer to him than ever before.' Poppy filled the kettle. 'Don't mind me,' she added, noticing Anthony's raised eyebrows, 'I'm not fey or anything, just short of sleep.'

'Ah.'

'You know I killed him,' she watched the kettle, 'made him laugh.'

'Not a bad way to go.' Anthony found a tray, assembled cups, sugar and milk, showing Poppy that he knew the house as well as she, perhaps better.

'The hospital seemed to think it reprehensible.'

'Hospitals.' Anthony dismissed hospitals. 'He was on the way out – his heart was a mess.'

'I am ashamed. I shouted at the sister, she implied Dad's death was inconvenient. I apologised later. I saw him again when they had. . . .'

They had moved him out of the ward, tidied him up, closed his mouth and eyes. His nose looked as though they had pinched it with

13

a clothes' peg. She had preferred his expression in death, rather ghastly surprised amusement.

'Let's take the tray into the sitting room.' She poured boiling water into the pot.

They had also shaved him, brushed his hair, given him a parting.

'You forgot to put any tea in.'

'Oh God.' She felt displaced, inadequate.

'Let me.'

She watched him make the tea, followed him when he carried the tray to the sitting room. 'I have nothing to offer you to eat.'

'Not to worry.' He sat on the sofa, legs apart, watching her. 'I watch my weight.'

Poppy sat with her back to the light. 'This won't take long, will it?' She wanted to be alone. 'Dad had nothing much to leave, had he? He wanted me to arrange this funeral, he seems to have set his heart on it. I rang the man. He wanted Furnival's Rococo Funerals, he. . . .'

'What?' Anthony leant forward. 'Who?'

'Furnival's Roco—'

'I heard you. I've heard of Furnival too. What will the neighbours say?' Anthony, discreet solicitor, was about to say it himself. 'You can't. . . .'

'I'm going over to fix it, it's what Dad wanted.'

'So far only a pretty odd pop star and a member, well, it's said he was a member of the IRA, have used—'

'Dad wants . . . wanted . . . .'

'It costs the earth to . . .'

'I expect I can pay by instalments.'

'You won't need to do that.'

'What?'

'There's rather a lot you have to know, Poppy.' Anthony sighed. 'Shall you pour or shall I?'

'Sorry.' Poppy poured, remembering that Anthony liked one lump and a drip of milk.

'I've given up sugar.'

'Oh.' Poppy fished hastily with a spoon. 'Sorry.' She passed the cup. 'Dad didn't even own this house.'

'That's right.' Anthony took a swallow of tea, testing it for sugar. 'You do; he put it in your name soon after your mother died.'

'Why? What an extraordinary . . . he never told me.'

14

'He wanted to save death duties. As a matter of. . . .' Anthony paused, the girl wasn't listening. What was she thinking? He watched her: she had a curious expression. He opened his briefcase, took out the will.

Laurel wreath, she thought. Why should Dad not have a laurel wreath? He would like it far better than a lot of rotting flowers, it had been a good suggestion from Furnival's Funerals: it would amuse him. He would have laughed, too, if she had told him Edmund's new girl was called Venetia Colyer, an upmarket name, far more sophisticated than Poppy. Poppy's mind wandered to Edmund holding Venetia against him under the bridge over the Serpentine, his face against hers, her naturally yellow hair blown across his eyes. Perhaps she should have pushed them into the water. It was an opportunity missed. His hand had been on what the French call the saddle, pressing her against his genitals.

'You are not listening, Poppy. I didn't come here to watch you daydream; pay attention.'

'I am, I will.' She sat up straight, fixed her eyes on Anthony. 'You had got to death duties.'

'I had got a lot further. I'll start again.' Anthony blew out his cheeks. He had finished his tea; he poured himself another cup.

'Sorry, Anthony. I am all attention.'

'Right then. It's all here in legal language.' He tapped the will.

'Oh.'

'I will put it into plain English.'

'Thank you.' Poppy assumed a trusting, expectant expression. Anthony wondered if she was as great a ninny as she looked.

'Your father put this house in your name to save death duties. You got that?'

'Yes, Anthony. How wonderful of him.'

One had doubted the wonder of it at the time, thought Anthony. However, 'So, should you want to sell it, you can; straightaway.' He watched her.

'Sell Dad's house?' The house where she had first made love with Edmund? Not very successfully, they'd been expecting Dad back from a trip to Brighton. Edmund had enjoyed it; he was, she found herself admitting, pretty selfish in bed.

'That's something for you to decide later. I only wish to make the point that you may, if you want to sell, sell.' Anthony suppressed a niggle of irritation.

'Thank you, Anthony. Point taken.'

'You will find – I shall explain to you – that you have not only the house and all its contents, but quite a substantial income and considerable capital sums banked in your name.'

'Gosh. Why?'

'Presumably your father did not wish to leave you destitute.' Anthony could be acerbic.

'I knew nothing about his money. . . .' Poppy was puzzled. 'I mean, he never talked, he never. . . .'

'Your father had a phobia that some man might want to marry you for your money. I used to tell him you had more sense.'

'Thanks, Anthony.' Poppy's mind strayed back to Edmund and Venetia. Venetia had money, Edmund made no bones about it, grant him that, 'I fancy being kept, Venetia has a safe income.' Would he be selfish in bed with Venetia, not bother whether she came or not, or would he feel he owed—

'Poppy!'

'Sorry, Anthony. I am paying attention, it's just that I don't understand. Dad was always rather economical, not mean, just. . . .'

'Careful,' said Anthony. 'Wise in his way.'

'Yes, yes, I see,' but she didn't see. 'Where did he get it, this money? I always understood my mother bought this house with her bit. I mean, he never earned it, he was always changing jobs; and for years he's done nothing at all, just travelled about. Where does it come from, this money? Are you his executor?'

'Well, no. Naturally he asked me – actually the bank is executor. As your father's friend, as his solicitor, I am here to tell you, to advise. . . .'

'The bank. Nice and impersonal. Great!' Anthony compressed his lips. 'I mean, you won't be bothered by me and a lot of trivia, that's all I mean.'

'A substantial inheritance is not trivia.' This girl is hopelessly unworldly, thought Anthony, even if she isn't stupid.

'No, no, of course it isn't.' Poppy drew in her breath, dismissing Edmund and Venetia and their possible orgasms. 'You haven't answered my question, Anthony. Where did this money come from? Do you know? I never had an inkling. Was my mother, after all, rich?'

'Certainly not your mother.'

16

Why 'certainly' in that tone of voice? What had Dad done? Anthony did not approve, whatever it was. 'Then what?' asked Poppy, alert. 'How?'

'Your father backed horses.'

'So that's where he went, he went to the races, he was a betting man.'

'Not to put too fine a point on it – yes.'

'Bully for him.'

Anthony frowned. 'And, ah . . . he nearly always won, and he—'

'Spent it on women?'

This girl, his reprehensible old friend's daughter, was making light of what might so easily have been a disaster. Frivolity was, he supposed, in the blood.

'Yes. You could say in a way that he did.'

'But he invested a lot of it?'

'He invested what he called Life's Dividends.' Anthony's tone was repressive.

'Sounds like Dad. Where did these dividends come from?' Poppy fixed Anthony with her dark green eyes.

'Not to put too fine a point on it' (why does he keep repeating himself?) 'these . . . ah, um . . . women.' Anthony dropped his voice, muting his tone.

'How?'

'Sums, large sums, left in wills. Quite legitimately, I assure you.'

Poppy let this pass. 'Had he been their lover?'

Anthony poured himself a third cup of tea, now grown cold. 'I have no idea,' he said coldly.

Silly old goat, thought Poppy watching him sip his chilly tea. Perhaps Dad saw to it these ladies who made wills in his favour had delightful, splendid times in bed.

In a way I am glad, thought Anthony eyeing her, that I am not the executor. He cleared his throat. 'Well, that's it, then. The bank will give you all the details. I have made an appointment for you with them tomorrow. I have put a notice of your father's death in *The Times*, and I will contact the undertaker for you.'

'Furnival's Funerals?'

'No, no, my dear. The best round here are Brightson's. You will find them very efficient and discreet. Most helpful—'

'He wants – he wanted – Furnival's Fun—'

'I know, I know. Trying to keep his spirits up, a sick man's joke—'

17

'Dad's joke is sacred—

'But—'

'I have a date to see them. More tea?'

'No, thank you.' Anthony stood up, pulling his waistcoat downwards.

'A drink then?'

'No, no, I must be on my way.' He made a last appeal: 'It would be, well, in rather well . . . rather dubious, er . . . rather frivolous.'

'So apparently was Dad.'

Poppy watched Anthony drive away. Viewed through the back window of his sensible car, he looked huffy. He was trying to manipulate me, she thought. It was cheek to put an announcement in the paper without telling me. Cheek to try and thwart Dad's last wish. He probably wants to buy the house cheap, she thought uncharitably, for a client who has had his eye on it for years. Perhaps he isn't an executor because he tried to manipulate Dad. 'It's okay, Dad, you shall have your wish,' she addressed the spirit of her progenitor as she went in search of food, suddenly ravenously hungry, not having eaten since that awful catastrophic evening with Edmund. What a remarkably tiring scene, she found herself thinking, as she opened a can of consommé. She felt that, if she cosseted herself, she might just possibly recover, a possibility she had not envisaged since the humiliating parting, the death of the affair. The end, she thought histrionically as she twisted the can-opener, of an era. She reached up to grasp a bottle of sherry from the cupboard, uncorked it and sloshed a liberal dose into the soup.

5

Victor Lucas tore the paper out of his typewriter, crushed it between both hands and threw it violently towards the grate to join a trail of similarly treated first paragraphs of Chapter Five of his fourth novel. Sourly, Victor viewed the mess of wasted paper, wasted effort. It was all too likely, at this rate, that novel four would join novels one two and three in the shredder.

Blocked, stuck, Victor decided to try the trick of studied inattention which, before now, he had found could jostle his lethargic muse into coming up with an idea or two. He would go out, get some exercise, buy something to eat for supper. He snatched up his jacket, pushed his arms into the sleeves, ran downstairs, slammed the street door and set off walking fast along the street towards the shops. As he walked, he considered his ex-girl Julia who had recently, out of the blue, after months of silence, sent him a paperback cookbook, *How to Cheat at Cooking*, by a pretty girl called Delia Smith.

To win her back when the affair was unravelling he had invited her to dinner in his flat. Bloody Julia had not been won back, had not enjoyed the meal he had cooked with such trouble: clear soup, veal in wine and cream sauce, green salad, wild strawberries (costing the earth). 'Too much Kirsch,' she had said in that clipped voice, 'you drowned the taste', and later adding insult to injury sent the cookbook.

He had hoped, now that they had gone platonic, that Julia would commission a series of amply paid articles for the glossy magazine for which she worked. 'Not a sausage,' Victor muttered, walking along, shoulders hunched. 'Sheer waste of money, waste of time, bloody bitch.' He headed towards the supermarket where he would buy himself a steak and Sauce Tartare in a bottle, as recommended by Miss Smith (or was she Ms? With a lovely face like that, more likely Mrs) or, considering his present economic state, some sausages.

Striding along, Victor passed the fishmonger where, on marble slabs, lay, on crushed ice and seaweed, oysters backed by black lobsters, claws bound, with tight elastic, Dover sole, halibut, cod, herring, shining mackerel and – 'Oh Christ!' exclaimed Victor, 'it's alive!' as a fair-sized trout flapped among its supine companions, in a shallow indentation on the fishmonger's slab.

'It's alive,' Victor cried to the fishmonger, a stern lady in white overall and fur boots. 'The poor thing's alive.'

'Come in fresh from the country,' said the fish lady complacently, 'from the fish farms.'

'But it's drowning,' cried Victor, desperate.

The fish lady nonchalantly picked up the fish and slid it on to the scales, which joggled as the fish threshed its tail.

'No, no, don't put it in newspaper. Haven't you a plastic bag and a drop of . . .' he fished in his pocket for money; the trout gasped, open-mouthed, 'water?'

'Your change,' said the fish lady.

'Keep it.' Victor was racing back to his flat, opening the door, the key shaking between his fingers, tearing up the long flight of stairs, gasping in sympathy with his prize, running the cold tap in the bath, jamming in the plug, gently releasing the trout: watching its extra-ordinary miraculous revival. 'How could anyone eat anything so beautiful?' he crooned to the fish which stationed itself, its head towards the fall of water, idly moving its tail and fins, keeping in position under the cold tap, its pink flanks iridescent.

Victor tried to remember what he knew about trout.

They needed pure running water. At this rate he would flood the house. He reduced the flow of tap water, cautiously let some run down the plughole. Who did he know who lived near, or had, a trout stream? Where could he take his protégé, where it would not be caught by some demon angler?

Presently, leaving the tap dribbling, he was telephoning his friend and cousin (more of late years an acquaintance) Fergus, explaining the trout's plight, imploring asylum.

'Well, well. Well, I never,' said Fergus. 'Yes, of course, bring it down, no problem. You can stay a night if you want, I've got a job for you.'

'An article?' asked Victor eagerly.

'More of a manual job, not so cerebral as your talents deserve.'

What does he want? Victor asked himself. I'm in no position to refuse. He strained to see how the trout was faring, but the telephone lead was not long enough.

'I'll pay you, of course,' came Fergus's voice from the country, 'and come to think of it, there might well be an article. Good for you, good for me.'

'Oh thanks, I . . . what. . . .'

'Put a lid on the container.'

'A lid?'

'Don't want it jumping all over your car, cause an accident!'

'Should I feed it? What about fish food, where can I get maggots?'

'No need. It can last. Come down the motorway; don't brake suddenly or you will bruise it. See you.'

'What's the job?' Victor shouted, but Fergus had rung off.

Presently, with the trout in a plastic bucket, holes punched in the lid, Victor wondered, as he drove past Chiswick to join the motorway, what Fergus had meant by 'good for you, good for me'. He had never entirely trusted Fergus since the occasion Julia had stood him up, preferring Fergus's company to his. 'He's so enterprising,' Julia had excused her conduct. Bet she went to bed with him, Victor mused as he drove carefully so that the water in the bucket should not slop. Not that I care now, he told himself truthfully: glossy mag Julia is not the girl she was, I can't stand what she's done to her hair. There was too the connection with Penelope which he preferred not to think about. Driving carefully, Victor wondered what enterprise Fergus was at present engaged in. He had last heard of him doing something in France, though what that something was his informant had forgotten.

'First things first,' Victor addressed his passenger. 'He has a stream through his orchard, he doesn't fish, your only risk will be an occasional heron.'

6

Les Poole, bank manager, placed the Carew folder on his desk. He delighted in the gift he imagined unique to himself, of observing himself as others might, indeed must, see him.

The desk was cleared for action except for the framed photographs of his dog, his wife and his daughter, familiar props, part of the furniture, well-worn, well-loved, he supposed, never being exactly certain. Time, he thought, peering at Marjory's photograph, time she got herself done again. That hairstyle was old-fashioned and the hair had changed colour, from brown to auburn (she was good about weekly visits to her hairdresser, keeping the grey parting under control). The scene was set for his pleasurable interview with Poppy Carew. Had she, one wondered, been born on Armistice Day? The father (what a character, should one consider him eccentric?) had been capable, if not of anything, of much, as the content of the folder proved. Les Poole looked at his watch, spoke into his desk telephone, 'Send Miss Carew in when she arrives.'

'She's here now,' replied Ida, pertly invisible in the outer office.

Poppy Carew came in, shook hands, sat down, smiled. 'How do you do, Mr Poole?'

In imagination, Les Poole had expected a tall girl with black, tangled hair, gypsy eyes, dressed in red. The real Poppy Carew was slight, medium size, with plain, straight, fawn-coloured hair, dark green eyes, black lashes, large mouth with rather too many teeth. She wore no make-up and a black shirt and skirt. She looked sensible. She will need to be, thought Les Poole.

'It is a rare pleasure to give good news,' said Les Poole, giving the folder a little shake, as though saying to it: wait until you are spoken to.

'Yes,' said Poppy, looking intelligent.

'Yes. Well, then. We come to the investments. Your father used to call them—'

'Life's Dividends.'

The bank manager frowned. 'The best birthday present she will ever have had, is what he called them to me.'

'My birthday is on Saturday,' said Poppy, thinking, And so is Dad's funeral.

'Ah, indeed, yes, well. Here is the list.' He glanced out at the late September sunshine. So much for Armistice Day. He handed a list from the folder across the desk. Poppy took it. She did not, he observed, paint her nails: he must tell Amanda (aged fifteen). 'A rich girl like Poppy Carew,' he would say, 'does not paint her nails black.' Amanda would answer, 'So what?' At least he would have tried. He watched Poppy read the list, eyebrows rising.

'Gosh,' said Poppy, handing it back as though afraid it might snap. 'Gosh!'

'There are too some capital sums,' said Mr Poole, bestowing his benison.

'So Anthony Green told me. What's it mean?'

'Your father meant it to mean that if you wanted, immediately, to buy a house, buy a car, go on holiday, you could do so without disturbing the investments which are your income.'

'An income from investments.' Was her tone derisory or respectful? Hard to tell.

'Yes, Miss Carew.' A girl like this should now say, Oh, do call me Poppy. She didn't.

I am stunned, thought Poppy. How did he come by all this? It's difficult to realise one's the child of a gigolo. She noticed the bank

22

manager was waiting for her to say something. 'I don't want a house. I apparently already own my father's. I don't want a car, Dad's just bought a new one. I might buy a little house in London.' I never want to see my flat again, she thought. 'A little house would be nice.' And she added, to please this harmless man (bet he never jilted anyone, far too square), 'It would be a good investment.'

Has she really got too many teeth, or is it her jaw formation? Marjory would know. If I were younger, I'd call that mouth sexy, thought Les Poole, a generous mouth. 'If the house is in a good neighbourhood it would be considered a good investment,' he said gravely. 'You might find one in an area which is coming up. I have clients who swear by Islington or Bow.'

'I don't,' said Poppy. 'I'd just like to get away from where I live now. I'll look south of the Park.'

'There's no hurry,' said the bank manager. Somehow this girl looked capable of foolish impetuosity. It wasn't just the mouth which was sexy; those breasts, well, leave the breasts, pay attention, she was asking a pertinent question.

'How much, Mr Poole,' she had taken the trouble to remember his name; quite a lot of people didn't, 'how much exactly is my income?'

Les Poole made pretence of studying the list as though for the first time, then named the sum calculated on the computer the previous day.

Poppy said, 'Wow! Shall I be stung for income tax?'

'I fear so. We shall, of course, always be happy to advise and help, Miss Carew – no charge of course.'

'Do call me Poppy,' said Poppy relenting, though not liking patronising avuncular men (I'm not *that* stupid).

'Thank you.' He paused.

Poppy looked expectant. What other surprise did this old boy have in store, what shock? 'Just one thing more. Your father left a letter for you, with us, in the event of his demise. . . .'

Why can't he say death? Dad's dead, bloody dead, stiff.

'It's in our vault, Miss Ca – Poppy, shall I send for it?'

'Yes please.' (Pompous ass.)

Les Poole spoke into the telephone, 'Ida, ask Mr Dunne to bring me the letter for Miss Carew.'

'Righty-ho, Mr Poole,' Ida crackled.

'She's leaving us to get married,' Mr Poole informed Poppy, who said, 'Really?'

They waited. Poppy's eyes roamed over the desk, the photographs, the blotter, Mr Poole's feet in neat black pumps, his perfectly creased trousers, navy blue socks.

Les Poole decided that Poppy's legs were long in proportion to her body, and approved. Marjory's would be better longer.

Mr Dunne brought an envelope which he handed to Mr Poole, who passed it across his desk to Poppy.

Mr Dunne swept the discreet eye of a future bank manager over Poppy and left the room.

Poppy eyed the letter addressed to herself, 'Poppy Carew', in Dad's large handwriting, with an exuberant 'Top Secret' flourishing right across the envelope under her name. She put it in her bag. She stood up, holding out her hand.

'Thank you very much indeed, Mr Poole, for all your trouble.'

'Delighted . . . of help . . . any time.' Her hand was small, dry, firm (no rings, he must tell Amanda).

'Would you perhaps be kind and come to Dad's funeral, Mr Poole? And Mrs Poole, if she would bother?'

'We would be honoured.' What a fool thing to say, the girl's father was nothing more than a—

'Saturday,' said Poppy. 'I'll put a notice of the time in the paper.'

'I can find out from Brightson's—'

'I don't think you'd find out much, but there will be a notice. Goodbye, Mr Poole. Thank you so much.'

She was gone, the letter hidden in her bag. It would have been interesting to know what was in it. One had some pretty funny clients, banking had its moments.

Pushing through the swing door into the street, Poppy was muttering 'Can't have him advising me on undertakers, like Anthony Green; it's too much. I'll read Dad's letter when I can find somewhere quiet, when I feel calmer.'

She got into her father's car, adjusted the seat once more to get it right for her length of leg, checked the mirrors, fastened the safety belt and headed towards the point on the map where, hidden in a fold of the downs, Furnival's Funerals had its establishment. As she drove, she wondered whether Dad would like Mr Poole to be at his funeral, or, for that matter, Anthony Green. Now I come to think of it, she thought as she drove, he must have despised all those respectable people: not very nice of you, Dad, while you were laying up store in Heaven, placing your bets, living it up with ladies. I wish I'd taken the trouble to know you, Dad, instead of panicking about interference. Perhaps you were too busy collecting Life's Dividends to interfere seriously. Wish I'd known you better, Dad: too late now. Never mind, you shall have your funeral. So she tried to stifle her feelings of guilt and remorse.

7

By the time Poppy found Furnival's, she was tired from driving up lanes which ended in farmyards, making three-point turns in the unaccustomed car, reversing when to turn was impossible, and when she stopped to ask the way at lonely cottages, the occupants were either out or professed ignorance. On the point of giving up, going home and ringing up Brightson's, as advised by Anthony, she spotted a painted board on a gate leading to a grassy track which said 'Furnival's Fine Funerals'. It led her gently up a valley, running parallel to a small stream until, rounding a corner, she came upon a group of faded brick buildings crouching, in secret isolation, under the downs. Parking the car beside a battered Ford, Poppy pushed through a door in a brick wall to find a yard, neatly cobbled, flanked on two sides by loose-boxes, from each of which, benignly, stared a horse.

In the middle of the yard there was a stone trough and a pump. A very old sheepdog lay asleep in the sun. Poppy walked towards the dog, who raised his head, flapped his tail but did not rise. Poppy looked round for a bell or knocker, but found none. She crossed the yard to a barn which formed the fourth side of the yard, opened a door and peered in. It was dark, but sunbeams, striking through cracks in the tiled roof, showed what she took to be a tractor, covered by plastic sheeting. Crossing the barn, she ventured through a door into an untidy garden, a-hum with bees feasting on golden rod and Michaelmas daisies. A weedy path led to a brick cottage, its door propped open by a stone. Poppy knocked, knocked again and peered in. A large cat, lolling on a chair, one leg hanging nonchalantly towards the flagged floor, stared at her with insolence.

Poppy called, 'Anybody there?'

The cat stared, Poppy called again. There was no response, only the sound of bees and rooks cawing, as they floated up the valley to a stand of beech. Poppy went back to the yard to wait. She presumed somebody would come, eventually, to tend the horses.

She idled round the yard, speaking to each horse, gratified by the friendly snuffling and whickering as they made her welcome. She breathed in the stable smell, enjoyed the silky feel of well-groomed necks and soft noses. The old dog lurched to his feet and walked beside her in amiable companionship. She began to relax from the pain of the last few days, appreciating the sunshine and the gentle animals.

One of the horses turned from nuzzling her face over its box-door, to lurch across and blow draughtily down its nose into a manger. At once, a baby caterwauled loudly. Startled, and unable to see more than tiny feet and fists, bunched in a reverse attitude of Muslim prayer, Poppy peered into the loose-box.

How to effect a rescue?

Gingerly, she opened the box-door. The horse swung round, laid back its ears and bared yellow teeth. Poppy retreated fast.

'What d'you want to wake him for? Bloody hell.'

A thin girl in black jeans and T-shirt, ink-black hair brushed up spikily, appeared at Poppy's side, pushed past her into the loose-box, slapped the horse's rump, 'Out of the way, there,' snatched up the baby, who at once stopped bawling. 'I told that sod not to put him there again.' She banged shut the stable door and walked away. Over her shoulder, the baby stared reproachfully at Poppy with round black eyes.

'Well,' said Poppy to the horse. 'Well!'

The horse, calm again, made a huffle-wuffle sound and stamped its hoof. Poppy went and sat on the edge of the water trough, shaken by the girl's anger. The old dog flopped down at her feet and resumed its snooze. The yard was silent. Poppy did not feel equal to following the girl and the baby. The large cat sauntered through the yard to sit a few yards from her, and stare offensively, unblinking. Seeking solace, Poppy opened her bag and took out her father's letter.

Poppy love,
1. Never lend, give.

2. Never marry unless you are certain sure you cannot live without the fellow.
3. Don't be afraid to back outsiders.
Love, Dad.

She put the letter back in its envelope. There was no indication of when it had been written. She felt no wish to ask Mr Poole, it would show how little she had known her father. Nor would she ask Anthony Green.

Resentfully, she mulled Dad's advice. Had he guessed that she lent money to Edmund? Had she been certain sure she could not live without Edmund? She was, she thought ruefully, without Edmund as she sat here in this stable yard, still living; and what did Dad mean by outsiders? She considered her father. He had been kind and, she supposed, caring. There had been a housekeeper to keep house, she had been clothed, educated, fed. Had he loved her, had she loved him? She felt unsure. He had been away so much. She had been away so much, first at school and then, after the rows over Edmund, away for good, only keeping a tenuous connection – thanking belatedly for the postcards. He sent her postcards from all over England. Even in childhood the postcards had dropped through the letterbox. What had he been doing? – he had no job. He had been (she stared back at the cat), he had been at the races with those ladies who produced Life's Dividends, she thought censoriously, remembering that Edmund seldom repaid her loans, took money she could ill afford as of right.

'Sod Edmund,' she said aloud, staring back at the cat, 'sod him, sod him, sod him.' At her feet, the old dog wagged his tail. 'And sod you too, Dad,' she murmured with amused affection, 'landing me up in this place, miles from anywhere, to fix you up with a rococo funeral.' I will miss him, she thought, miss the occasional lunches in London restaurants, when we chit-chatted of nothing and he pointedly refrained from mention of Edmund. Curse Edmund, she thought. If it had not been for Edmund she might have known her father, that small man with dun-coloured hair, bright brown eyes and engaging laugh. She rememberd the laugh, totally without malice. Perhaps that was his charm. He had charm, she thought, and loved her father as she sat in the sun on the edge of the water trough. 'Shoo,' she said to the staring cat, who lifted a leg and began to wash its parts.

27

Her reverie was interrupted by voices. Several rather wet dogs ran into the yard, followed by two men. One man was mocking the other.

'You were never so tender-hearted when Penelope nearly drowned that time,' he said, laughing.

'She could swim; besides, I wanted shot of her,' said the other.

'So you did, and did get shot. What a pain she was. Aha, here's my client, Miss Carew. I expected you to be much older.' He made a rapid inventory of Poppy's finer points. 'Down,' he said to a labrador who was preparing a boisterous greeting.

'Sorry we weren't here to greet you. Victor – this is Victor, Victor Lucas – had a—'

'There was a baby. . . .' stuttered Poppy.

'The infant Jesus, I'd forgotten. I put him down while we went to the stream.'

'A girl, your. . . .' Poppy hesitated to say 'wife', though this man had eyes not unlike the baby.

'That's Mary, its mother, one of my grooms. Found it, did she? Keeps house too after a fashion.'

'Yes.'

'That's okay then.'

'But the horse might have—'

'No, no, best baby-sitter on the place. Did Mary create? She shouldn't have left it with me. I told her I couldn't be bothered. My name is Fergus,' he held out his hand, he wanted to touch this girl, 'and this is Victor as I said.' He clasped Poppy's narrow hand and held it a moment. 'You've come about your father's do. Furnival's Fine Funerals, that's me, Fergus to you.'

'Yes,' Poppy did not dislike the handshake, but was shocked by the cavalier attitude to the baby. In her turn, she had visualised an older man, grey-haired, dignified. This man couldn't be much more than thirty and struck her as altogether too lighthearted to run a funeral establishment, almost jokey. On the other hand, she knew instinctively Dad would have warmed to him.

'Let me show you round,' said Fergus. 'Sorry to keep you waiting. Victor had a fishy friend who had to be rehoused. You've met the horses, I take it. Come and see the tack room and the hearse, then we can discuss the rest in the house over tea. Be a good friend, Cousin Victor, tell Mary to put the kettle on and, if she won't, tell one of the others.'

'They're out,' said Victor, who had not taken his eyes off Poppy since their meeting. He made no move to carry out Fergus's request.

'Well then, you do it,' said Fergus impatiently. 'This way, Miss Carew.'

He led the way to the barn. Poppy followed, taking stock of the tall dark young man not much older than Edmund but, unlike Edmund, magnificently fit.

'Do you jog?' she asked.

'Jog?' Fergus grinned. 'No need to jog if you have six horses and are humping bales of hay and mucking out all day.'

'I thought the girls did most of that,' said Victor dryly.

'Do you jog, Miss Carew?' Fergus ignored Victor, his dark eyes met Poppy's, his grin showed teeth Edmund would have envied, he being sensitive about his one gold-capped eye tooth.

'No,' lied Poppy, 'of course not.' (Why must I keep thinking so nastily of Edmund?)

'Do you jog, Victor?' Fergus decided, since he would not go and tend the kettle, to include Victor. 'You didn't jog from the fishmonger's, you ran like the clappers.'

Victor laughed, catching Poppy's eye.

'Victor lives in London. You must get him to tell—'

The roar of a motorcycle drowned Fergus's voice, as a heavy Yamaha bounced through the door into the yard, coming to rest by the drinking trough. Two figures, wearing heavy boots, studded leather jackets, jeans and crash helmets, got off the machine.

'You are late, girls,' shouted Fergus above the noise of the engine, as the rider revved it for the last time before stilling it. The riders took off their helmets and shook free a quantity of hair. 'Annie and Frances,' said Fergus. 'My stable girls.'

'Hi,' said the girls, quite friendly. 'Hi.'

'Put the kettle on, one of you.'

'Why can't Mary? It's still our time off.'

'She's feeding infant Jesu, found him in the stable.'

'His name's Barnaby,' said the girl, Frances, wheeling the Yamaha towards a shed. In spite of her tough appearance, she sounded maternal.

'Poor little bugger,' said the girl called Annie. 'He'd be much better off living with the family. I can't see the grandmother leaving him in a manger.'

Poppy made a lightning readjustment of the baby's parenthood.

Fergus, noting this, said, 'The father's called Joseph. The girls met on holiday on the Costa.'

Annie and Frances laughed, exchanging sly looks. Then, returning to the point where he had been interrupted by the Yamaha, Fergus drew Poppy across the yard towards the barn. 'As I was saying. Victor had this trout he brought from London. He knew it wouldn't last long in his bath; London water's passed through twelve pairs of kidneys before you drink it. Did you know that?'

'No,' said Poppy bemused.

'No trout, Victor thought, could stand that. Wouldn't survive like you or me, so he SOS-ed me and brought it here.'

'What was it doing in the bath?' Is this supposed to be a joke, Poppy wondered: perhaps Dad would find it funny.

Fergus explained the trout's career, Victor's dilemma, the mercy drive down the motorway. 'We were seeing it settled in the stream in the orchard. Victor's tenderhearted.'

'I am,' said Victor, still studying Poppy (what a super girl). 'Couldn't let it drown, could I?' he said, contriving to catch her attention, pleased that she seemed impressed by the saga, hoping to tell her more.

'He was quite different with his wife,' said Fergus, noticing Victor's attempt. 'She divorced him.'

'The trout was helpless,' exclaimed Victor, 'drowning, gasping.' He gaped at Poppy as the fish had gaped on the fishmonger's slab, trying, at the same time, to indicate that his ex-wife Penelope was not the helpless sort.

'Well it's okay now,' said Fergus, who had had enough of the trout. He took Poppy's elbow. 'Come and see the hearse.' He propelled her towards the barn. 'Be a kind friend and pull the sheet off, Victor.'

Victor gave a tweak to the plastic sheeting Poppy had observed earlier.

'That suit your father?' asked Fergus.

'Oh!' cried Poppy, overwhelmed. 'Yes.' Then, 'Where did you find it?'

'In France,' said Fergus, proudly. 'Restored it, then I found the tack, the fittings, bought the horses, broke them in for driving, got them used to wearing the harness, plumes and so on. Come and see.' Still holding her elbow, he led her to the tack room.

'Oh,' said Poppy, gazing at the ornamented harness, black ostrich

plumes, the richly caparisoned rugs. 'Dad will love it . . . would.'
She was moved almost to tears. 'It's exactly what he would want.'

Victor, who had followed behind Poppy and Fergus, thinking it
was time Fergus let go the girl's arm, that her hair was rather nice
even if it was mousy, and those were very nice shoulderblades, said,
'What about that tea?'

'Ah yes,' said Fergus, looking at his watch. 'Tea, and of course
. . . er . . . um . . . business.'

'Business,' agreed Poppy, pulling herself together, 'of course.'

'Come to the house, we'll have tea in my office,' said Fergus,
leading the way. 'I take it your father's in cold storage?'

Poppy did not answer.

'You want the funeral on Saturday, don't you? That's what you
said. Today's Tuesday.'

'Oh,' Poppy began to cry. 'God.'

'Oaf!' said Victor to Fergus. 'Tactless oaf. Cold storage. . . .' He
stepped towards Poppy who, through her tears, noticed him properly for the first time. Long, thin, sinuous, so slender he could be
drawn through a napkin ring; the shape of man poor Edmund would
have liked to be.

Oh fuck Edmund, she thought, laying her tearful face against
Victor's chest. Victor gave her a brief hug with thin but muscular
arms. (This is not the time, not in front of Fergus.)

'Tea first, and then business.' He quickly wiped Poppy's eyes.
'There.' Perhaps she's one of those girls who are in love with their
father, he thought. No, she can't be. 'Tea,' he said, repeating the
formula.

'Actually,' said Poppy, 'I'm pining for a drink. Is there any
whisky?'

8

The office, which was also the cottage kitchen and living room, was crowded, having to fulfil more roles than there was room for. Kitchen equipment overlapped with typewriter, account books and stationery. A pile of freshly washed baby clothes took up room on the kitchen table. The dogs pressed up to the stove, edging away from the cat. A gun was propped in a corner, a game bag in another. There were two top hats occupying one of the chairs: a heap of horse rugs in another corner and pieces of harness in the process of being mended or cleaned occupied more room. There was a long row of rubber boots by the door and the door itself groaned under the weight of coats and waterproofs hanging from hooks.

'Sorry about this,' said Fergus 'space is at a premium. We really need a much bigger house, but do come in and find somewhere to sit.'

The girl with spiky black hair now shared the chair with the cat. She had hitched up her T-shirt and was suckling the infant Barnaby, who rolled lollipop eyes at Poppy without interrupting the business in hand. His mother stared stonily at Poppy. Victor, averting his eyes, muttered greetings which the girl, Mary, ignored.

'Hi, Jesu,' said Fergus, moving towards a walk-in larder. Mary stuck out a foot, he tripped and nearly fell. 'Ouch!' he said, regaining his balance. 'Damn you.'

Mary said, 'Barnaby,' with soft menace, 'his name is Barnaby.'

'All right, Barnaby.' Fergus reached for a bottle of whisky. 'Miss Coquelicot needs a drink. Miss Coquelicot Carew, esteemed client of Furnival's Fine Funerals.' He poured a stiff tot into a tumbler and handed it to Poppy. 'Sit down, sit down; please sit down.' He smothered embarrassment with jocosity.

Poppy sat on a chair pushed forward by Victor and gulped the whisky which, travelling at speed into her system, began its revivifying effect. From a room above she could hear girls' voices and laughter, there was a sudden rush of water down a pipe by the cottage door, the scent of shampoo drifted into the kitchen.

'Out of interest,' said Fergus, filling a kettle and setting it to boil on the stove, 'why are you called Poppy?'

'Poppaea,' said Poppy, aglow with whisky. 'Dad was interested in the Romans.' No need to tell them he was a milkman.

'Didn't she get hitched to Nero?' Victor had no intention of being excluded from the conversation, and considered his erudition more shapely than Fergus's.

'He treated her bad, kicked her when she was in foal,' said Fergus, deliberately horsey to irritate Victor.

'Sod.' Mary switched the baby to her other breast and resumed her silence, ignoring Poppy. Her anger double-wrapped about her.

'Did you ever kick Penelope?' Fergus asked Victor. 'His ex-wife,' he informed Poppy. 'Very pretty girl.'

'Would have liked to but didn't.' Victor helped himself to whisky and watched Poppy.

'Soft-hearted,' said Fergus jeering. He collected cups and saucers from a varnished dresser which had one worm-eaten foot supported by a brick. 'Hence the trout,' he laughed as he rattled the china. 'Perhaps you are only a softie to cold fish: there must be a moral of some sort there. Don't you think so, Miss Carew?' He spooned the tea into a brown teapot.

'Do call me Poppy,' she used the whisky's false courage, 'silly name though it is.'

'I like it,' said Fergus and Victor in unison. Mary sniffed, narrowing fine nostrils, rolling supplicatory eyes at the ceiling.

Fergus found plates and knives. 'Any scones?' he asked. 'Or cake?'

'In the larder,' said Mary, not looking up, devoting herself to the baby.

'You realise,' said Fergus maliciously to Victor, 'that on that fishmonger's slab were oysters equally alive and lobsters, alive too; I know the shop.'

'They did not gape.' Victor put an end to the subject.

Poppy remembered her father in death. If this goes on, she thought, I shall never get anywhere. I came here for Dad, not to listen to these men girding at one another. She cleared her throat. 'Furnival's Fun Funerals—' she began.

'Aah!' cried Fergus. 'It was a wicked misprint. I shall sue the editor.' He put a plate of scones in front of Poppy. 'It's Furnival's Fine Funerals,' he emphasised the word 'fine', thumping his fist on the table.

'Dad seemed to have taken to the fun part.' Poppy felt embarrassed.

'Your dad must have been quite a character. Come on, eat your tea. Butter, jam,' he produced these from the larder, 'then we shall plot him a slap-up do, and Victor shall write an article which will be syndicated all over the country. You did not know Victor was a writer, did you?'

'Manqué,' said Victor, deprecatory, modest. 'Extremely minor.'

'Only up to now. We'll get him launched, won't we, Poppy?'

Poppy said nothing, not having previously met anyone with literary pretentions.

'Just a humble journalist,' explained Victor. 'Freelance.'

'Dad wouldn't want, I don't want, publicity,' Poppy took fright. 'I don't think. . . .' but perhaps Dad would enjoy publicity; how was she to know.

'Of course not, of course not,' cried Fergus. 'Now then, to business. Time to stop fooling.'

Mary put the baby against her shoulder and patted its back. It gave a prolonged burp.

Fergus said, 'Oh God! Sick next.'

Mary left the room, carrying the baby. Frances, her head wrapped in a towel, pushed past her into the room. 'I must use the telephone—'

'No, you must not. Push off, use it later, can't you see I'm doing business? This isn't a madhouse.'

'Not a bad imitation.' Frances retreated in a waft of shampoo.

Fergus shouted after her through the open door, 'When will you learn to wait for the boys to ring you? You frighten them away by your pursuit, you'll never have a lasting relationship this way.'

Out of sight Frances riposted, 'Your love life's not all that brilliant, and it's the telephone bill you fear for, not my single state.'

Fergus closed the intervening door.

'That's better. Now then. Time. Place. Four horses, you said. Wreaths? Mutes? Would you like a special coffin for your father, or to have whatever he's in draped with a pall? I have a fine black velvet I found in Stroud, or would you prefer purple?'

'Black,' Poppy whispered beginning to shake.

'Black it shall be, and where did you say your dad is now?'

Poppy began to cry again, more from the onslaught of whisky

34

than grief. (It's not Dad I'm weeping for, it's Edmund.)

'Butter her a scone, Victor,' said Fergus; then, as Victor did so, he said gently, 'I suppose he's stuck in the hospital morgue.' Poppy nodded. 'We can fetch him from there, you know, Poppy; would you like to have him at home until the funeral? We can arrange that too, he could lie in state.'

'At home,' said Poppy in a low voice. 'Please.'

'Right, I'll fix all that presently on the phone. Eat your scone now.'

Victor handed Poppy a scone, ready buttered, which she obediently ate.

'Drink some hot tea, try.' Victor was solicitous, pushing the cup towards her.

'All right.' She drank the scalding tea.

The two men watched her with concern. Fergus ruffled his thick black hair. 'I have so little experience,' he apologised. 'I know the rules and all that, but not how to behave to clients. We've only done two funerals. One was a pop person, bit of a shambles that, and the other—'

'Anthony Green, Dad's – I mean, my – solicitor said it was an IRA, he said—'

'No, no. It was a vagrant. We wanted a practice run. The poor devil had been sleeping rough. We gave him the works, it annoyed the Council who had to pay, it was not exactly the pauper's funeral they intended.'

'He was a wino,' said Victor, 'Mary said.'

'What if he was? He was entitled to something,' Fergus was aggressive, 'man in the image of God and so on.'

'Oh!' exclaimed Poppy. 'Oh!' She mourned for the vagrant, for her father, for the girl Mary and her baby, for Edmund, for the two men watching her, their expressions kind. 'I'm not usually lachrymose,' she cried, 'I feel so guilty, I hardly knew him. I never paid any attention to what he wanted unless to do the opposite. Oh,' she snuffled.

Wisely Victor and Fergus let her cry.

'I'm sorry,' she said presently, 'it's a whole lot of things, it's. . . .'

'I apologise for clowning,' said Fergus hoping to console.

'Me too,' said Victor. 'I am fundamentally serious.'

'Everybody feels guilty when someone dies.' He sat beside Poppy and offered a kitchen tissue. 'Mop.'

'What about your mum, is she . . .?' Victor asked.

'Died when I was a baby.' Poppy wiped her eyes on the tissue.

'So you can't feel bad about her.'

'I suppose not.' Poppy smiled weakly and blew her nose.

'That's better.' Fergus grew brisk. 'Now we plan. Come on.' He reached for a notebook. 'Name, address, hospital, parson or priest, church? Let's get the forms filled in.'

Poppy supplied the information, signed where told to sign, drank her tea, watched Fergus fill in forms.

'That's about it.' Fergus stood up. 'The rest I'll do on the telephone. Now come and meet the Dow Jones.'

'The who?'

'The average horses. It's a joke, you are supposed to laugh.'

Poppy obliged. 'I've met them,' she said.

'Come and meet them again. They are what shops call "seconds", not good enough to get into the Horse Guards or Police, but good enough for Furnival's.'

'What about eats?' asked Victor, following them out of the cottage. 'After the service people expect a binge.'

'Do they?' Poppy was appalled. 'I've never been to a funeral, I don't know what's—'

'Like me to help?' Victor offered eagerly.

'Would you?'

'Love to. Will there be lots of relations, dozens of friends?'

'I don't know.' Poppy thought of the providers of Life's Dividends, presumably dead. 'Not many friends,' she said, 'and no relations, we had no relations.'

'What a mercy,' muttered Fergus enviously.

'I suppose the village will come. I live in London, I hardly know . . . we didn't meet often. I think his best friends are dead.' I wonder who they were, she thought; clever old Dad.

Victor and Fergus exchanged puzzled looks.

'Tell you what,' said Victor. 'Now you've fixed everything with Fergus, suppose I follow you home and suss the situation, then I can arrange the catering. What did your father like?'

'Champagne.' Certainly champagne. Had champagne celebrated all those winning horses? Poppy visualised Dad in company with shadowy ladies at candlelit tables in intimate restaurants.

'I see.'

'And spicy Indian food, or Chinese.' The memory of a lunch with

Dad, and Dad shying away from the subject of Edmund as he bit into a particularly fierce chilli. He was so lovable in retrospect, she had hated him at the time.

'Tell you what,' said Victor again. 'I'll fix it all. The booze at least we can get on sale or return. I don't suppose your father's friends are great drinkers.'

What makes you suppose that, thought Poppy. It was drink that caused Dad's coronaries. 'I wouldn't know,' she said evasively.

Fergus noticed Poppy's expression. So her pa was a boozer.

'That's fixed then.' Victor assumed Poppy's compliance. 'I have an Indian chum in Shepherd's Bush who does a super take-away.'

'Come and meet the horses,' interrupted Fergus, furious with Victor. How dare he plot to go off with the girl, leaving him to slave. Spitefully, he wished he had not given the trout house room.

'I'm coming too.' Victor jumped up. 'I'm already brewing a superb article for Julia's mag, she won't be able to resist it, she might even come to the funeral.' He visualised a double spread, illustrated; he must alert a good photographer, and why not TV while he was about it or was that going too far?

Poppy, beginning to wonder whose funeral this really was, accompanied Fergus to the stable yard. Annie, Frances and Mary were filling haybags, removing dung and carrying buckets of water, watched by baby Barnaby propped against a bale of hay. Sparrows chirped, swallows swooped, a portable radio blared, bantams pecked round the stable doors. There was a smell of horse and saddle soap. The girls sang to the radio and called to one another in cheerful voices.

Fergus led Poppy round the yard, naming each horse. 'This one has a white blaze and two of them have white socks. We dye those bits black for the occasion. Mary's got the dye. She's a natural blonde,' he stroked an equine nose, 'gets carried away and dyes her own.'

'I see,' said Poppy. 'That accounts for her white skin. How thorough you are. Dad will – would – love this.' She looked again at the hearse, the tack room and the splendid harness, the sombre ostrich plumes. 'Do you muffle their hooves?' she asked, remembering something she had read, was it Sir John Moore after Corunna?

'No,' said Fergus, who had never thought to do so. 'That makes the scene a bit macabre.'

'How do you get to the, er. . . .'

'Location?'

'Yes.'

'I have horse-boxes and a lorry for the hearse. We get ourselves sorted out and hitched up half a mile or so from the pick-up or the church.'

'Like a circus,' said Poppy, giving mortal offence.

'If you say so,' Fergus answered stiffly. Observing this, Poppy felt irritation: whose father is having this funeral, who is paying for this jamboree? She felt furious: who is hiring Furnival's Fine Rococo Funerals? 'I expect you would like a cheque in advance,' she suggested, putting Fergus in his place (I bet Brightson's wait months).

'Spot on,' said Mary who was crossing the yard, baby on hip. She smiled brilliantly at Poppy, her previously hostile expression gone. Poppy caught a glimpse of the merry girl who had become entangled on the Costa.

'Certainly not!' exclaimed Fergus loftily. 'Payment when the customer is satisfied.'

'Ha, ha,' said Mary, walking away, 'ha, ha, ha,' on a rising note.

Fergus exploded. 'She's impossible since she had that child. Pretends to be unemployed. Draws single-parent benefit, knows all the dodges.'

Poppy did not respond.

'That poor man is dying to marry her, writes to her every day, utterly lovelorn. What it must cost him in stamps – telephones. Fellow's a fisherman. But she's too grand, says the county would never accept him. You wouldn't take her for county would you?'

'I—'

'Her pa's probably one of your father's friends, he's my landlord, actually used to train racehorses here, gives her a colossal allowance, sent her to Westonbirt or Roedean I forget which—'

'Neither,' shouted Mary, still in earshot.

'She enjoys slumming and playing the Gypsy Queen. I wish I'd never taken her on.'

'Just for the ride,' shouted Mary mockingly. 'The ride.'

Not thinking Fergus's relations with Mary her business, Poppy said, 'All the same, if you don't mind, I would rather give you a cheque now. Let's say half. How much?'

Without hesitation Fergus named a hefty sum. Poppy gave a mental whistle but, fishing her cheque book from her bag, wrote a cheque. It had better be good, she thought, underlining her signature. She handed the cheque to Fergus who pushed it quickly into his hip pocket.

Victor, breaking a thoughtful silence, suggested that it was now time they left.

'May I come with you in your car, I've run out of petrol?'

Poppy nodded.

As they drove away Victor looked back to see Fergus study the cheque, then wave it as though it had burned his fingers.

'He expects it to bounce,' he told Poppy; or perhaps, he thought, he's waving it in triumph.

'It won't bounce.' Poppy stopped the car. 'You haven't run out of petrol, have you?'

'Just thought I'd try.'

'Pretty feeble,' said Poppy. 'Run back for your car. I'll wait, and you can follow.' She had recovered her cool and wondered why she had wept; she blamed the alcohol.

'Okay.' Victor got out of the car unprotesting.

'I take it Furnival's Funerals are short of trade.' Poppy surprised Victor by her shrewdness.

'You could say that.' He reassessed her.

'M-m-m.' She drummed her fingers on the driving wheel. 'What are you waiting for?'

'Sorry.' Victor ran back to his car, the old Ford Poppy had seen when she arrived. While she waited, she thought of Edmund, the soul of convention, and how horrified he would be by the planned funeral, how he would have insisted on Brightson's, how he would, if asked, have prevented Dad lying, for his last days above ground, in his own house, how he would have implied this to be somehow insanitary. Oh Edmund, she thought, weakening, recollecting the feel of his body, the bristly hairs round his navel. Oh Edmund, impregnated with tact for all seasons, no wonder Dad did not like you. 'This is Dad's funeral, not yours,' she said out loud.

Catching sight in the driving mirror of Victor's car coming down the track, she put the car into gear, released the brake and drove on. How one wishes it were Venetia to feed the worms, she thought with venom; what a pity murder is illegal. She pressed her foot on the accelerator, deciding to wear Dad's festive dress in his honour. I am torn between the dead and the lost, she told herself histrionically.

9

Driving her father's car up to the front door of her home (she must get used to owning it) Poppy regretted her show of emotion. It had been ridiculous to cry on a strange man's chest, to give way to grief for Edmund. Naturally the two men thought her tears were for her father; it made her behaviour the more absurd. She decided to be businesslike with Victor, discuss the comestibles, show him the general layout of the house and nothing more. In decency she supposed she would have to offer him a drink. It occurred to her that if she searched carefully among her father's effects she might find some clues to his persona which now he was dead belatedly aroused her curiosity.

Victor, who had hoped to increase his knowledge of Poppy, found himself shown the ground floor of the house, the sitting room with the French windows opening on to the garden, the kitchen where he would assemble what he called the eats, the cloakroom, and that was all.

Poppy offered Victor a drink. He accepted a vodka and tonic, and was put out when Poppy did not join him but stood plainly waiting for him to leave.

Victor took a swallow of vodka. 'So,' he said, 'I will see about the drinks. Are you sure you want champagne?' If they discussed alternatives he could elongate the conversation.

'Sure,' said Poppy. 'Quite.'

'Right,' said Victor, 'champagne it shall be. You have shown me your fridge.'

'Yes.'

'I had better hire glasses, you may not have enough.'

'As you wish.'

'The food I can get from my take-away friend in Shepherd's Bush. Will you leave it to me to make a choice of little eats?'

'Of course.' Her flat tone indicated that they had been into all this already, no need to recap.

40

Victor sipped his vodka, spinning it out; she might not offer him another. He would have to leave if he put down an empty glass.

'If the weather's fine as it is today your guests can overflow into the garden.'

'Yes.' What guests? Who would come other than Dad's daily lady, Mrs Edwardes, a few curious from the village, local bores. She had invited Mr and Mrs Poole and Anthony Green. What a dreary party! She would have to invite the vicar. She tried to remember whether of late years Dad ever went to church. Had he not claimed to be quasi-agnostic? Was she doing right to have a church service? Oh Dad, look what you've let me in for.

'What about parking?' Victor sipped his drink letting it run back through his teeth into the glass.

'Parking?' Poppy was amused by Victor's ploy (does he think I don't notice?), watching her with his small pale eyes with dark pupils like a jackdaw's. 'Parking?' she questioned.

'Yes. All the cars and for that matter Fergus.' Grudgingly Victor mentioned Fergus.

'There's the road, the village green, there's the stable yard.'

'Stable yard, could one see it?'

'Sure. Have another drink,' she relented. 'I will show you the stables.' She watched Victor gulp the remains of the vodka, poured him another. 'Across here.' She led him through the garden. Victor, carrying his fresh drink, followed her.

'These are the stables, rather dusty and unused. The er – hearse horses could rest in them if—'

'Fergus has his horse-boxes, he can load up and go home after the ceremony. Get the horses home quickly after the job is what he'll want.'

What makes him think that? He looked the sort to want to join in the champagne drinking, eat the eats. The girls too looked as though they would appreciate a party.

'I have to talk to the vicar,' she said. 'I've got a date.' A grey lie, never mind.

'Right.' Victor gave up, downed his drink. 'I will ring you from London to confirm the logistics.' Victor was fond of the word 'logistics', brought to his attention during the Falklands War. He hoped one day to find a place for it in a novel.

'It's very kind of you.' Poppy walked with him to his car. 'It's extremely kind of you to be so helpful.' Without this man could she

41

have forced Edmund to help, appealed to his better nature? If he has one, she thought, sourly remembering the entwined figures by the Serpentine and other occasions when Edmund had not been altogether perfect. 'Well,' she said as they reached the car, 'goodbye and thanks again.'

'I'll be in touch. See you Saturday, 'bye.' Victor waved as he drove off. She saw through me like a sieve, he thought with amusement. Glad she lives in London, it will be easier to get to know her there. 'I won't live here,' she had said in her father's house. 'There may be a use for it, weekends perhaps.' I wonder how I can stop Fergus seeing those stables, mused Victor as he drove towards London, unaware that Poppy, looking at the dusty buildings, had decided to ask Fergus for his advice about them, perhaps rent them to him if he expanded his business.

Fergus was the sort of man Edmund detested and another type he loathed would be Victor with his thin intelligent face. Edmund had no time for intellectuals. I wish I had stopped by the Serpentine and spat in his eye, she thought, and went to answer the telephone which was ringing.

'Hullo, Vicar.' She recognised the hesitant insecure voice, not the sort to inspire confidence or lead one to higher things. Dad had once unkindly said 'not enough spunk'. 'Hullo, Vicar. Yes please, it would be very kind if you would come round or we can discuss it now.' She listened to the vicar, giving him half her attention while the picture of the girl with the spiky hair flitted across the other half. She supposed the baby's father was a Spaniard; if one went by the baby's face he must be a knock-out. The girl had been jolly rude. She must be unhappy to be so antagonistic. The vicar was talking about the grave.

'—the Sexton says he can just fit it in the old graveyard with your mother.'

'Dad will be pleased.'

'—and the service? Have you any particular—'

'As simple as possible, he would, I would like, jolly hymns, sort of rejoicing.'

'—?' The vicar mumbled a doubtful query.

'Yes, Vicar, I do mean rejoice. He's had coronary after coronary, *he* will be rejoicing all that's over.'

'If that's your – attitude.'

'Yes, it is.' Is he going to make difficulties?'

'Most laudable. I – er—'

'It's not laudable, it's what Dad would feel so I must too. Surely you who believe in the after-life agree.'

'I never knew your father well, ah – er – he never discussed his beliefs with me.'

'I think he hedged his bets,' said Poppy.

He would, wouldn't he, thought the vicar who, though he barely knew Bob Carew, had heard much said in the parish about Bob Carew's interests.

'To come back to the hymns,' said the vicar, retreating to safer ground, 'it's a bit difficult, it's—'

'No jolly hymns? Nothing suitable?' This vicar was eminently teasable.

'Suppose our organist, if I can get Mr Ottway to play – he's really very good – suppose we do away with hymns and ask Mr Ottway to play a lot of Bach.'

'Brilliant idea.'

'Oh good, then suppose, Miss Carew—'

'Poppy, please.'

'Thank you. Suppose I come round tomorrow and we make the final arrangements. I can get details and fix times with Brightson's.'

'Not Brightson's.'

'What?'

'My father wished to have a firm called Furnival's.'

'Oh.' The vicar's voice dipped. 'I see.'

'I saw them this afternoon. They will be in touch with you, Vicar.'

'Oh.' The vicar sounded alarmed. 'I see—'

'And I hope you will come back to the house afterwards.'

'Thank you.' On the other end of the line the vicar gathered strength. 'Do I really understand that—'

'Yes, not Brightson's, Furnival's, it's perfectly legit, Vicar.'

'Yes, yes of course. I'll telephone tomorrow.' He sounded apprehensive on the verge of protest.

'Thank you very much. Goodbye.' Poppy waited for the vicar to ring off and presently telephoned *The Times*, the *Daily Telegraph*, and the local paper asking them to put in a notice of her father's funeral, spelling the name Furnival, making sure they got it right.

Left alone, Poppy walked about her father's garden, trying to visualise him as he used to be when she was a child. Mowing the lawn, sweeping up leaves, weeding. But she could not see him. Here behind the lilacs she and Edmund had kissed. Here, out of sight of the house, they had lain on the grass on hot summer evenings, their bodies touching. Dad, where are you Dad? The leaves on the lilacs were now turned yellow, a hesitant breeze testing the quiet autumn air rustled the bushes, bringing back that moment when, sheltered from observant eyes by scented lilac and philadelphus, Edmund had pulled her down on to the grass, kissing her mouth, holding her body against his, hard, heavy urgent; had penetrated so that astonished she had whispered, 'Go on, do that, don't stop,' in her first exultant sexual success, 'go on, don't stop, don't stop,' with the selfishness of satisfied joy, and as it waned leaving her gloriously spent her father had called from the house and Edmund had frustratedly called her 'you fool, you fool, you put me off' and then 'damn your fucking father'.

The breeze dropped as quickly as it had risen, a leaf from the lilac drifted crisply to the ground. Dryly Poppy thought that never again had Edmund admitted her need before his own.

She bent down brushing the grass with her palm where this, her first sexual experience, had happened. Then the grass had been short dense deep green, springing, today it felt dry, brittle, rather dusty.

Poppy went back to the house. She would leave Edmund in the garden; the scenes she remembered were old anyway, seven, eight years old, an age of ignorance. She wandered through the empty rooms seeking her father, thinking now of the unhappy girl Mary, with spiky hair and the beautiful baby.

When the telephone rang it was Fergus.

'They will bring your father early,' his voice was kind reassuring, 'tomorrow.'

'Thank you. What time?'

'Nineish or even before.'

Perhaps with Dad actually in the house it would be easier to find him. She felt very tired. Climbing the stairs to bed, she decided she would sleep in the visitors' room. Edmund, so disliked by Dad, haunted her room. Poppy dismissed her fanciful thoughts. Dad was in his coffin and would be brought here tomorrow. Edmund would now be tucked up snug with Venetia in Venetia's flat after eating one of her delicious dinners. She was an impossibly good cook, spent lavishly on food.

As she was getting into bed the telephone rang in Dad's room across the landing.

'Hullo.' She stood in her nightdress and bare feet.

'It's me again I'm afraid.' It was the vicar. 'Sorry to bother you.'

'Yes?'

'I just wondered thinking about the service on Saturday and your wish for a cheerful hymn whether you had thought of any particular one so that I can apprise the organist. It is usual to have at least one hymn.' The voice was gently insistent.

'Oh, I—' Poppy stood barefoot holding the receiver 'Um – I – ' she searched her mind: 'The race that long in darkness—?' 'How dark was the stable?' 'There's a home for little children–'. Dad was no child for Christ's sake! 'Colours of day'? 'The King of Love—'? 'Oh Vicar, I can't.'

'Perhaps,' the vicar's voice was mild, 'perhaps you could leave it to me?'

'Please. If that's—'

'Nothing lugubrious, nothing mundane, nothing the Bishop would take exception to.'

'The Bishop? What's he got to do with—'

The laugh was both deprecating and dismissive. 'His job to criticise, Poppy.'

'I see.' I don't see, all I see is Edmund in Venetia's arms. Does he explore her teeth for stoppings with his tongue as he did mine? The vicar was still talking.

'—so if you leave it to me I will make sure you have something your father would like.'

'Leave it to you?' First Fergus, then Victor, now the vicar. There is nothing left for me to do. 'Do you know what Dad would like?' She felt doubtful.

'Certainly I do,' said the vicar.

'All right, Vicar. If you are sure I will.'

'Good.' He did not ring off, waited for her to thank him, end the conversation.

'Is there anything else?' he asked.

'No, no, nothing else. Thank you. I am sure you will make a suitable choice.' The vicar laughed again in an affectionate way. 'You have been so kind.'

'—my job.'

'Well good night, and thank you again.'

Has Venetia found out yet how he picks his teeth?

10

Late in the afternoon, Mary, baby on hip, came up to Fergus. 'Now you can pay the rent. And the feed bill.' Her tone was sarcastic.

'In part perhaps—'

'Father didn't rent you this place for free.'

'I wish your father would take a—'

'Running jump,' said Mary. 'I'm with you there.' Her tone was quite hearty.

'Really?' Fergus was surprised.

She watched Fergus. 'Have you thought about this place in winter?'

'Winter?' Her voice implied a catch.

'It gets snowed in. You won't find your business possible without a snow plough. Father's known it cut off for weeks, months, in some winters.' She waited for Fergus's reaction with relish.

'So that's why he rented it so cheap, the crafty bastard.' Fergus thought of Nicholas Mowbray's weather-beaten face, expansive gestures, fruity voice.

'He thinks I'll get over my horsey phase if I am frozen and uncomfortable.'

'You can nip back to Spain to warm up in Joseph's arms,' Fergus suggested.

Mary ignored this gibe. 'He thinks you're a sucker. He doesn't mind if you go bankrupt; all he thinks is that I might decide to try a job he would consider sensible if this one packs up.'

'Like secretary to an oil mogul?'

'I wouldn't last long.' Mary let off a peal of laughter. 'You should have checked the advertisement before posting it,' she jeered. 'You are not competent. You know I can hardly type.'

Fergus eyed her without animosity: her typing error had brought him Poppy's father. I am a simpleton, he thought. I rather took to Mary's father and his bonhomie: he is using me, I shan't pay the rent, there are far more urgent bills. Ruefully he considered the pile of buff envelopes on the kitchen mantelshelf.

Forgetting Mary, he stood looking down the valley, seeing all too clearly how cut off he could be. He thought, I could get the horses out, but where would I take them? His enthusiasm for his project had led him to jump at the cheap rent suggested by Nicholas Mowbray. He flinched, thinking of the monthly payments on horse-boxes, Land Rovers and the lorry. The horses are mine, he thought, seeking comfort, the tack and the hearse are mine. He looked round the yard for reassurance from the horses, as they watched from their loose-boxes. I refuse to be defeated, he thought, I must make a success of this. He said nastily, 'What a bloody little Cassandra you are. There's no necessity,' he cried angrily, 'for your single parent situation. I understand Joseph would like to make an honest woman of you, why don't . . .?'

'Do you want to get shot of me?' Her voice quavered upwards in thin defiance.

Fergus ignored the question. 'Wouldn't it be better for Barnaby?'

'Why are you so keen on marriage for me? You steer clear of it. You are as bad as my father, you want to see me pegged down.'

'I should have thought Barnaby quite a peg.' Fergus met the baby's eye. Barnaby smiled gummily.

'I can travel with him; a child is a carrier bag, a husband is a trunk.'

'You wish to travel light?'

'For the present.' Keeping her options open, Mary shifted the child from one hip to the other with a sensuous movement. Fergus appeared to have erased from his memory the horse-buying trip to Ireland when, for months, she had shared his bed. From Ireland, she had gone to Spain and returned with Barnaby. She stood looking down the valley, bleakly considering her options. She was glad she had planted the seed of unease in Fergus: he's too bloody pleased with himself, she thought, remembering him in Ireland. And, before Ireland, Fergus had had something going with Victor's ex-wife Penelope and, later, with the magazine editor Julia. 'You and Victor are pretty close friends, aren't you?' she said with sweet malice. 'Great sharers, keep your girls in the family.'

'So, so.' Fergus was not to be drawn. He was remembering Poppy's slip; circuses, he consoled himself, have winter quarters – so?

Standing beside him, baby on hip, Mary shied away from the thought of the extended family ready with its octopus arms to gather

her in, coddle her in its expansive bosom. I can't live in Spain, she thought, I could never get used to that crowd. I shall get no help from Fergus. Despairingly she looked at her child who looked back at her with his father's eyes. 'Oh!' Mary yelled in frustration. 'Oh!'

At this moment Annie and Frances joined them. Both girls now smelled of shampoo. Frances looked extraordinary, which was her intention, in a skin-tight mini-skirt which barely covered her pubic region, an immensely baggy black jersey worn under a man's string vest, on her wrists a jingling collection of silver bracelets. Annie, demure in a flowing black dress, bare feet, plethora of earrings, red caste mark between her eyes, a diamond clipped to one nostril, had not succeeded in disguising her Sloane Rangership. 'Coming to the disco?' they asked Mary. 'Help us sort out the local boys?'

'All right,' Mary was obliging. 'I'll come as I am,' she said. 'You do look an old-fashioned pair.' She eyed Annie. 'Are you from the Bazaar or the Souk?' Annie laughed. 'You won't mind baby-sitting Barnaby, will you?' She held the baby out to Fergus.

'No fear,' said Fergus, 'you can take your carrier bag with you.' He started walking back to the cottage.

'We can't squash three on to the Yamaha,' Annie was plaintive, '*and* a baby.'

'Take us in your car,' cried Frances to Fergus, 'be a devil.'

Fergus went into the cottage and slammed the door, locking himself in with his dogs. He wanted his supper. Fetching some chops from the larder, he watched from the window as the three girls wedged themselves on to the motorbicycle, and proceeded slowly down the track. They would return in the small hours in some local boy's car, noisy, part-drunk, happy.

'Such nice girls,' Fergus said to the cat Bolivar who wove silently through the casement window to sit, paws together, preparing to terrorise the dogs with basilisk stare and, hopefully, lick the frying pan when Fergus had finished with it. The dogs shifted uneasily on their hunkers, casting sidelong glances at the cat, licking their lips, unable, since he was a favourite of Fergus's, to attack as they would have liked. Fergus gave Bolivar a snippet of raw meat, respecting the cat, an entire tom, for having shown guile and agility in escaping the vet on the day of his intended emasculation. Something about Bolivar set him thinking of Poppy Carew's father, wondering whether there was any similarity. I must not make a cock-up of this funeral, ruminated Fergus, frying his chops. That's a lovely girl, she

48

shall have what her dad wanted, and who knows, he thought optimistically, it may lead to other work. Eating his supper, Fergus thought about Poppy and was a mite uneasy of the feelings she engendered. For, like Mary, he had a penchant for independence.

Having eaten, Fergus spent a session on the telephone. Then, plans made, he whistled his dogs and walked up the valley to the downs. Bolivar came too for the first quarter mile, spoiling the dogs' joy by his sinister presence. Since he had found the hearse mouldering in a barn in France, he had put his savings and everything he could borrow into his business, bought the horses, their harness, the vehicles. Rented the yard and the cottage from Mary's father and was only now, deeply in debt, ready to start in independent practice.

Overheads are terrible, Fergus shuddered, thinking of the pile of bills, the monthly payments, the rising bank interest. Treading the springy turf, he blamed himself for being so unsuspicious of Mary's father who had, long ago, trained horses here, out of sight of snoopers. He reached the top of the valley and looked along the stretch of downland where the horses had galloped. There was no evidence now, on the short turf grazed by sheep, of the unsound animals dosed with anabolic steroids, innocent collaborators who had displayed their paces to potential buyers. Standing on the sweet turf, hearing the ghostly breath and drumming hooves of horses long gone, Fergus felt lonely, afraid, vulnerable.

Mary's father now farmed in East Anglia, growing surplus grain for the EEC. He had not been specifically warned, but hinted, out of the racing world. The old boy network had netted him and, humiliatingly, let him go, as too small to fry. He saw me coming, thought Fergus ruefully, remembering Mary's introduction followed by the helpful offer at low rent of the cottage and stables.

'Any friend of Mary's . . . glad to help an enterprising chap . . . wonderful to be your own master . . . bound to make a success.' At this rate, I am bound to the bank, nothing belongs to me, my Dow Jones are in peril. Fergus stooped to peer in the fading light at a harebell still in flower in late September, and was glad that his landlord was too mean to spray and spread fertiliser, kill the harebells, thyme and Shepherd's Purse. He felt sorry for Mary having such a treacherous father; he forgave her her careless typing and arrogance, guessing that she was warning him to be careful of her father by telling him what could happen when it snowed. Winter, after all, is the dying time, the boom time for undertakers.

Had she not told Frances, a notorious blabbermouth, about the anabolic steroids and the end of her father's interest in horses? In Ireland buying horses, she had been invaluable, spotting defects he might have overlooked. He had been puzzled, at the time, by her esoteric knowledge.

Fergus straightened up as his dogs lit off in sudden noisy pursuit of a hare. He watched the hunt vanish over the hill, racing towards the moonrise, and waited for their panting, shamed return; standing on top of the quiet downs, watching the lights of distant cars on the main road and the sparkle of the town where Mary, Frances and Annie danced in the disco, almost he wished himself with them.

He knew Mary well enough to guess that Barnaby would be disposed of somewhere safe. And another thing, he thought, to Mary's credit. She had not tried to father the infant on him. It would have been possible, he would not have been able to disprove it. He had been galled and at a loss when shortly after Ireland she had vanished abroad without warning.

Many months later when searching for suitable stables he had run into her in Newbury. She had suggested her father as landlord. It had seemed natural to ask her to work with him again, she had brought with her Annie and Frances (to himself Fergus admitted that without Mary it was doubtful his venture would have got off the ground).

Watching the lights in the distance Fergus found himself hoping that it would be a long while before her love of travelling light inspired her to disappear a second time. A replacement would be difficult, well nigh impossible to find.

He recalled her hair had been long and thick-plaited like a corn dolly, oat coloured. Fergus winced at the thought of it now chopped short, often tinted an ugly black. He remembered the feel of the plait in his hand the temptation to yank it like a bell pull. She had been more approachable then, less abrasive, perhaps less competent?

She did not speak of her year in Spain; what meagre information he possessed was gained from Frances and Annie's idle gossip, gossip which Mary made no attempt to elaborate, lurking behind her habitual reserve, a reserve which bordered on the inimical tinged with not unfriendly mockery. Cheered by thinking better of Mary than he normally did, and by the exhausted return of his dogs, Fergus ran back down the track to the stable. As he ran, his eye caught a glint of moonlight on the pool in the stream in the orchard, where, that afternoon, he and Victor had loosed the trout. He peered into the water, fearing to see it floating dead on the surface (as well it might after its vicissitudes) but, noting Bolivar sitting still and enigmatic, watching the water, he assumed its survival and went to bed, to sleep and forget his anxieties. It was only when the girls returned in the small hours, with Barnaby yelling and their boy-friends shouting raucous good nights, that he woke to worry as to whether Victor, going off as he had with Poppy, had stolen a march on him. Damn Victor, he thought, and damn those bloody girls.

'Shut up,' Fergus flung open his window, 'shut bloody up.' The laughter trailed away then broke out again into bubbles of high spirits. Slamming his window shut, cracking a pane, Fergus thought they will wake the dead and the dead are my métier, as he drew the covers over his head to deaden the sound.

I I

Early the next morning, deserted by fickle sleep, Poppy lay in the visitors' bedroom thinking of her father. Although he had spoilt her as a child, never been angry, impatient or unkind, he had been much away leaving her with Esmé.

There had been between Dad and Esmé, a handsome woman referred to behind her back as 'The Spirit of Rectitude' an uneasy truce. She insisted on brushed hair and washed hands, had been known to tell Dad to change his gardening clothes before sitting down to tea. Childhood had been punctuated by sharp commands: 'wipe your feet', 'clean your teeth', 'go and have a bath', 'don't bring that filthy thing into my kitchen, take it out at once'. 'Your mother' or 'Mrs Carew' (depending on which of them she was addressing) 'would not like that'. When Esmé called on his wife's name for support Dad would laugh and say, 'She wouldn't mind, Esmé. You are inventing her, building her in the image of past glories.' (Esmé had once been Nanny to a diplomat's children and was not averse to putting the Carews down a peg. Poppy had never been sure whether Esmé had actually known her mother, her own memories of her were hazy. There were the photographs in Dad's room, the recollection, vague, of Mum leaving on a trip abroad, of time passing and the eventual realisation that she was not coming back. That somehow she had been negligent, had died. Life had carried on, orderly, rather dull, with Dad constantly away. 'Another card for you.' Esmé would sort the post, picking through it with suspicion, sniffing at bills and appeals. Where were those postcards now? Restless, Poppy got out of bed, crossed the landing to her old bedroom, crouched down by the chest-of-drawers and began to search. What a lot of rubbish, old letters, broken toys, odd socks, snapshots of cats and dogs, school groups, junk jewellery and snaps of Edmund. Oh Edmund, did you really have your hair cut like that? And oh, I'd forgotten you tried to grow a moustache (it had been unkind of Dad to laugh). And the postcards, bundles of them, the message always the same, 'Love from Dad, see you soon.' Poppy turned them over, looking at the postmarks. Cheltenham, Plumpton, Newcastle, York, Worcester, Wincanton, Newton Abbot, Chepstow, Brighton, Liverpool, Ascot. A litany of racetracks. He had been with those mystery ladies who dealt out Life's Dividends. Poppy sniffed the cards. Were the ladies beautiful, witty, sexy? Had Esmé known as she sifted the post what he was up to? Where was Esmé now? Alive? Dead? Esmé had liked Edmund, unlike Dad who had taken his instant dislike. She had encouraged Edmund, making him welcome, laying another place at the table (no trouble at all). She never did that for anyone else (can't have just anyone popping in without so much as a by your leave). Crouching by the drawer full of junk and memories, Poppy remembered Esmé's expression. She had been defiant, annoying Dad on purpose, getting a kick out of it. 'Edmund will do you good,' she had said. What had she meant by that? Had she meant Edmund will hurt you which was Dad's fear? I believe, thought Poppy, putting the postcards back in the drawer, I believe she fancied Edmund, how repulsive, eugh.

Soon after Edmund had become established as a fact, welcome or not, Esmé had retired, gone to live with her sister, showing no emotion at parting. Poppy remembered Esmé's voice, its rasping timbre. 'My sister wants me. You are old enough to look after your father. I've arranged for Mrs Edwardes to come in and clean, she will do for you well enough.' Esmé's voice had been contemptuous. Had the contempt been for the Carews or Mrs Edwardes? For us, thought Poppy, shutting the drawer, nobody could despise Jane Edwardes. At the time she had been shocked, realising that Esmé did not mind leaving, she and Dad had been a job, no more, she had wasted no emotion on them.

She didn't love us, thought Poppy, and to be honest we did not love her. Dad had suggested lunching out on the day of Esmé's departure. They had lunched in Newbury. Dad had raised his glass and said, 'Let's drink goodbye to Rectitude'. After another drink or two he had said, 'I hope Mrs Edwardes won't moralise or encourage followers', a dig at poor Edmund. (Why do I pity him, the swine, tucked up with Venetia.) Briefly Poppy considered finding Esmé, asking her what she knew of Dad's life. Impossible. As impossible as to ask Mr Poole or Anthony Green exactly when the various dollops of dividends had appeared and in what quantities. It was extraordinary to have lived in the same house as Dad and not know what he was really like, shameful to have shown so little interest and to let him die a stranger. Am I too late? Poppy asked herself. Perhaps he did not mind, she thought hopefully, but if Dad had not minded he would not have been so inimical towards Edmund filling her life for ten years.

And now Venetia. 'I hope she chokes him.'

Poppy re-routed her search into Dad's bedroom. It was rather eerie going through his drawers and cupboards. Orderly, neat, smelling faintly of Dad. Shoes, socks, underclothes, suits, shirts, photographs of Mum smiling and one very sad and beautiful by his bed. She searched the dressing-table drawers. Indigestion pills, heart tablets, cufflinks, nothing to introduce or betray. Downstairs she searched his desk, fingering receipts, bank statements, (might be a clue or two there, but the only ones kept were recent). A catalogue of a country house sale, writing paper, pens, paperclips, old indiarubbers, TV licence, dog licence (old Buster dead last year), racing calendars, snapshots of herself at school, on the lawn with her rabbit, in her bath (what a fat baby), none of herself with Edmund, Dad had not wanted any. (I don't need reminding.) Several drawers were empty. He must have tidied up, known he might die. Of course he had known. At another lunch – when, a year, two years ago? – he had said, 'I might go any time, not to worry, it's the only certainty and I've enjoyed my life, I only grumble about one thing and that is beginning not to bother me.' At the time she had thought he is coming round to Edmund, beginning to accept him. Now she realised, sitting back on her heels, feeling chilly in her nightdress, that what made Dad feel better were the first signs of Edmund's

53

impending desertion. Clever Dad, you noticed before I did. Was it then you wrote me your letter and put it in the bank to wait?

And now for the locked drawer, the drawer Edmund had prized open with his neat bit of plastic, the drawer full of old letters.

'Other people's letters are a laugh. Lush, slush, sentimentality, let's see the sort of stuff they wrote to each other in their day.' Edmund, giggling. Dad's letters to Mum and Mum's letters to Dad, tied in packets of ten or twelve with tape, the envelopes yellowed, the ink faded.

She had slammed the drawer shut, catching Edmund's fingers. He had black fingernails for weeks, months. He had hit her dancing about the room in agony. It was the first time he had hit her and she forgave him, crying, 'Sorry, sorry, I'm sorry.'

I'm not sorry now, she thought, pulling gently at the brass handles. She would find the key among Dad's things. The drawer opened sweetly, lightly, showing emptiness. Empty of Dad and Mum, empty of written evidence of their love. Dad had not trusted her, had withdrawn himself and her mother too.

She stood up remembering Dad coming into the house when he had been away, holding out his arms to hug her, 'How's my Poppy love?'

Outside the hearse came to a discreet halt, the driver rang the bell, his mate stood by the hearse, waiting.

Poppy put one of her father's old coats over her nightdress and opened the door.

'Miss Carew?'

'Yes.'

'We've brought—'

'Yes.'

'Indoors, love?'

'Yes.'

'A couple of chairs perhaps?'

'There are stools. Wait a moment.' She must hurry to let Dad into the house. She ran to the sitting room where his small television perched on a stool. 'Here,' she called, 'help me with this.' One of the men moved the television to the top of the desk, carefully displacing the silver photograph frame which held her mother aged seventeen. 'There's another upstairs.' The second man followed her, fetched down the stool.

As they carried Dad in Jane Edwardes drove up in her car. 'Thought I'd come early, get you some breakfast.' She put her arms round Poppy and hugged her. 'Heard he was to come home. Still in your nightie, don't catch your death.'

'I'm all right.'

They watched the men settle the coffin on the stools. They were quick, expert, tactful, did their job and left.

'Go and pick a few flowers from his garden while I make your coffee.'

Jane Edwardes handed Poppy secateurs. Poppy, walking in the dew listening to the birds in Dad's garden, remembered his favourite flowers and cut their stalks snip, snip, as he had done. A robin sang furiously asserting territorial rights. Edmund knew a lot about birds. Damn Edmund, don't come between me and my father, get stuck into Venetia.

Jane Edwardes had a bowl ready on the coffin. The house smelled of coffee. 'That's better.' She steadied a rose into place. 'Looks nice. My nephew works for Brightson's—'

Oh, not that again.

'Tells me you are having Furnival's.'

'Yes.' (Must I be defensive?)

'The old bastards had the monopoly far too long, my nephew says. He's thinking, my nephew that is, of applying for a job with Furnival's, says Furnival's will soon be the "in thing". That's what the young ones are saying.'

'Oh?'

'He, my nephew that is, my brother's son Bill, you know him?'

'Yes.'

'He rang up Mr Furnival and offered to give a hand Saturday at the funeral—'

'How very—'

'He thought, well we all thought, the village would like it, you know just to show—'

'What?'

'We loved him, always had a joke your father. He gave them many a good tip in the pub too.'

'Dad did?'

'Didn't you know?'

'No, no I didn't know.' I didn't know the village loved him, I didn't know he went to the pub. 'Thank you, Mrs Edwardes.'

'Come and eat your breakfast, love.'

'I'll come in a minute.' Poppy stood by the coffin. This oblong box held the man with the unmalicious laugh, now silent. The capable hands which would never again pick flowers. 'Pick flowers with the dew on them, they last better.' She touched the flowers in the bowl, the late roses, rosemary, pink daisies, a few late lilies. I am making myself think these morbid conventional thoughts. Those hands, those fingers used a biro to mark many a race card, how I wish I'd known his companions at the races. Those strong fingers tore up all your letters, destroyed your past, wrote me that last short note. An appeal? An order? A warning, a suggestion?

'Fergus thought you would like these.' She had not heard Mary come in. Did not recognise her at first. The black hair was washed clean and hung down as gold as Venetia's and as smooth. Mary looked prim in clean jeans and grey cotton jersey. She carried what looked like a black rug over her arm and held a wreath in her hand. 'If you lift the bowl of flowers I will spread it for you, unless you want to do it yourself.'

'Oh no.' She drew back from the coffin.

'Hold this then a minute, it's the laurel wreath—'

'Oh.'

As Poppy did not move Mary picked up the bowl of flowers herself. 'These are nice. From his garden?'

'Yes.' She watched Mary spread the pall over the coffin so that its edge, braided in gold, trailed down to the floor, replace the flowers 'Over his heart. Poor old boy, was it one of his coronaries?'

'Did you know him?' She was surprised.

'We used to meet at the races. I'd get him to mark my card. He had a nose for winners. Didn't know him well, people said he talked to the horses. There, that's better.' She put the bowl exactly in the centre. 'Of course he talked to the trainers too, and the wreath, how about that?' She propped the wreath at the head of the coffin. 'Made it myself, worked for a short time at a florists when I left school. It will smell nice when the room warms up.' She looked sharply at Poppy. 'It's bay, you know, not laurel. I pinched this lot from a garden I know. They won't miss it.'

'I—' She longed to ask Mary who had been at the races with Dad.

'There we are.' Mary brushed her hands together. 'Do I smell coffee?'

'Come and have some.'

'You been up all night?' Mary walked with Poppy towards the kitchen.

'Most of it.' She could not question this stranger.

'Fergus sent me to take a look round the church, get the lay of the land, where to unload and hitch up the horses, that sort of thing.'

'I see.'

'I've done that. Nice church, nice village. Oh great, coffee.' She took a cup handed to her by Mrs Edwardes and gulped it hurriedly. 'Thanks a lot. Got to rush or Barnaby will be yelling for his feed. Many thanks.' She put down the empty cup, 'See you Saturday,' and was gone.

'What a nice girl,' said Mrs Edwardes, watching her go with an approving eye.

Poppy stood watching Mary walk to her car, get in and drive slowly past. As she drew level, Mary wound down the window and leaned out.

'Did you love your father?' Her eyes were questing.

'I hardly knew him.' Why do I say that? It's the truth. Poppy met Mary's eyes.

Mary nodded. 'It happens.' She went on looking at Poppy, taking her in. 'I can't stand mine.' She smiled connivingly, slipped the car into gear, wound up the window and drove away.

12

Although he knew perfectly well that the trout was in Fergus's stream, on his return to London Victor looked in his bath to make quite sure it was gone.

The whole episode seemed out of context with his ordinary life. He screwed the bath tap, which was dripping, tighter. As he thought of the fish, his sympathy for its plight on the fishmonger's slab he relived the comprehension in Poppy's eyes when she heard the story from Fergus. She had appeared to think his action natural, even reasonable, she had given Fergus an appraising look when he joked about it.

A girl like that, thought Victor, putting a clean sheet of paper into his typewriter, was not in the same league as his ex-wife Penelope who would have snatched the fish, gutted, filleted and grilled it for supper.

An occasion, buried in his memory, came hauntingly back. Staying with Penelope's parents – they had lately become engaged – he had been strongly tempted to backtrack, call the engagement off. Across the lawn a rabbit had struggled, pursued by a weasel. Fear paralysed the rabbit so that its limbs jerked, its eyes rolled, it could hardly move its legs. Penelope, leaping out of the window, had snatched the rabbit and wrung its neck. (Sitting at his typewriter Victor winced, remembering the crack of bone.) As Penelope leapt and ran towards the rabbit Victor had assumed she was racing to the rescue. He had been shocked when she wrung the rabbit's neck, had been too much in love to protest.

I suppose I was in love, thought Victor, setting the paper in position, testing the new ribbon. Good job all that's over, he told himself stoutly.

The ex-wife Penelope jumped nimbly out of the window and wrung the rabbit's neck, he typed.

I am a moral coward. If I had trusted my instinct I would have saved a lot of time, emotion, money. I didn't mind when she nearly drowned that time, I didn't mind when she slept around with a whole lot of people, Fergus included. I am damn glad to be shot of her, it wasn't love, it was lust, he assured himself.

Yup, this ribbon is okay, just lust. Victor tore the paper out of the typewriter, crushed it into a ball, threw it towards the grate, inserted a fresh sheet, started typing his article for Julia.

Two hours later he'd got it right, Julia would publish the article in her glossy mag, Julia's mag would pay. In no way could this interesting original piece hurt Poppy's tender susceptibilities. Victor experienced the euphoria of a man who has written consecutive paragraphs of decent prose. He looked up Julia's office number and dialled it.

'Oh, hullo Victor, I've—'

'I've got the article for you, Julia, you won't be able to resist it.'

'Really?' She sounded quite friendly, the telephone suiting her contralto voice.

'Shall I come round with it and take you out for a drink? You're just leaving your office?'

'Yes, if you like. I've got a bit of—'

'We could go to that bar you like and if you like my article I'll stand you dinner afterwards.'

'I'm trying to—'

'And then we could—'

'Victor,' Julia shouted, 'listen, I have some news for you.'

'Oh Lord.'

'It's good news, no Oh Lord about it.'

'How's that?' Victor was suspicious.

'You know a year or so ago I said I'd show your manuscript to my publisher friend Sean?'

'Oh God. I'd forgotten. I'd rather forget.'

'No you wouldn't Victor. He got around to reading it. He likes it.'

'What?'

'Likes it. Wants to publish it. He'll pay you an advance, Victor.' Victor was silent.

'Victor, are you listening? This means money.'

'Julia.'

'Yes.'

'Is this novel about you know—'

'Your marriage to Penelope thinly disguised? Yes, it is.'

'I thought I'd thrown away all the copies.'

'You told me to throw it away when I'd read it.'

'And you didn't?' Who can you trust, thought Victor with glee.

'I thought it was such a marvellous portrait of old Penelope' (Julia pronounced the name to rhyme with antelope) 'that I kept it. She did give you a rough time, Victor.'

'Well.' Victor remembered the rabbit and the time Penelope nearly drowned. I could easily have helped her, he thought, but I didn't want to.

Julia was still talking. 'Then the other day I showed it to Sean and he loves it, it's as simple as that. Screams with laughter.'

'Laughter?' It's a tragic book, thought Victor, nothing funny about it. 'Oh Julia—'

'So bring your article and give me dinner.'

'What about libel?' Adjusting to having written a comedy (what's the difference, all great tragedies have a comic element) Victor remembered his novel. 'I wrote that book with my pen dipped in cyanide.'

'That's what Sean likes. He calls it stark. Penelope's far too vain to recognise herself, don't worry.'

'Julia, I love you, I'm on my way.'

As Victor walked jubilantly along the dusty late September pavement to the bus stop he thought about Julia. She will expect me to sleep with her after dinner, she will forget the brush-off she gave me, she'll forget she switched to Fergus. I shall tell her about my trout, Fergus's enterprise, well, the article is about that but I can tell her a few more details, Mary and her baby for instance. I am grateful for the introduction to Sean, he's a good publisher, well in a good publishing house, not afraid to take risks whatever that means, not that my novel's a risk. I could write a children's book about my trout or we could get it on television, a cartoon perhaps, bring in that fearful cat of Fergus's, Bolivar, no all that's been done. My luck has turned. Superstitiously Victor bowed to the new moon as he waited at the bus stop, turning round three times, jingling the silver in his pocket, wondering what to wish for.

He had a vision of Poppy's shoulderblades, mousy hair, long legs, funny teeth and tip-top tits.

But I call them breasts, he thought, climbing into the bus which had roared to an impatient stop. I shall take Julia to Shepherd's Bush and she shall help me choose the nosh, that will teach her to send me cookbooks. What a fool I am, thought Victor, as the bus jerked forward, how vain I am. Sean is Julia's current lover, I heard someone say so, sex with me doesn't come into it, we are platonic, have been for ages, I am just a writer with a novel she can lay at his feet, it costs her nothing. Better not wish too hard for Poppy, it might be unlucky. Victor glimpsed the crescent moon through a gap between high rise flats. I shall wish, he thought with a burst of generosity, I shall wish that Fergus makes a success of his enterprise, that my article brings me recognition and Fergus customers, that my book gets rave reviews.

Sitting in the bus on his way to meet Julia, Victor tried to adjust his mind to being a comic writer and mulled over some particularly felicitous turns of phrase which had tapped from his fingers. Re-reading his article as he rode along, Victor was pleased with his afternoon's work.

As he got off the bus Victor felt a pang of conscience. Poppy didn't want publicity, might not be pleased with his article. Julia might be inspired to come to the funeral, she was incurably inquisitive, might even bring Sean. I shall discourage her, Victor told himself, it's a solemn occasion, not a raree show. Then thinking yet again of his article he decided Poppy couldn't possibly take exception; it was faultlessly written, in excellent taste, restrained prose. The sort of taste Penelope made fun of. There's a fine line between love and lust when one is very young, thought Victor, wishing now that when he'd wished on the new moon he had wished never to think of Penelope again. It still hurt.

One of the things which hurt most was the drowning episode frequently brought up by friends as an example of his heartlessness towards his then wife. The most favoured version, which he had grown used to believing himself since it was the one most often recounted, was of the quarrel in the cove in Greece witnessed by onlookers, of his slapping Penelope's face, of Penelope in tears, diving off the rocks and swimming out to sea. That he had sat, not bothering to swim out to help or call for assistance when she got into difficulties.

In actual fact Victor remembered it had been Penelope who had slapped him so that taken unawares he had sat abruptly and bruised his coccyx while Penelope dived gracefully off the rock and swam off without a backward glance. He had lain back, eyes closed, nursing his injuries, physical and emotional. When he opened his eyes there had been no sign of Penelope. Worried, he had scrambled up the cliff to a vantage point and seen Penelope loitering along the cliff in her bikini, picking flowers, stopping to chat to groups of tourists. She looked very lovely and strange with her long wet hair and sun-brown limbs. She obviously made her usual impression. Busy making it, she had not seen him. He had hurried back to where she had left him and when she eventually rejoined him he had said, 'I wish you had drowned.' He could still remember her mockery. 'I don't drown easily.'

Going up in the lift to Julia's office Victor thought, I never felt protective towards Penelope as I did for the trout and do towards that girl Poppy. It was I, he thought, making his way past Julia's pretty secretary ('Julia's expecting you, Victor'), who was in need of protection.

13

'Haven't you got a nice black?' Mrs Edwardes stood with her back to the window looking at Poppy in the bed.

'Not really.' Poppy sipped the strong tea Jane Edwardes had brought her.

This was the fourth morning she had woken in the visitors' room. She felt rested after a night's sleep unmarred by memories of Edmund or pangs of conscience over her father. She felt positively cheerful. This, Dad's last night so to speak, had been dreamless. She had slept in peace in the visitors' bed, had felt that Dad after his fashion was at peace also.

It seemed a pity that he had to be disturbed from his position between the stools in the sitting room, to be carted to the church, endure the service, be carted again to the graveyard and buried out of sight, soon to be out of mind.

The days spent by Dad in his coffin in the sitting room had been friendly, pleasant, therapeutic. People had popped in to visit through the front door which she left open or in the case of some who were more intimate or perhaps shy (it was not possible to discern which), through the French windows from the garden. In almost every case these people, Dad's friends from the village and villages around, had something appreciative to say about him. They touched the coffin the way they would the sleeve of a friend. Some chuckled or laughed outright at some pleasing but private recollection. Some brought flowers, laying them by the coffin, promising a proper wreath on the day.

Poppy had grown used to Dad being there as one grows used to a new sofa after the first cultural shock, the replacement perhaps of a battered piece of Edwardiana by a new chesterfield from Habitat. She had grown used, too, to sprawling in this extremely comfortable bed, waking to the sound of sparrows chirping and the twittering of swallows ranged along the telephone wires in the road, gathering their wits, exchanging last messages before the long flight to Africa. They must go and Dad also. Today was the day, Saturday, Dad's funeral, her birthday.

'Haven't you got a nice black?' Jane Edwardes watched Poppy propped on her elbow drinking her tea in the large bed. The sheets slipped back as she lifted the cup, showing biscuit-coloured breasts with nipples Mrs Edwardes's grandmother would have called Old Rose. Jane Edwardes's grandmother had been a dressmaker and taught Jane the names of colours – Moss Green, Marina Blue, Nigger Brown, Old Rose, the fashionable colours of her day, the Thirties. Jane's grandmother would have run Poppy up a nice little Black Number for her father's funeral in a day if she had still been alive and no nonsense about wearing the dress Bob Carew had brought from Italy.

'It's my birthday. I always wear his present on my birthday.' Poppy put the cup in its saucer, laid it on the bedside table and, leaning back on the pillows, smiled up at Mrs Edwardes, not bothering to pull the sheets up.

The dress from Italy hung expectantly on the outer side of the cupboard door flaunting its simple elegance, its amazing juxtaposition of coloured triangles. Glancing sidelong at the dress Mrs Edwardes noted Moss Green, Lilac, Old Rose, Red Carnation and a blue which in some lights looked purple; her grandmother would not have known it as Aubergine.

'Delicious tea. Thank you.'

'There's a boutique in Newbury which has little black dresses—' Jane Edwardes tried again.

'I know it.'

Jane stooped to pick up Poppy's white cotton nightdress lying discarded by the bed.

'Can't sleep in them.' Poppy watched the older woman.

Jane shook the nightdress quite roughly, making her feelings clear.

'It's Dad's funeral, Mrs Edwardes.'

Jane sniffed.

The sun streaming yellow into the room was blacked out by a momentary cloud.

'I must have a bath, wash my hair.' Poppy slid out of bed and made for the bathroom.

'Bacon and egg for breakfast?' asked Jane Edwardes, accepting defeat.

'Yes, please,' answered Poppy warmly.

The sun shone in again illuminating a buttock as she went into the bathroom.

'Girls these days, I don't know. . . .' The older woman folded the nightdress, put it on the bed. 'Only wears it to walk about the house.'

Poppy turned on the taps. 'I'm going to keep that room as mine from now on,' she called above the rush of water.

'So that's how it is.' Jane commented as she went down to the kitchen. If asked she would not have been able to explain what she meant but inside she knew and quite liked the knowledge. There were two shades of lilac in that dress, she thought, taking the kitchen scissors to cut rind off bacon. Clever people with colour, the Italians. She'd noticed it last summer on the tour with her cousin when they'd seen Venice, Florence, Rome and that other place in six days. There might well be two shades of red and green in that dress. If she insists on wearing it I'll check, thought Jane, reaching into the refrigerator for an egg. I wonder whether she would eat two? She should eat a good breakfast, it's going to be a long day. Jane hesitated. One egg or two? That dress, though. Any other day but at your father's funeral! She went to the hall and, standing at the foot of the stairs, shouted: 'One egg or two?'

'One, please,' Poppy called from the bathroom.

Milan, that was the other place they'd seen. The dress came from there. What had he been doing in Milan? No need to ask. Jane Edwardes, standing by the refrigerator holding the egg, thought with tolerant affection of Poppy's father Bob Carew, hearing his voice, 'Like to flutter a fiver on the three-thirty at Kempton, Mrs Edwardes?' He'd always called her Mrs Edwardes, never Jane. The egg was pale brown, the same colour as the girl's skin. I was always good with colours, Jane reminded herself, comparing the egg with Poppy's tan. Bathes topless, one can see that, but wears the bottom bit. Bit's the word, thought Jane, recollecting the thin streak of white slanting across Poppy's bottom when she walked into the bathroom. Barely enough. Jane picked up the kitchen biro and traced a double V on the egg. Barely enough to cover her fluff. I don't know, I really don't. Sighing, Jane Edwardes went back up the stairs to stand in the bathroom doorway.

'You want a nice black dress on a day like this.' It was her last appeal.

'No, Mrs Edwardes, no, no, no.' Poppy looked up at the older woman's disapproval. 'I don't want,' she said and burst out laughing as she lay in the bath.

'No laughing matter.' Jane Edwardes was delighted to hear Poppy laugh. The first time she's laughed since he died. Laughs like him, she thought, remembering times when he would laugh. 'That animal won the three-thirty. I told you it would. You should have risked your fiver.' What a tease he had been.

'Come and eat your breakfast,' she told Poppy.

'Coming.' Poppy got out of the bath. 'It will be all right, you'll see, don't fuss.' She felt a surge of unseemly mirth, remembering Dad's affectionate mimicry of Mrs Edwardes' Berkshire vowels. 'It's what he would like.' She reached for a bathtowel. 'You know he would. And I like it. For once we are in agreement.'

Silenced, Jane went down to cook breakfast. Picking up the egg she doodled a bit more. 'Quite rude,' she murmured, giving the drawing a finishing touch. 'I should have taken up art.' She cracked the egg into a cup and crushed the shell, dropping it into the pedal bin, slightly ashamed of her lewdity.

Poppy came down in a white towelling robe, her wet hair screwed up in a towel. She sat at the kitchen table to eat her breakfast.

Jane poured two cups of coffee and sat across the table from Poppy. She was glad to see the girl sitting easy, tucking into her bacon and egg. She would never have thought before this that Poppy would take her father's death so hard. For the last few days she had looked all twisted and screwed up, her face tense with misery. Better today, though. Jane sipped her coffee. That boyfriend, that Edmund. Why wasn't he here to help the girl? Now her father was dead there was no need to keep away. Jane considered Poppy eating her bacon. Those two had been a matched pair, met when Poppy was sixteen or thereabouts, the girl crazy about the man, always rowing with her father, row, row, row, until she upped and left home to live and work in London, share a flat with Edmund. Running a thoughtful tongue round her molars, Jane Edwardes wondered whether she should enquire.

'Have another egg? It's no trouble.'

'No thank you, that was lovely.' Poppy held her coffee cup in both hands.

'Edmund coming to help, is he?' The words slipped traitorously out.

'I shouldn't think so.' Poppy stiffened.

'They didn't get on, did they?' The question needed no answer. Edmund was apparently consigned to the past.

'I must dry my hair and get dressed. Thanks for my breakfast.' Poppy stood up tense and nervous. Jane watched her leave the room and, cursing her ineptitude, deliberately smashed a plate to vent her feelings. *How was I supposed to know?* Bending to pick up the pieces she became aware of a man carrying something heavy shuffling backwards into the kitchen.

'Easy, Singh, don't push or I'll topple over.'

'Poppy,' shouted Mrs Edwardes, catching sight of a jowly brown face topped by a turban suffused by the strain of carrying a heavy box, sharing the load with the first man. 'Poppy!'

Shuffling backwards into the kitchen was not the way Victor would have chosen to present himself to Poppy who, answering Jane Edwardes's cry, came back into the room.

He was not to know that the laugh with which she greeted him was not mockery but surprise as she compared his unusually slender hips with the vast bulk of his companion.

'Where can we put this?' Victor gasped, his arms aching.

'On the table.' Poppy hurried to clear a space. 'What have you got there?' *How long he was, how narrow, his legs must be a foot longer than Edmund's, well, not to exaggerate, half a foot.* 'Here.' She spread her hands over the space she had cleared, 'Put it here. Hullo,' she said to Victor's companion who was averting his eyes from the cleavage rendered wider by her gesture.

'This is Singh, my take-away friend.' Victor straightened his back, noted Poppy drawing the robe across her chest, tightening its belt. 'The king of Indian nosh.'

Poppy held out her hand. Singh took it in polite silence.

'He has no English,' said Victor, grinning.

'Try not to be stupid,' said Singh in a bass voice with impeccable pronunciation.

'Well, very little,' said Victor to prolong the moment when he could watch this girl, her pale face topped by the white towel confronting Singh, dark bearded, blue turbanned.

'Enough to get an Honours Degree at the LSE,' said Singh, good-humoured, smiling with perfect teeth at Poppy who smiled back.

'But he doesn't like talking.' Victor spun out the introduction, 'so he took to take-away food.'

66

'It pays better than teaching, stupid.'

'So this?' Poppy indicated the heavy box.

'Thermos boxes, Singh's family's relics of the Raj, your eats for this afternoon. I thought if we unloaded now Singh could go back to London and I can return the empties tomorrow. Singh can't stay.'

'Alas,' said Singh, watching Poppy with shining dark eyes, 'I cannot.'

'Come on, Singh, two more boxes,' exclaimed Victor. 'They were used for tiger shoots when the Viceroy came to stay,' Victor told Poppy, hoping to see her smile again.

'On railway journeys, stupid. We never entertained Viceroys,' said Singh rather nastily, belittling Viceroys.

'How was I to know? Well, better get on with it, time is short, I have much to do.' Victor clapped his hands together smiling at Poppy.

'Come on then, stupid. He is a clown,' Singh said to Poppy as he left the kitchen, 'but he means well.'

'How can you be so cruel?' cried Victor.

'Can you manage?' asked Poppy. 'I have to dress and dry my hair.'

'Sure, leave it all to us, we have the booze in the van and glasses and plates and all that, actually it would be better if—'

'I were out of the way?'

'Well no, no of course not.'

'I'm just going, I must.'

'I'll help if they need anything,' said Jane who had been standing watching by the sink. 'I've seen photos of these things. The gentry used to use them at shooting parties and at races in the old days.'

'Stand by for a flood of reminiscence.' Singh came back carrying another box. 'These Thermos boxes unleash a cornucopia of memories. I shall have to stop using them, a terrible time waster.' He shot Jane a sultry glance. 'Young stupid here knows how to look after them, not to shut them immediately when they have been washed, else they smell musty.'

'I'll see to that,' said Jane busily. Poppy left the room to dry her hair and dress.

They can manage perfectly well without me, she thought, pulling off the turbanning towel, brushing her damp hair. They could manage Dad's funeral without Dad. They have all the trappings, the food, the drink, the Thermoses, the horses. As she combed her hair she watched the stout Indian leave the house, get into his van and drive off. From the kitchen she heard voices, Jane and Victor.

I'm very quiet, she thought, brushing her hair, and Dad's very quiet.

An Interflora van drove up, a man and a girl got out, opened the van doors and began to unload wreaths.

Oh God! Poppy stood watching. More trappings. I wish I could run away. Why did she have to ask after Edmund? I was all right until then, now I feel sick. Would they notice if I left them all to it? Brushing her damp hair, she wished she could jump into her car and drive away. They are all happier without me, I am *de trop*. She stood by the window looking out at the swallows on the telegraph lines. She felt isolated as one standing in a fog, the sounds from the outside world muffled and indistinct. They are arranging all this without me. They do not need me. They are carried away by their plans for the ritual, using me and Dad as a rehearsal for the burial of their own loved ones when their time comes. I wish it were over.

14

Half awake, Edmund experienced a feeling of unease. He lay still, setting his sleepy brain to define the grounds for this sensation. His mind clocking into gear, recognised the cause. It was not Poppy who lay warmly asleep beside him but Venetia Colyer, a longer version of womanhood than Poppy, quite a lot older and, he faced it bravely, cooler.

One of Poppy's assets had been her physical warmth. She had been lovely to cuddle on winter nights. It had been nice to feel her warm bottom in the small of his back as they lay back to back as he now did with Venetia.

Heigh-ho, thought Edmund, can't have everything. He consoled himself for his loss by enumerating Venetia's assets. She was beautiful, sophisticated, rich, well dressed. She had a marked talent for cooking, useful friends who were in touch with important people. Her flat was large, comfortable, finely furnished. For instance, the bed in which he now lay was perfectly sprung, something which could not be said of the bed he had shared with Poppy which, sagging in the middle, led to sexual encounters when he was too tired or felt he should have been too tired, having a fear of excess in these matters as do many keep-fit maniacs. Except that I am not a maniac, he told himself, I just mind my diet and exercise properly. Damn, thought Edmund, reminded of exercise. I must arise and jog in a few minutes and Venetia has now said that she will not jog with me. Only on occasion. Edmund recalled Venetia's upper crust voice which he revered saying 'only on occasion' making the occasion sound like a rare benison, a medal for good conduct.

Beside him Venetia shifted slightly in her sleep, her feet brushing against his calves. Her feet were cool, even chilly, after hours in bed when they should have been warm and friendly like Poppy's. Edmund resented in retrospect the last few nights when, getting into bed, Venetia had pressed her cold feet between his legs saying 'warm me, warm me,' as though it were something he would enjoy. He wondered, while resenting the temperature of his mistress's feet, whether if he gave her bedsocks it would set off her other irritating trait, sudden gushing tears spurting unheralded by as much as a moan from her large blue eyes. Superstitiously Edmund wondered what the third irritation would be, simultaneously crushing the sense of loss he still felt for Poppy. One has not lost something, one has discarded, he told himself sarcastically as he prepared to slide out of bed. Venetia would sleep on for another hour while he jogged round the Park solo.

Outside it was raining. Poppy would have exclaimed 'I feel chicken', but the rain would not have stopped her. Plucky little thing, Poppy.

Setting his jaw, Edmund trotted along Venetia's as yet unfamiliar street towards the Park, consoling his lonely state with the thought of Venetia's breakfast. Orange juice, crisp bacon, excellent coffee (she made much better coffee than Poppy, who made it in a tin jug), brown toast, Devon butter and Cooper's marmalade, which would be waiting on his return. 'Have I time for a shower?' he would say, as he had these last few mornings. 'Yes, but don't be too long,' Venetia would reply, her gold hair brushed and shiny.

Forgetting the temperature of Venetia's feet and her tendency to sudden tears, Edmund swung north towards Bayswater, taking care to leave the Park by Lancaster Gate and not by the old gate as he had yesterday, his feet from long habit leading him towards Poppy and the flat they had shared for so long.

Passing a paper shop Edmund stopped to buy a paper. He had been shocked to find Venetia's daily paper was a rubbishy tabloid not *The Times*. 'Buy your own,' Venetia had said, 'if you must have it.' People like Venetia, he had often heard, were mean in small things, hopefully generous in large. Perhaps this was the third irritation he thought with relief, in which case it was a blessing in disguise. Had not Poppy often taken his *Times* just to pore over the reviews, messing up the paper?

It had stopped raining. Edmund opened *The Times* as he walked the last stretch of pavement, running his eye down the column of births and deaths before turning to the City page. 'What's this, what's this,' Edmund exclaimed aloud and again, 'What's this?' He stood in the street re-reading the small announcement. 'Robert Carew, loved father of Poppy – suddenly – funeral Saturday.'

'Saturday – today is Saturday.' Edmund used the key Venetia had given him and went up to the fourth floor in the lift, infinitely preferable to climbing four flights as he had all these years, though climbing stairs kept one fit.

'I have to go to a funeral,' he said, kissing Venetia absently as though they had been married for years. She had consented to marry him all right, no problem there, but stipulated she should keep her name. 'I am fond of Colyer,' she had said (her divorced husband was Michael Colyer). 'Why don't you change yours by Deed Poll? Edmund Colyer sounds terrific.' Edmund had answered jokingly, 'I might well at that. I'll think it over.' There was time to think, they were not married yet. Why not Edmund Colyer-Platt? That sounded good, making the deplorable Platt, so awful in its single state, positively Who's Whoish.

'I have to go to a funeral today,' said Edmund.

'Whose funeral?' Venetia's ready tears spurted. 'I'll come with you,' she said, 'and spread the load.'

15

'Are you wearing this?'

Poppy did not know how long she had stood looking out of the window, hairbrush in hand.

Cars and vans had come to the house, flowers had been delivered, large sprays and small, brought by people coming up the steps, ringing the bell, handing their offerings to Jane who, invisible beneath the window, thanked and chatted before calling goodbye and closing the door. The sun moved round to shine directly into Poppy's eyes. Her hair was dry now. She had watched the young swallows make tentative flights, returning after each adventure to the communal safety of the telephone wire to twitter and preen, display flashes of white and chestnut against navy blue plumage. She had seen Victor leave the house to join Fergus, driving away in his old Ford, followed shortly after by Jane in her new Metro. Before leaving Jane shouted up the stairs: 'I am going home to change into my black.' Poppy had not answered. She remained by the window looking out at the swallows.

'Are you wearing this?'

Reluctantly Poppy turned towards a woman who stood in the shadow, holding the dress Dad had bought for her birthday.

'Yes.' How had this woman got in?

'Good,' said the stranger. 'Perhaps you'd let me help you dress?' she suggested. 'Your front door was open,' she answered the unspoken question.

'I'm all right.' Poppy was defensive.

'Of course.' The woman was old but erect. Poppy saw that she had beautiful legs, narrow feet, she wore a heavy white silk dress and coat, black hat, bag and shoes, she gave the impression of confidence and authority, she smiled at Poppy, amused, she held the multi-coloured dress so that it seemed to move towards her, anxious to be worn.

Poppy faced the stranger.

'I am a friend of your father's, used to meet him at the races.'

'Oh.' Poppy reached for her knickers, pulled them on, let the towelling robe drop, pulled a slip over her head. 'Tights,' she muttered.

'Here.' The tights were held out to her.

'Thanks.'

'Shoes?' questioned the old woman.

'Will black shoes do?'

'Of course.'

Poppy adjusted the tights, put on the shoes. 'Now the dress.' The dress was slipped over her head. 'Beautiful, just as we thought,' murmured the old woman.

'We?' Poppy stared at her. 'We?' she questioned apprehensively.

'I was with him when he bought it.' This woman had once been lovely, was beautiful in age. She smiled at Poppy. 'I helped him choose it, he asked my advice. We had met at the races. I hope you don't mind.'

'You are still alive.' Poppy thought of the anonymous leavers of Life's Dividends.

The other woman laughed. 'I was never in *that* category.' She read Poppy's thoughts.

'I just wondered.'

'Yes?'

'Are they all dead?' Here perhaps was someone who could enlighten, who had known Dad's companions, mistresses perhaps.

'I wouldn't know. Your father had lots of friends; some were lonely people afraid of going to the races on their own. Your father was kind to them.'

'Did he, were they—' Poppy bit off the rest of the sentence.

'He didn't necessarily sleep with them.' Life's Dividends were dismissed.

'There now, you look lovely, look at yourself.' She indicated the mirror. 'He would be very pleased, your pa,' she said, smiling at Poppy's reflection.

Poppy envied the stranger's assurance, her elegant clothes, the jewellery she was wearing, the waft of unusual scent. She had not known that her father had friends like this. She had not known her father.

'Here they come.' The old woman moved to the window. Poppy joined her.

Round the bend in the road into the village clip-clopped hooves, into view came the Dow Jones, rich harness gleaming, bits jingling, ostrich plumes waving. They drew the hearse, shining black and gold, its glass sides polished, its springs creaking, its wheels rumbling and crunching on the road. On the box Fergus, in black, tail-coated, top-hatted, rug wrapped tightly across his knees, held reins and whip, beside him Victor similarly dressed. Behind the hearse Annie and Frances in black also but hatless, while in front at the horses' heads Mary strode gravely.

'Beautiful!' exclaimed the old woman. 'I shall certainly book him for myself. I must make a note for my executor. Where did your father find them?'

'An advertisement in the *Field*.'

'Never missed a trick, your pa.'

The hearse came to a halt. Mary stood by the horses' heads as they stretched their necks and blew down their noses. Annie and Frances went into the house. Fergus and Victor jumped down from the box.

'Time you went down,' said the old woman.

'Oh my God!' Poppy shrank from what lay ahead, she shivered.

'Oh my nothing,' said her visitor briskly. 'You have to see him out of the house and follow behind him to the church. Brace up, don't be a ninny. Here, wear this.' She took off her white silk coat and put it on Poppy. 'I felt cold at my husband Hector's funeral. Look sharp,' she said. 'Play your part. Think how he's enjoying this.' She pushed Poppy towards the door. 'A bit of pageantry in this dark age, be proud. I can imagine him watching, can't you?'

Poppy walked down the stairs. She did not feel her father was there to watch.

Jane Edwardes had appeared wearing unmitigated black. Her husband John and her nephew Bill were with Fergus and Victor hoisting the coffin on to their shoulders. They carried it to the hearse. Frances replaced the laurel wreath on the coffin and helped Annie arrange other wreaths round the coffin and on the roof.

When the cortège started Poppy looked round for the old woman to thank her but she was gone. Obediently she paced behind the hearse carrying Dad's body through the village to the church. In later years when she smelled the smell of horses in harness she would sniff, reminded of that day but missing the illusive scent which impregnated the borrowed coat. She followed the hearse, her head up, glad now that Dad was having the funeral he wished. The half mile to the church was the proper distance to walk in the September sun with the swallows twittering from the telegraph wires and rooks cawing as they flew up the valley.

While the hearse drew Bob Carew at a walking pace and Poppy followed, lonely behind, the church filled with people.

They paused in the porch to give their names to the reporters, blinked as they adjusted to the dimness, muted their voices as taught by their forebears, shuffled their feet, found seats, greeted friends discreetly, looked around, remembered to kneel, pray or appear to pray before sitting back to wait for the service to begin.

Calypso Grant observed the congregation, sifting the locals from those from further afield, recognising people who had once gatecrashed parties now become almost professional funeral-goers who, in youth, had known or pretended to know all the party givers. They now come she thought, to watch their former hosts departing who knows where.

But, she thought, there are lots like me who really cared for Bob Carew, as his daughter does too late, while those who cared most for the dear man have preceded him. I wonder, mused Calypso, whether there is some splendid race meeting in the sky and they wait for him by the paddock rail to advise them which horse to back.

Beside her, her nephew Willy who had driven her to the funeral sat quietly, knowing no one, looking ahead at the pale stained–glass window behind the altar. He is thinking of his farm, the dear fellow, and is too nice to feel resentful of this boring afternoon I have let him in for.

I must register every detail, thought Calypso, so that I can tell Ros Lawrence what sort of job her son Fergus makes of being an undertaker. Ros makes no complaint but her new husband may not welcome Fergus's choice of career. Hector would have found it original. I've seen those stable girls before, Calypso thought. The fair one is old Mowbray's girl. What's the story? And I see he has roped in his cousin Victor to help. Without seeming to she docketed and placed the congregation.

The organist struck up gently and the people rose.

At the church gate Poppy stood, a slight figure, as the men unloaded Dad and carried him into the church. Somebody nudged her arm and led her in to settle her in the front pew alongside the coffin. She was unaware of Anthony Green and his wife, of Les Poole with his consort, of the eyes of the congregation watching her as she tried to concentrate on the service, on the words designed to consign her father to God's keeping. Did he believe in God? Did all these people, his friends believe in God? Why did I never ask him, Poppy wondered. Why did we never discuss serious matters? Why did we shy away and worry at the subject of Edmund? Oh, Edmund.

Beside his Aunt Willy Guthrie suddenly stiffened like a pointer. She followed his glance.

The organist let rip a burst of Bach then it was over and the bearers were preparing to carry Bob Carew out to the hearse for the short trip to the grave.

There was silence in the church except for the shuffling of the bearers and the mass breathing of the congregation as they waited.

The vicar moved round the coffin ready to lead it out.

Oh my God, thought Poppy, there will be a hymn. I should not have left its choice to the vicar, how can he know what Dad liked, he will have chosen some awful muscular Christian tune which will set my teeth on edge. She gripped the pew in front of her. The vicar glanced at her sidelong.

From behind the altar came a pure high note. A blackbird sang joined quickly by mistlethrush, thrush, robin, tit, finch and wren in delirious joyful chorus filling the church. The vicar did indeed know what Dad would like. She remembered then her father telling her how the tape had been made one spring morning in his garden. I will get him to play you the tape, Dad had said, if you are interested. She had not been interested. Instead they had squabbled over her life with Edmund.

She followed the coffin into the September light slanting now across the green, her ears full of birdsong, feeling grief, remorse, gratitude to the vicar. She did not notice the congregation waiting for her to pass, watching her. She did not catch their eyes. Behind her in the church the birdsong ran on until the tape ran out.

Standing by the grave for the final words as the coffin was lowered Poppy felt relief that Dad had had the send-off he wanted, satisfaction that in this at least she had given him something he wanted. It rounded off Edmund's defection.

People gathered round her as she shook hands with the vicar and thanked him.

'You will come back to the house?'

'Thank you.'

A heavy man in a tweed suit said, 'Hullo, you must be Poppy.' He smelled of alcohol and cigars.

'Yes.'

'The birds were an inspiration.'

'The vicar's.'

'Not a church-goer your father, it was the race tracks for him.' The man laughed fatly.

'Yes.'

'Used to take my aunt to Chepstow and he took Archie over there's mother to the National every year. Kind to the old girls your father, never accepted any reward, most charitable chap I ever knew, free with his tips too. My name's Ebberley.'

'Oh.'

'Let us give you a lift? Get you home in a flash.'

Yet again others were taking charge, knowing what she should do, doing it for her. She heard the strangers around her saying, 'Okay, see you in a minute at the house. Could do with a drink after that,' 'Hope there's something stronger than tea,' 'Sure to be some booze, Bob was never mean about booze.' They all seemed to know each other, substantial men with their competent high-voiced wives mixing with the neighbours from the village and villages around. Their voices carolling up.

'Excuse me, would you mind if I took my aunt's coat?' A man's polite voice. 'We have to leave.'

Flustered by the noise around her, Poppy took off the coat. 'Where is she, I must thank her? Won't you come to the house?'

'Over there.' He took the coat. 'Don't bother, we have to go.' He sounded angry. 'Goodbye.' She watched him join the old woman waiting in the car. She smiled and waved. The young man got in and drove away.

'Who is she?' cried Poppy embarrassed not to know. 'She was so kind, she seemed to know my father.'

'Calypso Grant, used to be quite a raver when she was young. Here, jump in.'

The man in the tweed suit was managing her, putting her into a car beside a wife who smiled a welcome, patting the seat beside her. 'That was Calypso Grant,' the man told his wife who said, 'Oh, Calypso, one's heard of her of course,' noncommittally.

Poppy, half in the car, hesitated, fighting suffocation. I am being killed by kindness, she told herself. She backed out, scrambling away. 'Please go on,' she urged. 'I must just see – I have to speak – do go on up to the house—' She escaped, doubling back towards Fergus and Victor waiting by the hearse for the cars to move, the road to be free. One of the horses threw up its head and neighed impatiently. People were getting into their cars, slamming doors, starting the engines. Frances and Annie stood at the back of the hearse. Mary was chatting to a group of people she seemed to know.

'You will come back to the house?' asked Poppy, looking up at Fergus.

'Love to.'

'I must, I'm doubling as waiter,' Victor said smugly.

'Put your horses in the stables, Victor will show you.' She needed to keep Fergus near her and Victor too.

'Stables? That'll be fine,' said Fergus, surprised.

'Didn't Victor tell you?'

'Victor did not.' Fergus shot a suspicious glance at Victor, who looked innocent.

'May I drive back to the house with you?'

'Of course you may, there's room on the box,' said Fergus.

'You are the only people I know here.'

'Stay with us then.' Victor drew closer to her. He would have liked to put an arm round her but not in front of Fergus.

'What I'd really like is to be alone,' cried Poppy.

'Have to wait a bit,' said Fergus.

'We'll stand by,' said Victor comfortingly.

Mary came up laughing. 'At least ten people have asked for your phone number, Fergus. This has been a wonderful advertisement. Half the bookmakers in the south of England are here and lots of the hunting crowd. You are going to be the in thing, Fergus, if you are not snowed in,' she teased, 'but no fun then.'

Fergus snapped 'Do shut up, Mary,' glared and muttered.

'What does she mean, snowed in?' Poppy looked up at the weather, set fair.

'My father rented him a pup,' said Mary and sketched the trap Fergus might find himself in.

'Don't let it bother you.' Fergus indicated the hearse. 'Jump up.'

Poppy scrambled up in her beautiful dress, showing a lot of leg in the view of the verger who was waiting to close the church and get

77

home to his tea, not that he objected to legs but not at funerals. . . .

Annie and Frances sat in a row with Mary, swinging her legs in the back of the hearse. 'Walk on, gee up,' cried Fergus cracking the whip.

The Dow Jones threw up their heads and lurched forward. Fergus drove through the village at a smart trot. People returning to their homes looked amused or disapproving at Poppy in her multi-coloured dress sitting on the box between Fergus and Victor.

'They don't look too pleased,' commented Victor.

'How else am I supposed to get home?' cried Poppy. 'I was offered a lift but it was with strangers.'

Victor and Fergus felt jointly pleased not to be so considered.

'Why don't you rent my stables as winter quarters,' suggested Poppy when they arrived, speaking as though the idea had just occurred to her. 'I'll introduce you to my solicitor, you can fix it up with him. I shan't be here much,' she added, dashing Fergus's spirits. 'Do the place good to be used,' she said. 'You may have the house too, if you want it. Let us get this dreadful wake over.' She must play host to all the people who had known Dad and very likely Life's Dividends too. It pleased her to think that it was Life's Dividends who were paying for the party, forking out for the champagne.

16

As the Dow Jones clattered round to the stable yard Victor acknowledged a shout from Julia Wake who, having parked her car, was heading towards the house in the company of Sean Connor.

'Who are they?' Poppy asked but who cares, she thought, the church had been full, strange faces outnumbering the familiar ten to one. With the funeral ordeal over came euphoria, sparked off by the novelty of the drive from the cemetery. High on the box between Fergus and Victor she was exhilarated by the horses tossing their heads, black plumes dancing, bits jangling, the snortings, the pounding hooves on the road, the eager canter quickly repressed by Fergus. 'Whoa there, steady.'

'That's Julia Wake, she edits the magazine I told you about.' (Had he told her?) 'The man with her is Sean Connor, he's in publishing, he is very interested in my novel.' Victor hoped Poppy had been as distrait as she looked during the ceremony, had not noticed the photographers, not being sure how well she would receive his article when it got into print.

'A novel? How exciting. Are they coming to your party?'

'Your party,' Victor corrected her.

'I hardly feel it's mine, it's been organised by you. Shall you rush ahead and pop the bottles?' Poppy jumped down from the box as Fergus drew up in the stable yard. 'Run on,' she said to Victor, 'all these people will be dying for a drink.' She waved towards the house. 'I'll follow in a minute,' she said, quashing his desire to linger.

Victor, hoist perforce in his role as caterer, went reluctantly ahead to the house.

'Now,' Poppy switched to Fergus, 'let me show you the stables.'

They left the horses to Frances and Annie and toured the yard. Fergus, expecting shabby desolation, was astonished as he looked into loose-boxes, tack room and coach-house. 'It's in good nick, all it needs is a lick of paint and a few repairs.'

'Dad would have liked to have horses here, it would have been one of his dreams. Like to rent them, what do you say?' She looked at Fergus.

Fergus said, 'It would be a bloody miracle. You've no idea of the terror that's gripped me since that bitch planted the fear of snow. If I were snowed in I'd go bankrupt.'

'Her father took you for a ride; why?'

'He wants to muck up Mary's life, wants her to be respectable.'

'Fathers do,' said Poppy dryly.

'He was getting at her through me. If I go bust she'd lose her job.'

'Charming.' Perhaps I was lucky with Dad, he only talked, she thought. 'I'll introduce you to Anthony Green, he'll be in the house. Rent it for a year and see how things go,' she suggested. 'Oh!' she exclaimed as Fergus hugged her. 'Ah!' she said as he kissed her mouth.

'Sealed with a kiss.' Fergus kissed her again. 'More?' he suggested, enjoying himself.

'Well,' said Poppy. She had not been kissed by anyone other than Edmund since she could remember, not like this. Fatherly pecks on the cheek by Dad, avuncular cheek-touching by Anthony Green, certainly nothing of this sort. 'Well.' She felt cheerful and, to her surprise, roused. She smoothed her dress, shook out her hair. 'No more,' she said, laughing. Fergus desisted.

Poppy watched while the girls took the horses out of their traces and loosened their bits. They brought haybags from a Land Rover. Mary watched also, holding the infant Barnaby who had materialised with the haybags. He held out plump arms to Fergus and said, 'Dada, Dada.'

'I'm not your bloody Dada,' said Fergus. 'Wait till you are of age, I'll sue you for slander.'

Mary looked down her nose.

'Dada,' insisted Barnaby, bubbling spittle. Poppy felt happy, with Fergus and the girls watching the horses chump their hay, swish their tails, sigh gustily, break wind, phut, phut, phut of sweet smelling gas. She was in no hurry to go into the house.

'There will be no booze left if you don't come in,' Victor shouted jealously from the kitchen door.

'Okay, we'll come.' Poppy led Fergus and the girls towards the back door.

They were met by a wall of sound from the sitting room, hall and overflow into the garden.

Friends from the village and neighbourhood raised their voices in competition with Dad's friends from the outer world. Bookmakers, gypsies, racing men, smart suited in tweed and pinstripe, shiny-shoed, boomed and bellowed while their wives and mistresses yelped and trebled as they snatched and nibbled at the Indian eats, gulped and swilled champagne, greedy for the life from which Bob Carew had so recently absented himself.

Poppy strained to hear snatches of conversation, hoping to piece together a picture of Dad through his friends.

'The last race at Doncaster was when—'

'Cast a plate at Plumpton so the second favourite won.'

'You marinate it in white wine. Try it.'

'Man cannot live by bread alone, he needs butter.'

'Haw, haw, haw.'

'Knew Furnival's mother, very pretty girl Ros. I shall book him for my exit.'

'Don't you think it was in rather dubious taste?'

'Oh come on, makes a change from the usual humdrum do.'

'Apprenticed himself to an undertaker, they say, rather

enterprising.'

'Went to France, found the equipage there—'

'Why France?'

'Why not—'

'A papist contraption—'

'But why?'

'Search me. Search *la femme*. Any more of that bubbly?'

'That chap over there drowned his wife.'

'Victor something—'

'That's right. Writes. Wish I could drown mine. Victor Lucas, that's it.'

'I keep forgetting names.'

'Too much alimony. It's old age creeping up on you.'

'Ha, ha, ha. You too.'

'Isn't that girl Mary Mowbray, Nicholas Mowbray's daughter?'

'It's said she had a baby by a wog. That must be it. I say! Anything goes these days.' (Mary was observed sitting on the stairs suckling Barnaby, glass of wine in hand, legs apart.) 'Looks like one of those Virgins and Child in the National Gallery.'

'Don't be profane, darling.'

'The ones in the Gallery wore longer skirts.'

'Something funny in her breeding, her grandfather is supposed to have slept with Tallulah Bankhead.'

'Who's Tallulah Bankhead?'

'Oh come on. Yes please, just one more.'

'No, no I mustn't, I'm driving.'

'It's got a cough, been scratched.'

'What about that horse he backed at Ascot? Wasn't it fifty to one?'

'You mean Epsom, funny thing that, Stewards' Inquiry as near as dammit.'

'Steroids?'

'Well – one doesn't—'

'Beating about the bush—'

'What bush, whose?'

'Haw, haw, haw.'

'No, I mustn't drink any more or my wife will insist on driving.'

'Splint.'

'There's always York.'

'It wasn't a splint, it was—'

Hemmed in, Poppy looked round. She was trapped among the

loud voices. She felt as invisible as her parent so rapidly forgotten by his friends.

Across the room an old woman plastered in pancake make-up with blue eyelids waved. She recognised Esmé looking like a man in drag. She had no wish to speak to Esmé, felt safer where she was.

Jane Edwardes shuffled to and fro through the crowd hospitably. 'Let me refill your glass.' She knew everybody. She laughed and chatted, she was enjoying herself wearing her black.

Victor, a tray of empty glasses in his hand, was pinned against a wall nearby. Poppy edged towards him. Near Victor, Julia and her friend Sean were shouting. (Impossible not to shout in this uproar.) Poppy strained to hear. Sean was giving Victor his opinion of the novel. Soon Victor would be known, up and coming, acclaimed. Julia shouted Sean down to give Victor a witty resumé of the characters in the book (surely he knows his own book, thought Poppy). Sean recaptured Victor's attention, dousing Julia. 'I like it, I like it,' he said. 'A lot more than your first efforts. Come and see me next week, come to lunch, I'd like to publish, there are just a few things of course that need—'

'Such as?' asked Victor, hackles anxiously rising, glass halfway to his mouth.

'Nothing much. Well – er – once again as in the first book you've failed to check your foreign bits.'

'Which?' queried Victor suspiciously.

'I'm no linguist of course but if Urdu or Armenian are hard to check the same isn't true of French.'

'Oh, what—' hackles rising.

'Well, just glancing through of course, I noticed for instance "*compotes*" which takes a circumflex neither in French nor in English. And "*comme il faut*" with two intrusive hyphens, "*marché noir*" with two erroneous capitals.'

'Aah—' Victor gargled.

'"*Tiree à quatre épingles*" written as it *shouldn't* be in the masculine and "*vieux jeu*" in the plural whereas that idiom always takes the singular, "*ceci n'empêche cela*" the "*pas*" left out – true, skipping the "pas" sometimes gives the distinguished touch but where you use it it gives a false note and "*femme d'un certain âge*" with the circumflex missing.'

'Oh,' whispered Victor, outraged.

'That's just a few I noticed as I whizzed through. Sean took a long swallow of champagne. 'I must read it more thoroughly before we—'

'Just a few. No linguist,' breathed Victor, mortified, flushed.

'But I love it. It fits nicely into our spring list,' insisted Sean extending his empty glass to Mrs Edwardes passing with her tray, taking a full one. 'I love your book.' He looked tenderly at Victor as though unaware of the pain he was inflicting.

'I—' began Victor, choking with spleen.

'And of course,' Sean gulped wine, 'it's the funniest book I've read for years. The way you've disguised the black humour with obvious sentimentality, pretending it's a tragedy is masterly.'

'Aah—' It was hard to tell whether Victor was mortally wounded or exalted to the spheres. 'Aah,' he breathed deeply. 'So glad you latched on to the hilarity,' he said, almost choking on his bile.

With detached insight Poppy decided Victor was about to hit Sean, ruin his literary career, remain a writer manqué for the rest of his days. She flung her arms around Victor's neck. 'Kiss me, don't hit him,' she said in his ear, 'quick.'

Victor obliged, pressing his mouth hard on to hers. 'This is because I once called him a poof,' he said, catching his breath, 'he's getting his own back.' He kissed Poppy again.

'And is he?' She came up for air.

'Both, my darling, both hetero and homo.' Victor kissed her yet again.

Fergus, watching from across the room, thought bloody hell, there goes the march I stole on him, and began to shoulder his way across the room.

'Artful little bitch,' said Sean to Julia. 'Doesn't miss a trick, does she? Who is she?'

'Our hostess,' said Julia. 'You've had too much to drink, nearly lost yourself an author.'

'I couldn't resist a small tease. I abhor the ignorant use of Franglais.'

'You are a snob because your mother was French,' said Julia, laughing.

Poppy was interested to find how much she enjoyed kissing Victor, quite as much as Fergus who had a different technique. She was after all enjoying Dad's party.

Fighting his way through the throng Fergus reached Poppy. 'What about that introduction to your solicitor?' He put his arm round her waist.

'Of course.' Poppy disengaged herself and led him towards Anthony Green who had found an armchair in a safe corner of the room. 'Anthony, this is Fergus Furnival. I want him to rent the stables for his business, and the house, too, perhaps.'

Anthony struggled to his feet. 'I say, I see. Is that wise?' he asked, peering cautiously at Fergus, reaching into his breast pocket for his spectacles.

'The stables are empty. They will go to ruin. My father would like Fergus to use them, so would I.'

'We can of course go into it.'

'Go into it tomorrow.' He is going to delay, prevaricate, make difficulties. 'Just work out a fair rent and lease the stables to Fergus for a year, then if we are both happy with the arrangement he can renew the lease.'

'I shall have to—'

'Look sharp.' Poppy finished Anthony's sentence for him in a mode he would never have used. 'I want him to have them so make out a simple lease, dear Anthony, or shall we go to another solicitor? You do do leases, I take it?' Poppy sized Anthony up with her green eyes, looking, had she known it, exactly like her father Bob Carew at his most obstinate.

'We can make an appointment. There is no rush, I take it.'

'There is a great rush, it may snow.'

'I can pay the rent in advance,' suggested Fergus, remembering Poppy's cheque lodged in his bank, not yet spent.

'Nonsense,' said Poppy. 'You'll be quick about it, won't you, Anthony? I want the horses in the stables as soon as possible. Cut the red tape or I'll put them in rent free without a lease.' She put a daughterly arm round Anthony's neck and kissed him, aiming the kiss close to his mouth. Anthony squeezed her waist in a not quite avuncular way which made his wife, who was watching, decide that it was time to go home and that it would be safer if she drove.

Poppy helped herself to another glass of champagne from a passing tray and found she liked the party even better than a few minutes earlier. It seemed a pity that Dad, who was responsible for this happening, should not be here but no matter. Drink up, she could almost hear his voice.

She continued to enjoy the party until Edmund, coming unexpectedly from nowhere, took her roughly by the arm and dragged her away.

Accounts later varied.

Victor and Fergus maintained that their way had been blocked by intoxicated guests when they struggled to reach her. Annie and Frances differed as to whether Poppy had put up more than token resistance. Mary maintained that Poppy had passed her on the stairs where she sat nursing Barnaby shouting 'I *must* go to the loo first,' before joining Edmund in the car quite willingly. Innumerable people saw Edmund bundle her into a car and drive off towards London.

What nobody present had noticed was Venetia watching Edmund both in the church and at the party, nor did they observe her, when Edmund drove Poppy off in what was Venetia's car, go to the kitchen, pour honey over the floor so that feet passing through the kitchen would carry stickiness throughout the house, working it into rugs and carpets. Minutes later she hitched a lift to London from a fellow guest, made agreeable conversation, and declined an offer of dinner.

Reaching her flat before Edmund was likely to arrive (she assumed he would take Poppy to a crowded restaurant where she would be embarrassed if she made a scene), Venetia set to work on Edmund's clothes. She stuck up the cuffs and flies with Superglue, folding each garment with precise attention, nor did she neglect the pants, socks and pyjamas. Then, packing a bag, she hailed a taxi and went to spend a weekend with her mother at Haslemere, from where she phoned the police to report her car as stolen.

17

With surprise on his side Edmund held a tactical advantage. Not expecting him, she had not noticed him. Edmund congratulated himself. He noticed too that Poppy, who held her liquor weakly at the best of times, was rather drunk. She must be, he thought, kissing the undertakers, snuggling up to Bob Carew's sly solicitor, ignoring the dignity of the occasion by riding back to the house on the hearse.

He waived the thought that the ride on the hearse was prior to the champagne. She might have had a fortifying drink before the service.

Telling himself that he must stick to the point, get Poppy away, wait until later to reproach her for the ludicrous horse-drawn hearse, the ghastly tape of birdsong instead of a decent hymn, the lack of dignity among the guests at the house. (The scene had resembled what one had read of Irish wakes, not that even they had Indian food and champagne, from what one had heard a slosh of the hard stuff was more probable.) Above all, he was disgusted by the wearing of that frivolous dress. Where on earth did it come from? The whole scene, thought Edmund, driving fast towards London, was one one would hope to forget, an undignified pantomime in the worst possible taste, making a mockery of a solemn occasion.

Edmund maintained a lofty silence keeping Venetia's car in the fast lane, treading on the accelerator when challenged by other cars.

I must keep a clear head, he thought. He had restricted himself to one glass of champagne. I have to sort Poppy out. (For the moment he set Venetia aside.) Get her back to our habitual footing, she will need me when she sells her father's house and realises her assets. There are some quite decent pieces of furniture which will come in useful, the rest can be sold at auction. We can move into a larger flat now her father is dead. Now he is out of the way we can get married and start a family – if I want to.

I shall keep my options open, thought Edmund, think it over carefully. There is a lot to be said for the Poppy I know against the Venetia I am discovering.

Allowing himself a quick glance at Poppy, Edmund's mind strayed to Venetia's ready tears and cold feet.

No need for an immediate decision, thought Edmund, remembering Venetia's income. One should approach marriage with caution, divorce was by all accounts a financial disaster. One could keep Venetia as a mistress or vice versa. Poppy needs me, I must look after her, she probably feels a bit sad at the loss of her disreputable father but, he assured himself, she will get over it, she is a resilient girl.

Slumped in the seat beside Edmund, Poppy, aware of her intoxication, had the sense to keep quiet. If I speak I shall say something I regret, she told herself, something irreparable. I shall sit here in this infernal car which stinks of Venetia and wait. She stared ahead at the road waiting for her eyes to regain their focus, letting her thoughts stray.

She enjoyed the movement of Venetia's car, Edmund had always been a good driver. She wondered what he wanted.

Does he want to get me back? she asked herself; after all, he threw me away in favour of Venetia. Has he heard that I now have money? I shall not tell him if he hasn't.

He will be planning to sell Dad's house which may be worth quite a lot. He worked for years as a house agent, he will know its value.

Or is he just being dog in the manger? Is he furious that I organised the funeral without consulting him (not that he was there to ask). He would not admit he wasn't there, he will say, 'Why didn't you telephone when your father died', be hurt, blame me?

'Why didn't you telephone when your father died?' asked Edmund, slowing the car as it began to rain, switching on the wipers.

Poppy did not answer.

'I find it extremely hurtful.' Edmund sounded aggrieved.

Poppy bit her tongue.

'After all—' said Edmund, leaving the sentence to float between them.

After all, he left you, Dad would say if he were alive and Dad would laugh that chuckling laugh, not the shout of triumphant joy which had killed him.

'It was a coronary, I take it,' suggested Edmund.

Poppy failed to reply.

She remembered Dad's note. What had it said? Give, don't lend. Don't marry unless it's impossible to live without the fellow. Back outsiders. What, in Dad's book, were outsiders? She could have asked any one of those friends of Dad's, those bookmakers, that woman who had lent her coat. The man who took it back. Fergus, Victor, were they outsiders?

'We will have dinner at Luigi's,' said Edmund as they drove into London. 'I've booked a table.'

Poppy kept mum.

If Edmund had booked a table at Luigi's, their favourite restaurant for special occasions, it would have been for Venetia.

Poppy marvelled, rediscovering Edmund.

'I thought you would need a good meal and cheering up after your ordeal.'

'Does he take me for a doormat,' she asked herself. A complete fool? What else have I been for the past ten years, she answered herself, an imbecile.

She felt despairing, lethargic. Without the energy to protect herself, she let herself drift as Edmund willed.

Arrived at Luigi's, she combed her hair and washed her hands in the cloakroom, smoothed her dress. It looked great by electric light, flattering her eyes, making the colour of her hair quite interesting and – the sign of a good dress – it looked as fresh as it had when offered to her by that old woman on its hanger.

Edmund sat waiting at a table in the middle of the room. In the space of a week it had become Venetia's favourite table, she liked to be in the centre of the restaurant to be viewed from all angles, no back to the wall banquette for her. Poppy joined him without comment. The waiter gave them each a menu.

Edmund ordered smoked eel, fillet steak, chipped potatoes and spinach. He would finish, Poppy knew, if he had a chink left, with Stilton. He must, she thought as she studied the menu, have borrowed the money from Venetia. As ever, his fear of putting on weight was defeated by his love of food.

Poppy ordered a dozen oysters (Edmund's eyebrows rose), grilled Dover sole, matchstick potatoes and a green salad. 'Then I'll have an artichoke with sauce vinaigrette.'

She chose on purpose so that I shall have to order both red and white wine. (Edmund prided himself on his knowledge of wine.) He consulted the wine list, recklessly ordered two bottles, red and white. Damn her eyes. She knows I can't stand the hours she takes eating an artichoke.

Poppy ate the oysters in slow appreciative silence, enjoying the salty juicy flesh as she bit the poor live creatures. She was beginning to feel rather cheerful, her alcoholic fog lifting. She wondered why she had never before tested the pleasure and power of silence. She watched Edmund tackle his eel, knew he expected her to offer him a glass of her white wine with it, refrained.

She sipped her wine, watched the room full of chattering diners.

Edmund started talking again. Getting on with her meal – the sole was delicious – she listened.

'This new job of mine means quite a lot of travel.' He bit his steak, forked up some chips.

What new job? Ah yes, he had this new job in a travel agency, it had thrilled them both in those faraway days – at least two weeks ago – before he had left her for Venetia. He was to earn twice the money he made as a house agent and there were, he had said, excellent perks. Edmund was still speaking. 'So I thought we'd go as I have the tickets. We fly from Gatwick. It will set you up, you will get over your loss, you can lie in the sun while I do what business I have to do. The climate's lovely at this time of year, still hot of course. I thought we'd go the day after tomorrow which gives us time to pack. I have to get some decent clothes suitable for the job.'

You'll like that, commented Poppy in her silence. What marvellous nerve. He plotted this for Venetia, why the switch? Poppy started work on her artichoke, dipping each leaf in the sauce, letting the sauce smear her chin to see whether he would notice.

Edmund averted his eyes and went on talking (a week ago he would have hissed 'sauce on chin, love, wipe it'), he described the African town they would visit, the sun, the sea, the beach, the food, the trips to visit the Roman antiquities, the Arab cities, the markets. He has done his homework thoroughly, read the brochure, Poppy thought, in her silence stripping off the last artichoke leaf, preparing to savour the last delicious bit, the heart. Edmund's new job was to plan tours for his new company, undercut, if possible, the opposition.

The waiter took away Edmund's plate. He had not the heart to order cheese, he crumbled a roll. He had run out of puff.

Poppy sipped her wine, dabbled her fingers in the finger bowl, dried them on her napkin. The oysters had been restorative, the sole delicious, the artichoke fresh and perfect. She felt very well. Glancing at Edmund under her lashes she thought, He doesn't look too good, he's got himself into a difficult situation.

Edmund had never before not savoured fillet steak. The last piece had nearly choked him. I should not have brought her to this restaurant full of memories. I should not have sat her at this exposed table where everyone can see us. I must not lose my nerve now. He said, 'Poppy, listen. I love you. I cannot live without you. I have behaved—'

'Coffee, madam?' suggested the waiter. Poppy nodded and smiled at the waiter.

'I have behaved badly, please forgive me. The Venetia thing was mad, an aberration.'

What nonsense, thought Poppy, how banal.

'I am very unhappy, quite dreadfully unhappy—'

That's right, lay it on with a shovel, thought Poppy in robust silence.

'Please, darling let's begin again—'

Whatever for? She kept silence.

'I love you so much, forgive me and—'

The waiter poured coffee, rattled the cups, moving them unnecessarily, lending an ear.

'I will try and make it up to you, Venetia doesn't mean a thing. You mean everything to me, you always have. I love you so.' Edmund stared at Poppy and to his horror, moved by his own eloquence, began to cry.

Raising his eyebrows the waiter moved away.

Across the table Poppy began to cry too. Edmund's speech was maudlin muck, patently fake, having the tear-jerking quality of massed bands, God Save the Queen or A Hundred and One Dalmations.

Poppy did not produce the swift gush of tears that were Venetia's but two slow oily drops which hovered for a second before oozing economically on to her cheek. She wiped them away with her finger.

'More coffee,' suggested the waiter, coming back.

'The bill please,' said Edmund keeping his voice level with an effort.

'You had better return Venetia's car.' Poppy spoke to him for the first time since the parting.

'You are quite right. I shall.' He paid the bill, calculating the tip. I shall not give him extra because he saw my tears. Churchill wept and Wellington, dammit.

They went out to Venetia's car. He was too cautious to touch her, she might jerk away. They drove to Venetia's flat in silence then on arrival: 'Come up and give me a hand with my packing,' he said from force of habit. 'It will be quicker,' he added to placate her. 'I cannot help my male chauvinist piggery,' he joked feebly expecting her to contradict him, which she didn't.

Poppy followed him into the lift thinking he would have stood aside for Venetia, minded his manners.

Edmund let himself in at Venetia's door, put the key down where she would find it, making sure that Poppy noticed his action, laid the car keys beside it.

In the bedroom on the bed Venetia had stacked Edmund's clothes:

90

'She's guessed,' said Edmund, embarrassed. He fetched his suitcase from a cupboard in the hall and prepared to pack.

'What's this? What on earth?' As the full extent of Venetia's act became clear Poppy, who had up to now felt detached and ambivalent, made up her mind.

'Okay,' she said. 'I'll come to Africa.' Was it possible, she thought, as they went down in the lift, that Edmund qualified as an outsider? That Dad was, as she had always maintained, wrong?

18

Anthony Green had not expected to see Fergus again, imagining Poppy's proposal to rent her house and stables an idea born of the effervescence of champagne, which would subside as fast as the bubbles and, the day after the funeral, be forgotten. He was not pleased when his clerk told him Fergus was in the outer office.

Agreeing to see Fergus, Anthony decided that the quicker he discouraged him the sooner he would be rid of him.

As Poppy's solicitor, though not the executor of her father's will, Anthony had anticipated advising her to sell the house and invest the proceeds while she thought through what she wished to do with her life. He had yet to discover whether she wished to marry or start a new career. With capital behind her, her horizon had altered. He would advise her to take time, make no hasty decision. He hoped that with the connivance – though connivance was the wrong word – of Les Poole they should between them steer the proceeds from the sale into gilt edged harbours.

Still in search of a better word than connivance Anthony rose to greet Fergus, standing behind his knee-hole desk in his tweed jacket and corduroy trousers, it being market day in the town and many of his clients farmers or country people. Fergus's clothes, aged jeans, flannel shirt, none too clean jersey and torn leather jacket strengthened his resolve. They shook hands.

Fergus, with few illusions about the speed with which Anthony would be prepared to work, yet expected to discuss terms of a lease of Poppy's stables and with luck the house. He was not expecting the whole project to be blocked, which Anthony proceeded to do with a fine example of circumlocution delivered at ponderous pace while he fingered his pen and patted some papers on his blotter as though to say, 'I have to sign these documents, you are wasting my time, please go away.'

Fergus broke in, cutting him short. 'Has Poppy changed her mind about renting me the stables? It was her idea, Mr Green. There was mention of the house, too.'

Anthony hesitated. Naturally it was Poppy's idea, true daughter of Bob Carew. He was here to stop such ideas coming to fruition. He must put a stop to the spirit of Bob Carew living on in his daughter.

'Why don't we ring her up, Mr Green, settle it one way or the other? She was perfectly sober when she had the idea, though possibly not when she told you about it. If she has changed her mind there will be no need for me to bother you any more. May I borrow your telephone, her number is—'

'I know her number, Mr Furnival.' Anthony failed to conceal his irritation.

'Well, then.' Fergus sat back smiling.

'There are er—'

'References? You need references?' Fergus queried.

'Of course.' Anthony snatched at the proffered straw. The conversation was taking an annoying turn, but references will slow him down, put a brake on this indecent haste. A person with a mounted undertaker's business – for some reason he could not define Anthony saw Fergus as mounted on his black horses so irreverently called Dow Jones – no person proposing to run such a business would produce reputable references. Anthony smiled thinly at Fergus across the desk. 'Of course we shall require references, that goes without saying.' He let his tone hint at patronage.

Fergus reached a long arm across the desk for the telephone at Anthony's elbow and dialled Poppy's number.

'I say!' Anthony was beginning to be angry. This young man was impossible.

'Poppy?' Fergus was speaking. 'Did you or did you not offer to rent me your stables and possibly your house?'

'Of course I did.' Fergus held the receiver away from his ear so that Anthony could hear Poppy's voice.

'What's the problem?' asked Poppy.

'Your solicitor seems to have doubts.'

'Silly old ass. I'll talk to him, I can't write, I haven't time, I'm going away, you were lucky to catch me, ten minutes more and—'

Fergus said, 'I'm in his office, speak to him now. I shall give him references and so on.'

'Don't bother about references—'

'I'd rather bother but I am in rather a hurry, winter is nigh.'

'It's in my soul.'

'What?'

'Nothing. Business looking up?'

'You could say that. Here's Mr Green.' Fergus surrendered the telephone to its indignant owner and sat back, taking care that Anthony should see that he did not listen.

Anthony listened; he found it hard to get in more than the odd word since Poppy let fly in a voluble rush expressing her ardent definite wish to rent to Fergus, begging him to act fast before the weather closed in, elaborating on the dangers of snowdrifts and the duplicity of Nicholas Mowbray.

Fergus wrote three names, three addresses and telephone numbers on a sheet of paper and waited for Anthony to finish his conversation.

Anthony replaced the receiver rather flushed. How dare the girl who had sat on his knee as a small child (well, if she hadn't, she could have) be so peremptory. She had brushed aside his rearguard action, almost ordered – 'She seems quite anxious to rent you her premises,' he said cautiously. Fergus said 'Good,' keeping his eyes on his sheet of paper. 'These are my references.' He pushed it across the desk.

Anthony, still ruffled by the tone Poppy had seen fit to use, took the paper. The names of Fergus's references leapt from the page. 'These are?' he asked keeping his voice in neutral.

'My stepfather, my godfather, my uncle. Should you require others—'

'These will do very well, I dare say.' On no account, Anthony told himself, admit that you had not guessed Fergus was one of *those* Furnivals. How could one possibly be expected to connect an undertaker with such – well, not to put too fine a point on it – exalted people. God help poor old Brightson's, he whispered to himself. 'Well now, suppose I make you a lease for a year and we review it at the end of that time with the prospect of renewal. Would that suit you, Mr Furnival?'

'Yes,' said Fergus. 'Fine. How long will that take?'

'Let's say a week since you are in a hurry.'

Fergus extended his hand. 'Thanks, I'd like to move in pretty soon.'

'Of course,' said Anthony, generous in defeat. 'May I wish you every success in your enterprise. I dare say you will make your fortune—'

Standing up, a head taller than Anthony, Fergus said, 'Success isn't just money Mr G. Bob Carew's funeral meant his daughter felt better because she gave her father something he had wanted. She felt guilty about him. Taking the trouble to have me and my horses goes a little way to assuage the guilt.'

'Guilt?' Anthony frowned.

'Didn't you feel guilty when your parents died?'

'No,' said Anthony, who had never crossed his parents.

'How unusual, lucky you.' Fergus looked at him with interest. 'We could have a fascinating conversation on the subject of guilt but I won't waste your time. I must be off. Goodbye.'

Watching Fergus go, Anthony thought that after all connivance had been the right word to use in that context; it would have been wrong to manoeuvre Poppy into selling her house. He would see to that lease right away.

He rang for his clerk.

Crossing the street to a telephone box with the intention of alerting his parent of the probable requests for references so that she, with her charm, could warn his stepfather, godfather and uncle, Fergus thought, What did Poppy mean implying that her soul was wintry? Was he imagining a hint of desolation in her voice, had he been optimistic in thinking that the funeral had cheered her? He remembered kissing her and wished he could do so again soon. He dialled her number but the telephone rang in an empty flat. 'Going away,' she had said, 'lucky to catch me.' Where? She had said nothing at the funeral of any such plan. He considered telephoning Victor and asking him, since he was in London, to go round and find out but dropped the idea feeling jealous. Victor had kissed her too, would be only too ready— He dialled his mother's number. 'Hullo, darling,' she said, 'we were all thrilled to see you on television, all my friends are determined to have you when their turn comes.'

'Not too soon, one hopes.'

'Someone has to start or you'll go broke.'

'Are you offering?' he asked laughing.

'Not yet, but it makes one think. Bob Carew wasn't that old, he drank of course and had a dicky heart.'

'Did you know him?'

'Anyone who went to the races over the last twenty years would know him. He had a pretty daughter, I believe.'

'Yes, Poppy.'

'Is that her name?' His mother's interest quickened. Fergus would have liked to discuss Poppy with his mother but he ran out of change.

By the time he had got more change and reconnected himself with his mother he no longer wished to discuss Poppy, she was as yet too fragile an idea to discuss with his parent whom he quite erroneously considered robust. He therefore confined himself to the matter of references. His mother laughed and promised results. Thoughtfully replacing the receiver, she prayed that Fergus would not get hurt. Was he aware that Bob Carew's girl lived with that rather awful young man Edmund Platt? If not, it was not for her to volunteer the information.

19

Looking down at the clouds from her corner seat, Poppy absented herself from Edmund sitting in the gangway seat which allowed him to stretch his legs as he sat half turned away reading the evening paper. The clouds did not look like cotton wool or whipped cream, just layers of cloud turning pink in the sunset. It had been raining when they left London, it would be raining still. '*Il pleut dans mon coeur*—' how did it go? Her mind wandered in search of poet and poem, she was too apathetic to concentrate. Victor would know or Sean Connor with his knowing superiority. She would certainly not ask Edmund, sitting beside her in his new suit. Was it '*pleur dans mon coeur*?' For a moment she conjured Victor with his thin face, jackdaw eyes. How could anyone be so slender without appearing scraggy? She glanced sidelong at Edmund's muscular legs. Victor merged into Fergus, black-eyed, burly, flat-stomached. Until he stood up one didn't see Edmund's slightly convex stomach, a convexity which worried him and was the cause of the jogging before breakfast.

Got it, it was '*pleut*' not '*pleur*'. Cry, cry! Cry for what? I cried for Edmund, she thought, and here he is, here we are, I have him, snitched back from Venetia. Poppy's lips twitched as she looked down on the clouds. Venetia had no inhibitions, no false restraint. I never glued up his flies, she thought, I just let him go and wept for him. But here he is. She turned further away from Edmund, laying her head back, pretending to sleep. She would feel safer when Edmund put down the paper and buried himself in his Dick Francis. I paid for that too. She peeped under her lashes as Edmund folded the paper and reached for his paperback, cracking its spine in his strong fingers. I paid for the suit, the book and practically everything in his suitcase. He even bought new sunglasses, the French kind one is supposed to be able to stamp on with impunity (I must try it).

When he had spoken the expected words, 'Will you lend me some money?', not 'can' or 'would you mind', but 'will', expecting her to say yes which she (immediately, almost apologetically) had she felt she had regained along with her lover her identity. Or, she thought, as Edmund turned the first page of his thriller, almost, almost regained, for never before would she have had the cheque book ready and pen in hand. Always before she would have believed the words 'I'll pay you back of course', carried credibility.

To be fair, she thought, glancing at his well-clad legs, sometimes he repaid her, sometimes he didn't, but this time she had not listened not bothered, just written the cheque.

He thinks he owns me and everything that is mine, she thought resentfully, suiting her miserable mood to the thrum, thrum sound of the aeroplane. Yet, she thought, conscious of the man beside her, I suppose I love him.

A stewardess pushing a trolley along the aisle stopped. Edmund ordered a large whisky, jogged her elbow. 'Drink, darling?' She kept her eyes shut. 'I think she's asleep.' Edmund reached for the wallet in his hip pocket. The smell of whisky, the desire to sneeze. She suppressed the sneeze with an effort. Who was it Dad had told her who maintained an orgasm was a sneeze, no more. Peter Quennell, that was who. What could he mean? How come Dad knew Peter Quennell; writers were not his line at all. Used he perhaps to go racing? With Dad gone it was too late to ask. I rate my orgasms higher than a sneeze, thought Poppy.

Edmund read his book, drank his whisky in measured gulps. A beautiful man, Poppy thought. It was not just the wonderful legs in the new trousers, the magnificent torso, the muscled arms, the thick neck (did I say thick?), the handsome face, the golden hair (ears a bit too small but one should not quibble), the whole man was marvellous, had he not been in the Olympic team, well not quite, almost, spare man or something. I love him, I've got him back, what am I to do now, she asked herself in misery.

Beside her Edmund snapped his fingers for attention, ordered another drink.

So indifferent had she been, she had not even asked exactly where they were going. 'A place in Africa' might mean anything. Leaning back, feigning sleep, listening to the thrum of the engines, Poppy let her mind play back the last forty-eight hours.

She had been too astonished at Edmund's appearance at the funeral party, his whisking her away in Venetia's car to be either pleased or sorry. Edmund had never before been impetuous. She had been a little drunk, on the defensive. She perversely enjoyed the dinner at Luigi's, felt much the better for it, resolving in future never to order fewer than a dozen oysters.

On the way to Venetia's flat to return the car and collect Edmund's clothes, she had decided to leave him. Get shot.

The drive across London had been long enough for her to compose what she saw as a firm but unhurtful paragraph (she would later put it in writing to make doubly sure) of parting, civilised, definite, kind, final.

The parting words remained unspoken. Venetia's revenge put a strange gloss on the situation. She had felt sorry for Edmund, protective even, her instinct had been to comfort and console. In no time they had found themselves back in the flat they had shared for so long, lying in the bed which sagged in the middle, doing what they always did.

So, thought Poppy, as the aeroplane bore them through the night towards Africa, the wounds in the fabric of their relationship were mended, the holes cobbled together, preparations for the trip planned for Venetia (not that Edmund would have admitted it) kept them busy. Edmund borrowed the money, bought his new clothes, rushed her to the doctor for the necessary injections, made sure she too had the right clothes, took her to Boots to buy anti-diarrhoea pills and suncream, to Hatchards for a supply of holiday books. He was as attentive and caring as one could wish a lover to be.

Perhaps, thought Poppy, I am being ungenerous in thinking he is suppressing the things he would like to say, his objections to the funeral service, the horse-drawn hearse, the oddity of Dad's friends, the multicoloured dress, the dawn chorus, Fergus and Victor.

Just one small sentence muttered under his breath had escaped as he made love to her. 'That will teach you to kiss those yobboes,' gasped as he reached his climax long before she was ready for hers.

Was he going to order another drink? Yes, he was, and the intelligent stewardess was ignoring him. Shortly there would be a plastic meal on a plastic tray, he would order wine. Poppy hoped the flannel disguised as bread would absorb the alcohol. Possibly she would pretend to wake, make herself agreeable. One providential thing, she thought behind her closed eyes, was that he had been in the lavatory when Fergus telephoned, had not heard her tell Anthony to lease Fergus the stables and the house.

Edmund jogged her elbow, put a hand on her knee.

'Wake up, darling, dinner.'

She opened her eyes, kept silent.

'Might as well eat it, shall I order a bottle of wine?'

He ordered a bottle of wine.

He looks beautiful, poor fellow, when he has had a few drinks, she thought, carefree, pink.

The stewardess brought the plastic trays with plastic food in plastic packets. Poppy buttered a roll and handed it to Edmund who accepted it, munched.

The stewardess brought the wine, poured it into their plastic mugs.

The engines went thrum, thrum. Around them fellow passengers, keeping their elbows close to their sides, picked with urgent fingers at packets of butter, examined the secret parcels of food disguised as meat, cheese or whatonearthcanthisbe.

'I thought,' Edmund gulped the wine, spoke close to her ear, 'that when we are married I'd call myself Platt-Carew.'

'What?' The wine halfway to her mouth rippled in its beaker.

'There's nothing to stop us now your father is dead.'

'God,' she murmured. (Threat? Exclamation? Prayer?) She swallowed some wine.

'You never liked my surname any more than I do, lots of people take their wife's name. You have a pretty name and will probably like to keep it.'

'I shall.'

'Good, that's settled, glad you agree.' Edmund picked at one of the mystery packages and uncovered what appeared to be a wodge of beef.

'It's not.'

'What?' Edmund half turned towards her.

'You never asked me to marry you.'

Poppy bit on a roll, put it back on the plastic dish, buttered it and tried again adding some St Ivel cheese, could not swallow, gave up, spitting it into her paper napkin.

'Love! I took it for granted. You can't expect me down on one knee in a plane.' Edmund laughed, drank his wine. 'Shall we order another bottle, they have a way of shutting the bar.'

'No.'

'No more wine? Come on.' Edmund drank.

'No.'

I can't think what I am doing on this plane, thought Poppy. I can stop loving Edmund if I want to, it's not obligatory. Perhaps I only stuck to him because of Dad's objections, now that Dad is dead I am free. If Dad had died sooner I might have stopped loving Edmund long ago. Yet he is a very beautiful man, she thought weakly, turning towards Edmund, looking him over. Perhaps I can teach him to be less selfish. I must think this over, keep a clear head, wait until I am less tired.

'I'll think about it,' she said.

'That's settled then.' Edmund kissed her cheek, 'Eat your dinner, darling.'

Poppy pushed the tray away, feeling forlorn. She felt a longing to talk to another woman, found herself thinking of Mary and baby Barnaby, wishing she knew her better. Normally she feared other women in case they might rob her of Edmund and Edmund for his part distrusted her female friends, subtly denigrating them so that she was more isolated than most women of her age.

That is not how I wanted to do it, thought Edmund, drinking his wine, but, he reassured himself, it will be all right. I hope I appeared more confident than I am. Better the girl that one knows, I dare say. Time has proven that I love her. He turned to take Poppy's hand in his, to hold it reassuringly but she had stuffed both hands in her pockets.

I shall get to know Mary, Poppy thought, and then it occurred to her that, improbable though it might seem, it might be fun to get to know Venetia.

20

Edmund had not been the only person in the church to concentrate on Poppy.

While most of the men in the congregation let their eyes stray discreetly, recognising friends they wished to buttonhole after the service while their wives took stock of their neighbours' clothes, state of health, stage of decrepitude, Calypso Grant's nephew Willy Guthrie, having sighted Poppy, was unable to take his eyes off her.

It was not, he thought, that she was particularly pretty, it was the general ensemble, even the imperfections which struck a chord in his heart. He had a full face view as she came up the aisle and a long stare at her profile during the service. He was pleased that his aunt had deputed him to retrieve her coat when the service was over.

'Once Bob's in his grave she will feel warmer.' What exactly did she mean? 'You can ask for it back, for by then it is I who will be feeling the chill.' An old person being fanciful.

Willy looked forward to introducing himself, asking for the coat, finding something felicitous to say. He believed in the impact of words. He hoped she would smile at whatever he said and that later at the drinks party it would be possible to chat and pave the way for future meetings *à deux*.

He was therefore aghast when Calypso, on leaving the graveside, asked him to fetch the coat saying that she was cold as she had predicted she would be, tired and more than ready to go home. 'You don't wish to go to an awful drinks party, do you?'

Willy made a faint unspoken protest, his aunt appeared impervious. 'Think of all the noise, all those hearty men heehawing and their wives screeching. I am too old for that sort of thing, and champagne, for if it's anything to do with Bob Carew it will be champagne, upsets my stomach at this hour. Run for the coat, dear Willy, I shall wait in the car.'

Forgetting his felicitous phrase, Willy mutinously went to get the coat. He was rewarded by Poppy's smile and a grateful flash from her green eyes which in the church he had thought to be brown. As he carried the coat, still warm from her body, back to his aunt Willy decided that what was always said about her was right, she was an utterly selfish old woman who had never been anything else. He started the engine of the car and drove off stifling his disappointment.

'An attractive girl.' Calypso settled in the seat beside him.

'Was she?' Childishly Willy attempted to hide his chagrin.

When they arrived at his aunt's house Calypso stepped out of the car and slammed the door. 'If you drive fast,' she said, looking in at Willy, 'the party will still be going on, the most boring people will have left, the fun beginning. Have a good time.'

'But—' said Willy.

'I wanted to come home, you wanted to go to the party. Hurry.' She was mocking him.

'How—'

'Go on, Willy, off you go and tell me about it later.'

'Are you—'

'I am all right. I shall change my clothes, then take the dog for a walk. Off you go.' Even with her face close to his so that he could count the wrinkles, he could see what people meant when they said she had been a lovely girl. 'Not as selfish as all that.' She was laughing now, teasing him.

'Thank you.' Willy turned the car and drove back towards Poppy Carew. As he drove he whistled a Bach Cantata and allowed himself to hope that in some neat way things would work out so that, the party over, he would be able to take Poppy out to dinner and who knows – or if this was too fanciful a scenario he would be on such terms that it would be natural, in a day or two, to telephone, fix a date, carry on from there. He forgot that a few short days before he had boasted of his freedom. As he drove he composed felicitous phrases and congratulated himself that there would be no overlap: his long affair with his late girl Sarah had ended not with a bang or even on a sour note, it had unstitched like a seam no longer able to hold together. He felt perfectly friendly towards Sarah, a very nice

101

girl, but in retrospect surprised that he had ever felt desire. He felt the same towards several other girls who had occupied his time and his heart. Was it heart though, Willy wondered, searching, as he drove, for felicitous phrases, or merely sex? The sensations both mental and physical aroused by Poppy were utterly different. It is different each time, he told himself, but heretofore I have found things to say while now even imagining myself faced with the girl, hoping to impress, I am struck dumb, can't think of a thing and I have yet to speak to her. It was rather ridiculous, thought Willy, to feel like this when all he had to go on was her appearance, he had not even heard her voice properly. That at least, thought Willy, driving fast, can be rectified. What if she has a voice which grates on the nerves? Willy scotched the idea, it was too awful.

Reducing speed as he reached the village, he drove past the church and the graveyard where Bob Carew lay cool under a mound of flowers and along the village green. The line of cars which had stretched from the church to the house was nearly gone, a few people were standing chatting by their cars before driving away. Willy stopped the car by the house. The front door was open, the hall empty. He listened.

From the back of the house he heard a raised voice, a row of some sort was in progress, somebody was very angry, a woman's voice expostulating, a high keening coloratura.

'My rugs, my carpets, it's ground into the parquet, I'll kill whoever did it, my kitchen, the stairs, have you seen the landing? A whole pot *and* a tin of golden syrup, look at it, look! Don't move, you'll make it worse, oh, I could—' The voice drowned a muttered chorus male and female. Willy had the impression that the lament was repetitious, could it be Poppy making this gruesome racket? Mystified, he took a few steps towards the sound and peered into what proved to be the kitchen. At once the voice shouted: 'Don't come in here you'll grind it in. Who are you? What do you know about this? Was it you? Your idea of a joke?'

'Not a joke,' said a voice from the chorus.

'Not funny at all,' said another.

Willy felt the woman's blast of anger; an oldish woman was doing the shouting, three girls in the background and two men he recognised as the undertakers the chorus. There was no sign of Poppy.

Silence fell. Willy introduced himself. Interested faces stared. One of the girls was holding a baby. He was suspected of something malign.

'I came to see Poppy,' he said bravely, 'er – Poppy Carew.'

'She's gone,' said the larger undertaker.

'Evaporated,' said the thin undertaker.

'Whisked away,' said one of the girls.

'Dada, dada.' The baby held out its arms.

The undertakers laughed, releasing pent up merriment.

'What—' began Willy.

'Some joker has poured honey and syrup on the floor, it spread all over the house on people's feet. Mrs Edwardes is furious. This is Mrs Edwardes.'

Willy smiled placatingly at Mrs Edwardes and said, 'My name is Willy Guthrie.' Mrs Edwardes looked unlikely to believe it.

'I am Fergus. This is Mary, that's Annie, Frances, the infant—'

'Barnaby.' Mary jogged the baby. 'And Victor.' Fergus indicated Victor.

'How awful.' Willy grasped the cause of the brouhaha. 'Who did it?' He deftly cast the ball back into Mrs Edwardes's court.

'The Mafia,' suggested Mary, grinning. Mrs Edwardes drew in her breath, she was off again unless—

'Why don't we clear it up?' suggested Willy. 'I'd be glad to help.'

'So who did spread the treacle?' asked Calypso later that evening when Willy had recounted his experience. 'It was good of you to stay and wash the floors, it was not after all anything to do with you.'

'I was able to talk to them, get to know them.'

'Ah.'

'Yes.'

They sat on either side of the log fire he had lit to cheer the autumnal evening, Calypso, resting after her tramp through the woods (working off the depression engendered by the funeral), waited for Willy to tell her more. She would not ask again who had spread the treacle, she thought she knew, her eyes had ranged round the congregation, not got stuck on one object like Willy's.

They had washed the kitchen floor and mopped through the house cleaning the sticky footprints from rugs and carpets. Like a general with his troops, Mrs Edwardes had issued orders to her depleted workforce for as soon as Willy offered, Fergus and the girls remembered the hearse and the horses and the urgent need to load up and get them home which left Victor, who it transpired was only standing in as assistant undertaker, having no proper role in the Furnival outfit. As they worked Willy listened to Victor ingratiating himself with Mrs Edwardes; it seemed Victor too was interested in Poppy's whereabouts.

'I did see Edmund in the church,' said Mrs Edwardes, emptying the bucket of dirty water down the sink, 'but he was with another girl, not sitting as you'd expect with Poppy.'

'Oh,' said Victor, encouragingly tilting his voice to a questioning tone, '—is?'

'Since her Dad couldn't stand the sight of him, it may be that Edmund was being tactful.' Mrs Edwardes made this sound improbable.

'Perhaps he was,' Victor led her on, 'being tactful.'

'But I got the impression,' Mrs Edwardes raised her voice above the sound of fresh water pouring into the bucket, 'earlier today, this morning to be exact, that Edmund is no longer persona grata.' She turned off the tap.

'Oh,' said Victor, 'why was that?'

'Persona grata he has been for a very long time, years, I should say, eight years to be exact, yes I'm right, eight.'

'Ah,' said Victor, 'eight.'

'But not with her Dad. Oh no, Edmund was persona *not* grata with him.'

'Non,' murmured Victor.

'I dare say you're right.' Jane Edwardes was undampened. 'I got that impression from Poppy this morning when she was eating her breakfast. Bacon and egg, didn't want two, I offered another, she seemed a bit off Edmund, if you get my meaning.'

'Oh.'

'Quite off, I'd say. If you knew girls as well as I do you'd know the signs.'

'Of course.'

'Then suddenly at the party, I don't suppose you noticed, you were all very busy talking. No, you didn't notice.' Mrs Edwardes looked round. 'Got any more of that washing powder? Carpet shampoo's what we need but I've run out.'

'This do?'

'Thanks, that's fine, not much more to do now, is there, Mr—'

104

'Guthrie, Willy.'

'At the party?' ventured Victor, manoeuvring the conversational wheel.

'Just this bit, that's the lot. I can check tomorrow when it's dry.' Willy admired Victor's restraint.

'As I say. All of you busy talking when in rushes Edmund, catches sight of Poppy, drags her off and in two jiffs they are gone. I don't know what happened to the girl.'

'What girl?'

'The girl he was with. Came into the church with him, nice looking girl, a bit older than Poppy but as I say nice looking, wearing a decent black dress, very suitable not like—'

'Like?' Victor dared.

'Well,' Jane shrugged disloyally, 'nobody could call the dress Poppy was wearing suitable.'

'I thought it very pretty,' said Victor rashly.

'Pretty all right.' Jane Edwardes twisted a floor cloth in her strong hands, wringing it over the sink. 'There. That's it then, that's the lot. Thank you very much both of you. I'll be shutting up now.' It was plain she was waiting for them to leave. 'Got a lift back with somebody else, I dare say.'

'Who?' asked Victor who had lost the thread.

'The girl in the suitable dress,' said Willy speaking to Victor for the first time.

Victor laughed. 'Come and have a drink in the pub.' He was convinced that Poppy would be returning to her father's house that night, wished to fill in time.

'No thank you, I have to get back,' Willy declined thinking that if Poppy had been as it seemed abducted, she was not likely to come back. On the other hand it was just possible that his aunt might know where he could locate her in London. He was loath to ask Victor for Poppy's address and so declare his interest. Victor was clearly a rival.

'I am thinking of taking a few days off some time soon,' said Willy casually as he prepared to leave for his farm, after supping with his aunt. He had decided to keep quiet about his sudden passion for Poppy; Calypso was used to a fairly rapid turnover of girls in his life and might class Poppy as just another of the many, not realising that she was unique, too precious to discuss.

Calypso, who had found Willy's company irritating during the

105

meal, guessed that the sultry mood he appeared to be in could be attributed to the moment in the church when he had sighted Poppy.

'Your pigs will come to no harm, you have left them before,' she said.

'Well—' said Willy.

'You have fallen in love with Poppy Carew, I saw it happen at the funeral. *Coup de foudre*,' stated Calypso, cutting short Willy's reluctance, tired of waiting for him to confide.

Willy laughed unconvincingly.

'It happens,' said Calypso blandly. 'If one can hate at first sight equally one can love. It runs in your family. Your uncle Hector got it when he clapped eyes on me. I thought all he wanted was a healthy girl to breed an heir by. Later of course I adored him.'

Willy thought, this was not the picture of his aunt painted by her peers and that anyway no comparison could be made between an old uncle he had barely known and himself.

'So what are you going to do about it?' pressed Calypso, assuming Willy's tacit agreement.

'I have to find her,' said Willy, yielding.

'Ask if you need any help.' Casually Calypso prodded the large dog who screened the heat of the fire from her legs. 'Move.' The dog flicked his ears back, settling his haunches more firmly on the rug. 'Good luck,' she said, as Willy bent to kiss her goodbye.

'Thanks,' said Willy, 'I may take you up on the help.' There were times when he found his aunt extremely trying. This was not one of them.

21

As her ears began to pop and the stewardess made sure the safety belts were fastened, Poppy regretted her hauteur during the preparations for the journey. A new place in Africa might be anywhere. Judging by the length of the journey, North Africa was their destination. It was now too late and she was too proud to ask Edmund which country. If I had any wits I would have listened to the captain on the intercom, she thought, as the plane lost height, her ears popped and the engine whined then roared preparing to land, arriving with a triple jolt to taxi to the disembarkation bay.

Experiencing a spasm of fear, she thought of how beautifully birds came in to land, twisting their wings to brake against the wind, extending their feet ready for contact. She thought particularly of mallard measuring their descent exactly, their clever feet touching the water so that there was no bumping, jarring or shaking, just a long V of ripples on a still lake.

She looked out at lights, a glimpse of buildings, as the plane swung taxiing in a half circle. Fellow passengers raised their voices eager to get out of this metal tube, release the straps holding them, stretch their cramped limbs.

Edmund, stuffing his Dick Francis into his briefcase, was anxious to stand up and ease the new trousers cutting into his crotch.

'There's a fellow meeting me. Representative of the Tourist Board,' he said offhandedly. Poppy did not answer. He would be nerving himself to think clearly, to be ready for his business talk, hoping to make a good impression. He should not have drunk all those whiskies.

'He will be waiting at the Customs, see us through,' said Edmund, 'he'll have a car.' He checked their tickets were safe in his jacket pocket. 'Got your passport?'

'Yes,' she said, undoing her safety belt, giving Edmund a quick glance, noting with sinking heart his out-thrust lower lip, sure sign of too many drinks. Hope for the best, she told herself, standing up, collecting her hand luggage, following Edmund out of the plane into a dark North African night.

They waited with the other passengers by the carousel, yawning, tired, dousing the anxiety that their particular bag might have acquired a will of its own, gone elsewhere to a friendlier country, might not turn up whirling round on this piece of technological nonsense which replaced the human porter who might, just possibly, hoping for a tip, have greeted one with a smile.

Poppy looked round at hawk-nosed men, holsters on hip, watching them. Guards? Police? Customs men? She was not going to ask Edmund. Fleetingly she thought of Singh's bulky figure carrying the Thermos boxes of delicious funeral meats. Had he got them back, had Jane Edwardes cleared away the débris, tidied the house?

Was her home still there?

Her bag appeared lying upside-down, shaken by the carousel, the strap torn, the label with her name on it shredded. She grabbed it as it passed. Edmund looked irritated, thrust out his lip, the carousel went round twice more.

'Where the hell? Bloody inefficient—'

'There, it's coming, catch it—'

They pushed their trolley towards Customs. Haughty, expressionless men gestured at cases. 'Open.' Their fingers roughly probing among nighties, knickers, dresses, disarranging so that the case would be hard to shut, picked out books, ruffled pages, peered.

'We might be in Russia,' a man complained.

'There's nothing subversive or even porn in my bag.'

'Didn't like my duty free—'

'Muslim country,' said another in explanation. 'Dry.'

'Pay attention to that, do they?'

'Wouldn't know, this is my first visit.'

'That must be my man.' Edmund hurried, lip back in place, smiling, expansive, to shake hands with an Italian-suited individual, dark glasses blotting his eyes. He introduced Poppy who shook hands, failing to catch the name as muttered by Edmund, not really listening, thinking it rash of Edmund to refer to this individual as 'my man', it being more likely to be the other way about.

Their luggage was put into the boot of a black Mercedes. They sat three abreast on the back seat, Edmund in the middle, Poppy silent, ignored by the two men who talked immediately of the new hotel to which they were going, the prospect of opening the country up to the expected tourist boom, its troubles being now over.

Half listening, Poppy wondered which country in this part of the world did not have troubles. She was by now, as well as tired, hungry. She regretted passing up the meal on the aircraft.

They drove fast passing other cars with blaring horn, shaving close to contemptuous camels, terrifying cyclists wobbling out of the dark, nagging at lorries clinging desperately to the crown of the steeply cambered road, overtaking with a snarl and a howl, car lights briefly illuminating humble overloaded donkeys, errant goats, palm trees, dogs.

Poppy shut her eyes as a limping dog dashed across the road, the car bumped, the driver laughed a short yelp of glee. She strained her ears, heard nothing more. Dear God, let it have been killed outright.

Edmund went on talking. 'How far out of town is the airport?'

'Some thirty miles. In a moment the road runs along the sea by the new boulevard and the beach where we build The Cabana complex among the palms which I show you tomorrow. They should be a great attraction, bring many tourists. We transplant the palms of course from the famous oasis.'

'I see.'

Had they not seen the dog, felt the bump? Poppy's mouth was dry, she no longer felt hungry, drawing away from Edmund into her corner.

'And there is our sea. See the waves are phosphorescent, see how they light up as they reach the sand, are they not beautiful, romantic?'

'Difficult to see, it's very dark.' Edmund craned his neck to look out into the dark past Poppy.

'I think perhaps there will be a storm maybe, an autumn storm.'

'Rain?' asked Edmund, not expecting rain, pained. 'Really?'

'But not to worry. Storms are short. Here is the hotel, as I told you, not quite completed but it is superb. The other passengers on your plane go to the old ones, you only are complimented with the best. Under this archway, here you are, please, welcome.'

The car stopped under a portico. 'No doubt Miss Carew would like to mount straight up to the room?'

'I expect she would.'

'And we go to the bar for your nightcap?'

'Great.'

Poppy drew breath, breathing in a lungful of wet concrete-smelling air. She watched their bags collected by a servant in khaki uniform.

'You go ahead, darling, make yourself comfortable, I'll be up in a minute.'

He was pretending not to have noticed the dog. Perhaps he had not noticed the dog.

She did not look at Edmund, said a polite good night to their guide, followed the servant with the bags to the lift. The room was large, airy, twin beds, fitted cupboards, bathroom. It might be any hotel room in any country. The servant put down the bags, she tipped him with English money, he left. She opened the window, looked out from a balcony into inky darkness, the sound of distant surf, palm trees rustling and with the smell of wet cement a whiff of jasmine.

Perhaps he had not noticed the dog, he was busy talking.

He had his work, it was important that he should succeed in this his first venture in the new job.

Perhaps he had not noticed. He could not have helped the dog. Nobody could help the dog.

A few cars patrolled along the sea road. She watched their lights. Her watch had stopped, it must be pretty late. The hotel was silent, almost as though it were empty. She ran water in the bathroom, bathed her face, washed her hands, her hands would not stop shaking. Stupid.

Better to unpack and go to bed, be asleep when he comes up.

She heaved her bag on to the bed, picked out the lovely dress, Dad's present, carried it to the cupboard to put it on a hanger to hang it perhaps outside the cupboard where she could see it, be comforted. She opened the cupboard door, screamed a small controlled choking scream, shut the door in haste. bent to pick up the bedside telephone.

''Allo?'

'A gentleman in the bar. Please find a gentleman in the bar. Mr Platt, Room Thirty-eight. Get him fast.'

'*Comment?*'

'Oh— Un *monsieur. Il y a un monsieur dans le bar, appellez le vite, s'il vous plaît.*'

She waited taking deep breaths.

'Plat?' a puzzled voice.

'Yes. *Oui.* Platt. P – L – A—'

'*Pas de messieurs.*'

'What?'

'No gentleman. Bar empty. *Fermé. Chiuso.*'

'God!'

'*Comment?*'

'Send somebody up, Room Thirty-eight. *Vite.* At once. *Subito.*'

'*Subito.*' The line went dead. This is ridiculous.

It seemed a long time before there was a knock on the door. Two servants standing, moderately interested.

Poppy showed them the occupants of the cupboard, a group of very large reddish cockroaches clustered halfway up the cupboard, fidgeting in the electric light, waving long sensitive feelers.

'Ah!'

'I want another room, I can't sleep here.'

'*Comment?*'

'Another room. *Une autre chambre. Ein anderer – un altro—*'

Confabulation, shrugging of shoulders. One of the men flipped at the cockroaches with a towel from the bathroom.

'No. *Non. Nein.* Another room—' She pushed the dress back into the bag, zipped it shut, made herself plain by signs and single words. One man seemed to understand Italian, the man who had flipped with the towel. Now he craftily captured the cockroaches in it, shook them away out of the open window.

'*Ecco!*'

'I still want to move.'

'*E pericoloso sporgersi.*' The man leaned out laughing, demonstrating the insects' departure, smiling ingratiatingly, expecting to please with his little joke.

'I—'

The man pointed at the bed. '*Allora! Dormez bien. Gute Nacht.*'

'*No.* Another room. The bloody things will come back.' She knew she was being irrational. '*Un altra camera. Ein.* Oh God, I can't speak German. For Christ's sake move me.'

'Okay.'

At last another room far down the corridor, the servants anxious to please, by now opening each cupboard door exhibiting its pristine emptiness. The drawers too pulled out, virgin clean, bringing more towels to augment those already in the bathroom, running the water. (See it runs?), testing the lights, the telephone. Everything in order. '*Alles in Ordnung*'. Accepting tips. English money again. Good night. Good night. Poppy locked the door after them, washed her hands again, undressed, got into bed, covered her face with the sheet, prayed for sleep.

He *must* have noticed the dog.

Perhaps he had *not* noticed the dog.

Had Victor and Fergus helped Jane Edwardes clear up after the party? Perhaps the girls had helped? The girl with the baby, Mary? Why had she not telephoned from London, she was after all responsible, it was her father's funeral, asked Mrs Edwardes whether everything was all right, told her that she was letting the house and stables to Fergus. Yes, Mrs E., all those horses, yes, Mrs E., that's what I said.

Am I having a nervous breakdown?

What about her job? Had she or had she not made it clear when she telephoned them about Dad's death that she was not coming back?

What had she said? Had she made herself clear? Memory failed her. Why worry about that now, a bit late surely.

No, I am not having a breakdown.

And Edmund? Not in the bar? There were other bars. There were always other bars. She had seen this film before.

What would Venetia Colyer do under these circumstances? Or Mary with her dyed and spiky hair pomaded into points, tiny upright striking spears?

Poppy switched on the light, took the dress Dad had given her for her birthday and hung it near her on a chair so that if by some miracle she slept it would be in view when she woke. Then she got back into bed, laid her head on the pillow, switched off the light.

Neither Venetia nor Mary would have got themselves into a dump like this boiling with cockroaches with a man like Edmund. When they didn't really want to.

We have no joint destination, she thought, Edmund and I.

Somewhere in the night a donkey brayed, expressing, as no other beast can, all the sorrows of the world.

22

In an empty bar Edmund sat with Mustafa from the Government Tourist Board, a half-full glass of whisky before him. He was aware that his host barely succeeded in hiding his feeling that it was a long time since he had met the plane, that everything that could be discussed between them that evening had been mulled over multiple times, that it was time to call it a day.

I have one more thing to say to him, thought Edmund, it is important. Why did I tell him the whole story of my life with Poppy, my love for Poppy? Edmund tried to remember. How did Poppy come into this important thing he had to say, ah of course, got it, here goes.

'I know the car's well sprung. Trust the Krauts to make a good car,' he began.

'—?' Mustafa hummed.

'Yes. That's what I said. No, not better than a Ro— Ro— What? I said Rolls Royce, didn't I? Ro Ros are the very best, we all know *that*. You agree?'

'—' he sighed politely.

'Of course. Even Arabs— God—. I've lost the thread. I was saying that we ran over a dog, you must have noticed.'

Mustafa lit a cigarette, blew smoke towards the ceiling.

Edmund ploughed on. 'Poppy noticed. Went stiff as a board with horror.'

Edmund's host glanced secretly at his watch, caught the eye of the barman.

'Yes.' Edmund answered Mustafa's silence. 'As I say. Too polite, too tactful to protest of course, but horrified.'

'A stray dog.' Mustafa drew in a lungful of smoke.

'Grant you, a stray maybe, but your driver ran over it. I felt the bump even though we were in the second best car. I say, that's funny. Second best.'

'So?' Mustafa let the smoke drift out of his mouth finishing with a sharp puff.

'He should have stopped.'

'Stopped. Why?'

'For appearance sake. Taken the dog's number.'

'No use, no point, no number—'

'Of course no use to the *dog*, it was dead, wasn't it, but if you want to attract the British tourist you have to stop when you run over a dog, it's essential.'

'Ha ha ha.' The marvellously comic Brits.

'No laughing matter. Preferable of course *not* to run over a dog in the first place. The British tourist doesn't want to spend his hard earned pounds running over dogs.'

'You say—'

'I'm telling you. I say nothing matters, my precious Poppy says (well she didn't, too polite wasn't she, a tactful girl), nothing matters as much as dogs, better a child.'

'A child?' Mustafa straightened from a lounging position.

'Yup,' said Edmund wisely. 'For some reason, yes. Herod is a secret hero with some sects in the UK.'

'Ah?' He must make enquiries, sects could be a serious cause of disturbances. 'So?'

'I say. What's the time? Lord, it's late. You've kept me talking while what I've been meaning to do is take my precious Poppy in my arms and tell her how much I love her. I've loved her for years.'

'You will marry her?' Mustafa feigned interest, he was sick of the subject of Poppy.

'Of course. Her father died the other day. Didn't like me, influenced her against me or tried to. I told you that didn't I?'

'Yes.' Twice over, thought Mustafa, in truth, in triplicate. Can't stand it again.

'Didn't succeed though, did he? Told you that too. Now then, look here, I can't sit up all night talking to you when I have to comfort Poppy. Shall I tell you—'

'No.' Mustafa released a glint of impatience.

'Oh, I see. Okay I won't, but let me tell you the British won't stand for killing dogs, it isn't done.'

'She did not notice,' unwisely Mustafa answered.

'Of course she bloody noticed. She noticed the *dog*, the bump, the shit driver laughed. Christ, that laugh could cost you all Thompson's Tours, much better Herod.'

'Who is this Herod?'

'Wouldn't go down well here, he was a Jew as far as I can remember.'

'So?' Bristle concealed by cigarette smoke.

'So,' said Edmund with a flash of sobriety, 'I must leave you. Meet you tomorrow in the hotel bar. We can get down to business then.'

They drove back, conversation exhausted. Edmund knew they had arrived when he smelled wet cement. They said good night. The night was beautiful, moonless. Edmund looked up at the stars. He felt an overwhelming love for Poppy, he wondered as he went up in the lift why he had not insisted ages ago on marrying her. Soon he would be in bed, hold her warm in his arms, too tired tonight for more than that but her warm bottom in the small of his back held familiar allure. He would not wake her, just creep in (ah, here we are), no need to put on the light. He stood to accustom his eyes to the dark, moved forward, arms outstretched. 'Oh hell, twin beds, creep into this one, tell her in the morning when my head has stopped roaring how much I love her.' He pulled off his clothes, slipped into bed. He must not take Poppy so much for granted. He lay down, remembered his watch, wound it, put it on the bedside table, laid his head on the pillow. What had he told Mustafa? My love is a fire which inflames my soul. Oh dear God! I'm drunk. The classic way to make a fool of oneself. For some reason it seemed all Poppy's fault he had made a monumental cock-up of the job, first try.

23

When Calypso Grant's husband Hector returned from the 1939–45 war he bought land to plant his dream wood, an idea born in the treeless Western Desert which had become an obsession.

He found his location, a bowl of land with a stream meandering through it dotted with oak and limes. On the side of a hill overlooking the land a tumble-down house. He bought the land, restored the house and spent the rest of his life planting trees.

By the time Hector had planted wild cherries in a series of loops, circles and curves to spell his wife's name, Calypso, who had originally scoffed at her husband, became bitten by the bug. Together they planted beech and oak, chestnut, hornbeam, sycamore, pine, larch, rowan, birch and more limes to scent the air. They encouraged an undergrowth of spindleberry, blackthorn, hawthorn, hazel and wild rose. Among the scrub they set honeysuckle to ramp. In open spaces they encouraged gorse. When the wild cherries flowered spelling, as Hector intended, his wife's name, they had rivalry from hawthorn, rowan and horse chestnut. Between them they had planted clumps of box, philadelphus and lilac, planning that at almost every turn of the year there would be the reassurance of sweet scents. Forty years on, walking through the wood in the evening, Calypso doubted whether anyone flying over the wood would read her name spelled in blossom but there was no part of the wood which did not spell Hector for her.

To wild anemones, primroses, bluebells and foxgloves they added in open glades drifts of fritillary, spring and autumn cyclamens, windflowers, daffodils and narcissi.

In the centre of the wood they widened and dammed the stream to make a lake, bordering it with reeds to form a haven for wildfowl and warbler. The wood as it grew was colonised by innumerable birds and wild animals.

115

As she walked in the wood the day after Bob Carew's funeral Calypso thought of her husband, how he would have enjoyed the funeral, especially the tape of birdsong in the church, a dawn chorus comparable to the chorus in the wood which had delighted their springs.

Pausing by a clump of hazel wound about with honeysuckle, thinking of Hector, she breathed in to catch a last elusive whiff of honey. Instead, sneaking from the far side of the hill on a north-east breeze, she smelled pig.

Some years before his death, to protect his wood from an encroaching developer, Hector had bought the land over the hill and with it a group of derelict farm buildings. He restored the buildings and leased the land to a dairy farmer. To the dawn chorus was added the comforting sound of lowing cattle.

The lease expired, the farmer died and Calypso rented the farm to Hector's nephew Willy Guthrie who had chosen an agricultural career. Tiring of milking cows, Willy switched his attention to pigs and presently prospered, growing what his aunt referred to as Happy Hams, pigs who lived in comfort, lolling at night in deep straw in the barns, roaming freely by day in family or adolescent groups in large paddocks with ample fresh water piped to their troughs.

In exchange for not losing their tails, having their teeth extracted, sleeping on bare concrete, imprisoned in the sweatbox – conditions of the modern pig – the prospective Hams surrendered their lives after a period of cheerful carefree growth to become sides of bacon and high-class smoked ham similar to Jambon d'Ardennes which Willy smoked himself in a barn converted into a smokery. These hams under the brand name of Guthrie he sold at high prices to upmarket restaurants and delicatessens.

Calypso, scenting pig, forgot Hector, noted that the wind had swung to the north-east, the only and fortunately rare wind to bring hint of pig, remembered that she had news for Willy garnered from carefully selected telephone calls. She was fond of Willy, who reminded her of her late husband, not so much by physical resemblance but by genetic quirks. Hector had never been as Willy was, gangling as though his limbs were not only loose but double jointed, giving his movements a disconnected quality which some people found irritating but which she found endearing. Where Hector's eyes had sparkled like jet, Willy's were brown velvet. It was the intonation when moved, the catch in his voice which made her stop, remember with a pang that she would never hear that voice again.

With her hand raised to pick the last honeysuckle and hold it to her nose, Calypso hesitated. She left the honeysuckle where it was and set off towards her house to telephone Willy. Her dog, who had been patiently waiting for her to make a move, followed.

'Willy?'

'Yes, Aunt.'

'What are you up to?'

'Just about to stroll round the enterprise, scratch a few backs perhaps.' His voice was depressed.

'Leave all that and come and see me.'

'Okay I'll come, love to.'

'Have you had supper?'

'Not yet.'

'Come and share mine.'

'Thanks, I'd like that.'

'Good.'

'I'll be over as soon as I've settled the pigs.'

'Don't bring Mrs Future.'

Willy laughed. Mrs Future, a sow of exceptional intelligence and charm, born the runt of the family, was, after being reared on a bottle by Willy, under the impression that she was entitled to accompany him wherever he went, tripping merrily at his heels, raising pleased smiles from the neighbours in her early and adolescent youth but now, a mature sow, her appearance in people's houses and gardens raised protests, complaints even.

'It's okay,' Willy reassured his aunt. 'She farrowed last night, she can't leave her piglets.'

'I hesitate to worry you but there was a bit of a whiff when I was walking in the wood just now, of dung.'

'Not to worry, that would be Harry Arnold who took a load away to muck spread it, suits his land, the pong is gone.'

'Right.'

Calypso uncorked a bottle of wine, setting it to breathe in the warmth of the kitchen, debated what to give her nephew to eat, decided on pasta with a garlicky sauce, the aroma of which would stifle any lingering hint of pig Willy might bring with him. In her youth, she thought with amusement, she would have sent him off to bath and change his clothes if he dared bring evidence of the byre with him. In age she was sensitive to young people's feelings. As she chopped onions and garlic for the sauce she debated whether or not to tell Willy the result of her telephonings. She was still undecided when he arrived, coming in by the kitchen door, stooping to kiss her cheek.

'Smells delicious, brought you a ham. I had a bath after your remarks and changed. Have I kept you waiting?'

'No. Hang it on the hook on the larder beam. You must let me pay you.'

'No, no.'

'I insist.'

'No, no, I owe you.'

'Whatever for?'

'Taking me to Bob Carew's funeral.'

'I hope this doesn't end in tears,' Calypso exclaimed as she poured the saucepan of pasta to drain in a colander.

'If it did it would be worth it,' said Willy. His aunt drew in her breath with a hiss, reminded with a fierce pang of Hector. She watched Willy scatter Parmesan on his pasta, twirl it round his fork and eat. She was glad that love had not impaired his appetite. She offered a second helping.

'No, thank you.' He sipped his wine, stared gloomily at his empty plate then, looking up at her, said bleakly, 'What am I to do? I can't find her.'

'Where have you looked?'

'I tried the daily woman, Mrs Edwardes, at her father's house. Not much joy.'

'And?'

'She gave me Poppy's London address and the address of her work. She's left her job and her flat is empty. Nobody answers the door and the telephone rings and rings.'

'Sad.'

'It appears that Fergus Furnival and his cousin Victor are trailing her too, no luck for them either.'

'Ah.'

'And Poppy's solicitor who is arranging the lease for Fergus – he's renting her house and stables by the way—'

'Swift work.'

'Yes, very. Well, the solicitor hasn't got her address, bit annoyed about it Mrs Edwardes says, complains of being rushed.'

'It's good for solicitors to be rushed.' Calypso offered fruit.

'No thanks.' His appetite blunted, Willy sat looking glum.

Thoughtfully Calypso peeled a peach.

Willy burst out. 'I must find her. I've got to. Please don't laugh.'

'I am not laughing,' said Calypso as sharply as she could with a mouthful of peach. She swallowed. 'It's not funny.' It's quite possibly sad, she thought. He sits there reminding me of Hector behaving in this painfully old-fashioned way. Why me, why must he drag me into this? I am old, I manage to keep my equilibrium. Why should I be bothered with Willy in love?

'What about the man who swept her off, her lover?' she asked, conscious of her brutality.

'I don't think he matters,' said Willy.

'She went away with him, you told me. You told me he burst in on the party and dragged her away.'

'I don't think she went willingly.'

'If she did not want to go she could have called for help, made a scene.'

'Perhaps she felt embarrassed—'

'Come off it, Willy.'

'There may have been a reason for going with him. I'm sure she didn't want to.'

'What makes you think that? You weren't there.'

'A gut feeling.'

'Now we have guts. Extra-sensory perception next.'

'Look, Aunt, if I had been there I would have stopped her. Victor and Fergus who could have stopped her were otherwise occupied, the one coping with the solicitor the other with a publisher – he's written a novel, I gather – it all happened very fast. If I had been there—' Willy looked distraught.

'So now you blame me for making you drive me home when you wanted to stay—'

'Not that. You needed to get home. You sent me back. I was too late, that's all, but I feel there was a reason to make her go with him.'

'I can only think of one reason if she is not in love with him,' said Calypso laughing. 'She went with him to prevent another girl getting him.'

'Aunt!' Willy was shocked.

'It doesn't mean she has feet of clay, it would be a very normal reaction, the sort of thing I'd have done at her age.' Calypso chuckled.

'Oh.' Willy was thoughtful, not sure he wanted Poppy to resemble his aunt when young.

'Coffee?' suggested Calypso.

'Please.'

They were silent while Calypso made coffee. She was surprised to find herself anxious for her nephew, Hector's nephew, she corrected herself, it being her habit, of which she was proud, of letting others, particularly the young, make their own mess without interference. 'How sure are you,' she asked quietly, 'that it's love?'

'As certain as I could ever be about anything.'

'But you don't know her.'

'Did you know much about Hector? Did he know you?'

'What has that got to do with it?'

'Just that I want to spend the rest of my life with Poppy. Uncle Hector must have felt the same about you.'

'I didn't realise it at the time.'

'But you did later. You said you did. Poppy can't realise it either. We haven't even spoken to each other or rather I said something about taking your coat back and she smiled. I didn't hear what she said.'

Calypso stared at Willy whose voice as he spoke of Poppy waxed lyrical.

'She isn't a virgin; I was,' she said, hoping to bring him to earth.

'You may have been a virgin but—' Willy flushed, hesitated, fell silent.

'But what?'

'Oh you know, the catty things people say about you being a – er – man eater. All those old women and—'

'The old men?'

Willy laughed. 'The old men all wish they'd been in my uncle's shoes.' He watched his aunt, they regarded each other smiling.

'So you are certain?'

'Yes.'

'Very well. I think I can find out where she's gone.'

'You can?' Willy's voice whooped up exultant.

'Not that it matters.'

'Why not?'

'Because you will be lying in wait for her when she comes back.'

'Oh no I won't. Wherever she is I shall go and find her.'

120

'Oh my!' Calypso admired his spirit, refrained from asking whether this was wise.

'So how can you find out where she is?' To Willy it seemed wildly improbable that his old aunt could help him.

'By talking to the girl Poppy snitched him from.'

Willy gaped.

'She was in the church with Edmund, she's called Venetia Colyer.'

24

When Edmund found Poppy on the terrace overlooking the swimming pool she had finished her breakfast and sat talking to Mustafa who was making himself agreeable.

Edmund felt at a gross disadvantage as they turned towards him, eyeing him through their dark glasses. Taking his own sunglasses from his shirt pocket, blotting out his hungover eyes, Edmund regretted encouraging Poppy to buy such dark ones, he could not see her eyes, her mouth gave nothing away.

Mustafa called out 'Hi', smiling and, 'Have you had breakfast?' snapping his fingers at a hovering waiter. 'Refresh the tray.'

'Just coffee please.' Edmund sat beside Poppy. 'Black.'

'Delicious figs,' said Poppy in neutral tone, pointing to bits of bruised fruit skin on her plate, bearing, Edmund saw with a pang, the marks of her teeth.

Mustafa called out 'Coffee' and something in Arabic.

Edmund wondered whether Mustafa knew they had slept in separate rooms, did he perhaps know where Poppy had spent the night, there had been neither hide nor hair of her when he had surfaced. He was not going to ask Poppy where the hell she had been or what she thought she was up to, in front of Mustafa. He felt betrayed and bitterly resentful, he had had a terrible fright waking to find her gone, she might at least have left a note. He felt choked with whisky-fumed self-pity and love.

'I was suggesting Miss Poppy might like an expedition to the Roman amphitheatre while we do business today. There will be parties going in buses from the other hotels, easy to arrange. The amphitheatre and the theatre are interesting if you like that sort of thing.'

'I'll think about it,' said Poppy politely.

'The archaeologists who worked for our government were partially British.'

'How partial?' asked Poppy gravely.

'From Cambridge,' said Mustafa.

'Not Oxford?' (So that's how she's going to be, thought Edmund, little bitch.)

'A bit of both, no matter.' Mustafa was careless of universities. He was aware from the servants of this girl making a fuss the night before, she had not mentioned the matter to him, it would be indelicate if he brought it up. The servants had been cringing but with a hint of mockery describing the scene. The girl had made a fuss over a few immigrating locusts, the servants said, calling them cockroaches. Mustafa realised that the offending insects probably were cockroaches yet preferred, as the servants did, to think of them as locusts. Clever beasts to get into such a new hotel, though in truth it had stood half built for a long time. Edmund had slept in the room too drunk to notice the girl's absence. The information on this score was reliable. If Edmund and Poppy represented what one must expect of the new wave of European tourists and their women it would be as well to make it clear once and for all that in this country visitors were expected to make use only of the room they had booked, not move around as the girl had done. Not that it mattered. Edmund was guest of the State and the hotel still empty, incomplete. The girl was talking, projecting her remarks at a point between himself and Edmund. Mustafa jerked to attention.

'Such extraordinary camber,' she was saying. 'That road we came along from the airport last night, so steeply cambered it was not like the roads you see in most countries, was it an old road?' She turned towards Mustafa, 'Pot holes too.'

A servant brought coffee for Edmund, collected Poppy's used cup and plates.

'Yes, an old road. The new road is under repair,' said Mustafa, 'it will soon be open again.' That sounded all right, he told himself, no need to tell her the main road had been cleared for troop transport hurrying to take up station at the airport. These things happened, it was unfortunate but not necessary to inform visitors of every slight disturbance. Their currency was too welcome.

'And so crowded,' continued Poppy, 'so many people and animals at that time of night. Camels and donkeys and—'

'Travelling in the cool of the night,' said Edmund, breaking into the chat, fearing mention of the lame dog; he remembered it lame.

'The weather isn't hot,' said Poppy. 'I'm wearing a jersey and what seemed rather funny was they were all travelling away from the town, it looked like the flight from Egypt.'

'Your sense of direction!' exclaimed Edmund in sarcastic contradiction.

'You usually say how good it is,' said Poppy saccharine sweet.

'Ah,' said Mustafa lightly. 'There is a tribal caravan trek at this time of year. Simple people, they move out to an oasis.' The girl was likely to be ignorant of local geography and the explanation was in part true.

'Really,' said Poppy. 'I see.' Politely sceptical.

'Forgive me a moment while I telephone,' said Mustafa rising. 'Then perhaps we start on our tour of the town, the beaches, the Cabana complex to be starting with, the Office of Tourism? You meet the Minister.' Edmund should be impressed.

'Certainly,' said Edmund. 'I am ready.' He was gratified.

'And you,' said Mustafa to Poppy, 'you like to join the bus to the Roman antiquities?' He was sure she would.

'I think I'll just fan about in the garden.' She leant back smiling.

Mustafa went to the telephone.

'Garden,' said Poppy with a laugh, 'great piles of cement. The *garden*,' she stressed the word contemptuously, 'the garden isn't half made, the whole place reeks of wet cement. I bet the workmen pee in it.'

'Shall you bathe?' asked Edmund. 'The pool looks nice.' Would Venetia have been more helpful?

'Very nice. If you weren't so pi-eyed you'd see it's empty.'

'It will all be finished very soon.' Edmund ignored the gibe. It was true, if he had looked he would have noticed the emptiness of the pool. He looked at it now. There was a suspicious-looking thing like ordure in the far end. 'Soon all this will be peopled by tourists.'

'Cockroaches.'

'What?'

'Never mind.'

'It would help me if you went to the Roman sights and let me

123

know what they are like.' It was as close as he could come to an appeal.

'I think I'll stay in the garden or I may explore the town.'

Edmund swallowed his resentment. At least she had not brought up the squashed dog, he did not feel up to that just yet. They sat uneasily silent until Mustafa came down the steps from the hotel. He had missed the chance to find out what had happened to Poppy the night before. If he had not been so heavy on the booze there would have been no problem, no mystery.

'Well then,' Mustafa rubbed his hands together, 'everything arranged. We drive along the coast after visiting the Minister of Tourism.'

'Oh, the Minister,' said Poppy. 'Oh.'

'Will you be all right?' On his feet now, preparing to leave with Mustafa, Edmund lingered by Poppy. If only she'd take off those bloody glasses.

'She will be all right,' said Mustafa pleased with his telephone call. The airport was quiet now, they said, excitement over, arrests made. The road was clear, everything under control. We'll keep an eye on the girl, they said, there is nothing to see.

'Are you sure you don't want to see the Roman ant—' began Edmund.

'You know how I hate conducted tours,' snapped Poppy.

'Well—' Edmund stood hesitating looking down at her lolling in the garden chair, her long legs crossed at the ankle. 'Is there anything I can get you before I go?'

Poppy shook her head.

Edmund walked away with Mustafa. 'Goodbye then,' he called over his shoulder, hurt. She watched them go down the steps to the road, get into a car and be driven off. She wiped a tear with a finger before it could roll down her cheek.

25

Edmund, introduced to the Minister of Tourism, took a violent dislike to him, loathing his thick greying hair, macho moustache, red lips, even teeth and above all his extremely healthy general appearance. Not having jogged for several days Edmund was pervaded by guilt. This emotion generated a sort of second wind which cleared his mind to such an extent that he was able to conduct his business with zeal, efficiency and dispatch, surprising the Minister whose information relayed from Mustafa via his secretary prior to their meeting had been to the effect that Edmund was to all intents and purposes a pushover.

Edmund's success with the Minister did Mustafa no good but no harm either since he was the nephew by marriage of the Minister's wife. He was amused by Edmund's transformation since it proved his grandmother's theory (she was partly French) that no Englishman was to be trusted. With this in mind he excused himself and went into the outer office where he arranged for a message to be transmitted to the Minister to the effect that it would be as well to take Edmund out of the town for a few hours, visit the Roman city perhaps, be usefully occupied a hundred kilometres away while the troop transports returned from the airport, one never knew with such perfidious people what interpretation they might put on what they saw. There was no need for Edmund to hear of yesterday's unrest. He returned to the Minister's office in time to watch him receive the message on his office telephone, accepting it with understanding calm.

Mustafa thought if the opportunity arose it would be amusing to test another theory his grandmother held about the English. Taking off his dark glasses he flashed an enigmatic smile at Edmund. Edmund remained expressionless, not wishing to show pleasure at having scored, from his employers' point of view, a variety of vital concessions. He was not bothered that Mustafa signalled that he was aware of his success, it was up to Mustafa to run with the hare and hunt with the hounds, he was that sort of wog. Thinking these thoughts he relented and returned Mustafa's smile.

The Minister was now suggesting that their official business over, minor points conceded on both sides thus showing a proper spirit hopeful for the future of tourism, it would be a pleasure and a joy if Edmund allowed him to drive him to the Roman antiquities, the city, the theatre, the amphitheatre, only a few kilometres along the coast by the sea; a few hours off from affairs of State would do no harm. Edmund found himself sitting beside the Minister in his Porsche, driving at speed along a road parallel to the sea while Mustafa followed at a more sedate pace in the Mercedes. Too late Edmund thought that it would have been possible to bring Poppy, then consoled himself that she had had the chance and refused. He set himself to listen to the Minister's description of the Roman city they were to visit, excavated, he assured Edmund, by archaeologists from London University. Edmund thought briefly of Poppy's earlier tease about Oxbridge.

The Roman city impressed Edmund enormously, it was so large it had swallowed up several busloads of Scandinavian tourists with their guides. The buses were parked, silent, glinting in the sun, while their drivers gossiped with a group of herdsmen who were building a fire of driftwood on a slight elevation on the dunes overlooking the ruins. They had with them several disappointed looking donkeys and some flop-eared goats whose charming little kids with enormous knees attracted Edmund's eye. Poppy would have loved them. He made himself listen to the Minister's historical dissertation on the city, its rise, its prosperity, its fall. Having eaten no breakfast and nothing since his meal on the plane, his attention flagged, hunger vied with intellectual interest. Would it be eventually possible, he suggested by way of a diplomatic hint, a good thing even, an encouragement to tourism if the Minister's government built a restaurant near the ruins where hungry tourists would spend their pounds, dollars, Deutschmarks, nothing vulgar naturally.

'Hungry are you?' asked the Minister who had spent a long time in England and was familiar with the expression 'cut the cackle'. 'You English march on your stomach like Napoleon?'

'He was French.' Edmund disliked the Minister more than ever. 'A Corsican actually.'

'Look.' The Minister pointed towards the car park.

'I see. The buses are driving away.'

126

'Not that. See, there is Mustafa. I sent him to arrange a desert meal in your honour. Can you see him?'

'Yes.' Edmund followed the pointing finger in time to see one of the men hold up a kid by its legs while another man slit its throat.

'Delicious,' said the Minister, 'roasted with herbs over the open fire, you will never have tasted anything like it.'

'I dare say not.' Edmund's throat was dry. Thank God Poppy had not come with him.

'So while the lunch cooks we swim,' said the Minister. 'Work up an appetite.'

'Okay,' said Edmund cravenly turning his gaze towards the sea.

'You don't have to eat its eyes,' said the Minister, evilly mischievous.

Edmund said nothing.

They reached the beach, a deserted expanse of sand beaten by creaming rollers.

'Race you to the water.' The Minister dropped his trousers, Edmund followed suit, running into the sea, diving under so that the water would drown the sound of the startled bleat, the vision of the exposed throat. It would be nice to catch the Minister by the foot, pull him under, drown him, but curse him, he swam like a porpoise.

Back at the picnic site the Minister excused himself. 'Eat your lunch,' he said, 'enjoy the al fresco.' Mustafa would be his host, he himself had urgent business, it had been a pleasure but now alas . . . He drove away in his Porsche.

'Now eat,' said Mustafa.

The kid was delicious, tender, redolent of herbs. Not far off one of the men milked its mother. 'You would not like milk to drink,' said Mustafa, 'the vessel is filthy, these are ignorant men.'

'Oh, ah, I—'

'I have brought you something else.' Mustafa produced a bottle of wine and glasses from the Mercedes. 'They can make us coffee,' he said, 'we have work to do.'

'So has the Minister, urgent business.'

'If you call it business.' Mustafa took off his glasses and stared at Edmund. 'You look better,' he said looking away.

'I was not ill.' Edmund defended himself boldly, holding out his glass for a refill. 'I take it the Minister has a beautiful wife,' he said. One must not let these fellows get the upper hand.

'Very beautiful.' Mustafa laughed, crinkling up his eyes. 'You understand it all.'

'Well,' said Edmund, pleased, 'one does—'

'Now coffee.' Mustafa handed him a tiny cup of gritty coffee. 'Then we drive back, inspect the sites for the Cabana complexes, visit the hotels we have already built, the site for the golf course, the tennis courts and the stadium. I will show you the plans for the stadium.'

'You never mentioned a stadium.' Edmund felt he might wilt. 'Won't tomorrow do?'

'Of course. Have some more wine, finish the bottle.'

'I think I have,' said Edmund, surprised. 'I rather like you without your glasses,' he said, not guarding his tongue.

'So, to work.' Mustafa let Edmund's remark drop. 'And when we have done our work I will show you a private bar where you will—'

'What?' Mustafa's tone made Edmund suspicious. 'What will I?'

'Nothing important. They have a pastis like in France, you will enjoy it in the cool of the evening. Arak.'

'Maybe,' said Edmund watching Mustafa's curious velvety eyes. 'Put your glasses on,' he said roughly, 'and let's get on with it.'

'Okay, okay,' said Mustafa, gently mindful of his grandmother.

26

'Are you listening, Willy?' said Calypso on the telephone.

'Yes, Aunt.'

'Then take this down. I have the name of the country, the town and the hotel they are at. Shall I start?'

'Please.' Willy wrote rapidly as Calypso dictated.

'Thanks,' he said. 'You are a perfect marvel.'

'You fly from Gatwick, there are three flights a week, there may be one tomorrow.'

'I'll soon find out.' Then, 'I thought,' said Willy, 'that they were entirely into oil in that country. This must be something new.'

'They are enterprising people, they look ahead. When the oil runs out there will still be tourism to net the dollars.'

'I see.'

'What about Fergus and Victor? What are they doing? Were they not in the hunt? Perhaps they are not really serious,' suggested Calypso.

'I checked. Fergus is moving his business into Poppy's stables, he wants to get settled before a rush of orders bogs him down.'

'Is he expecting a flu epidemic or Legionnaires' Disease, or does he rely on *anno domini*?'

Willy laughed. 'He's of sanguine disposition, he feels after the press and television coverage of Bob Carew, business will perk up. Did you read Victor Lucas's article in Julia Wake's magazine? There's mention too in *Horse and Hound* and *Country Life*.'

'I did and Lord Hatchet's letter to *The Times*, objecting, is a marvellous advertisement. I wonder who put him up to it.' Calypso chuckled. 'And what of Victor?'

'He's bogged down by his editor who wants a mass of alterations to his novel done immediately so that the book can get into the spring list.'

'Have you made friends with those two that you know so much?' Calypso was curious.

'No, no. I gave Mrs Edwardes, Bob Carew's daily lady, a ham, one of Mrs Future's nephews actually.'

'Don't, Willy! I must have my hams anonymous. How *is* Mrs Future?'

'Terrific. So clever too, she gauged her last litter exactly a piglet to each teat.'

'The result of hormones?'

'You know I don't give them hormones, she just is the perfect sow.' Willy enthused.

'Who are you leaving in charge, Arthur?'

'Yes, he copes well if I have to go away.'

'Will he control the smell?'

'Of course he will. Don't tease.'

'Take plenty of money. Are you okay for money?'

'Yes, thanks. I can't thank you enough. I am eternally grateful. How, by the way, did you get all this information. Did you extract somebody's teeth by torture?' Willy was curious.

'I telephoned Venetia Colyer as I promised. She volunteered it.'

'Good Lord!' Willy whistled.

'She's no slouch when she wants something. She wants Edmund

Platt back.'

'Good Lord!'

'One wonders what she means, almost one feels sorry for him.'

'Good Lord!'

'Don't keep saying "Good Lord", Willy, try a bit of variety.'

'Sorry, it's hard to grasp this aspect—'

'According to Venetia this Edmund of Poppy's, although not a particularly nice character – who is when it comes to that and you really look among the débris – is very attractive. Girls would like to have had him rather in the way antique dealers like to have a collector's piece in their shop window.'

'Oh.'

'Venetia says Poppy's had the monopoly for far too long and she, Venetia, wants him before he goes off.'

'Oh.'

'Some girls are like that.'

'Oh.'

'Not Poppy of course.' Was Calypso making fun of him? 'So Venetia's not averse to getting him back, says she knows it's perverse but she would not mind keeping him permanently.'

'Oh!'

'Don't keep saying "Oh", Willy, you've no idea how irritating you sound.'

'Sorry.'

'When shall you go?'

'Tonight.'

'Let's hope she's still there.'

'That's a risk I have to take.'

Willy's tone reminded her of Hector. 'God speed,' she said, replacing the receiver. 'I hope I've done the right thing, not buggered up his life,' she murmured to her dog who, wagging his tail and rolling his eyes towards the door, indicated that a walk in the wood at twilight would be the right thing for a dog.

Following her dog through the wood, it occurred to Calypso that by aiding Willy she was guilty of hindering Fergus.

When Fergus's mother Ros, a friend of years, had heard that she intended going to the Carew funeral Calypso had agreed to report on Fergus's enterprise.

'If you are going to this do will you let me know whether Fergus is going to make a success of his crazy idea, or a fool of himself? I am

130

worried sick for him. I can't interfere, he is so touchy, all I can do is stand by and pray,' Ros had vented her maternal anxiety. Calypso had agreed; the request was simple enough. I went to say farewell to Bob, she thought irritably. I can tell her the horses were beautiful, the turn-out impeccable, the hearse dignified, the service moving, that, as funerals go, it was a success. I can tell her it's the sort of thing Hector would have liked, that will reassure her. One does not anticipate the undertaker falling in love with the chief mourner or one's nephew, level headed and sensible, to fall arse over tip for the same girl. I shall censor the news of Poppy, give her a glowing report, stick to the hearse and horses. 'What she's really worried about is all those pretty stable girls,' said Calypso aloud to the dog.

The dog thrust his head up under her hand, nudging for a caress.

27

As soon as Edmund and Mustafa had gone Poppy felt regret. She should have been nicer to Edmund, told him about the cockroaches, told him why she had changed rooms, why she was not there when he came to bed, enlisted his sympathy, he was after all supposed to love her. But no, she told herself robustly, he had gone off on a round of the bars with Mustafa, he was never loving or sympathetic when drunk, he had looked pretty poached when he turned up this morning.

So how to occupy her day?

She looked beyond the empty pool and the half-made garden to the sea, choppy and uninviting, and decided to change some money, explore the town.

The man at the desk explained in halting English that there were as yet no facilities to change travellers' cheques in the hotel. She would have to find a bank, the hotel was not yet geared for tourists. Poppy thanked him, looking round the empty hall, wondering whether she and Edmund were the only guests. The emptiness was a little eerie.

'Three months,' said the desk clerk, holding up three fingers. 'Finish in three months, *drei Monaten*.' This explained perhaps the smell of wet cement, the desultory work being done in the garden, the empty pool. Perhaps there had been a pause in the building of the hotel during which the cockroaches had moved in.

'Taxi?' suggested the desk clerk.

'Thanks, I'll walk,' said Poppy.

Settling her sunglasses on her nose, she set off for the town. She had all day, she would do what tourists do, explore, buy postcards, find a museum perhaps, sit in a café.

Arriving in the dark the night before, she had not noticed the environs. Outside what was to be the hotel garden there was an expanse of ground where there had been buildings. Bulldozers were at work levelling the ground, earth-moving machines scooped and scraped, lorries churned up dust with their enormous wheels turning the landscape barren. She looked back at the hotel and guessed that in the near future there would be other shoebox hotels, swimming pools, bars, all the complex thought necessary for travellers, but we are not travellers, she thought, we are tourists, packaged into manageable parties by people like Edmund and Mustafa. She picked her way across the waste ground to the road leading into the town and eventually found herself in a large square surrounded by municipal buildings, offices and banks.

The population did not seem very large. There was little traffic but armed men stood in groups at the street corners and as she looked about for a Bureau de Change a dozen army trucks drove through the square. In the trucks soldiers looked at her with lack-lustre eyes over the tops of their weapons. As she stood watching, several busloads of tourists passed the army trucks, overtaking them and driving out in the direction of the sea. Poppy surmised they were heading for the Roman city and congratulated herself on resisting Mustafa's plan to herd her with them. She located a bank and went in past an armed policeman to change her traveller's cheques. The clerk who attended to her asked whether she wished to change Deutsch-marks or dollars and let his face fall when she admitted to pounds. He rallied however when she spoke to him in Italian and asked her where she was staying. When she told him he exclaimed and said that the hotel when it was complete would be the most magnificent on the North African coast. Poppy felt it would be unfair to complain of the smell of cement, the empty pool and the insect lodgers. He wished her a happy holiday and, slightly cheered by this brief human contact, she left the bank and its armed guard to buy picture postcards and find a café where she chose a table in the shade from where she could watch the passers-by.

Waiting for the waiter to bring her coffee she was conscious that people at other tables in the café stared at her with interested disdain. She became aware of being a woman alone; such women as there were in the café were old, caring for children, the majority of the customers male. Pretending not to notice Poppy addressed her postcards, sipped her coffee, taking her time to write a postcard to Jane Edwardes, another to a girl she was not particularly friendly with at her late job. There had been no camels for Venetia Colyer, a psychedelic view of a sunset with palm trees would have to suit. There was no possible message for the woman who had stolen your lover when you had got him back. She stared down at the blank card pondering this conundrum, wrote one word. Quickly she scribbled a card to Mary, care of Furnival's Fine Funerals, adding 'much love to infant Barnaby' remembering his lollipop eyes. It crossed her mind that it would be fun to be here with Dad even though they would squabble about Edmund. They had never been abroad together, she had made an excuse the only time he had suggested it, inviting her, she remembered with a pang, to the races in Paris. If he were here would she be able to tell him what she now felt about Edmund (and what may that be, asked her inner self), would she feel tempted to ask his advice? The very idea amused her, she finished her coffee, paid and tipped the waiter. The clientele had stopped staring at her and were watching the people in the street who were all drifting in one direction, taking a street which led out of the square. One by one the men in the café got up, joined the crowd, drifted away with it.

An occasional gust of wind swept through the square stirring bits of paper, billowing out the robes worn by the older men. Poppy noticed that what women there were about were hurrying against the tide of men, dragging children with them. In casual search of a postbox she let herself be carried along with the crowd which, funnelling out of the square into a long colonnaded street, seemed to grow thicker by the minute. As she walked down the street on the look-out for a postbox she was puzzled that shopkeepers were putting up their shutters; was it perhaps a holiday or siesta time or was everyone going to a football match? All round her men spoke in low muttering voices or walked silently so that the street was filled with the shuffling slapping sound of feet. Far ahead there was the

133

sound of shouting; the crowd hurried forward. Poppy began to wish herself elsewhere, having a claustrophobic fear of being hemmed in, suffocated by numbers. She tried to keep close to the side against the shop fronts, closed up now so that it was no longer possible to go into one and take refuge.

Suddenly noisily with shouts, hooting and cries two armoured cars forced their way through the crowds who were pressed and heaved against Poppy. She held on tight to her bag which held her freshly changed money and her passport. If I lose it, she thought, Edmund will be furious but at least he has my return ticket. A man trod on her heel, pressing up against her in haste. The pain as his foot scraped down her Achilles tendon was acute. She threw herself against the wall to get out of his way.

The street ended abruptly, opening into an open space with rising ground on the far side and a vista of palm trees on a road leading away to open country down which swayed what looked like the procession of the night before, women, children, dogs, donkeys, camels, the poor of the city on the move. On the corner of the street as it debouched on the open space was an iron pillar against the wall. Poppy held on to it while the crowd surged past her.

In the middle of the space under a plane tree, surrounded by the crowd, were army trucks, armed soldiers faced the crowd which murmured and muttered repeating a sort of groan which grew to a demanding rhythmic shout. The breath of the multitude stank and Poppy found herself taking quick shallow breaths, denying her lungs the odour of anger.

Quite suddenly the crowd hushed. In the silence from behind the trucks two men were hoisted up: ropes put round their necks thrown over the branch of the plane tree, they were pulled strangling up.

The noise the crowd then made was terrifying.

Stifled by the sour smell of the people, Poppy turned towards the wall, her clothes drenching with sweat, she began to claw her way through the crowd. As she fought her way inch by inch part of her noticed the postbox she had been looking for. She stopped, opened her bag, took out the postcards, dropped them into the box, struggled on.

Later she was running along the water's edge on the beach, her thin shoes soaking in the shallow waves.

A flight of weary swallows came in low from Europe to pause and recoup before continuing their journey across the Sahara.

Poppy tripped, stumbled, sat by the water's edge trembling, exhausted.

She bathed her sore heel as the sea advanced and receded over her feet.

She pushed her hair back, congratulated herself that she had not lost her bag, found a comb, combed her hair, remembered that she had written no message on Venetia's postcard beyond the one word, wondered what Venetia would think when she received it, wondered how long it would be before Edmund found her.

Time to get back to the hotel. She stood up, straightened her dress, looked about, found her bearings, walked limping along the beach until she reached the town. Here she climbed up to the road which circled the harbour. It forked and led her back into the town and into the square where long ago she had found the bank and cashed her traveller's cheques. In the square was a newspaper kiosk she had not noticed that morning. It sold foreign papers. She bought a *New York Herald Tribune*, went and sat in the café she had visited earlier in the day, ordered a brandy. People looked at her curiously as she lifted the glass with hands that shook. She felt better when she had drunk it. She stopped trembling and ordered another.

She opened the paper, found what she was searching for, an unimportant paragraph on an inner page.

An unknown sect had thrown a bomb. The airport had been occupied by troops in case of trouble. People from the desert in the town for the celebrations (what celebrations?) had evacuated by night, taking their livestock and goods with them, their camels – the dog, there was no mention of the dog – the main road into the town from the airport had been closed by the army, the old road was heavily congested. A few arrests had been made, everything was now calm, riots slight, no panic.

A few arrests.

A few hangings.

Poppy folded the paper carefully and sipped her brandy.

Sipping her brandy, steadying her nerve, she discussed with herself why she was more afraid here than she would have been at home. There are after all kidnappers, hijackers, rioters, terrorists everywhere these days, all sorts of innocent and ignorant people mixed up with such things. Don't be so silly, she told herself.

It is the not understanding the language just hearing the sounds which is so frightening, she answered herself.

That dreadful silence when the crowd grew still, that greedy silence while the soldiers put the ropes round the men's necks. The crowd holding its collective stinking breath, its lust. The roar of satisfaction when the dangling men kicked as though they were dribbling an airborne football.

Snap out of it, she told herself. Pull yourself together, she told herself in Esmé's voice of long ago. She had hated Esmé.

Edmund was going to be furious when he got back from his day's work with Mustafa and the Tourist Board and found her still out. She sipped her drink, looking about her, outstaring neighbours at the café tables with arrogance.

There was rather a jolly family party two tables away. A young couple, three well-behaved children, a much older woman, some sort of baby-minder and fond grandparents, very bourgeois, very sedate, happy. Poppy exchanged a secret smile with a little girl who looked about three.

What to tell Edmund?

Edmund was not the man to understand the almost sexual smell of the crowd observing death or their sense of appeasement when the soldiers—

Her hands were trembling again, she picked up the brandy with both hands, gulped.

A thin cat shot out of the inner café and wove its way through the tables to disappear with the speed of light. Poppy thought of the cat Bolivar's contempt as he outstared her in Furnival's yard.

Would Fergus understand?

Would Victor Lucas, so tender-hearted over his rescued fish? He was supposed to have drowned his wife. What was it she had overheard at Dad's wake? She sipped her brandy, one could not believe everything one heard.

One could not believe everything one saw either.

Poppy snapped her fingers for the waiter, finished her brandy, paid the bill.

'Get me a taxi.'

It was so easy. The waiter found her a taxi, she told the driver where to go and in no time was on her way to the hotel.

It was almost dark as she drove along the sea front, past the waste ground to the hotel, dark enough to see the phosphorescent waves roll on to the sand.

Edmund had not yet come back.

Poppy went to her room and had a long bath, soaking in very hot water, easing the pain of her scraped heel, soaking away the sour smell of fear.

Edmund had not come back when she got out of the bath.

The multicoloured dress was on its hanger in the cupboard. Poppy put it on the chair by the bed, got into bed and covered her face with the sheet.

28

Penelope Lucas met Venetia Colyer in Harrods food hall.

'Hullo,' she said, kissing Venetia's tendered cheek, 'charging a few bits and bobs to your ma's account?' she joked, knowing Venetia's shopping habits, swift to deliver the first thrust.

'Paying for my own cheese actually, Penelope dear.' Venetia laid her smooth cheek briefly against Penelope's. 'And how is Penelope?' She pronounced the name to rhyme with 'antelope', having recently gossiped with Julia Wake on the telephone.

'You've been talking to Julia,' said Penelope, good-humoured. 'She wears her jokes to death. Did you see Victor's article about that super funeral in her magazine? A huge puff for Fergus.'

'I was there actually.'

'At the funeral?'

'Yes.'

'Really! Did you see Victor? You must have, he couldn't have invented all that about the horse hearse, the horses dressed in feathers and the mutes.'

'Victor was principal mute.'

'Gosh! How did that come about? I know, don't tell me. The Furnival man paid him, he's fearfully strapped for money.'

'He won't be strapped long. Sean Connor is going to publish his novel.'

'Whatever next!' Penelope was genuinely surprised. 'Is he getting a good advance, I wonder?'

'Ask Julia, she might know.'

'Can't very well, Victor and I are divorced, she might think I was after his money.'

'So you would be. Wait a sec while I buy my cheese, then let's go and have a coffee.'

'Harrods is too expensive for me.'

'What are you doing here then?'

'Just looking. It's all so pretty, a lovely still life. I like watching the Japanese tourists taking photographs in the butchers' department.'

'I'll stand you coffee, wait while I get my cheese.'

'And a bun,' Penelope stipulated, accepting.

'Anything you like.' Venetia moved to the cheese counter.

Penelope watched. Venetia's hair in the artificial light was the colour of Wensleydale. She bought Brie, Parmesan and Goat. They repaired to a coffee bar and settled at a corner table. Venetia ordered coffee and cakes. 'So what's your news?' she asked, scanning Penelope's face with her bright eyes.

'Nothing much.' Penelope hesitated then, making up her mind, asked, 'Did Julia tell you which of Victor's novels Sean is publishing, he's written three.'

'His last I think.'

Penelope let out a cry. 'That one, it's his version of our marriage, I never thought anyone would publish it.'

'Why not?'

'All our rows, almost verbatim, masses of four letter words, abuse and some pretty intimate sexual revelations.'

'You do let rip when cross.' Venetia put two lumps of sugar into her coffee. 'Sugar?'

'No, thanks. I'm trying not to. I could sue him for libel.'

'Great publicity. How did you come to read it, he's written it since you parted company.'

'I still have the key of our flat. I went to look for something I wanted and as the manuscript was there I had a quick flip through. I thought it well written and terribly sad.'

'Julia says Sean finds it irresistibly funny.'

'Other people's miseries are.' Penelope sipped her coffee, made a face, weakened, put in a lump of sugar. 'And what's with you these days?' She turned an appraising eye on Venetia. 'Didn't I hear you had a new man, Edmund something?'

'Platt.'

'What a name!'

'He can change it to Colyer.' Venetia was equable.

'But Colyer was your ex,' Penelope demurred.

'True, but it's a name I like, I shall keep it.' Penelope raised her eyebrows. 'It's nothing new,' said Venetia defensively. 'A contemporary of my Granny's married a big title, rather a pretty one, then she married a Mr Jones but she kept the title. I shall stick to Colyer.'

Penelope stirred her coffee, watched Venetia. 'It's coming back to me. Your Edmund Platt is the man who's been living with that girl Poppy Carew for absolutely years. You must know who I mean, her father's the man who always backed winners.'

'That's right.' Venetia bit into an éclair. 'Try one of these, they're super.'

'A great judge of what horse would like which course, that's her father.'

'Got it in one.'

'The Poppy girl's father started life as a milkman then took to the turf, became the terror of the bookmakers.'

'How do you know all this?' asked Venetia, mildly curious.

'An old friend of my aunt's used to talk about him, she went racing with him, I think. My mother swears she left him money but you know her stories, she gets carried away with her powers of invention, she should write—'

Venetia finished her éclair, licked her fingers.

'I *say*.' Penelope turned to look at Venetia. 'The penny's dropped. It was Poppy Carew's father's funeral Victor wrote about. He's dead.'

'Would have to be—'

'And you went with Edmund,' Penelope's voice rose.

'That's right.'

'What a nerve. Did she see you?'

'Don't think so.'

'Well!' said Penelope.

They sat thoughtfully stirring their coffee for some minutes.

'Has Victor put how he tried to drown you in his novel?' Venetia moved in to attack.

'Of course not.' Penelope was momentarily tempted to defend Victor, to tell the truth about the famous drowning.

'Can't think how you went on living with him so long after-wards.' Venetia started on a fresh éclair.

'I didn't leave him because of that—'

'These are too rich, I can't manage two.' Venetia laid the wounded éclair on her plate.

One should think of the starving third world, thought Penelope. 'I've often seen your Edmund.' She turned again to look at Venetia. 'Big tall man, fearfully good-looking, fair, lots of muscles.'

'That's the one.'

'Jogs in the park, used to be some sort of athlete?'

'That's him.'

'Drinks.'

'What?'

'Drinks too much.'

'Nonsense.'

'Darling! It's coming back to me. I've seen him about with Poppy. He drinks too much and gets bad tempered, sticks out his lower lip like this.' Penelope stuck out her lower lip.

'Only when he's bored. He's been too long with—'

'And he won't drink too much with you?' Penelope's eyebrows rose, her tone implied 'Pull the other one'.

'Of course he won't.'

Penelope gave the shriek of laughter which had charmed Victor in their early days but engendered murderous feelings during the latter part of their marriage. Venetia felt that Penelope was venturing too far.

'That sort of man gets awfully fat, if he lasts,' Penelope persisted, her tone foretelling heart trouble for Edmund.

'I like fat men who drink,' said Venetia comfortably. 'Edmund will last.'

'I was only thinking of your happiness, darling.'

'That's great of you.' Venetia gave the discarded éclair a push.

'Is he around? Would one be allowed to meet him?' asked Penelope sweetly.

'He's abroad on a business trip to North Africa.' (No, you would not be allowed to meet him.) Venetia helped herself to more coffee. 'You needn't think I don't know Edmund's weak points – more coffee? Oh, I've finished the pot – where was I?'

'Weak points.'

'Yes. Well of course he has weaknesses, who hasn't? One must

140

balance them against, well—'

'Terrific in bed?' Penelope slipped a quick thrust under Venetia's guard.

Venetia laughed, leaving the question unanswered. 'Oh Lord, is that the time? I must go.' She waved to catch the waitress's eye. 'Oh, I pay as I go out of course. What's this I heard about Victor and some old trout?'

'What?'

'Something about settling her in Berkshire near the Furnival man, I didn't catch it all. Must rush.' Venetia gathered up her shopping, pecked Penelope's cheek. 'It's been marvellous to see you, see you soon,' and she was gone, walking fast back towards the food halls where she extravagantly bought a pound of smoked salmon, congratulating herself that she had not let slip to Penelope that Edmund was not alone in North Africa but accompanied by odious Poppy Carew, may she rot.

Stung by Venetia's thrust, Penelope sat on in the coffee shop. She could not visualise Victor with an older woman, had difficulty visualising him with any woman other than herself, it was after all her he loved she who was irreplaceable. He had no right, no business with anyone else. Why, she asked herself dolefully, had she allowed Venetia the last word? She should have kept her, hinted of an Edmund with an interest in little boys perhaps, suggested that soon he would develop not only into a fat man but a fat man with the spongy complexion of a drinker, boozer's flush. Edmund was not likely to write a novel about Venetia. Penelope sought comfort in the thought that Victor had written a book about her, then remembering the parts she had read she was appalled that the quarrels, the memory of which had hitherto been privately dear to her, should be made public. Her eyes filled with an uncharacteristic rush of tears. She resolved on a vengeful expedition to Berkshire soonest.

29

Edmund woke. It was quiet, the bed was luxurious. He stretched out a hand, feeling for Venetia, moving his legs out of reach of her feet in reflex action. She was not there. He drifted back to sleep.

Below in the garden sparrows chirped, the wind stirred the fronds of the palms making a gentle scraping noise. He woke again.

A shaft of sunlight stabbed through the drawn curtains as the wind blew in to part them then sucked them closed again. He opened his eyes, looked round, sniffed, smelled wet cement, remembered.

He was at least in the right hotel but not with Venetia.

Steady, he told himself, take it easy, it will come back.

Moving his head with care, he observed the room in the half light. It was not the room he had previously occupied, similar but a different shape.

Hanging over a chair he recognised Poppy's frock, the dress of many colours. What brilliant instinct had brought him safely to her room? Where was she? Moving with caution, Edmund rolled over. The adjoining bed was empty but had been slept in. There was a familiar dent in the pillow, sheets thrown back. Had she been in the bed when he came in? Take it easy, he told himself, it will unfold.

He lay on his back, eyes closed, cudgelling his memory.

They had arrived, he remembered, waiting by the carousel for the luggage, he had been with Poppy not Venetia. Surely the idea had been to bring Venetia on the trip. They were after all getting married (this bit was muzzy). Why had he brought Poppy, something wrong there. Sort that out later.

So, he remembered their arrival, then something about a dog. Oh God yes, poor dog.

Meeting the Minister with Mustafa in the Office of Tourism, yes.

A picnic somewhere near the sea, a goat, a kid. Oh Lord, yes.

The swim, the Roman ruins, the meal, the wine, rather good claret. Why had Poppy not been there?

After the picnic the drive back to the town in the Mercedes with

Mustafa. Quite a long drive through stony desert. Then what happened? It had been evening by that time, almost night, the sea had been phosphorescent along the harbour wall. Edmund lay on his back breathing deeply, filling his lungs; if his lungs cleared his head would clear. He cajoled his memory, come on I must remember, something must have happened.

A bar. Mustafa had persuaded him to try the local pastis, they called it something else here, right, he'd got that, he'd tried the pastis, well several, pretty potent, what then? (Arak, it's called Arak.) A memory floated back. It *can't* have happened, he told himself, as the blood flooded his face, his heart thumped, his neck grew hot, his ears roared.

Jesus, it had happened, he knew it, Christ!

He remembered leaving the bar, getting into a car, not the Mercedes they had used all day, another older car which smelt of what? Got it, cannabis. There had been two youths, had they been in the bar? No matter, come back to that later, no don't, it's not important. He remembered them all in the car, the two youths not much more than boys, Mustafa and himself driving to a house somewhere outside the town and then all too clearly it came back, that room with the divan, the boys, Mustafa in a corner smoking a cigarette, watching.

And I enjoyed it.

Edmund lay with his eyes shut, trying to close his mind also.

At first in the car driving out of town he had thought that they must be kidnapping him, one of the boys was armed, the driver had a weapon beside him on the seat, had Mustafa by then been armed too?

The youths were beautiful, olive skin, softly curling black hair, sensual mouths.

Edmund was drenched with sweat as he lay thinking. He had his job to finish, the survey of tourist possibilities for his firm. There was the stadium to visit, the details of the hotels to note. The ultimate cost of tours to discuss with the Tourist Board, spy out what goes on with such tours from other countries already ongoing, loose ends to tie up, finish the job, write the report.

A sharp rap on the door made him jump, chilled the sweat on his body.

Poppy called from the balcony: 'Come in – *entrez – avanti – herein*'. As she came through the curtains from the balcony she laughed, 'I don't know what language they use so I use all the ones I know.'

The sun illuminating her mousy hair from behind made a curious halo effect. She opened the bedroom door to let in a waiter carrying a tray. He took it through to the balcony, put it down on an iron table with a clatter. Poppy thanked him. 'Thank you – *merci* – *grazie* – *Danke*.' There was the welcome smell of coffee.

'I left you to sleep,' she said, 'you came in late.'

The servant went away closing the door behind him.

'Thanks,' said Edmund, sitting up in the bed, pushing the hair out of his eyes, ignoring the pain stabbing his temples.

'Why don't you have a shower? I'm starving so I shall start breakfast,' she said.

Edmund dragged himself out of bed, went into the bathroom, stood under the shower, let the water wash, wash, wash it all away.

She had been very quiet out there on the balcony, leaving him to sleep. What state had he been in when he came in during the night? What had he said? Had he said anything? Would she tell him what he had said supposing he had said it? If he had been legless he would hopefully though not necessarily have been speechless too. Venetia would tell him at once without hesitation. Poppy was quite another kettle of fish, close.

Listening to the swish of water in the shower Poppy poured herself coffee, hot, fragrant, civilised. Her hand shook as she poured. She added milk and sugar, lifted the cup with both hands, drank.

'Ah,' she sighed, 'that's better.'

She buttered a roll, ate ravenously, wondered when she had last eaten. I shall not tell him what happened yesterday, he would probably not believe me, it would do no good, she shuddered, drank more coffee.

'Let's have a nice day,' she said as Edmund joined her, wrapped about the waist by a towel; he was really a beautiful man to look at, even his feet were elegant. 'Have you got to work or could we go somewhere together, swim perhaps, enjoy ourselves?'

'Why not,' said Edmund accepting a cup of coffee. (I can't possibly tell her, never, never, never.) 'I can take the day off, finish the job tomorrow,' he said. 'This is good, just what I need.' He gulped the restorative liquid. 'That fellow Mustafa is a bit of a bore in large doses, we can dispense with his services today.'

'Lovely,' said Poppy, looking across the palm tops towards the sea. I had better not suggest aspirin, she thought, it only irritates him.

'It's a long time since we spent the day together,' said Edmund, who had lately spent his free days with Venetia.

'Ages,' said Poppy thinking of Venetia, had she posted that card, did Venetia know what *chameau* meant? 'Did you have a successful day?' she asked in the tone of voice which expects no answer.

'You could say that.' Edmund chose a roll, buttered it. 'How was yours?'

'So, so,' said Poppy, 'so, so.' She put on her sunglasses, handed Edmund his, wondered whether anyone had yet trod on them. 'Sun's very bright,' she said. If we can keep this up nothing need have happened, nothing will have happened.

There was an English language paper by the breakfast tray. Edmund picked it up, glanced at it. 'There seems to have been some political trouble just before we arrived. All quiet now it seems.'

'Oh really?' said Poppy.

Edmund put the paper down, helped himself to more coffee, looked out across the palms towards the sea, burst out laughing. How could Venetia's feet be so permanently chilly, she must have a funny sort of metabolism.

'The cupboard in the first room they put us in was full of cockroaches,' said Poppy.

'Oh darling,' said Edmund, still laughing, thinking of Venetia's feet. 'Why didn't you tell me?'

'You weren't there to tell,' said Poppy lightly. And you weren't there when they hanged those men either. She clipped up her secret thoughts.

30

Willy Guthrie's intention of flying in search of Poppy on the first available plane got a setback when he found no airline called at the desired destination for two days. With mounting impatience he prowled his farm, trying not to drive his stockman mad with repetitive instructions for the duration of his absence. He sought solace watching the young porkers hop, skip, chase each other in short grunting rushes, root thoughtfully along the hedges, gobble their balanced diet from their speckless troughs. He found no solace. Communing with Mrs Future, admiring her aerodynamic Zeppelin shape, catching the beady intelligent eyes peeping at him from the shade of ears shaped like arum lilies, he sought comfort. It was some years since, tiny, pushed aside by her siblings, squashed almost to death by her mother, she had lain in Willy's arms feeding from a bottle. She had rewarded him with almost as much companionship as a dog, he had derived a lot of pleasure driving to market with a pig beside him. Walking the fields with Mrs Future was something he missed now that, full grown, she regularly brought litters of little Futures into the hard world of hams.

There was no trace of sentiment in Mrs Future's eye as she twitched her mobile snout, took from his hand a proferred carrot. Willy felt that Mrs Future would consider, were she human, his emotions *vis à vis* Poppy rather ludicrous, without place in the real world.

Scratching Mrs Future's flank with a stick kept specially for the purpose, Willy dreamed of Poppy as he had seen her standing alone in the front pew at her father's funeral. 'You don't know what it is to be lonely,' he said to the pig, lifting her large ear to peer into her little eye. The sow's eye gleamed red in the evening light. 'When your litter have grown a bit we will take them for a walk under the oak trees,' said Willy. 'You love acorns.'

Mrs Future turned away sashaying back to the litter in her byre. It was sentimental to think of her as any different from the other breeding sows lolling in their comfortable quarters, rows of piglets laid along their flanks in pale pink harmony.

To the uninitiated each sow identically resembled the next. Except for their past relationship Mrs Future might just be one of the many, indeed the pig's rather nonchalant attitude inclined to hint that now that she had better things to do their special relationship was at an end. Rebuffed, Willy experienced a fresh pang of loneliness, his mind veered away from the pig to speculate on his aunt in her house on the other side of the wood and her uncharacteristically helpful attitude towards his love for Poppy. Had she murmured something about risk? He searched his memory. Did she suggest love was a *risk*? Was that her opinion? Surely a risk worth taking? Uneasily Willy set out to walk off his fretful anxiety, tire himself so that he would not lie sleepless before his journey. As he walked he remembered

Calypso visiting his smoke-house, inspecting the cadaver of a pig split neatly in half ready for smoking. 'That is what I feel like,' she had said, turning away. Willy had wondered what the hell she meant. As he walked along the wood path Willy discovered what she had meant for he felt he would never be whole without Poppy just as Calypso could never be whole without Hector. Here was the endemic risk in loving. There is no knowing, thought Willy grimly, whether I shall ever experience that wholeness. Pig farmers cannot afford to be morbid, he told himself.

I can perfectly well live without Poppy, I have up to now, he persuaded himself.

The word mawkish occurred to him. He had survived other loves, he thought robustly, there was no need to be mawkish.

In the fading light the wood grew dark, occasional yellow fern, precursors of winter, lightened the way. In the still hour when the night's inhabitants roused themselves, Willy waited under a giant oak, survivor of a long gone forest towering among the young trees planted by Hector. He promised himself to do some coppicing for Calypso during the winter. On the edge of the wood a cock pheasant cried, was still. From the oak a tawny owl flew out silent about its hunting. Willy sighed with satisfaction, walked back over the hill, came finally to his farm, turned on the harsh electric light, cut himself a sandwich, poured himself a beer, switched on the radio for the late news. 'Terrorists, attempted plot uncovered, attempt on ruler's life, shots fired in the streets, three men arrested, executed, calm restored.' He waited for the weather report, went up to bed, slept. The distant sound of a train rushing through the night blew in on the night air.

At cockcrow Willy woke, shaved, bathed, dressed, checked his bag, put passport and tickets in his breast pockets, ate a hurried breakfast, carried his bag to the car and drove across country to Gatwick.

Arriving early, he wandered round the departure lounge, drifted through the duty free shop, read the titles of the books on the bookstall, bought a newspaper and a couple of weeklies, impatiently waited for time to pass. Ruefully he envied the sangfroid and ease with which habitual travellers drifted along just in time to board their planes. In the past he too had been a carefree traveller. At last, time relented, he boarded the plane. Once airborne he felt elation; in a matter of hours he would find Poppy, what happened after that was up to the Almighty. In an attempt to keep calm he opened his *Spectator*, tried to read.

Halfway through the third article he realised with a jolt that he was reading about the country of his destination, went back to the beginning of the article. 'The country's past record is by no means peaceful, the present troubles are due—' Frowning, Willy read on. Plot, counterplot, suppression, terrorists, kidnappings, bombs had a familiar ring, he was not unduly disturbed. Reading about trouble abroad, he had always understood, was quite different to being actually present where it took place. The odds were, if you were on the spot you would notice nothing. Uneasily Willy cast his mind back to the previous evening's news. Where and in what country had the reported trouble been. If it was in Poppy's country her man (even to himself Willy refused to think of him as her lover) would take care of her and all governments took care of tourists. Willy put down the *Spectator*, searched his newspaper, found nothing, no mention even in the stop press. Reassured, he dozed.

Roused by the steward for the midflight meal, he was picking at the packets on his tray when the intercom crackled and the captain made an announcement. The weather along the North African coast was of such turbulence that the plane must alter course and land in Algiers. The airport at their proper destination was temporarily under water.

Willy could not believe his ears. He checked with his neighbour who agreed; he too had heard the announcement. It was confirmed by the stewardess.

Willy shouted, 'God damn the bloody plane I want to get off.' His neighbour, much amused, ordered a large whisky and offered one to Willy who fretfully refused.

The plane altered course in the direction of Algiers. Philosophically the passengers ate their meal.

The captain apologised for any delay and inconvenience caused, promised that the passengers would be accommodated at the airline's expense in the best hotels. The plane would land in forty minutes. Presently the plane lost height in a series of stomach-jolting jerks, groaning down through dark rain clouds. Willy watched the ground rush up, saw lashing rain, palm trees waving like dishmops.

'Much worse along the coast,' shouted Willy's neighbour. How did he know? 'Often happens in autumn, equinoctial gales—' What a know-all.

The plane landed, splashing on to puddled tarmac, taxiing through sheeting rain to the terminal, stopped. The aircraft doors open a voice hailed, '*Que messieurs les passagers descendent—*'

'Here we go,' said Willy's neighbour. 'Wonder what dump they'll put us in.' Wretchedly Willy followed him out of the aircraft to Customs to wait dejectedly in line. Dispirited, sniffing the smell of Algiers, garlic, spice, petrol fumes, thirsty earth, listening to the mix of French and Arabic, thinking that at any other time he would have been amused, interested, pleased by this diversion in his proper journey, Willy let his eye wander across the Customs hall to a group from another plane standing by their baggage, queuing for the Customs officers. A man and his wife were squeezing shut their suitcases, cursing each the other's attempt to help. Next in line behind them a girl obeyed the Customs official, opened her case.

Willy exclaimed, shouted, leapt over a barrier, grabbed the girl, held her. 'Poppy.'

She looked at him astonished without recognition.

'I saw your dress, I knew it at once.' The multicoloured dress lay on top of the case.

The Customs man poked brown fingers down the sides of the case. 'Okay.' Poppy pushed the dress back, shut the case. The man moved on to the next passenger. Someone called to Willy, 'Hey, Monsieur.'

'I think they want you back over there.' She had a frightful black eye, she looked awful, her nose was swollen. She picked up her case, moved away.

'Monsieur—' An official harried Willy to get back where he belonged.

'Wait for me,' Willy shouted at her retreating back, '*wait*'.

'We are all headed for the same hotel.' Willy's neighbour from the plane knew even this.

'Your case, Monsieur, open it.' The man was impatient. Willy complied, craning his neck to see where Poppy had gone. The Customs man took his time. Willy memorised his face so that some day, even if it were in the after life, always supposing there was such a thing, when he had the time he would come back and hit him. The man relinquished his futile search, moved away. Willy snapped the case shut, nipping his urgent fingers, ran. She was standing in the next hall.

'I waited,' she said.

'Thank God,' said Willy.

'Do I know you?' she asked.

'You will,' said Willy. 'Give me your case, let me carry it for you.'

31

Having made sure by an unanswered telephone call that Victor was out, Penelope let herself into the flat. She wondered whether Victor knew that she still had a key, how much he would mind that she had quite often in the years since their divorce let herself in to pry. While she had a strong aversion to anyone poking their nose into her own affairs, she persuaded herself that her interest in Victor was excusable.

Inside the door she listened.

The tap in the bathroom dripped as it always had, defying DIY efforts and even the arts of a visiting plumber.

Outside the window on the parapet pigeons strutted and cooed as they always had. The noise of traffic passing in the street was deadened by the dry leaves rustling in the plane trees.

Penelope went into the bathroom to give the tap a futile nostalgic twist. Victor had filled the bidet with socks, they soaked in grey unappetising water, she was almost tempted to wash them. The bedroom had acquired an austere masculine air: pillows heaped against the centre of the headboard, the duvet pulled askew, suggested a solitary Victor. His clothes had edged across to her side of the hanging cupboard, he had left the doors open, a carelessness which had been a continual source of irritation during their marriage. Unable to resist interfering, she shut the doors.

In the living room she inspected the desk and was surprised at the number of receipted bills. Things were definitely looking up for Victor. She fingered through a pile of letters finding none of interest bar one from Victor's mother. Opening it she read, pursing her lips, breathing in, closing her nostrils in imitation of her former mother-in-law who had the haughty appearance of a llama. Victor's parent congratulated him warmly on the acceptance of his novel while hoping that it was not as autobiographical as the previous unpublished manuscripts. 'Some hope,' muttered Penelope. You were very unfair to poor Penelope, wrote Victor's mum. I know she can be irritating but so, my goodness, can you. 'Hallelujah!' said Penelope loud in the silence. You get it from your beloved pa, wrote Victor's mother, and went on to give some routine and boring news of Victor's family. Penelope returned the letter to the pile.

In Victor's typewriter a pristine sheet of paper, Page One, Chapter One. 'The day I decided to drown my wife dawned crystal clear.'

'Hey,' said Penelope, 'this *is* fiction.' She knelt by the grate to inspect crumpled sheets of paper. Victor had written, 'The day I decided to drown my wife dawned grey and—'

'The day I decided to drown my wife dawned thundery—'

Penelope addressed herself to the desk drawers. 'I must really clear out this mess,' she muttered, momentarily forgetting her divorced status. 'Oh bugger.' She shut the drawer. There was no trace of what she feared, nor was there anything to indicate the existence of another woman in the kitchen, no alien garlic crusher, nobody's favourite knife. After a final look round she let herself out and drove west out of London, towards Berkshire, in search of Fergus.

Leaving the motorway at Junction Thirteen Penelope headed towards the downs. She drove slowly with only the vaguest concept of Fergus's whereabouts. Victor's article giving Furnival's Fine Funerals its splendid write-up had left the location of the enterprise enigmatically vague. 'A beautiful secret valley in the Berkshire Downs' did not get one far. While hoping to extract information about Victor from Fergus Penelope was unsure how best to set about it. After their brief affair Fergus had moved, apparently jointly, with Victor into Julia's embrace, but now if gossip was true Julia was seriously committed to Sean Connor. Penelope was friendly with Julia who presented no threat; she was interested in the unknown quantity hinted by Venetia in Harrods. 'Though why I bother—' Penelope talked to herself. 'Victor is just an untidy habit I have given up, or should give up if I had it.'

On the outskirts of a pretty village two workmen had just finished erecting a sign which read *Furnival's Fine Rococo Funerals* in large letters, in smaller lettering, *Director Fergus Furnival*. 'What luck,' said Penelope parking her car by the side of the road, peering up at the house, 'but this village isn't particularly secret—'

The men who had put up the sign collected their tools, got into a van and drove off. Penelope stood hesitating in front of the house.

From a window on the first floor Mary, baby Barnaby in her arms, watched. Penelope walked round to the back of the house. Mary moved from the front bedroom to watch Penelope's progress from the bathroom at the back.

Penelope reached the stable yard and went round it, peering into the loose-boxes. Two Dow Jones put interested heads over their box-doors to observe her progress. Penelope, who did not trust horses, gave them a wide berth. She inspected the tack room, opened the double doors of the carriage house, looked in on empty darkness, walked slowly back towards the house through the yard, hesitated outside the back door, went round to the front.

Mary ran downstairs and opened the front door with a jerk as Penelope was putting her finger on the bell. Penelope jumped.

Mary said 'Yes?' on a note of query.

'Oh,' said Penelope. 'Ah, I am Victor Lucas's wife, Penelope Lucas.'

'Yes?'

'We are divorced of course—'

'Yes?'

'I was wondering whether—'

'Yes?'

'Whether Fergus, I am a friend of Fergus—'

'Yes?' Mary was enjoying this.

'Whether,' Penelope refused to be disconcerted, 'whether Fergus knows where I can find – er – Victor?'

'Yes.'

'Yes, he knows?' Was this girl half-witted or plain bloody-minded? 'Does he know?'

'Yes.'

'There is something I have to talk to him about, something I need to tell him.'

'Yes?'

'I believe he has a friend somewhere near here who might – er – Venetia Colyer said that—'

'Yes?'

'Do you know Venetia?'

'Yes.'

'Is Fergus out?'

'Yes.'

152

'Perhaps you can help me.' Penelope caught baby Barnaby's eye, round, black, appraising. Without deflecting his gaze from Penelope he stuffed a hand in the opening of Mary's shirt, grabbed her nipple and sucked. Penelope took a step backwards. 'Isn't that baby a bit old to be nursed?'

'Yes.'

'I thought so.' Penelope held out a finger which Barnaby snatched and held in his tight infant grip. 'Are you being irritating on purpose?' she asked.

'Yes.'

Penelope laughed and waggled her finger in Barnaby's fist. He stopped sucking Mary's nipple and tried to stuff Penelope's finger in his mouth. Penelope snatched the finger away.

'You'd better come in.' Mary pulled the door wider, jerked her head towards the kitchen. 'We aren't settled in yet, we only moved the day before yesterday, Fergus and the girls are doing a funeral near Wallop.'

'Oh.' Penelope followed Mary to the kitchen.

'Sit down.' Mary nodded at a chair.

'Thanks.' Penelope sat. An old dog got to his feet, came across the room to sniff and wag, retreated to lie by the stove.

'So you are looking for Victor,' said Mary. 'He lives in London.'

'Of course he does. It's a friend of his who—' Who? What? Who is this friend I am so het up about whose existence is hinted at by Venetia. Venetia never meant good. Must I ask this rude girl as Fergus is not here? Penelope regretted her impulsive journey. 'If Fergus is out I can telephone or come another time—'

'Didn't you go for a spin with Fergus?' Mary's eye, though not dark and round like her child's, was more penetrating.

'What d'you mean?'

'Screw, didn't you screw with Fergus?'

'Well, really I—' Penelope got to her feet.

'Yes or no?'

'Well, yes – um – what business is it of yours what I – er – we. It wasn't for long.'

Mary grinned. 'Just placing you. Sit down, have some coffee.' To Penelope there was something menacing about the offer.

'I – I ought to go.'

'Oh come on, you can't come all this way for nothing.' Mary put Barnaby on the floor, filled the kettle. 'What do you want poor old

Victor for, what's his friend to do with you?' As she spooned Nescafé into mugs Mary sized Penelope up. 'I bet Victor never *really* tried to drown you,' she said, looking at Penelope, amused.

'Of course he did,' Penelope said defensively.

'And this friend?' asked Mary. 'What's your interest?'

'Nothing, it's nothing.' Penelope was harassed. 'Just something Venetia said when we met the other day.'

'I know Venetia.' Mary handed Penelope her mug. 'Sugar? Milk?'

'Just milk please. I thought Fergus's place was more isolated.' Penelope took stock.

'It was. He's rented this from Poppy Carew. He did her father's funeral. You read about it?'

'Yes. I did. Victor's article and—'

'Poppaea has disappeared with Venetia's new man—' Mary chanted. 'Poppaea!' mocking the name.

'Oh.'

'This man is Poppaea's *old* man, he left her, I guess, an educated guess, for Venetia.'

'Gosh.'

Mary sipped her coffee watching Barnaby crawl across the floor to join the dog who licked his head. 'There's an interesting connection if you are interested in Victor.' She switched her eyes back to Penelope. 'Both Fergus and Victor have their sights on Poppaea. They do seem to like the same girls those two, you, Julia and now Poppaea, funny isn't it?'

Penelope put down her mug. 'Then what the hell is Victor doing installing some old trout in Berkshire?'

'Is that what Venetia told you?' Mary looked enchanted.

'Yes it is.' Penelope was outraged. What business had this girl to pry? Why had she let slip Venetia's mischief? That she was herself prying did not bother her at all.

'And you think Fergus can tell you where to look?' asked Mary, deceptively mild.

'That was the idea,' said Penelope stiffly.

'Are you jealous, do you want him back or just dog in the manger?' Mary teased.

'Of course not,' said Penelope hotly.

'You go up the road a few miles, take the fourth turning on your left, the second on your right, follow that road until you get to a humpback bridge and a track which goes up into the hills beside the stream. It's possible you will find what you are looking for.'

'Oh.' Penelope got to her feet. 'Thanks,' she said grudgingly.

'Not at all,' said Mary, picking baby Barnaby out of the dog basket, walking with Penelope towards the door. 'If when you are there you should see a large tabby cat please catch him and bring him here, Fergus is frantic, misses him terribly. He was out hunting when we moved, Fergus has been back to look three times already, he loves that animal.'

'But—'

'Surely you can catch a cat.'

'I doubt it.' Penelope loathed cats, longed to refuse, was afraid to.

'He'll be starving by now. Fergus will be eternally grateful.' Mary spoke with enjoyment.

'I don't think—' protested Penelope.

'I'll give you a tin of sardines to entice him; not allergic are you?' Mary turned back to find sardines, opened a tin. 'There, lure him into your car, keep the windows shut as you drive or he'll jump out.'

'I don't know anything about cats,' protested Penelope weakly.

'Then now's your chance to find out.' Mary was propelling her out of the house. 'You may also find out a lot about Victor, the great softie.'

'I—' Penelope was out of the house and in her car.

'Fourth turning on the left,' Mary pointed. 'Then follow the track into the hills after the humpback bridge.' She put the tin of sardines on the seat beside Penelope. 'His name is Bolivar,' she said. 'Let me know about Victor's friend when you come back. I would be interested to hear your opinion.'

Mary's mocking tone so infuriated Penelope that she leant out of the car window and shouted, 'I'm not going to bother about a bloody cat, Fergus can catch it for himself.'

'Oho, what spirit!' Penelope's tormentor leaned in through the car window to stare at Penelope at close quarters; from her arms Barnaby reached in to stroke Penelope's face. 'Pitty, pitty.' Mary snatched his hand away. Penelope flushed.

'You bitch. Why are you so bloody?' The two women glared at each other across the baby's head. Barnaby crowed, reaching pudgy hands towards Penelope.

'He likes me.' Penelope pursed her lips, blowing a kiss towards the baby. 'Is it Fergus's child?' she asked. 'Those eyes—' Mary stared at her, stony faced. 'And something about the mouth—' Penelope

155

persisted dangerously. 'When one's – well, you know what I mean obviously – one sees people from a different angle when one's—'

'Jesus,' murmured Mary holding the baby against her face, staring down at Penelope. 'Christ.'

'Who are you anyway, what's your role around here?' Penelope felt a sadistic desire to wound this woman who would not let her touch her child.

'I'm part of the scenery.' Mary was recovering fast.

'I didn't know Fergus was fond of scenery, that's not a side of him I know.' Penelope reached back for the safety belt. 'Is your baby teething?' she asked, looking up at Barnaby from whose open mouth trickled a stream of saliva. With her arm stretched up behind her, her hand fumbling for the buckle, she showed in her open shirt a pretty cleavage.

Mary dipped Barnaby forward so that his spittle dropped between Penelope's breasts. 'You don't see much scenery when you're flat on your back,' she said. 'Mind you remember the cat,' she called over her shoulder as she moved back into the house.

Penelope started the engine, put the car in gear and drove off. As she drove she composed apt rejoinders, tart replies, crushing last words she might have inflicted on the girl with the baby had she been fast enough on the rejoinder.

32

Victor, waiting to be served, watched a hurried spectacled youth buy mackerel, next a thickset woman hesitate between halibut and Dover sole, making vocal allusion to her husband, his penchant for shrimps or oysters with or without cream in the sauce. Victor costed her silk shirt, cashmere sweater, St Laurent jeans, gold bracelets, double row of pearls. How many advances for novels would pay for all that? Shifting his shopping basket from one hand to the next, he exercised his mental arithmetic.

The fish lady, apparently patient, ran a sardonic eye over the marble slab. The loquacious customer changed her mind, decided her husband would enjoy ray *au beurre noir* which, with out of season asparagus miraculously grown in Israel and new potatoes ditto, might deceive him now in October to believe it spring.

'Spring,' said the fish lady, slapping the ray on the scales, naming the price, wrapping the fish. 'Spring,' she said with lofty contempt for the seasons, looking past the customer's head at the street and its passers-by.

The woman took a notecase from her Hermès bag. Victor goggled at a wad of fifty pound notes; he opined that the metier of mugging would show greater dividends (always supposing one had the nerve) than writing.

Unmoved, the fish lady took the money, gave her customer change, handed her her fish, turned to the next customer. 'Yes?' Victor had watched this man when in the early halcyon days of their marriage he had shopped with Penelope, unable to bear her out of his sight, carrying their shopping in the very basket he now held. The man now being served invariably bought lobsters, taking his time, discussing the particulars of each crustacean as the fish lady lifted them for his inspection, their bound claws forlornly semaphoring. Penelope had voiced the opinion that the man was homosexual, Victor thought not but in those early days rarely contradicted his wife.

The present loneliness of shopping sharpened his powers of observation so that he took note of people's dress and mannerisms in case they might fit into some brief paragraph of a future work.

'Yes?' said the fish lady, jerking him out of his reverie. 'Yes?' Contempt in her voice.

'Oh! Half of unshelled prawns please.'

Why should I be humbled, he thought indignantly. Not all of us can afford lobster and sole. Prawns with brown bread and butter make an excellent lunch with salad. 'The salmon looks nice,' he said for the sake of saying something. The salmon wore a leering expression and had an undershot jaw. 'Cock,' said Victor to illustrate that he wasn't a complete fool, could tell the sex of salmon, hopefully insult the fish lady.

The fish lady did not answer but weighed the prawns indifferently.

'All girls,' said Victor, listening to the prawns tinkling frozen into the scales. 'All the prawns I buy have eggs.'

'Scotch,' said the fish lady, referring to the salmon. 'Iceland,' she handed Victor his prawns, took the money he proffered. 'Wait a minute,' she paused by the till. 'Or Greenland.'

'I gave you the exact money,' said Victor defensively.

'Your change,' said the fish lady, handing Victor some coins.

'Oh?' Victor was at a loss. 'Why?'

'You neglected your change,' said the fish lady, turning towards the next customer, 'when you bought your trout,' she tossed over her shoulder. 'Yes sir?' She was already in spirit with another.

The old bitch, thought Victor morosely as he turned towards home. She used to call Penelope 'ducks', now she pretends not to know me, doesn't call me anything. Feeling excluded from the human race he made for home, for his desk, to lose himself in his work.

As usual Victor approached his novel at an angle hoping to take it by surprise, to be at work on it before he or the novel became aware. He ate his lunch, buttering brown bread, sipping a glass of lager, peeling the prawns, crunching them, swallowing a lot of the shell as he ate. Penelope had said the roughage was good for him, she never bothered to peel her prawns thoroughly, sucked the contents of the heads, then licked her fingers.

Victor, eating his prawns, listening to the lunchtime news, thought of Penelope's fingers and other more delectable parts. By writing about her it was his intention to expunge her from his system so that he could the better concentrate on Poppy Carew. Finishing his lunch he tossed the débris into the pedal bin, washed his hands and went to the telephone where he dialled Poppy's London number. There was not, as there had not been for days, any answer. 'Still away.' Victor sat down at his desk. 'Not back yet.'

He read: 'The day I decided to drown my wife dawned crystal clear.'

He tore the paper from the typewriter, crushed it between both hands, tossed it towards the grate. He would answer his mother's letter lying in its envelope on top of the pile. The very act of typing would lead him smoothly into the novel by artful trickery.

Re-reading his mother's letter Victor felt mounting annoyance. What right had she to criticise, not for her to find Penelope irritating, not for her to denigrate her ex-daughter-in-law. Even though their divorce was several years old, Victor still had difficulty in thinking of Penelope as ex-anything. I shall exorcise her by writing about her, Victor told himself.

'Dear Mother,' he wrote. 'Thanks for yours. Are you coming up for the Horticultural Show or the exhibish at the Hayward? We might have a bite and go together. So glad you are glad about my book' (two 'glads' in a sentence but never mind, this is only a letter, she's lucky to get it). Victor tapped a little more about his novel, the advance he was to receive from Sean Connor, Sean's connection with Julia. His mother deplored Julia whom she had once accused of hooking him, did she know what a hooker was? Poor mother, he thought, as he typed, spacing the lines widely to fill the page, recommending a new novel she would enjoy (get it from the library), giving her a pungent piece of family news which might not yet have reached Somerset of a second cousin twice removed discovered in buggery. She would enjoy the use of the word 'buggery', feel 'with it', an expression she was fond of. I must telephone her soon, thought Victor as he typed 'with much love as always—' Poor old thing, she wishes me to be happy, she always says 'how lovely to hear your voice', she has no bloody business to find Penelope irritating, it's not for her— Victor tore the letter out of the typewriter, signed it, folded it, crammed it into an envelope, licked the envelope, addressed it. Now for the novel.

'The day I decided to drown my wife dawned clear and sweet—' Oh God what bilge.

How sweet had been Penelope in those far-off days when they decided to go to bed after lunch, take the phone off the hook – oh God, he was thirsty, those prawns, so salt. Victor left his desk and went into the kitchen for a glass of water, gulped it down as he looked out between the fat little pillars of the parapet at what they had laughingly called 'our view', a view constricted to a piece of pavement at the corner by the pillar-box outside the paper shop. Often and often Victor had waited for Penelope to come into view, stand hesitating, looking left and right at the traffic before stepping off the pavement and out of sight. And Penelope had done the same. Lovers watching.

On the parapet the pigeons strutted and cooed. Victor flung the window up. 'Fuck off,' he shouted. 'Fuck off.' He slammed the window shut, drank another glass of water, felt even less like working, gave up. Hoping to expunge Penelope in another way, he ran down to the street, got into his car and drove.

As he drove Victor made slighting comparisons between his ex-wife and Poppy, hands, feet, fingers, noses, hair, eyes, teeth, arms, legs. The trouble was he had never seen Poppy naked so that comparisons stopped short. Were her tits brown or pink, was her bush mouse like her hair, or astonishingly dark and secret like Penelope's, darker than the hair on her head, or even her eyelashes? Penelope, who had not bothered him seriously for weeks or even months, imposed herself between him and Poppy.

When he got around to drowning her in his novel would she cease to torment him?

33

Willy walked with Poppy to the airport bus carrying her bag with his own. She walked stiffly, holding her head high, her shoulders unnaturally straight. He stood aside to let her climb on to the bus, blocking the way to the other passengers so that she need not hurry, then he followed her to where she settled in a seat next to the window, stood between her and their fellow travellers while he heaved the bags on to the rack, then inserted his bulk into the seat beside her. The torrential rain streaming down the window made it impossible for anyone looking in to see Poppy; within the bus he shielded her with his body. Her bruised face, dishevelled hair, the way she sat ravelled into herself reminded him of the rabbits dying of myxomatosis he had seen as a child, too stupefied, too blind to get out of the rain. Then he had joined his father in awful retching sorties to shoot or club the miserable animals, putting them out of their misery. Sitting with Poppy in the bus Willy experienced the rage of pity and fury he had had as a child magnified tenfold.

It was clear Poppy had not been in a car accident.

The passengers all seated, luggage stowed, the driver brought to an end an altercation he had been having with somebody out of sight, climbed into the driver's seat and started the engine. The bus trundled slowly through the downpour out of the airport, crawling through wind and flood towards Algiers. After a quarter of a mile the bus stopped to take on board a policeman whose cape and boots streamed water on to the floor of the bus. The policeman shouted and gesticulated at the driver who yelled back, released the hand-brake and jerked onwards. The policeman continued to shout to make himself heard above the noise of the engine and the roar of the storm, the driver constantly taking his eyes off the road to confront the policeman, yelled back.

In the bus the passengers sat glum, barely exchanging a word, lighting nervous cigarettes, their collective breaths steaming up the windows.

Beside Willy Poppy made a small desperate movement, glancing up at the window.

'Want some air?'

She nodded.

Willy stood up, swaying with the movement of the bus, leant across her and forced a window open. In rushed wind and rain, there was a stormy protest from the seats behind in nasal American.

'Would you rather she vomited?' Willy shouted savagely. 'That better?' he asked, resuming his seat. 'Let them get wet.'

She nodded slightly.

The drive was long, several times the road was blocked by floods and débris. The driver stopped, cursed, shouted, reversed. The policeman got out, got in again, directed a detour. Eventually the furious sounds of the gale altered their tone, they sloshed through partly built-up areas, then streets.

Willy said, 'If you would like to give me your passport and so on I will see about rooms, then you can get to bed and rest.'

Poppy did not answer but opened her bag, found her passport and handed it to him. Her knuckles and the backs of her hands were blue, he had the impression that she was near the end of her resistance, could not hold out much longer. He said, 'Soon be there.' She huddled in her seat like an old woman.

The policeman shouted, the driver changed down, crashing the gears, and drove in a rush up a steep hill. It was like driving up a watercourse, and floodwater whooshed over the bonnet in a muddy wave, the policeman stood beside the driver shouting encouragement. They proceeded thus for half a mile, then the bus stopped, the policeman and the driver slapped one another's backs, laughing. The bus had made it. Triumph. The fellow passengers, breaking out of their torpor, gave tongue, struggled with their luggage, urgent to get out.

'Wait till the rush is over.' He was afraid she might be knocked

161

down. Poppy waited. Willy lifted down their bags. 'Okay now, can you manage? Follow me.' Between the bus and the hotel storm water rushed in a foot-deep torrent. 'Wait.' Willy splashed to the entrance, dropped the bags in the shelter of the portico, came back to where she stood on the step of the bus, held out his hands, led her through the water into the hotel lobby, noticed that she flinched, was lame.

Willy sat Poppy on a sofa beside their bags. 'A little more waiting.' Elbowed his way into the hubbub round the reception desk.

Twenty minutes later they were in a large room on the fourth floor with a panoramic view over the harbour where little boats tossed like corks and large vessels strained at their moorings.

Poppy's face under the bruises was grey, her lips bloodless. Willy searched and found whisky in the hotel refrigerator, held a glass for her.

'Sip it, try.' She sipped, swallowed, coughed. 'And again,' he said, 'good girl. Now I'm going to put you to bed, we'll see about a doctor later.'

'No,' she refused violently.

'Okay. We'll see. Come on now, let's get these wet things off.' He eased off her shoes. 'Some joker's trodden on your heel.' He helped her out of her clothes. 'Afraid we have to share a room, lucky to get this one. The hotel is full of tours who thought they were going to trek across the Sahara, or go up into the mountains, and oil people diverted on their way to Libya, all stuck here until the weather clears, none of them meant to be here at all. There, let me ease this over your head, that's better.' Willy went on talking as he extricated Poppy from her clothes, fetched a towel from the bathroom, wrapped it round her. There was a dark bruise on her collarbone. 'Is your bag locked?'

'No.'

'I'll find a nightie.' Willy unzipped her bag, put the multicoloured dress aside, found a nightdress. 'Here we are.' Helped her put it on. 'It would be a good idea if I bathed that heel and your face could do with—' Willy stopped, not trusting his voice.

Poppy stood up, holding on to the back of a chair. She was stiffening up. He helped her to the bathroom, sat her on the lavatory and bathed her face carefully. 'Now your heel.' She let him bathe it, winced with pain. 'Fine. Strong enough to make the bed? No? Never mind.' He picked her up carefully. 'This is how I used to carry Mrs

162

Future. Mrs Future is my prize sow, I brought her up on a bottle, I am a pig farmer. There you are.' Willy pulled back the bedclothes, eased Poppy into the bed. He hoped that if he kept talking it would overcome some of the strangeness of the situation. 'I'll put your dress where you can see it when you wake up. I always put something she knows near Mrs Future if I change her sty—'

'Oh,' she was crying, 'my—'

'Hey, hey no need to cry, not now. You are safe, try another sip of whisky; that's better, lie back now.' He gentled her as he gentled his animals when they were afraid or disturbed, concentrating on her need for rest and quiet.

'Don't—'

'I won't leave you. You go to sleep. I'm going to get out of my wet things, might even have a bath. If you wake up and I'm not here I shan't be far off, you will be perfectly safe.' Willy went on talking in the reassuring voice he used for Mrs Future as he drew the curtains, blotting out the gale and the ugly churned-up sea. Then he moved a chair within Poppy's vision and laid the multicoloured dress across it. In the dim light he peered anxiously down at Poppy's bruised face on the pillow. 'By the way,' he said, 'my name is Willy Guthrie.'

Poppy giggled.

'I thought you were in shock.' Willy bent closer.

Poppy's bloodshot eye met Willy's. 'Just knackered,' she said.

34

Ros Lawrence stood listening. The October sun warmed her back. She hesitated to ring the bell, the house was so quiet, but since the front door was open she supposed there must be someone about. With her finger by the bell she looked into the hall watching the dust dance in a shaft of sun. She felt an intruder.

Finding herself five miles from the village she had given in to an impulse she was now inclined to regret. It would have been politic to ring up, say she was coming, better perhaps to leave now, drive away, telephone, fix a date and visit later when expected. Having decided on this course a shuffling noise attracted her attention.

From the darkness at the back of the hall a baby crawled. Ros watched the effortful progress.

The child wore a loose T-shirt which inched itself up round his neck as he shuffled down the hall pushing himself backwards into the sun which lit a sunburned bottom, a roll of dimpled flesh at the waist, heavy head covered with dark curls. The baby pushed with determined hands, thrusting with plump legs, gasping and grunting with concentrated effort. As he came to Ros's feet he collapsed on to the floor, laid his head down, slid into sleep.

Ros watched the child, wondered whether she dared touch him, pull the T-shirt into a position less likely to throttle or whether to creep away without waking him. But if he woke he might continue his progress, crawl into the road, get himself run over.

Entranced, Ros watched the child, leaning against the lintel, her hand by the bell, counting the baby's soft breathing in the still October afternoon.

Down the road the church clock struck the hour. There was a clatter of jackdaws. The baby slept far away at her feet.

Ros bent down, carefully touched the baby's nape, he sank closer to the ground, splaying out tiny feet, lying like a frog. Ros was absorbed.

Then she noticed bare feet by the child's head, narrow ankles, brown legs disappearing into an indigo skirt. She looked up, smiling. 'Yours?'

'Yes.' Mary watched Ros warily squinting into the sun.

'He crawled down the hall backwards, he tired and fell asleep.' Ros smiled at the dark baby's mother, admiring her hair bleached almost white by the sun, blue eyes startling, dark.

'He is learning, some days he can only manage backwards.'

'Quite a long crawl.'

'Yes.'

'What's his name?'

'Barnaby.'

'What a good name. I am Ros Lawrence.'

'Fergus's mother?'

'Yes. Is he in?'

'Out. He's doing a funeral near Wallop. He won't be long if you'd like to come in and wait.'

'I should have telephoned.' Ros excused herself. 'I found myself

164

only a few miles away. I should have warned him.'

'Should you?' Mary looked amused.

'I dare say he would rather I did. I don't like people dropping in on me unexpectedly.'

'It depends who. Like some tea? Why don't you come in.' Mary bent to pick Barnaby off the floor. He woke, stared at Ros with enormous black eyes, smiled.

'Oh.' Ros stared back. 'Oh, he's—'

'I expect,' said Mary turning to lead the way to the kitchen, 'that you need to see what your husband has given Fergus a reference for.'

'It seems rather nosey,' Ros apologised. Barnaby kept his eyes on her, staring over his mother's shoulder.

'No, it doesn't. Come in. I'll show you round. Like to hold Barnaby while I make us some tea?'

'May I—'

'Of course.' Mary handed Barnaby over. 'Half a tic, I'll give you a towel in case he pees on you.'

'I wouldn't mind.' Ros sat, made a lap, felt the round little bum settle against her thighs. 'How old is he?'

'Eight months, nearly nine.' Mary reached up to a shelf for the teapot. 'I brought him back from Spain.' Putting cups and saucers on the table, reaching for the milk, Mary continued casually, 'The father's called Joseph.' Ros watched her. 'It was one of those accidents.' Mary stood waiting for the kettle to boil. Barnaby chucked his head back hitting Ros's solar plexus with a thump. 'The other girls, Annie and Frances, who work for Fergus too, found boys to go around with, I found this Joseph type.' Ros said nothing. 'He writes a lot, telephones, he's a lonely sort. Fergus thinks he's a waiter or a fisherman or something.'

'Spanish?' asked Ros casually.

'No.' Mary warmed the pot. 'His family's Swedish, they run one of the hotels. Fergus calls Barnaby the infant Jesus, it's his sort of joke. My name's Mary.' Mary made the tea, her back to Ros.

'Ah.' Ros flushed with shame for Fergus.

'It's supposed to be witty.' Mary set the pot down.

'I hope you clout him.' Ros held the naked baby between her hands.

'I don't bother.' Mary poured tea. Ros raised her eyebrows.

'Milk? Sugar?' asked Mary.

'Just as it is please.' Ros bent to kiss the child's head, breathing the indescribable smell of the very young. 'He's – er—'

'Yes?' said Mary on the defensive.

'Absolutely gorgeous.' Ros let out her breath.

'Oh – well – when we've had tea shall I show you round? Two of the horses are here, the other four are out with Fergus. You would like to see it all, wouldn't you? The whole set-up?'

'Well – Fergus might prefer me—'

'He won't mind. I'll show you the house as well. Bit of luck Poppy letting it to Fergus, wasn't it? She's away somewhere, Fergus can't wait for her to come back.'

Ros was silent. Then, filling in a pause, said, 'I knew her father.'

'So did I. A nice bloke, a genius for picking winners. They say he won a fortune.' Mary laughed. 'Others say that he was left money by women.'

'He was kind,' said Ros, 'to lonely people.'

'Yes. More tea?' Mary was suddenly wary.

'No thanks.' Ros, sensing Mary's change of mood, kept silent, her hands stroking Barnaby's plump legs, tickling his toes. His nails were like pink pearls.

'Fergus is greatly taken with Poppy,' Mary said flatly.

'And she with Fergus?'

'I wouldn't know. She has another sort of entanglement. Shall I take him?' Mary held out her arms as Barnaby began to whimper. 'I'm still breast feeding.' She unbuttoned her shirt.

'I nursed Fergus.' Ros surrendered the child reluctantly.

'That was nice for you.' Mary was distancing herself. 'And for him,' she said dryly.

Ros stood up. 'I think I won't wait for Fergus. Will you tell him I came? I'll telephone, let him ask me over.' Ros bent to kiss the baby's head. 'Goodbye Barnaby. Don't bother to see me out, don't disturb him. He looks so happy.'

'Thanks, goodbye then, it's been nice—'

'I'll see you again now I know the way. Goodbye.'

Ros went out to her car. 'What do they think they are playing at,' she muttered. 'What a fraud.' She accelerated, driving away from the house in a mood of dangerous exhilaration. The smell of the child was in her mind, she felt a fierce longing to bath him, wrap him in a towel, stay with him, rolling him on a rug in front of an open fire on a winter's night, feel again the fierce joy of motherhood, hear the delighted chuckle and shriek of a happy baby. I shall box his ears, she

166

promised herself, puzzling over the mixture of sensations, the turmoil which assailed her.

'I have not felt like this since first love at sixteen,' she told her husband that night. He, being an understanding man, took off his reading glasses, turned out the bedside lamp and took his wife in his arms.

'It's all very well for you,' she cried, bursting into tears, 'to be so detached. You are only his stepfather.'

'Amen to that,' said her husband.

35

Curled in a foetal position Poppy lay in the bed where Willy had put her. Demented rain slapped and smashed against the windows, gusts of wind whistled and howled, draught seeping in from the storm rattled the shutters which kept it at bay.

Her eyes hurt, her head throbbed, her hands ached. If she moved her arms the bruise on her collarbone was exquisitely painful. The pains of her body counterpointed the savagery of the weather.

Nothing broken, she reassured herself, just lie still, wait, and it will go away. This is nothing to the storm I left behind in cockroach country. Poppy groped for consolation, distancing herself from the last few days, from the unfinished hotel, the smell of wet cement, the insect infestation, the violence, the squashed dog, the hanging men—

With a glint of satisfaction she thought, The epilogue with Edmund is over.

Since she felt in no fit state to review the past week she dropped a closed portcullis over her mind. Start again at the moment where Willy Guthrie had materialised in the Customs. Last seen reclaiming the coat lent her by that friend of Dad's. What was he doing here, apart from being fantastically kind?

Arriving in this God-awful storm, Poppy thought, I'd just about run out of puff.

Was this man, she puzzled, part of Furnival's Funerals or a friend of Dad's? She did not remember him with Fergus and Victor. Would Fergus or Victor have gathered her up, brought her here, put her to bed without one question asked?

Putting aside the enigma of Willy, she considered Fergus and Victor, being kissed by Fergus and kissed by Victor. It had been agreeable, exploratory, loving; remembering the two men she was surprised by a twinge of desire (not done for yet) but curiously the desire was in essence equal for both. Poppy let her mind dwell on Fergus and Victor as potential lovers. It was so long since she had considered any man other than Edmund in such a role (never for more than a minute, never seriously). Fergus, she thought, would be a taker afraid to give, but an experience not to be ignored. And Victor? She thought of Victor's extreme slenderness. The fit of bodies would be a fresh experience. Edmund's hips were wide and muscular (banish Edmund). She thought with tender curiosity of Victor. Sleepily, for she was growing sleepy, she cast her mind back to the afternoon that she had met the two men, remembering the old dog in the stable yard, the younger dogs, the offensive insolence of the cat, the girls who shampooed their hair in the room above the kitchen while Fergus worked out the cost of the funeral. And Mary, brooding, sulky and enigmatic, holding that lovely baby. Sitting there as aloof as the cat she did not fit with the girls who harassed their boys on the telephone. Then, sliding into sleep, Poppy remembered Mary sitting on the stairs in her father's house during the wake and the smile she had given her as she ran up to the lavatory before leaving with Edmund. 'Watch your step,' Mary had said, her tone conveying female solidarity at variance with her words. Had she or had she not called after her when she passed her going down, 'Give the bugger hell'?

From a chair by the window, his back to the storm, Willy watched Poppy relax her foetal position, lay back her head in sleep, let her limbs lie free. He tiptoed across to look down on the sleeping girl before leaving her to go in search of arnica for her bruises. Even if he could find it she did not look the type to welcome raw steak on her eye. We are imprisoned here by the gale, he thought, she can spend its term resting while those bruises fade.

On his way down in the lift Willy considered ways and means of wreaking revenge on whoever had beaten Poppy up. Garroting done slowly might be good for starters.

An American lady, also stranded by the weather, observing

Willy's expression, pressed herself against the side of the lift and scuttled out to join her husband when they reached the lobby.

Returning presently with supplies Willy let himself quietly into the room, disposed of his parcels and stood looking down on Poppy sleeping now on her back, head thrown back, arms flung out, legs apart, snoring.

Willy bent to look at her. She reminded him in this abandoned attitude of Mrs Future as a piglet. The only human characteristic Mrs Future had acquired was the knack of sleeping on her back, trotters in the air. This in her now mature years she no longer did nor, Willy thought, his lips twitching, had Mrs Future ever snored.

Poppy opened her good eye: 'Was I snoring?'

'Yes.' Willy straightened his back. Poppy drew her legs together, folded her hands protectively across her chest.

'I got some arnica, there's a chemist counter in the hotel shop. I thought it might help your bruises.'

'Thanks.' She drew her hands under the coverlet.

'And he also – that's the chap in the shop – suggested some stuff to put in your bath, have a good soak he said, or I think he said, my Arabic's lousy, non-existent actually.'

'Mine too.'

'That makes two of us. Anyway, I bought some. It smells nice, sort of aromatic, it might be worth a try.'

'Thanks,' she said again. 'I'm sure it's marvellous.'

Why must she be so bloody polite? 'Oh well.' Willy looked away. (That is the most awful shiner I have ever—) 'Actually what I thought would be of immediate help is some booze. I nobbled a couple of bottles of champagne, it's in the fridge, and the barman's promised to keep us some more in case we are stuck here long. He'll defend it from our American cousins. There's a large party of them stranded en route from Morocco; it's okay. They really prefer Scotch.'

'Oh.'

'Like a glass now?'

'Please.'

'Great. Got anything to put round your shoulders when you sit up?' (Cover that bruise at least.)

'No, no – I—'

'Try this.' Willy fetched a cardigan given the previous Christmas by Calypso.

169

'Soft.' Poppy fingered the material. 'Cashmere.'

'My aunt gave it to me. I'll open the bottle.'

'The one with the coat?'

'That's the one.'

While Poppy got her arms into the cardigan, wincing as she moved, Willy clinked glasses, uncorked champagne in the anteroom. He came back to hand her a glass, sat distancing himself from the bed so that she would not feel threatened.

Poppy sipped in silence.

'This storm has got itself into the newspapers.' Willy broke what threatened to be too long a pause.

'That doesn't make it any better.' She swallowed.

Willy refilled her glass. 'You have one hell of a shiner.' He took the bull by the horns. 'Was it an accident?' (Of course it was no accident.)

'Not exactly.'

'Oh.'

'A fight, actually.'

'Ah.'

'He's got a broken leg.' Poppy sipped her champagne, not looking at Willy, remembering the scene in that other hotel bedroom when Edmund— 'He's in hospital,' she said.

'I was planning to garrot him.'

Poppy laughed. 'That's sweet of you.' Laughing hurt.

'But since somebody's broken his leg—'

'I broke it.'

'Bully for you.'

'With a chair.'

So with a vinous half truth Poppy joined the legendary figures of Victor, famous for drowning his wife, and Mary, known to all as the girl who had a child by a wog, to become celebrated as the girl who broke her lover's leg with a chair.

36

It began to rain as Penelope bumped up the track and a nasty little wind got up as she reached the group of buildings which had been the headquarters of Furnival's Funerals. She was tempted to turn round and drive back from whence she came. Only the memory of Mary's jeering voice and Venetia's fluting in Harrods prodded her on.

She switched off the engine, reached for her coat and got bravely out of the car.

Pushing open the yard door she found herself among empty loose-boxes where bits of straw shuffled into corners. An empty Coca-Cola tin rattled along the gutter; the doors of the boxes creaked.

She walked across the yard past the empty stables, sniffing the stale scent of horse. She kicked the Cola can which shot away rattling noisily, coming to rest against the water trough. The wind dropped, she listened. Nothing.

Leaving the yard Penelope shouldered open the doors of the coach house, walked boldly across its darkness and out into the garden, sighted the cottage, strode up the neglected path, seized the knocker, knocked.

Getting no answer, she knocked again. Above the door a window rattled on a loose latch. Penelope shielded her eyes, peered through the window into the kitchen trying to make out signs of occupation. Then she tried the door, found it locked. Exasperated she walked round the cottage peering in at the windows, unable to decide whether or not there was anybody living here.

I could write a note, she thought. Who to, she answered herself? You don't know who the woman is, who to address your note to.

The rain, up to now light, renewed its energies, slanting unpleasantly down from the top of the valley. She left the exposed doorstep, ran across to the coach house. As she pushed open the door there was a clatter and a crash, an ominous growl. Penelope's heart jumped into her throat. Something pushed against her legs, she shrieked.

'Oh God!' She was furious. 'Fergus's bloody cat. I am supposed to catch you.'

Bolivar pressed his bulk against her legs, purring throatily.

Penelope thought of all the trashy stories she had read where stupid girls were frightened by cats in empty buildings.

'Get off.' She kicked at Bolivar. 'Stop doing that. I hate cats. Follow me to the car and I'll give you your bloody sardines, then you can sit in the back and I'll drive you back to Fergus and that horrible girl. He should give me a reward for this,' she said, opening the coach-house door, slamming it shut, crossing the yard to her car.

Bolivar ran ahead of Penelope, his ringed tail in the air, exposing a tender triangle of gingery fur round his anus, jauntily displaying his balls.

'Here you are, you beastly animal.' Penelope took the tin of sardines from the car seat, laid it on the ground.

Purring loudly, Bolivar set himself to eat.

Penelope got into the car out of the rain and sat waiting for the cat to finish its meal. As Bolivar ate slowly after the first gulp she drummed her fingers on the steering wheel impatient to be off.

'Hurry up, for Christ's sake. I've had enough of this place, there's nobody here.'

Bolivar paused in his eating to lick his chops, shake the rain off his coat, stare around. 'If there is anybody here she must be out. I'm not going to wait.' For some reason she felt very nervous.

Bolivar resumed his meal, crouching intent and thoughtful over the sardines.

'Buck up,' ordered Penelope. Bolivar rasped his tongue round the tin, sucking up the last drop of delicious oil then sat back and began his toilet.

'Oh for God's sake, you can do that in the car, jump in.' Penelope opened the car door.

Bolivar moved away.

'Come on, get in, I'm not going to pick you up.' Penelope made to shoo Bolivar into the car.

Bolivar stepped aside.

'Blast you, get in I said.' Penelope reached down to pick Bolivar up. Bolivar scratched her.

'Bloody fucking beast.' Penelope lunged to grab Bolivar. Bolivar skipped aside. Penelope gave chase.

Bolivar ran ahead, enjoying the game, cantering tail up, as before, beautiful tabby flanks gleaming in the rain. Had Penelope been a cat lover she would have appreciated that here in Bolivar was a truly beautiful specimen of domestic cat.

Penelope stopped running, altered tack. 'Puss, puss, puss,' she called in her sexiest voice.

Bolivar sauntered down a grassy slope to the stream, crouched like a tiger to drink, his pink tongue lapping the clear water, the tip of his tail twitching in rhythm with his tongue.

The rain stopped as suddenly as it had started. Bolivar sat on a flat stone and resumed his interrupted toilet.

'Bugger you,' Penelope cooed between clenched teeth. 'Come on, pretty puss. Puss, puss, puss.' She approached the cat slowly.

Bolivar ignored her.

Holding her breath Penelope crept closer. Two feet from Bolivar she pounced. Her outstretched hands gripped empty air. The grassy bank overhanging the stream gave way. She crashed into the water, twisting her ankle in an agonising wrench, banging her knee on a stone, bruising it badly.

Stunned by the pain, Penelope hauled herself out of the water, sat on the bank, took off her shoe, watched her ankle swell and blood seep from her knee.

'Oh God, oh God, that woman will come back and find me like this,' Penelope moaned, 'I must get away.' She snatched up a stone and threw it at the cat. Bolivar did not flinch, he watched, sitting still again, whiskers fanning outward. Now in her wretchedness Penelope remembered Mary giving her the sardines. 'Lure him into the car,' she had said, 'lure him in.' Not put the fucking tin down in the open.

Bolivar moved, he nudged up against Penelope weaving a sinuous caress. 'Fuck off, piss off,' said Penelope gritting her teeth, close to tears.

Bolivar repeated his gesture, catching Penelope's eye, pressing his arched back against her side.

Penelope ignored him. The pain in her ankle was growing worse, it was beginning to throb quite horribly. She dipped her foot, ankle and all, into the icy stream. 'Oops!' Courageously she kept it there. She splashed water over her bruised knee. Bolivar was interested.

Holding her foot in the water, trying to keep still, breathing in shuddering gasps, Penelope felt disgusted respect for the cat who now sat out of reach on his stone, gazing down into the water trickling over a pretty little waterfall into the pool. From time to time Bolivar licked his lips.

Following Bolivar's intent scrutiny Penelope saw a fish idling in the current, lazily steering with its semi-transparent tail and fins. The water was so clear she was able to count its spots, view its pink-tinged flanks. Watching the fish, keeping her foot in the pool, she became aware of mud seeping through her clothes to chill her bottom and thighs, oozing icily through her skirt.

'I have to get away.' Penelope withdrew her foot from the pool, tried to stand. Impossible, she crumpled, the pain was awful. She went down on hands and knees and began to crawl back to her car.

Bolivar, interested, kept pace.

Penelope had managed twenty painful yards when she heard a car coming up the track. Her first reaction was to shout 'Help!' Then, no, oh no – that woman – I can't – won't. Penelope lay flat out of sight of the track. I'll get away when she's gone into the house, she thought, I can't possibly confront her like this. Conscious of her muddy and dishevelled appearance, painful ankle, bruised knee, Penelope lay face down on the wet grass.

'What on earth?' cried Victor, running down the slope to visit his trout. 'I say! Oh God, it's you, darling. I thought the car looked familiar. What are you doing here? You are hurt. What happened? Who did this to you? Let me see. Oh my love, my poor, poor love, don't cry. It's all right, I'm here now. Here, use my handkerchief. Oh, my darling. Put your arms round me. That's right. I'll get you to a doctor. Gosh, you are soaking, you'll catch pneumonia. Your poor ankle, look at that knee. Jesus, it's swollen. How on earth – I say, what's Bolivar doing here – trying to catch my trout, the old faker. Don't cry, darling, it's all right now, I'm here.'

'The cat did it,' said Penelope viciously.

37

Victor helped Penelope into her car. 'You'd better let me drive.' He took off his jacket, rolled it into a ball. 'Cushion your foot on that, then it won't get jarred going over the bumps.'

'Thanks.' Gingerly she eased herself into the seat.

'If you came to fetch Bolivar,' Victor went on, 'we'd better drop him off at Fergus's new place on our way to a doctor. Fergus will be able to recommend one. Bolivar can sit in the back, he'll be all right there.'

Penelope, so lately rescued, felt it unpolitic to say 'Just try and catch him'. Remarks of that ilk had sparked off many a row in the past.

Victor bent down, picked Bolivar up. Bolivar pressed a sheathed paw against Victor's cheek, chucked him under the chin with his head. 'Gorgeous animal,' said Victor, 'how come you got left behind in the move? You must have been out hunting or after the girls, you old rogue.' He put Bolivar on the back seat. 'Better wind the windows up in case he takes it into his head to leap out.'

Penelope wound up her window, Victor closed his.

'Perhaps he doesn't like cars,' Penelope ventured.

'Nonsense, I bet he drives everywhere with Fergus.'

'What about your car?' asked Penelope.

'I'll come back for it.'

'Are you leaving the keys in the ignition?'

'Yes,' said Victor, who had forgotten them. 'Why are you always right?' he asked bitterly.

Penelope sniffed danger.

'Nobody comes up here,' Victor justified himself. 'Right, let's be off.' He started the engine, turned the car.

In the back Bolivar began to scream.

'I don't suppose he's ever been in a car,' Penelope shouted.

Victor yelled, 'The poor fellow's frightened, he'll settle down in a minute.'

Penelope's answer, if she made one, was drowned.

Bolivar bounded caterwauling from side to side of the back seat. Penelope shielded her head with her hands in case he took it into his demented head to leap over into the front of the car.

Victor laughed. 'At least we can't have a row with this racket going on,' he bellowed.

Penelope stopped her ears with her fingers.

For the ten miles to Fergus's new establishment in Poppy Carew's house and stables Bolivar kept up an ear-piercing, growling, panic-stricken yowl. The only thing which prevented Victor from stopping the car and letting Bolivar out was the thought of the many, many times in the future when, supposing they were re-united, Penelope would say 'I told you so'.

At last reaching Poppy's house, Victor stopped the car, switched off the engine and sat still, his ears tingling in the sudden silence. Penelope kept her ears blocked and her eyes shut.

On the back seat Bolivar now sat quiet and wary, his eyes brilliant with suspicion, his tail lashing.

'How clever you've been. I never thought you'd catch him. Sardines did the trick, did they?' Mary ran to greet them. 'Hullo, Victor, what are you doing here?' she shouted through the closed window, cheerful and pleased.

'Went to visit my trout,' shouted Victor, beginning to wind down the window.

'Don't do that! He might run away, he's never been here, he might be frightened. Keep it shut,' shouted Mary. 'Wait while I fetch Fergus, he's just got back.' She disappeared into the house. They heard her voice still, 'It was a very successful funeral, went without a hitch. Fergus, Bolivar's arrived!'

'Am I in Hell?' muttered Penelope.

'That was Byron on his wedding night—' Victor, not one of those men who fancy themselves in Byron's shoes, waiting obediently for Fergus to appear, wished that there might be a time when he was not in perpetual disagreement with his ex-wife then, feeling an unwonted rush of affection for her, leant across and kissed her cheek.

'What did you do that for?' Penelope took her hands from her ears.

'Love,' said Victor.

Penelope said nothing. In addition to the throb of her twisted ankle and her bruised knee she was trying to assimilate the revelation she had just been posed by Mary. Then: 'I feel such an utter and

176

complete fool,' she whispered.

'Why?' Half expecting her to snatch it away, Victor took her hand.

'I *say*! Clever girl, found and caught my Bolivar.' Fergus came out of the house, bounding down the steps, putting paid to any explanation Penelope might see fit to make. 'Thought you didn't care for cats, Penelope. Here, just let me get at him. Come along, my treasure, you've no idea how worried I've been.' Opening the car door, Fergus gathered Bolivar tenderly into his arms. 'There, there, what a dreadful time you've had. Never mind, it's all over now.'

Penelope and Victor exchanged glances.

Moaning with joy, Bolivar nestled against Fergus, pressing his furry bulk against his chest, his purr rumbling fit to choke in his throat.

'It's Penelope who's had a dreadful time,' Victor yelled in exasperation. 'There's nothing wrong with your bloody cat. Penelope's hurt, I must get her to a doctor.'

'Really? Why?' asked Fergus, distracted from Bolivar, sighting Penelope. 'What on earth have you been up to, you *do* look a mess. Did Victor get around to trying to murder you again?'

'One of these days your jokes will get you into serious trouble.' Mary pushed Fergus aside. 'Shut Bolivar up somewhere until he's calmed down, butter his paws. You come with me,' she said to Penelope, 'you don't need a doctor. I'll fix your wounds. Help me get her up to the bathroom, Victor.'

'Bossy boots.' Fergus stood aside.

'And when you've shut the cat up, tell one of the girls to make a pot of tea. Come on, Victor. Lean on both of us,' she said to Penelope. 'Get cracking, Fergus, light the fire in the sitting room while you are about it and find the whisky. Keep an eye on Barnaby while I'm busy.'

'Christ!' Fergus, hugging Bolivar, watched Mary and Victor help Penelope into the house and up the stairs.

'And tell Frances and Annie they can't go out tonight, there's far too much to do,' Mary called from the stairs.

Fergus gaped. 'What's got into her?'

'Your mother came to see you this afternoon,' Mary called from the landing.

'My ma? What did she want?'

Mary did not apparently hear. 'Leave her with me,' she said to Victor as Penelope sank on to the bathroom chair. 'I can cope better without you.'

'I—' said Victor.

'Go on, you're only in the way.'

Victor looked at Penelope's face smeared with mud and tears. She made a tentative movement. Victor bent down, she put her hands on his shoulders. They kissed carefully, neither spoke. 'Okay, see you later.' Victor straightened up and left the room.

'Cry into this.' Mary handed Penelope a roll of lavatory paper. 'I honestly think you'd do best by getting into a hot bath, you're soaked. Let me help you out of your clothes. I'll lend you some of mine.'

'You're kind.'

'Just interested in the boomerang effect of whatever it was Venetia started—' Mary turned on the taps, helped Penelope undress. 'Have a good soak while I find a bandage to strap up that ankle. I'm sure she didn't intend you to meet Victor.'

'It was a ploy, probably directed against Poppy Carew. Oh, that's lovely.' Penelope lay back in the bath. 'Didn't you say when I was here earlier on that both Fergus and Victor are interested in Poppy?'

'Exactly. Quite funny as things—' Mary began to laugh.

Penelope joined in.

Fergus in the kitchen buttering Bolivar's paws, looked up nervously.

'Listen to those two. What can they be laughing at?'

'Us, probably,' said Victor. 'Where d'you keep the whisky?'

'It's on the dresser.' Fergus placed Bolivar in the dog basket. Bolivar shook his paws, sniffed, then started to lick them.

Victor poured them each a drink. 'When did you move in here?'

'Few days ago. Mary's getting us straight. It's lucky we moved. I'm wonderfully busy. We buried a retired hunt servant today and I've got two funerals in the next six days, an industrialist whose widow aspires to be county and a gypsy's grandmother from near Romsey. Mary's wonderful on the phone with that voice of hers, she talks posh to some, cosy to others, can't think how I'd manage without her.'

'What happened to Poppy?' Victor looked round the kitchen, reminded of her existence.

'No idea.' Fergus sipped his whisky. 'Her father's daily lady doesn't know either. Isn't she in London?'

178

'No,' said Victor, 'she isn't.'

'Oh.' Fergus looked at his cousin thoughtfully. 'I thought—'

'What did your mother want, d'you suppose?' Victor headed Fergus off, not wishing to discuss his intentions vis à vis Poppy with Fergus or to hear Fergus's plans. If Fergus was busy he would have little time to spare chasing Poppy. His own intentions were ambiguous.

'I don't know,' said Fergus, reminded of his parent. 'She doesn't usually drop in unannounced, she's supersensitive to interference herself.'

'Happy with your role as undertaker, is she? How does it fit in with the family image?'

'She persuaded my stepfather to give me a reference, it gave Poppy's solicitor a salutory shock.'

'I should have thought—'

'What?' asked Fergus suspiciously.

'That he was used to all sorts with Poppy's father's friends. What a *bouillabaisse* at the funeral.' Victor laughed.

'Not all of them fishy. Didn't you notice Calypso Grant?'

'Was that who it was? I wonder who spread the treacle. That was a fishy act if ever there was one. Must have been somebody with a grudge.'

'We must ask Poppy when she reappears.'

'Aren't you going to look for her?'

'How can I?' said Fergus. 'I'm up to my eyes with work. Are you going to look for her?'

'I'm pretty busy with this book of mine at the moment.'

'I see,' said Fergus. 'And Penelope?'

'Well—' said Victor. 'I—'

The cousins paused like hunting dogs who have temporarily lost the scent.

'What were you doing up at my old place?' Fergus poured Victor more whisky.

'I was stuck in my work. I went to visit the trout, see whether it was still alive, get a bit of inspiration.'

'And is it?'

'Yes, I think so. I forgot to look.'

'Eh?' Fergus looked at Victor. 'And you took Penelope with you?'

'No, I found her there—'

'What was she doing? Why did you push her into the stream? How

179

did she find her way there?'

'I don't know. I didn't ask her. I didn't push her—'

From the bathroom above the kitchen there was a shout of feminine laughter, followed by a spate of chatter.

'She seems all right now,' said Victor dubiously.

The laughter above them was renewed.

'Hilarious,' muttered Fergus. 'I wonder what the joke can be.'

'Us,' said Victor positively.

Listening to the laughter the two men felt threatened.

'I wonder what my mother wanted.' Fergus skated rapidly round his conscience. 'It's ages since I heard Mary laugh like that.'

'Ganging up,' said Victor.

'Pessimist.' Fergus was robust. 'Still, I'd better light the fire, as she said.'

38

Willy's personal experience of black eyes and bruises was limited to an occasion in adolescence when he had been involved in a car smash. Watching Poppy sleep he tried to remember how long his bruises had taken to fade. He was anxious for Poppy, anxious too to get back to his pigs. All very well to leave Arthur in charge for a few days but the prospect of much longer irked him. He did not like the hotel, inefficient and sloppy with its resentful undertones of past French glories. The atmosphere created by fellow stranded travellers with their hysterical impatience to continue their interrupted tours made him jumpy. He worried about running short of money, and worse; now that he had found Poppy, there was a barrier of silence between them which he resented.

She was not, he thought, watching her sleep, capable of breaking anybody's leg. It was at least doubtful. This must be some sort of joke. Not knowing Poppy he could only guess at her idea of humour.

Since she was, he supposed, in the grip of some sort of trauma, it would do her good to unburden herself, break this stubborn silence, but how to bring this desirable effect about?

He must not force her.

Long ago in his early days of farming he had forced Mrs Future's great-aunt to move from a sty where she was settled and content into another where it was easier, from his point of view, to care for her. Mrs Future's great-aunt had retaliated by eating her entire litter, presumably acting on the theory that they were safer inside than out.

It was two days since he had found Poppy. During that time she had volunteered no information, had been politely grateful for his care but most of the time she had slept, shutting herself away out of reach.

Tired of watching the storm outside, Willy stretched out on his bed and tried to read the only paperback he had with him for the third time. The complexities of Len Deighton bemused him, the book fell forward on his chest, he fell asleep.

Waking in the dark, Willy listened for the storm; its frenzy seemed a little less. Next he listened for Poppy's breathing, heard nothing, sat up, reached for the bedside lamp, pressed the switch, it did not work. Cursing, he blundered to the door, tried the switches, none worked. He opened the door into the corridor, that too was inky dark. Below in the hotel there was the confused sound of dismembered voices clamouring up the lift shaft. Back in the room he made for the window, looked out. There were no harbour lights. There was no moon.

Afraid for Poppy, he felt his way round the room, felt her bed, found it empty. Thinking he might have mistaken Poppy's bed for his own he searched the second bed. This too was empty.

Suddenly afraid, Willy shouted, 'Poppy!' screaming 'Poppy!'

'I'm here,' she called, 'in the bath. The lights went out.'

'Are you all right?'

'Getting cold.'

'I thought you'd run away.' His fear was still with him. 'I thought you'd gone.' He felt his way to the bathroom. 'I thought something had happened to you, I was terrified.'

'I was soaking in that stuff you brought me, it's delicious, helps a lot. Can you find me a towel? There's a bathrobe hanging on the door.'

Feeling for the robe Willy was surprised to find himself shaking. 'I have it,' he said.

'Thanks, heave ho, up I come.' She splashed up out of the bath

181

beside him. 'Where are you? What's the matter?'

'Thought you'd gone.' He felt for her wet body, wrapped her in the bathrobe. 'God, it's dark. Am I hurting you?'

'No, it's all right.'

'Don't get cold.' He held her bundled against him, smelling her hair under his chin.

'When the lights come back,' he said, 'I'll tell you I love you.'

They were pressed against the edge of the bath.

'Perhaps until then we could sit somewhere comfortable.'

'The bed—'

'Yes, okay. Why don't we get in?' She was shivering.

They felt their way to the bed. Willy pulled back the bedclothes. They lay facing each other. Poppy put a hand over his heart.

'Your poor bruised hands,' he said.

'They are getting better. Much better.'

Why did I tell her I love her? Blurt it out like that in a bathroom. Clot. Enough to put any girl off.

Outside the storm whooped up with renewed vigour. Further along the hotel's façade a shutter broke loose, clattered in anguish against the wall.

Should he go down, try to find out why there was no light, when it would come on again, join in the confusion raging in the lobby? He held Poppy damp in the bathrobe. She was speaking, her breath warm against his throat.

'I was awful to Edmund on the plane. I should not have come with him. I did it to spite Venetia. It seemed a good chance when he snatched me away after Dad's funeral. A surprise, that, because he had left me the week before. He's in love with Venetia. He wants to marry her. He never wanted to marry me, we just lived together. I suppose he had this impulse – I didn't like to make a fuss in front of strangers and in a way it was a bit of a joke, a poke in the eye for her. I thought I'd say No in private, No, it's over, then when I saw what she'd done I was sorry for him and I gave in, came on this journey. It was sheer cussedness and stupidity, crazy, a colossal mistake. But he assumed I loved him, assumed I would marry him, started talking marriage. He must have guessed I have money now, it couldn't be anything else. It was so crass. There were these insects, awful things, we ran over a dog and then those men I saw. They hanged them, sort of hoisted them up—' Willy held her, said nothing. She went on – 'He went out for the day, disappeared, came back so pissed he got

182

into the wrong room, no, it was the second night he was pissed, no, both nights. Then in the morning I could see something terrible had happened to him, he was hangdog and hung over, so I said let's have a lovely day together and we did. We picnicked and swam and drove out to an oasis in the desert and made love. Just like old times. When we got back he started drinking again, he can be awfully disagreeable when he drinks. Well, we had this bust up, this row, he hit me, knocked me down, stamped on my hands— I got frightened.' Willy held Poppy tight. 'Then I broke his leg with a chair.' Still Willy held her, she felt his heart beating under her hand.

Willy held his breath.

'I swung the chair with both hands. I heard the bone crack.' She went on, 'I was glad. I packed my bag, sent a telegram to Venetia and sent for Mustafa to cope, get Edmund to hospital or whatever. (Actually I did that before I packed my bag and alerted Venetia.) Oh, Edmund—' Poppy paused to feel the familiar pang, felt nothing. 'Then I got a taxi to the airport and got on to the first plane out. That's how I landed up here.' Poppy gave a long tired sigh. 'Sorry to bother you with all this.'

Willy held her, said nothing, content to piece the facts into some sort of sense later.

'It's remarkable,' said Poppy conversationally, 'how really nasty I become when I'm unhappy. It's not only me. Look at Venetia. She would never have done that to Edmund's clothes if she hadn't been unhappy. I can't help admiring her though. (He's such a beautiful man.) Then there's Mary, the girl with a baby, she's miserable, it sharpens her tongue. I dare say Venetia's happy enough now. Am I boring you?'

'No.'

'Say if I do. I'd got cold in the bath, the water wasn't all that hot to start with. I'm nice and warm now.'

'Good.'

'Are you worrying about your pigs?'

'No,' said Willy untruthfully.

'I wish the lights would come on.'

Willy stirred. 'I don't.'

'Oh.' She sounded sad, then, 'It's true what I told you about Edmund's leg and the chair, but we did not make much love when we picnicked and it wasn't such a lovely day. It was a good try, that's all. I credit myself with trying. To be quite truthful it was one hell of

183

an awful day. What are you doing?'

'Guess,' said Willy.

'Wow!' said Poppy presently, 'that was – Oh, I wish the lights would come on.'

'I can tell you in the dark,' said Willy.

'No, please don't. That's not what I want.' Poppy took fright, she had no wish to get involved with the pitfalls of love. 'Edmund never did it like that,' she said.

'I'm not all that keen on hearing about Edmund's performance,' said Willy huffily.

'No, I suppose not, how tactless, it was meant to be a compliment. Tell me about Mrs Future then.'

'You remembered her name.' He was amused.

'Of course.' Poppy lay in Willy's arms enjoying herself. Suppose I take this man on as a pleasure man? It's ages since I experienced pleasure. I've never had this sort of delight. What would it be like with Victor? With Fergus? 'Oh! Are we doing it again? It's nice like this in the dark, isn't it? Do you mind my talking?'

'No.'

'I am enjoying this – mm – yes, go on doing that. Yes, yes. If it hadn't been for the power cut we might not have – Oh! – Yes! – Oh! – Do you suppose there are people stuck in the lift?'

'Oh, oh Poppy—'

'Sorry, I made you laugh at the wrong moment—'

'It's never the wrong moment.' He had not heard her laugh before.

'Do you then think laughter and copulation are compatible?'

'Absolutely.'

39

Frances and Annie leant against the kitchen door, sharing a packet of crisps, minding their business. This comprised waiting for Frances's latest man to telephone. Frances called him a man although he was still sixteen. 'He has the requisite parts,' she had said when chal-

184

lenged on his tender years by Annie, whose present choice was twenty-three, and dissolved into giggles. Frances was eighteen, Annie eighteen also. They were evolving from horsestruck chrysalises into boystruck girls.

They had finished work, fed and watered the horses, swept the yard, cleaned the tack, polished the hearse and now anticipated the evening's entertainment, lolling against the kitchen door, looking out at the yard.

'It's much better here than up in the hills.' Frances smoothed the front of her dress. Her new man liked her in skirts.

Annie wore a kimono bought in a secondhand shop in Pimlico and baggy trousers *à la mode* from Miss Selfridge. She had slanted her eyes with eyeliner. Both girls' hair was freshly washed and set to look as though they had been drawn roughly through a hedge backwards.

'How long since Joseph telephoned?' Annie crushed the empty crisp packet between her hands. The crackle caused several horses to look out of their boxes hoping for lumps of sugar.

'Not since we moved down here.'

'Perhaps she didn't give him the new telephone number.'

'Perhaps she's tired of him telephoning.'

'Is that what you think?'

'You know what *I* think.' Frances rolled her eyes.

'Telephone!' Annie ran to answer it. She came back after a few minutes. 'It was some woman wanting Fergus, said she is coming round.'

'A client? Did you tell her he is out?'

'She said she'd come and wait for him to get back.'

'Where is he?'

'Walking the dogs.'

'Are you two going out?' Mary called from a window above their heads.

'Yes. Coming with us? D'you think she heard us?' Frances whispered.

Annie shook her head.

'No thanks,' called Mary.

Bolivar came out of the kitchen swaying his body so that he brushed against the girls' legs without seeming to pay them attention. Frances bent to stroke his back, letting his upward waving tail run through her fingers. He sauntered on to sit in a patch of setting sun.

Lowering their voices the girls discussed what Annie thought of Joseph, then, bored by this overworked unrewarding theme, switched to Victor and Penelope.

'I wonder.' Annie caught Frances's eye.

'I bet you,' said Frances.

'But will they actually remarry?' Annie mused.

'Positive,' said Frances.

'Rubbish,' said Annie. 'You were positive he was keen on Poppy Carew. He once tried to murder Penelope, he might try again.'

'After or before marriage?'

Lolling in the kitchen doorway the girls gossiped about Penelope and Victor last seen driving off to London in apparent amity. They would come back later to retrieve Victor's car.

'Nothing like that happens to us, nobody tries to murder me,' Annie complained.

'Our lives have barely begun.' Frances was an optimistic girl.

They stopped chattering to watch Mary, carrying Barnaby across the yard, get in her car and drive away.

'She's not exactly sociable these days.'

'Never really was.'

'Telephone. I'll get it.' Annie ran to answer it. Coming back she said, 'They are on their way, let's wait in the porch.' They moved to sit on the front steps. Annie tore open another packet of crisps. 'Have one? Who's this?' A car drew up by the house. 'A client, d'you suppose? At this hour?'

Annie and Frances watched Ros Lawrence get out and walk towards them. They assessed her clothes, her hair, lack of jewellery, excellent skin for her age. They sent out feelers to gauge her mood. Widow? Grieving parent? Friend of the deceased?

'Hullo,' said Ros. 'Is Fergus in?' She was nervous. 'I'm his mother,' she introduced herself.

'He's walking the dogs,' said Frances.

'Oh,' said Ros. 'Oh. I had hoped to see him.'

'He won't be long. They don't allow dogs in the pub so he'll be back. Won't you come in and wait for him,' said Annie, politely welcoming. 'We thought for a moment you might be a client.'

'Not yet.' Ros smiled, hesitated. 'I should have telephoned or written perhaps.' Annie looked at her curiously, recognising the voice on the telephone. I must sound odd, thought Ros, but surely it's perfectly natural to call on my own son, nothing to be frightened

186

of. ('Mind your own business,' her husband had said, 'don't interfere, he's a grown man.') 'I just thought I'd like to see him.'

'Naturally,' said Annie, puzzled.

'We work here. We are the grooms,' said Frances, trying to put
Ros at her ease (what a jumpy lady), 'and the mutes if they are
needed. I am Frances and this is Annie.'

'Of course,' said Ros. 'I've heard all about you.' He hasn't told me
about them, did he tell me about mutes? I can't remember. They are
pretty girls if they'd give themselves a chance. 'It's nice here.' She
looked up at the house.

'Very convenient,' said Annie.

'Much better than up on the downs,' said Frances. 'Why don't you
come in and sit down, he won't be long.' Annie waved Ros into the
house. 'We are supposed to be going out but Fergus will be back any
minute.'

'Here they come,' said Frances, relieved, as the boyfriends
drove up. 'Will you be all right if we leave you? We are going to a
party.'

'Of course. Have a good time.' Ros watched the young people go,
went into the house, sat on a sofa in the sitting room, got restlessly
up, looked at the bookshelves, fingered a pair of field-glasses,
remembered Bob Carew wearing them round his neck at New-
market, missed him, not as a close friend but as someone she had
always been pleased to see, always felt the better for meeting. Had he
really named his daughter after a racehorse? Had he worried about
her as she worried now about her son Fergus?

She listened to the empty house.

If I went upstairs I could pretend I'd gone to the lavatory, she
thought. With a quick look round I could work out who sleeps in
which room, with whom. God, how base! She suppressed her
curiosity, resisted the urge to explore, moved to the safer ambience
of the kitchen and on out into the yard to talk to the horses.

'Hullo my beauties, hullo.' She patted necks, stroked noses. 'And
Bolivar, how are you, how do you like it here?' She caressed the cat
who accepted her tribute offhandedly. She wished Fergus would
come in, feeling increasingly nervous, remembering her husband. 'I
would hesitate to interfere,' she had said.

'Which is exactly what you want to do,' he had answered.

'But I must find out what is going on,' she had said. 'I am his
mother.'

'All the more reason,' he had said, 'not to poke your nose in.'

'Oh Fergus,' she exclaimed, as Fergus came into the yard with his dogs. 'Thank God you are back.'

'Why, what's happened?'

'Nothing, nothing. I've been here such ages I was beginning to think I'd better come back another time, let you know beforehand, warn you.' She heard herself being querulous, tried to stop.

'I saw you arrive from up on the hill—'

'Oh, you did? Well, it seemed a long time.' Ros was defensive.

Fergus bent to kiss her. 'I'm back now, come along in and have a drink. Didn't the girls—'

'They went out, a party or—'

'Of course. Always on the go those two. They chase more boys than I have fingers or toes. Veritable Dianas. Isn't Mary about? She would look after you.'

'The house seems empty actually. It was about—'

'Well, come on in.' Fergus put his arm round her shoulders. 'Have you had supper?' He reached for the whisky, poured Ros a drink.

'I must get back. Henry will be waiting.'

'And how is my step-papa?'

'Fine, fine. What I came for – was—'

'Yes?'

Ros, courage evaporating under Fergus's kindly gaze, procrastinated. 'Well, I came to see how you are getting on now you've moved.' She sipped her drink. 'Could I have a little more water in this, it's very strong?' Trying to sound normal she succeeded in sounding nervous.

'Of course.'

'I used to know Bob Carew. Your father and I often met him at the races. This house was his, wasn't it?'

'Yes. We buried him. I'm renting it from his daughter.'

Fergus's face softened at the thought of Poppy, Ros noticed. 'I saw it on the local television and somebody wrote an article about you which I read in a magazine at the hairdresser's,' she said.

'Yes, Victor.'

'Oh, oh yes of course.' Ros sipped her whisky; it was still much too strong, drinks went straight to her head these days, some sort of bye-blow from the menopause. 'Of course,' she said again, 'it was Victor.'

Fergus looked at his mother over the rim of his glass. What's the matter with her, has she repented of marrying Henry, is she afraid to tell me she's made a cock-up, she can come and stay here if she wants to think better of it, get shot of him. 'What's the matter, Mother?'

'Nothing, nothing's the matter.' Ros gulped her drink. Where's my sangfroid? Why am I afraid of my own son, my only child? Mind the whisky. 'How are the dogs?' (Idiot question, the dogs are fine, sitting round us, wagging their tails, waiting for their dinners, it's a shame to keep them waiting.) 'Would you show me round? I'd love to see it all.' She made a circling motion with her glass.

'Of course. Come round the yard and see the horses.' Give her time and she'll tell me what her worry is. I thought she was happy with Henry. In many ways he's a lot nicer than Father ever was, got more humour, hasn't got his filthy temper. Fergus frowned as he led the way out to the stables. 'We had a good funeral a couple of days ago over at Wallop and I'm booked for two more this week,' he said cheerfully.

'How splendid. Soon you'll have so much work you – oh, I thought that horse had a white blaze.'

'He does. So does number three. Mary dyes it and their white socks.'

'Oh Mary. Of course I was—'

'Sometimes she dyes her hair at the same time.' Fergus laughed tolerantly. Ros looked at him sharply. 'Come along and let me show you the house.' Ros followed him in and up the stairs. 'You looked round the ground floor, I take it.'

'Sort of.'

'I hope the girls haven't left everything in a mess.' Fergus led her upstairs, began opening doors. 'That's Annie in there, Frances here. Bob Carew's daily lady comes to us now, she's quite a dragon, keeps us in order. You must meet her some time, she's what your mother would have called a treasure.'

'Oh.'

'Good so far.' Fergus glanced through a doorway. 'Nobody daring to be untidy. Mary's in there with Jesu.'

'Who?'

'Her child—'

'Fergus—'

'And I'm on the next floor out of harm's way. This room used to be the spare room. Mrs Edwardes – that's the daily lady – says Bob Carew's lady visitors used to stay in it; d'you suppose they were his mistresses?'

'I think—'

'Apparently Poppy has reserved it for herself or did before the funeral. I thought if she'd like to use it for weekends she could still have it. A lovely girl, isn't she?' Fergus's voice warmed.

'Never met her.'

'But you knew her dad, the one we buried?'

'Yes, of course. Fergus, I came—'

'Yes?' Fergus turned his black eyes on her. 'Yes?'

'Nothing. I wasn't—'

'Would you like to stay the night, Mother, have Poppy's room, have supper with me, I'm on my own?' Give her time to sick up whatever's bothering her, something is, it must be serious, I've never seen her quite like this. 'You could telephone Henry.' If my stepfather is ill-treating her I shall have to—

'No thanks, darling. I'd better get back.' She took fright.

'Have another drink, then.' Loosen her tongue. I must find out what the trouble is. Fergus, sensing his parent's distress, felt growing concern as he led the way back to the kitchen, poured her another whisky.

'I really shouldn't,' said Ros, taking it. 'I have miles to drive.'

'Then stay the night.'

'No, no.' The prospect terrified her.

'Why don't we sit where it's comfortable in the sitting room. I'll light the fire, come along.' He led the way. Ros followed, panic constricting her throat, why, oh why, had she come? Damn Henry for being right.

'There, sit there.' Fergus pushed her into an armchair.

Ros sat, reminded of a rabbit with a stoat, the part of the stoat was being played by Fergus, her only child.

'Well, now. What's really worrying you?' Fergus leant towards her, his elbows on his knees. 'I don't see enough of you, Mother.'

Somehow she must get herself out of this ridiculous situation. She took a large swallow of whisky. 'Henry and I thought, well I thought of it and he agreed, well of course he agreed' (what he'd actually done was fall about laughing), 'we—'

'Yes?' Fergus leant forward listening, sympathetic, caring, he was really very fond of his mother, no reason not to be.

'Would you like a coach?' Ros shot her inspiration out with a rush.

'A coach?' Has she gone off her rocker?

'Yes. I thought for your business it would – I mean with a coach you could—'

'I've got a hearse, Mother.' He was patient.

'I know, darling, it's just this, I thought if I gave you a coach, I saw one advertised in Bath—'

'It's very generous of you but what would I want with a coach?'

'You could do weddings,' said Ros inspired.

'Aha! It's out. You are snobbishly opposed to funerals.' He felt betrayed.

'NO!' She flushed.

'Yes, you are. You don't like having a son who's an undertaker.'

'No, darling, it's not—'

'Or my stepfather doesn't like having a stepson who's an under-taker. It lowers the tone. Well, he must bloody put up with it.' Fergus's short-fused temper exploded. 'He can stuff his coach up his fastidious arse. I thought you were embarrassed about something when I came in, had some awful worry you couldn't bring yourself to talk about. I see it all. You want to bribe me to chuck my business for a fucking coach for weddings.' Fergus spat out the last word. 'Well, you can tell him I am not interested in weddings.'

'I can see that!' Ros too had a temper.

Ignoring her, Fergus went on, 'I've worked my balls off to get my business off the ground. I'm beginning to do really well. I am not interested in marriages, they always fall apart, look at Victor reduced to killing Penelope—'

'She's still alive,' shouted Ros, infected by Fergus's rage, choking on her own agitation.

'I am interested in burials, in death, there's money in death and I am making it,' Fergus shouted. He was standing up now, towering above his mother.

'I am very glad for you,' Ros too stood up, put down her empty glass, 'delighted, though you may not believe me, you are so touchy.'

'I am *not* touchy.'

'I didn't come about offering to give you a coach, that was off the top of my head on the spur of the moment, an idea engendered by terror.'

'What did you come about, then?' Fergus stood looking down at his mother.

'Your child,' said Ros.

'My *what?*'

'Your child, Mary Mowbray's baby.'

Fergus stared at his mother. 'Mother, you must be mad.' He spoke very gently. (A good psychiatrist, this looked serious.)

Ros said nothing, watching him.

'That baby's father is called Joseph, mother, he's a Spaniard, in Spain, he's a waiter or a fisherman or something.'

'A figment.'

'You do not suppose I'd—'

'Yes.'

'Come on, Mother, you have the wrong end of the stick. She brought it back from Spain, I tell you.'

Ros sat down again. 'And I tell you, Fergus, that that child is the spitting image of you as a baby. I should know, I am your mother. It was a great shock when I saw him the other day. I can show you photographs of yourself when you were his age which could have been taken yesterday of that child and—' She held up a hand as Fergus tried to speak. 'I can also show you photographs of your father at the same age. Same thing, identical. The Furnival genes are mighty strong.'

Leaving the house, Ros passed Bolivar on the doorstep sitting in the dusk, whiskers twitching in anticipation of the night's business. She kicked his flank.

'That's not like you, Mother,' Fergus cried desperately.

'But that baby *is* like you.' Ros jumped into her car and drove off.

'You will have an accident if you drive like that,' Fergus yelled after the departing car. 'You are insane.' He shivered, feeling very cold.

40

When Edmund saw Venetia tripping towards him he was amazed.

The hospital ward was long and airy, the beds widely spaced, his bed the last in the row. As Venetia advanced the heads of the bodies in the other beds turned to watch her progress. He had time to wonder whether the Muslim patients would be shocked by Venetia's dress of fine cotton speckled with minute yellow flowers, semi-transparent, so that as she approached, with the light behind her, it was possible not only to see her legs but her whole silhouette. As her breasts bounced in time with her stride Edmund was pleasurably stirred.

'Edmund.' She took his hand in hers. 'I came as soon as I could.'

'Venetia.' He watched tears gush, roll down her cheeks, drip on to his hands. 'How marvellous, darling, don't cry.'

'I can't help it.'

'I love to see you cry but do stop.' He reached up to kiss her wet face. 'Sit down, he's offering you a chair. How did you find me?'

The young doctor who had escorted her was indeed offering a chair. Venetia thanked him profusely, sat. Her tears ceased. She tossed back her yellow hair. She looked like the Primavera in the Uffizi, beautiful, radiant.

'How did it happen?'

'How did you get here?' They spoke in unison.

'I had an accident.'

'I got your message, caught the first plane.' Edmund held her hands while she took stock of his predicament. His leg, heavily plastered, slung upwards in a sling, rendered him immobile.

'Is it painful?'

'Not now.'

'How brave. Was it a car crash?'

'Not exactly.'

The young doctor who had escorted her said something in Arabic, repeated it in English, 'I screen.'

'Not at the moment, thanks all the same. Oh I see, mis-understanding.'

Venetia laughed and Edmund too as the doctor drew a screen round the bed, creating a zone of privacy before leaving them.

'Well?' She looked at Edmund. 'What happened? Tell.'

Edmund stroked her hands, watched her face, he loved her yellow hair, such a definite colour compared with Poppy's mouse. Her eyes were not as pale as he remembered. 'Are your feet cold?'

'Of course. I am adapted to a warm climate. Come on, tell me what happened. Was it something disreputable?' She was not to be sidestepped into a discussion about the temperature of her feet.

Edmund looked past Venetia at the North African sky, the storm

193

was over, the palms in the hospital garden still, in the distance a glimpse of quiet sea. He was trapped. 'It's a long story, rather boring.' He was guarded.

'Not to me,' said Venetia. 'The sooner you start the better. I didn't come all this way for a silent sulk. Shall I fill you in about me?'

Edmund nodded.

'Right. You go off with this girl Poppy. You bring her here instead of me. I was really looking forward to this trip, Edmund. Anyway, this is no time for reproaches, she must have had some sort of hold over you.' (Oh she had, she had, cried a private part of Edmund. What have I lost?) 'So I won't nag, not now, my love. Days pass. I get an impertinent postcard from the girl, nothing from you. Then two or three days later a message which merely says "Broken leg" and the hospital address, signed Edmund. I take it you sent it?'

'No.'

'She did, Poppy?'

'Must have.' Edmund looked anguished.

'And where is she?' Venetia looked round as though to repulse Poppy should she appear round the hospital screen.

'Buggered off.'

'Oh my. You'd better begin at the beginning, take it slowly, I have all the time in the world.' Venetia wriggled, settling her haunches in the hospital chair. For no reason Edmund remembered a French tourist remarking to his friend *'en voilà des belles fesses'*. He had been disgusted at the time but now – 'I'm still pretty confused,' he said.

'Don't prevaricate.'

'You won't like it.'

'Oh come on, Edmund, don't be stupid. If we are getting married we can't have secrets. I know some people do but I like things clear cut.'

'You may not want to marry me when I've told you.' (Did a still voice whisper, 'Make a bid for freedom'?)

'Let me decide that.'

'You're a bully.' Poppy had never bullied or badgered, it was not her style.

'I am.' She accepted his tribute. 'I'm lots of things. I was captain of hockey at school. I have cold feet. I cry easily but I am as hard as the nose cone of a rocket, so begin.'

194

'Ah.' Edmund squeezed her hand. He'd been pretty lonely lying here since Mustafa brought him in the ambulance. 'I love you,' he said. It was probably true, he thought, he had loved, perhaps still loved, Poppy but there were so many no-go areas in the girl, so much privacy, so much from which he had been excluded. Venetia on the other hand was much easier to love. She might be hard compared with Poppy but she was as clear as a bell, an open book (any more clichés? whispered Poppy's vanished persona).

'Tell all, don't edit.' Venetia jerked him back into her orbit.

'Of course not,' said Edmund, who proposed to do precisely that. 'I'll start.'

'Right.' She was alert.

'You know about the job? Yes. Well, it went quite well, very well allowing for the fact that I've never dealt with non-Europeans. My opposite number here is called Mustafa, very friendly fellow, you'll like him. I got the hang of the set-up, what the Tourist Board's proposals are. The Minister took me out to lunch and a swim by the Roman city. You might like him, he makes a good impression.'

'Did Poppy go with you?'

'I thought it better to leave her behind. I needed to concentrate on work.'

'What did she do?'

'Amused herself, I suppose. There was a pool at the hotel.' No need to mention its emptiness.

'That must have been when she bought the postcard.'

'What postcard?'

'Never mind, go on.'

'Well, I dealt with the tourist officials and got the picture, where they will have a Cabana complex, what hotels there are, where they are building more, the stadium, how many tours they will accommodate at a time, and so on. What hotel are you staying at, by the way?'

'I came straight here from the airport, I was so worried about you.'

'My darling, thank you.' Edmund held her hand. 'I'd better get you into one of the older hotels. The one they put us, me, I mean, in is not really finished, smells a bit of wet cement—'

Venetia laughed. 'Go on, don't bother about my hotel, get to the drama.'

'The drama, as you put it, is really very small.' Indeed as he talked,

195

holding Venetia's firm hand, gaining confidence from her presence, the hell of the preceding days was shrinking. 'After we had finished our business, Mustafa took me out with some friends.'

'Where was Poppy?'

'She wasn't feeling well, tummy upset, that sort of thing. The trots.' (How am I doing?) 'We did a round of the bars to get the local colour. I'm afraid the Arak round here is pretty potent.'

'You got pissed.'

'You could say that. Yes, not to put too fine a point on it, I drank too much.'

'Yes?' Venetia remembered somebody, who was it? Of course, Penelope in Harrods. 'Yes, go on.'

'Well then—' Edmund lowered his voice, pulled Venetia closer. 'It was rather, well very embarrassing.'

'Go on.'

'Mustafa's friends – come close, I don't want the whole world to hear.'

'I don't suppose they understand English.'

'Even so. His friends, these two—' Edmund searched for a word, unwilling to call the boys boys. 'These two chaps started making advances to me.'

'Were they pretty?'

'Darling! They were boys.' Hell, it had slipped out.

'What did they do? Did they fondle your cock?'

'Venetia!' Edmund closed his eyes, remembering the shocked delight, the caressing, the smell of musk (surely people only smelt like that in pornographic books), the light brown skins, lovely, yes lovely black loosely waving hair. 'No, of course not.'

'Did you like it?' She seemed to be enjoying this.

'Of course I didn't.'

'Lots of people would.'

'I hope you don't take me for one of them.' Edmund genuinely huffy, caught Venetia's eye, saw she was laughing. 'Because I'm not.' He dismissed the experience to the realm of non-event. If in future years there were moments of sexual nostalgia or plain reminiscent lust he would be able to handle them.

'So what happened?' Venetia felt vaguely disappointed.

'I am afraid when I got back to the hotel I simply passed out.'

'Was Poppy better by then? Stopped trotting, no more squitters?'

'She was asleep. She was quite all right next day. We spent the day

together, swam, went out to the oasis, picnicked, that sort of thing.'
(Made love.)

'Was that when you had the accident?'

'No. It's pretty idiotic. I broke it falling over a chair, Poppy—'
Edmund stopped. This was too painful.

'Poppy what?' Venetia pressed him, 'Did she get drunk or what?'

'I don't think I – I don't like to—'

'Come on, darling, she's gone, left you in the lurch, tell me what
happened. She got drunk and then what? No need to protect her to
me.'

Edmund drew a deep breath. If anybody ever needed protecting it
had been Poppy. 'She was throwing herself about, making a scene,
she abused me for leaving her alone while I did my job.' He supposed
this sounded all right to anybody who did not know Poppy.

'You couldn't help that.' Venetia was indignant for him. 'So what
did she do? She must have known you were here to work.'

'Well,' Edmund passed a hand across his eyes, brushed back his
fine fair hair, 'I tried to calm her. She got hold of a chair and I tripped
over it and my leg snapped. I heard the bone go.'

'Oh poor you. She hit you with it.'

'Stupid isn't it, actually she—'

'What a vicious thing to do, break your leg.' Venetia sat holding
Edmund's hand. 'What a vile bitch,' she exclaimed.

Edmund squeezed her fingers, she squeezed his back.

Edmund felt drained, exhausted.

Let it rest there, what did it matter now, she was gone, wasn't she,
whatever he said would twist on his tongue.

'I don't see why you should linger here.' Venetia switched her
mind to more immediate matters. 'I am sure I can get you home on a
stretcher or in a wheelchair. I take it your company insured you?'

'Oh yes.' Edmund lay now with his eyes closed. If Venetia could
swallow the leg-breaking episode, absorb the boys, what were a few
lies on an insurance form?

'Leave it all to me, I'll get us home in no time.' She sounded
incredibly competent. But Edmund still felt a niggle of fear.

'What I told you, the – er – party with Mustafa, the Arak and—'

'Don't worry, love. I don't mind boys, it shows you have a
rounded personality. Getting pissed released your nascent inhibitions, it was healthy to seduce the little catamites.'

'But I—' Was a trap yawning?

'We'll keep it between you and me, it would not have happened if Poppy hadn't kidnapped you, forced you to bring her here and broken your leg—'

Edmund could not but admire Venetia, she was so sincere, sitting there in that lovely dress, fixing him with those baby blue eyes, holding his hand between both of hers, those hands which had Superglued the flies of all his trousers. No mention of that, he observed ironically. She was still talking: 'It was all that bloody girl – anything that happened – not your fault at all.' She absolved him.

Edmund was glad to have the ordeal over.

In future years the tale of the broken leg would be perfected by Venetia, dined out on. His slight rather arcane limp which added so much to his attraction would be blamed on Poppy, boost his reputation.

41

Poppy waking saw Willy standing with his back to her staring out of the window, his attitude one of leashed energy.

'Are you fretting to get back to your pigs?' She sat up pulling his cardigan round her shoulders.

Willy turned round. Earlier he had watched her asleep, calculated the length of the eyelashes which shaded her bruised eye, minimising by their length the damage. The backs of her hands which had been purple had faded to green blotched with yellow. She no longer seemed to feel her injured collarbone.

'I was watching the harbour.'

'Thinking of your pigs.'

'Yes,' said Willy, 'among other things.'

'We must find out when we can get seats on a plane then. The storm is over, isn't it?'

'Yes, all over.' Willy looked down at placid water mirroring the ships and boats barely rocking, a group of resting seagulls. We are no longer prisoners, he thought regretfully. 'I went down earlier, the streets are drying up, we could look round the town when we've found a plane, booked our seats,' he said.

'Why not?'

Without the storm to pen them in there was constraint between them. Willy felt resentful. While sleeping she had distanced herself from him, as though forgetting their shared delight.

They went down the stairs to the lobby – the lifts were still out of order – and joined the people clamouring round a harassed airways official attempting to make himself heard above a polyglot hubbub.

'Nothing will get sorted out for ages, let's find a café.' He drew her out into the street.

From a stall Willy bought figs. 'We can eat these with our breakfast. You like figs?'

'Yes.' She remembered the figs she had eaten that first morning while Mustafa watched her, waiting for Edmund to appear in the half-made garden by the empty pool of that cement-stinking hotel.

They found a café, sat at a table in the sun. Willy ordered coffee and rolls. Poppy put on her dark glasses.

Willy peeled the figs, Poppy watched his fingers, very different from Edmund's, which were strong and hairy even though he was such a fair man. For so dark a man Willy, apart from his thick hair, was remarkably hairless. She remembered her father's voice, 'Can't stand hirsute men.' He had been referring to Edmund though he had not said so specifically. Willy looked up, caught her eye, smiled.

'I was thinking of my father.'

'Tell me about him.' Willy shared out the figs, putting the ripest on her plate, wondering whether, were he a painter, he would be able to capture the nuances between the peeled fruit and her bruised hands.

'I know so little about him.'

'You loved him?' Willy remembered her at the funeral, solitary in the front pew beside the coffin.

'Yes, I suppose I did. I think I love him now. Before, I had such awful guilt.'

'Oh?'

'He could not stand Edmund Platt.'

(So that's the bastard's name.)

Poppy bit into a fig, swallowed. 'Delicious, much nicer peeled. I raked the flesh from the skin with my teeth before. Dad so disliked Edmund that whenever we met we either quarrelled or we talked of things that didn't matter to either of us. If I'd known—'

'Yes?'

'If I'd known Dad was such a gambler I could have learned a lot from him. He was always away when I was small. I realise now he was at the races. He sent me postcards from Brighton, Chepstow, Newcastle, York, Liverpool, Epsom; he was racing mad. I am called after a horse which won the Oaks, Poppaea.'

Willy laughed.

Poppy grinned.

'My favourite pig is called Mrs Future; some damn fool knowbester told me, "There's no future in pig farming,"' said Willy.

'Good for you.' Poppy took another fig, helped herself to coffee. 'I would like to know who Dad went to the races with,' she said.

'Why particularly?' Willy took the fruit from her and peeled it.

'He seems to have had friends who left him money when they died. Women.'

'Ah.'

'They must have been old, older than him, because women live longer than men and a number of these ladies made—'

'Wills in his favour?'

'They remembered him. He called them Life's Dividends. His solicitor, Anthony Green, let that slip or the bank manager, I forget which now. What I wondered was whether—'

'He slept with them?'

'Well, yes.'

'Does it matter? Is that to do with your feeling guilt?'

'No, no. I feel guilt because I never talked to him properly, because I excluded him from my life, was not interested in his, because I refused to listen to him when he was right.' (So she agrees he was right.) 'Because if I had not been so pig-headed and selfish I could have known him, been friends with him, loved him.'

'You might even have gone to the races with him.' Willy, laughing now, watched her.

'Exactly,' Poppy put down her cup, 'even if he didn't take me racing I could have known him. At his funeral complete strangers came up to me, said they loved him, met him at the races, or that he used to take their aunt or someone they knew racing. I'd never met any of these people, hadn't the remotest notion who they were, didn't know their names, was too embarrassed to ask. I felt a fool, a stranger, me, his daughter. That girl with the funny hair who works for Fergus Furnival knew him, was fond of him, said he marked her card for her at the races and even an old lady who lent me her coat knew him.'

'My aunt Calypso.'

'Of course. She is your aunt.' Poppy looked at Willy as though he might turn suddenly into his aunt. 'She knew Dad. She'd advised him when he bought my dress. She guessed that I wondered about all those ladies, she said something to the effect of not being in that league—'

'She wouldn't be. If she can't have my uncle Hector she doesn't want anybody.' And if I can't have this girl I don't want anybody, Willy thought savagely. 'I do not feel you have more reason than most to feel guilty,' he watched her covertly.

'Well, I do. I would like things to have been different.'

'Vain regrets.'

'I would like this minute to hear him say "I told you so",' she exclaimed.

'Retrospective generosity.'

'You are mocking my guilt.'

'My aunt could probably tell you about your father, she would give a fair picture.'

Poppy swallowed the last of her coffee, looked across the pavement at the passing traffic, did not answer. Would it or would it not be a good thing to know Dad? 'He left me a letter,' she said, 'more of a note really.'

Willy did not enquire its contents.

'You are anxious to get back to Mrs Future.' Poppy turned towards him. 'We had better see about a plane.' She stood up, putting an end to the conversation.

Willy paid the bill. 'And where will you go?' he asked. 'Your flat or your father's house?'

'Neither,' Poppy exclaimed before she could stop herself. The thought of the flat she had shared with Edmund horrified her. 'I have rented Dad's house to Fergus Furnival,' she said, 'I can't go there.'

'Job?'

'I chucked it when Dad died.'

'Why don't you,' Willy kept his voice level, walking back towards the hotel, 'stay with my aunt. It's just an idea, while you make up your mind. She will like to have you.' (She will because she is fond of me.) Then, as Poppy said nothing, he said, 'Stupid of me, you must have dozens of people you can go to, endless friends.'

'No, no I haven't.' Poppy stopped at a street corner as though she was interested in the people thronging the pavement, milling about them, crossing and recrossing the street, dodging the cars and carts, shouting, arguing, bargaining, jostling them as they stood, an alien pair. 'Edmund was clever at keeping me to himself,' she said. 'I liked it in a way but it means I have no intimate friends. I can't really tell you about Edmund but I'll try,' she said, standing close to Willy now, looking up in his face. 'I was in love with Edmund and I lived with him for years.' A fat man in a hurry bumped into her so that Willy put his arms round her to keep her balanced. 'Edmund drank too much.' Poppy spoke in a flat voice. 'Only on occasion but when he was on a bender he got rough. Why am I telling you this?' she cried sharply, then, not expecting an answer, went on. 'He started before we left London and he drank on the plane. When we arrived he carried on drinking. He went off without me on the first evening with Mustafa. That was when I met the cockroaches and after we'd run over the dog; it was lame. Then the next day he went off again, he was doing his job of course, he is an ambitious man, a beautiful man too. I said no I would not go with him, actually I don't think he asked me to, that was when the men were hanged—' Poppy clenched her fists on Willy's chest. 'They were strung up, literally strung up on the branch of a plane tree, I shall never— I couldn't speak of it to Edmund. It was too— Then afterwards the next day we tried or I tried, perhaps we both did, to have a day together but I've never felt so apart from anybody. Poor Edmund, it was a pretty awful day for him, he was hungover and stuffed to the eyeballs with shock at what he had done the night before. He had buggered two Arab boys – I know, when in Rome, but you don't know Edmund, he's pure, he was terribly shocked. Well, I did not mind because by that time I knew what I'd really known for ages, that anything with Edmund was over, that I didn't love him, that I'd only come to North Africa to annoy Venetia, so why should I mind? Of course when he first left me for Venetia I was mortified, humiliated but by then I'd realised I'd been freed. But Edmund felt so guilty, so ashamed, he wallowed in shame like a born-again Baptist. He'd enjoyed himself, these Arab boys are lovely, look around you. That evening he got drunk again and rough – well, violent. That's how I got my black eye and so on, my heel had been trodden on earlier in the crush at the hanging. Where was I? Oh yes, he was quite anxious to kill me and I was frightened, he's big.' Poppy paused, looking up into Willy's face, oblivious of the crowd about them scurrying about their business like ants or strolling slowly, in discussion. 'He was coming at me again so I grabbed a chair to put it between us and he fell over it. His leg cracked like a whip. That's what happened. I did not intend to break his leg. He screamed, I sent for a doctor, an ambulance and for Mustafa. They got him to hospital. I sent a cable to Venetia. She really wants him. I packed my bag and caught the first plane out. Oh Willy, I would so dearly love to tell this to Dad, it would have made him so happy!' She looked round at the crowded pavement. 'What a place to tell you, how extraordinary. I bet Mrs Future would never do anything so foolish.' She tried to laugh.

Willy started her walking. Keep calm, keep sane, he told himself. Put off the garroting until you have nothing else to do. 'We had better get you on to the plane,' he said, 'I am taking you to stay with Calypso.' He led her back to the hotel. Some day, if she wanted to, she could elucidate the little matters of cockroaches, lame dogs, hangings, what mattered was that she had unbottled, let it come pouring out. They went up to their room in the lift which was working again.

As they crowded into the lift Poppy said, 'I was boasting when I told you before that I broke Edmund's leg, actually I was scared stiff, just trying to fend him off. The first way I told you made me sound quite brave and aggressive. I wasn't.'

'Of course not,' said Willy, amused by the expressions of their fellow travellers pretending not to listen. 'I think if your father were alive and you were a racehorse he would put his shirt on you,' he said.

42

'Where do you want to go?' asked Victor as they got near London. 'Where are you living these days?' It made him feel peculiar not to know where Penelope lived, it was embarrassing having to ask.

Penelope did not answer, perhaps she had not heard, she was probably living with some man she would rather he did not know about. Whoever it was had a lot to answer for, letting her go off by herself to have a lonely accident, he should cherish Penelope better, prevent her risking her life, almost dying of exposure. Penelope's predicament in the empty farm grew larger in imagination as anger of her imaginary lover's behaviour stirred his loins, making him bold. 'Come and have something to eat with me before I drop you off,' he suggested, 'or are you expected?'

'I am not expected.'

'So you will come?'

'Yes, I will.'

'Good,' said Victor, pleased. 'We will buy something to cook on our way. I haven't got much in the flat. What would you like?'

They discussed possibilities and methods of cooking as Victor drove. Penelope was surprised at some of Victor's suggestions. When they had been married he had been barely capable of boiling an egg unsupervised, but now he was suggesting barbecued lamb chops, veal Marengo, Italian beef, a variety of risottos and several quite sophisticated pastas. Uneasily she wondered whether she had missed some clue on her clandestine visits to the flat, whether there were not, after all, another woman. 'I think I'd like fish,' she said, 'is our fish shop still there? I hanker for shellfish; what about mussels?'

'Of course it is.' Victor drove through the streets in silence until they reached the fish shop, drew to a stop by the kerb.

'Why,' cried the fish lady at the sight of Penelope, 'it's little Mrs Lucas! How are you, ducks?' She trotted across the pavement in her white overall and fur boots. 'Where have you been this long time? Nice to see you.' She looked through Victor.

'Super,' said Penelope, 'lovely to see *you*. We want something delicious for supper, what do you suggest?'

Victor was reminded that one of Penelope's talents was to deceive people into believing that they made decisions for her.

'You did like mussels when you had time to prepare them; have you time? Eating them tonight are you?' The fish lady ignored Victor sitting at the wheel, leaning into the car, speaking past him at Penelope. 'I've some lovely sole, or there's halibut.'

'Let's have mussels. Would you like mussels, Victor?'

'Yes,' said Victor averting his gaze from the sad black lobsters and the bowls of trout on the marble counter. 'Yes, I would.'

'I've sprained my ankle,' said Penelope to the fish lady, 'slipped and twisted it, look it's all strapped up.' She raised her foot.

'Shame,' said the fish lady. 'You should be more careful, ducks.' She looked balefully at Victor, blaming him.

'I'd better get out and pay,' said Victor. 'Don't move, darling, rest your foot.' The fish lady would talk to Penelope all night if allowed.

'Okay,' said Penelope, 'buy lots, let's make pigs of ourselves.'

Victor followed the fish lady into the shop, watched her weigh the mussels.

'How's the trout then?' she asked *sotto voce*, dropping two final mussels into the scales, ping, ping.

'What?'

'You know,' she kept her voice low, 'the one that was alive, gave you such a turn, ate it did you?'

'Certainly not,' said Victor annoyed. 'It's living wild in a stream in Berkshire.'

The fish lady laughed. Victor had never before seen her laugh. 'You're a writer, aren't you?' She spoke kindly as though he were mentally retarded. 'There's your supper.' She poured the mussels from the scoop into a plastic bag. 'Enjoy them.' She twisted a fastener round the bag's neck with strong fingers.

Victor paid.

Getting back into the car he said, 'She's glad to see you, she's always very offhand with me.'

'She doesn't like men,' said Penelope. Victor supposed this was probably true. 'She seemed to know I write, how the hell does she know?'

'Standing in that shop all day she must get to know everything there is to know about the neighbours.' Penelope remembered a month or two before, when buying a modest mackerel prior to snooping in Victor's flat, she had told the fish lady that Victor was writing a novel. 'We need brown bread and butter, a lemon, parsley and white wine,' she said.

'I've got wine,' said Victor. 'If you wait I'll run to the supermarket. Fend off traffic wardens while I'm gone.'

'Okay.' Penelope watched Victor run, his thin legs streaking down the street.

The fish lady crossed the pavement, leaving a customer to wait. 'Never told you how he bought a live trout, did I? He tells me it's alive and well in a stream in Berkshire.'

'I know it is,' said Penelope.

'Oh,' said the fish lady, disappointed.

'You've got customers waiting,' said Penelope repressively and sat waiting for Victor's return from the supermarket. But as they drove away she waved and the fish lady waved back.

Victor helped Penelope up the stairs, his free arm round her waist, their parcels gripped under his other arm. Reaching the top floor he released her, fumbled for his key. 'Same old flat,' he said, standing aside to let her pass.

'That tap still drips.' Penelope hobbled across the hallway into the bathroom to give it a twist.

'Sorry,' said Victor.

'I rather like it,' said Penelope standing with her back to him.

Victor smiled to himself, tipped the mussels into the sink in the kitchen and started scrubbing them.

Penelope came out of the bathroom, pulled the kitchen stool to the sink, perched on it to ease her ankle and joined in the scrubbing of mussels.

'If I had a carrot, an onion and garlic we could have them Marinières, I've got bay and thyme, I've run low on veg, should have thought of it in the supermarket.' He had raced round the shelves, hurried through the checkout, fearful that left alone Penelope would take the opportunity to scarper.

'Do you know how to cook Moules Marinières?' Penelope looked at Victor quizzically.

'Yes.'

'Been giving dinner parties?' Who had he been cooking Moules Marinières for or with, who had taught him all these new dishes? Penelope jerked the plug out of the sink to change the water before Victor was ready. He dropped the knife he was using and, searching for it among the mussels, managed to slice his finger. 'Sorry,' said Penelope, watching him suck it.

Victor, sucking his finger, considered whether to say no he never gave parties or yes he often did, neither reply being exactly true although in a sense he was giving a dinner party tapping it on to his typewriter. He had not thought to give his characters either Moules à la Béchamel which they were preparing now or Moules Marinières. It was an idea he must consider. The problem had been whether Penelope, who in the book was tentatively called Louise, should be murdered before or after dinner.

'You will have to make the sauce,' he said, 'unless you want my blood in it. Sauce Béchamel tinged with blood.'

206

Penelope limped round the kitchen finding the ingredients. Victor put a large pan on the stove, adding a cupful of water, transferred the mussels into the pan. While they opened in the heat (poor things, what a way to die) he drew the cork from a bottle of wine, poured a glass for Penelope and one for himself.

'Penelope' he toasted her.

'Victor,' at one time she would have added darling. 'For God's sake, put an Elastoplast on it,' she said.

They concentrated on their cooking, eating the mussels straight from the stove. Penelope's sauce was delicious. 'I read your article about that funeral,' she said, 'it was very good. It made the affair moving and dignified when it could have sounded way out and funny. I thought it gave Fergus a jolly good puff without a hint of vulgarity.'

'Thank you.' Victor watched his ex-wife, comparing her with Poppy who had since the funeral occupied the forefront of his mind, had even twice wandered into his dreams. 'I took part,' he said.

'What do you mean?'

'I was a mute, I helped shoulder the coffin, and afterwards I organised the food. I got it from Singh in Shepherds Bush. Do you remember him? I got lashings of champagne on sale or return for booze. I don't think there was much left over to return, it was quite a party.'

'I haven't seen Singh for ages.' Penelope reached for the bottle to refill her glass. 'Saw him in the street once.' ('What do you want to leave Victor for, silly girl?') 'Tell me more. What part does that girl who strapped my ankle up play in Fergus's outfit, is she or are all those girls his mistresses?'

'I think they just look after the horses. I got the impression—'

'Yes?'

'That Fergus was interested in Poppy—' said Victor reluctantly.

'The corpse's daughter?'

'Bob Carew, whose funeral it was, his daughter, yes,' said Victor coolly. His ex-wife's nomenclature, though technically correct, seemed rather offensive.

'So you are interested in Poppy, too.' With feline agility Penelope made the deduction.

'I hardly know her,' said Victor who was out of practice with Penelope.

'You sound as if you did.' Penelope wiped her plate with a piece of

207

bread.

'Have you finished with Fergus?' asked Victor catching up, rather enjoying this.

'Oh, Fergus was just a hop, skip and a jump,' said Penelope, dismissing Fergus. 'We never ate enough of these things.' She dipped her bread into the last of the sauce. 'Did we?'

Victor got up and peered out of the window along the parapet. It had grown dark while they had supper, Penelope had switched on the lamp. 'They roost here now,' he stretched his neck to catch a glimpse of the pigeons, 'I rather like it.'

Penelope remembered being waked by the birds' mating calls all year round, pigeons' sex life, similar to humans, is not restricted to the spring.

'I am writing a novel,' said Victor.

'I heard that you had one accepted,' said Penelope. 'Congratulations. Which one is it? I was afraid to ask.'

'The one about us.'

'Oh.'

'In the one I am working on now I murder you.'

'Should I be flattered? Are you getting a good advance? Who is your publisher?'

'Sean Connor.'

'Julia's beau? Are they getting married? You and she finished your little trot together?'

'What a lot you know,' said Victor, wondering whether Poppy Carew gathered gossip as Penelope did almost with the speed of light. 'I am going to wash the dishes,' he said. 'I can't stand getting up to a mess in the morning, it puts me off work. Why don't you rest your foot?'

'Thanks, I will.' She watched Victor collect the used plates; he had become positively old-maidish under somebody's influence or was it living alone? Limping, she went to the bathroom to wash her sticky fingers and then into the bedroom to look out of the back window at the anonymous backs of the houses in the next street. There had been times when it was possible to catch glimpses of other people's lives. Truncated from the waist, women rinsed their tights to hang them over the bath, men shaving in the early morning, shadows of both sexes running past landing windows down to the street. Once they had had to complain to the police during a noisy three-night-long party, on another they had listened to ghastly screams and been too

208

shy to do anything. On hot summer nights, there had been radios blaring from competing stations. She shut the window, bent to examine Victor's bedside books. Dylan Thomas, Graham Greene, Gabriel Garcia Marquez, Alice Walker. A notebook full of scribbled ideas, many crossed out and *How to Cheat at Cooking* by Delia Smith, much thumbed. Penelope smiled widely. Maybe, possibly, she would give him *One is Fun* by the same author.

When Victor had finished the dishes and put everything away, he took two glasses and the bottle of brandy given him the previous Christmas by an uncle and never used. They could finish the evening on the sofa watching the box.

But Penelope was not on the sofa. She was in the bedroom, in the bed.

'I've moved your clothes back to your side of the cupboard,' she said.

Victor put the brandy and glasses on the bedside table and undressed in silence.

I shall pretend she is Poppy Carew, he told himself, as he pulled his shirt over his head and dropped his trousers. I can use this situation in my novel, he thought, feeling rather agitated as he pulled off his socks.

Or, he can kill his wife Louise, *then* sleep with Poppy Carew, he thought as desire made him lusty. I still don't know what colour her bush is, but for the moment – he got into bed – this discovery ('Move over a bit, darling or I'll hurt your ankle,') must wait.

'Oh dear God,' said Victor, 'I am home.'

43

From the top of the hill Calypso looked down on the house she and Hector had restored. Faded pink brick striping through the wisteria leaves, yellow now after an early frost, a fit background for climbing roses, and the magnolia which still drenched the evening with the perfume of its flowers, its scent mingling with that of nicotiana planted under the windows. From the yard pigeons flew up with a clap to circle over the garden, then settle on the tiled roof, a variegated flock, the original too perfect white having long since mixed with wood pigeons.

When she walked down through the wood she would find the flagged terrace warm in the autumn sun, sit and plan for another year for the wood and garden, more bulbs, more flowers, more scented shrubs. Used now to living alone, she relished an uninterrupted evening. Before returning to the house she used field glasses to scan the wood, note where a tree ailed which might be replaced, where it would be politic to thin. Beyond the wood on the far side of a meadow between the trees and the road she would plant a triple line of lombardy poplars to reinforce her privacy. 'I can live to see them started,' she said to her dog, conscious of the slight stroke she had suffered three years before which left her limping a little when tired but otherwise unimpaired. The warning stroke had not been repeated. She thought of it only when one of her contemporaries died or at older friends' funerals. She had been aware of it during Bob Carew's service, he being much younger than she, and decided to miss the party after (a decision she now regretted) and then been distracted from morbid thought by Willy's entrancement with Poppy.

Swinging round to scan the wood towards the farm Calypso remembered with amusement that her son Hamish, summoned from the Highlands, had believed her dying but Willy, smuggling a tiny Mrs Future into the ward under his jacket, had mocked his older cousin saying 'Death blew her a kiss', making her laugh before being discovered by a nurse and sent packing.

'No sign,' said Calypso to the dog as she adjusted her binoculars to watch Willy's stockman going about his work with the pigs, 'no sign yet of the lovers.' She put away the field glasses, went down through the wood to lie on her garden chair, soak up the last of the sun's warmth beating up from the stone-flagged terrace, listen to the pigeons and the distant sound of Willy's bantam cocks crowing from the farm. She was none too pleased when, comfortably settled, eyes closed, face lifted to the sun, she heard a car arrive on the far side of the house.

I shall not answer the bell, she told herself, but the dog, giving her away, rushed barking into the house and out to the front to greet the visitor rapturously.

'Bloody animal.' Calypso lay still, hearing the bell ring, keeping her eyes closed, hoping whoever it was, seeing nobody but the dog, would, with luck, go away.

'Calypso?' a woman called. 'Are you there?'

Calypso did not answer.

'Your dog betrayed you.' Ros Lawrence came out on to the terrace through the French windows. 'Am I disturbing you?'

'Yes,' said Calypso, 'you are.'

'You are not doing anything,' said Ros, confirming some people's opinion that she was not all that bright. 'I'm sorry,' she pulled up a chair, 'I have come to you for help. For help,' she repeated distractedly, 'help.'

'You should know that I am the most unhelpful person of your acquaintance.' Calypso stressed the last word, lay looking up at her visitor who, although seated, gave the uncomfortable impression of hovering above her.

'And your advice.' Ros looked down at Calypso, irritatingly reposeful. 'Your advice.'

'I never give advice.'

'I know. Most people volunteer, press it, that's why I have come to you.'

'Oh Lord.' Calypso swung her legs off her long chair. 'Come indoors.' She did not wish to share the loveliness of her terrace. Ros followed her into the drawing room. Relieved of her weight, the wicker chair on which she had briefly sat creaked in relief.

'Sit down if you can find a clean space.' Calypso waved at chairs and sofa. 'Dog hairs everywhere, mud, pig mess—'

'Shall I go away?' Ros drooped. She looked round Calypso's beautiful speckless room, no trace of dog hair anywhere. 'I can see I'm not wanted, not welcome.' She accepted the hint, refused to take it.

'I'll get you a drink, sit down.'

Calypso left the room, followed by the dog. 'I shall send you to the Lost Dogs Home,' she hissed at the wagging animal. 'You may like uninvited guests, casual droppers-in, I don't. I shall send you back to Hamish, he had no business to give you to me. He knows I don't like dogs. Why must he interfere? I don't need guarding, I don't need protection, you are too soppy anyway. I never had all these people charging in before you came. I lay doggo until they went away.' Resentfully Calypso put the whisky decanter and glasses on a tray, filled a jug of water, plopped in ice. She carried it back to the drawing room where Ros sat perched on the edge of an armchair in woeful silence.

'Strong or weak?' Calypso asked.

'Strong,' said Ros, 'please.'

Calypso poured the drinks, handed Ros hers, sat opposite, sipped, waited. Ros, recently remarried after being widowed, was now presumably regretting it.

'Aren't you going to ask me what the matter is?' Ros spoke with barely suppressed agitation.

'No,' said Calypso. 'You may later regret telling me.'

'I have to tell someone. Henry won't listen, he says—'

Calypso sipped her drink. The dog now sat with his back to her, watching Ros with more sympathy than she. She kicked him gently with her toe. There was much to be said for the Catholic Church, a captive priest in a confessional under holy oath of secrecy, she thought, watching the younger woman. If not the new husband what could it be? She was not overly interested.

'I have made a complete and utter fool of myself and alienated my son,' cried Ros in violent anguish, 'my only child.'

'Easy done.' (So it's her son.) Calypso remembered remarks she would have rather left unsaid, made over the years to Hamish. 'We are all guilty.'

'He's my only child, Calypso. It's Fergus, you know what his father was like, Fergus is very like him.'

'Of course, Fergus.' The father had been notoriously irritable but who could blame him, married to Ros. 'How is he? I went to Bob Carew's funeral. I have asked Hamish to have him and those super horses for me when it's my turn. I was impressed, I hope he will be successful. The times call for someone like him.' Calypso forced herself to be kind. 'He has style.'

'Thank you.' Ros drank her whisky, gazed round the room, jealously admiring the older woman's possessions, wondered now why she had come, wished she hadn't. Her pain returned with a rush. 'What am I to do?' she shouted, almost choking in agitation. 'What – am I – to do?'

Calypso raised her eyebrows.

Ros finished her drink, put down the empty glass, half rose to go. 'I should not have come to bother you.' She sank back in the chair.

'No bother,' Calypso lied politely.

Ros leant towards Calypso. 'Fergus has a child,' she enunciated painfully, 'it's there in the house he's rented from the Carew girl. He has the house and the stables, his horses, the hearse of course, and three girl grooms – Henry let him use his name as a reference for the Carews' lawyer – one of the girls has a baby!' Ros waited for Calypso to say something. Calypso stayed quiet. Ros continued: 'It's beautiful, quite beautiful. The mother is Mary Mowbray, you know who I mean, her father Nicholas used to breed horses.' Again Ros waited for Calypso to say something. Calypso, no baby lover, made no comment. Ros went on. 'The child is called Barnaby. He is lovely, Calypso. Fergus refers to him as Jesus, it's a disgusting joke. You look puzzled?'

'I am.'

'Apparently the mother Mary went to Spain and returned with the baby. She had a friend there called Joseph.'

Still Calypso remained silent.

Ros gasped, trying to restrain tears. 'It's the spitting image of Fergus at the same age and of his father as a baby. I am not inventing,' Ros shouted as though Calypso had accused her. Her tears began to fall.

Calypso reached for a box of tissues from the table beside her, handed one to Ros, on second thoughts passed her the box.

'Thanks.' Ros wiped her eyes, pulled a bunch of tissues from the box. 'The thing is, Fergus seemed to have no idea. The girl had not told him. Can you believe it? I feel, oh God, I feel such a fool. I shouted at him, told him the baby is his, bellowed at him about the strength of the Furnival genes—'

Calypso burst out laughing. 'Sorry.' She swallowed her laughter. 'Sorry.'

'Well may you laugh,' cried Ros in anguish. 'I would laugh if this happened to anyone else, but it's my grandchild. I don't suppose Fergus will ever speak to me again. Why couldn't I keep my trap shut?'

Why indeed, thought Calypso, interested in spite of herself.

Still Ros wept. 'Henry is no help, he says a century ago there might have been dozens of tiny Furnivals scattered round the parish. Thank God for contraception. What am I to *do*?' Blowing her nose, Ros stared at Calypso.

'Quite a surprise for Fergus,' said Calypso dryly.

'It was, it was. What am I to do?'

'Oh, don't ask me,' said Calypso, bored by the repetitions. 'I can't

213

give advice. I try hard not to. I remember how tiresome and interfering my family were when I was young. Unsought advice is against my principles.'

'I'm seeking it—'

'Fergus isn't.'

'You are *not* helping me,' cried Ros as though Calypso had offered to. 'I know I should not have interfered but I did – I did.'

Surreptitiously Calypso looked at her watch. She always meant to time Ros's stream of complaint. This was a good opportunity. No need to actually listen, just sit and let it flow, she had heard the gist; Ros could only repeat what she had already told with embellishments.

As far as I can remember, Calypso thought, on previous occasions it took a good half hour before she ran out of puff when she was complaining about Fergus's father, his foul temper and infidelities. One had a certain sympathy for the man. Calypso lowered her eyes, suppressed a smile. Of course this was a little different. The girl Mary was a character worthy of investigation and Fergus must be wonderfully short of vanity not to recognise himself in the child. There were men without vanity; Hector, for instance, had always been a man unaware of his looks. Ah, Hector, Calypso slid into thoughts of Hector. Hector's lovely voice. Now Ros, pitching into her lament, had a very trying voice. She had had enough of this feast of boredom.

I wish she'd go away, thought Calypso, shrinking from Ros's dilemma, retreating into her protective thoughts. (We should have planted more sycamores, she thought, they are underestimated trees, they grow fast.) Why should I get involved with Ros's troubles? I hardly know her. I can't help her, it's bad enough to have to have Willy chasing wild goose after Poppy, he may get badly hurt, I shall mind that very much, my equilibrium will be upset. What a bore this woman is. 'Have some more whisky.' Grudgingly she remembered her manners.

'No, no thanks. I must go. You've been very kind, I knew you would help.'

'Not kind at all.' Nobody ever accused Calypso of lying.

'I suppose you're right.' Ros attributed words to Calypso. 'I have said too much. I will shut up and not interfere, let them work it out for themselves as you say. You are so right. I knew you would help me. You do though admit it's hard for me – my first grandchild?'

As far as you know, thought Calypso. 'Oh, Willy.' She jumped up as Willy came into the room. 'When did you get back?' Her relief at seeing him conjoining with the relief from the embarrassment of Ros showed plainly in her smile.

'Just arrived,' said Willy kissing her cheek. 'May I have a drink? Oh hullo.' He noticed Ros crouching now like a frightened partridge in the armchair, tissue at the ready. 'How do you do. Am I interrupting?'

'I am just leaving.' Ros sprang hastily up, put aside the box of tissues. 'I'm on my way.' She was embarrassed. 'Thank you, Calypso, for all your help.'

'It was nothing,' said Calypso gravely.

'I'll see you out.' Willy walked through the house with Ros, watched her drive away. 'What was all that about?' He returned to his aunt.

'Trouble.' She put Ros aside. 'Are you alone?'

'Alone.' Willy helped himself to a drink, patted the dog who was craving attention, sat in the chair vacated by Ros, stretched out his long legs, stared into his glass. Neither of them spoke.

The dog lay down with a sigh, laid his nose on his paws, watched. Calypso waited.

Willy put his drink aside, sat forward with his face in his hands. 'I had hoped,' he said presently, 'to bring her back here. I thought perhaps you would have her to stay, she didn't seem to have any place she wanted to go. I thought you wouldn't mind. I thought she'd agree to this—' He stretched out his hand, stroked the dog's head. 'But she changed her mind, decided not to, refused.'

'M-m-m,' murmured Calypso, 'm-m-m.'

'Well,' said Willy, jumping up, 'better see to the Futures,' false heartiness in his tone.

Calypso winced. 'Come to supper presently?' she suggested.

'Another night, but thank you. I have much to do after being away.'

'Of course. You must see to the Happy Hams. I haven't heard of anything going wrong but you must check.'

'I am poor company.' Willy apologised.

'Take the dog. He welcomes uninvited guests. He needs a run, he's in disgrace.'

Willy bent to kiss her, started to speak, thought better of it, walked away, his shoulders despondent.

215

'Go,' Calypso said to the dog, 'run after him, you dumb animal, he can do with your company. Go.'

The dog jumped up and ran after Willy, catching up with him on the edge of the wood. Calypso called, 'Take the dog, keep him for the night.'

Willy looked back across the garden. 'I remembered Mrs Future's aunt,' he shouted across the flower beds, 'and what happened there.'

Reminded of Mrs Future's aunt's malign act, Calypso laughed. 'So?'

'So I left her alone. I was afraid of rushing her.'

Willy and the dog disappeared into the wood. Calypso, resuming her place on the terrace, lay listening to the pigeons on the roof, the hum of the bees among the Michaelmas daisies. It was at odd moments like this that she most missed her dead husband whose family genes she thought with amusement seemed stronger in his nephew Willy than in his son Hamish. She had taken it for granted that Willy would find Poppy, hoped he would bring her back with him. She was curious to hear what had happened but too wise to ask. She did not need Ros's example to stress the inadvisability of family interference, however well meant.

44

In the train from Gatwick to Victoria, in the taxi to her flat, Poppy was ashamed of her vacillation. In Algiers she had agreed without reservation to Willy's suggestion that she should stay with his aunt. Looking out of the taxi window on to the wet streets of London and the umbrella-shuffling crowds, she felt again how easy to do what Willy suggested.

But in the plane things had become different. She had felt she needed to distance herself from him, go back to the flat she now hated, be alone to decide without pressure what, if anything, she wanted next.

In Algiers, wrapped about by the storm, she had jumped headlong into rapturous sexual pleasure.

In the foreign streets she had told Willy more about Edmund than she ever would in England. The circumstances of their meeting, the intimacy born of her injuries, the odd manner of their being together, had made her talk as strangers proverbially do in trains, safe in that there will be no future contact.

The trouble was that Willy had no intention of letting her go, for him their being together was no casual affair. If she only wanted him as a pleasure man he would rather back out than know her on such terms. 'All or nothing,' he had said. They had exchanged angry words on the plane sitting with trays of uneaten food in front of them, cocooned by the hum of engines, too close in their seats, unable to move apart, their very proximity a hindrance to calm discussion.

He had told her, turning towards her, his long legs cramped in the aircraft seat, his back half turned on a somnolent fellow traveller, that he had decided at her father's funeral that he loved her, that he must marry her, that this was, for him, final.

She had said, 'You did not tell me this in Algiers, it is ridiculous. When you saw me in the church you did not know me, we had not spoken, you could not know you loved me. It was pure imagination.' She shied away.

'It was and is love,' he said. 'A bolt.'

'Just an idea,' she scoffed.

'A great idea. I would call it inspiration.'

'Absurd,' she mocked.

'You have not found me absurd these last days and nights.'

'You gave me great pleasure,' she admitted stiffly.

'So?'

'Pleasure is not love.'

'The two are knit.'

'No.' She had loved Edmund, hadn't she? How to tell Willy about life with Edmund without giving herself and, incidentally, Edmund away. She had already said too much.

'You thought you loved that bloody man who beat you. I bet you never shared delight. You just persuaded yourself you loved him. *That* was imaginary.'

'It was not.'

'You have been happier with me than ever with him.'

She would not admit this, she was handling this all wrong, planes brought out the worst in her, had she not been sulky with Edmund on the outward flight? 'I have a lot to sort out, things to do. My father's business,' she had excused herself, trying to sound reasonable. 'I left home in a rush. I need to be alone. Why are you looking at me like that? What's so funny?' She was puzzled and irritated that in the midst of a serious desperate discussion Willy should start laughing.

'I may tell you some day. Not now. Okay, go ahead, be alone, sort yourself out, I'll wait.'

They had not parted happily.

The taxi stopped outside the flat. Poppy paid the man, stood with her bags on the wet and greasy pavement, nerved herself to use the key, climb up the steps. Inserting the key in the lock she noticed that a shop on the corner had changed hands in the short time she had been away, changing from a small grocery into a rather brash branch of a well-known bookmaker. Would Dad have called in there, did he place his bets by telephone or did he only bet on the course? As she unlocked the street door she thought she knew Willy better than Dad and damn Willy for laughing, curse his private joke. Resentfully she let the street door slam, crossed the dark and shabby hall to climb the stairs carrying her bag up one flight, up another flight and another to the top. Had he guessed, she wondered as she toiled up out of breath, her arms aching from the heavy bags, had he guessed what a rotten selfish lover Edmund had been, had he guessed from her joyful reaction that she had never known any better?

There are other fish, Willy Guthrie, she thought, as she searched her bag for the flat key. Where the hell has it got to, not lost, surely? Other fish such as slender intellectual Victor or Fergus, travelled, debonair, kind, enterprising – ah, here's the key – both of these had looked at her with interest, had shown their inclination and intention in their kiss. What had pig farmer Willy Guthrie got that they hadn't got? What had he to laugh about? She unlocked the flat door, pushed it rustling across uncollected mail littering the floor, slammed the door shut.

A dying bluebottle struggled buzzing on its back.

She had not shut the refrigerator door properly, it hummed as it had all her absent days, ice frosting down on to the tiled floor, a freezing reminder of useless activity during her travels.

The flat smelled stale and dry. Worse, it was permeated by Edmund.

Quickly she switched off the refrigerator, ran to open the

windows, began feverishly and at once searching the rooms for Edmund's belongings, throwing books, tapes, clothes, shoes, sports equipment into a heap, rummaging systematically through drawers and cupboards for anything, everything that was his. It was amazing what a lot of unvalued dross he had left, not feeling it worthy of Venetia Colyer. Off the wall came his Hockney print and a picture of the Lakes he had given her. Out of the drawers came clothes, from the kitchen plates, cups, saucepans, dishes he had contributed to their joint living, his tape recorder and radio from the bedroom.

While she exhausted herself limping about in a frenzy the fridge began to drip. She heated a knife over the gas on the cooker and prized ice from the sides of the cabinet, throwing chunks into the sink. From inside the fridge she snatched a lump of Cheddar cheese Edmund had bought. When? Weeks and weeks ago to make Welsh Rarebit. Threw it among his possessions. Yuk!

She found suitcases that were Edmund's, packed them with his things, crushed them shut, set them out on the landing. For the rest she heaped it on to his sheets, tying great bundles by the corners, heaving and dragging them out of the flat. Out, out, out.

She swept up their joint mail from the mat, sorted it, sat at the kitchen table, took pen, readdressed all Edmund's letters, bills and circulars c/o Venetia Colyer, ran downstairs and along the street to the pillar box and posted it.

Back in the flat she finished defrosting the fridge, wiped and swept the floors, shut the windows, turned on the bath.

While the bath filled she undressed, scattered drops of pine essence on the kitchen and bathroom floors, dolloped a generous gush into the bath, stepped in shakily exhausted, lay back in the fragrant delicious water, closed her eyes to appreciate relief and freedom. Opening her eyes minutes later she saw on the shelf above the bath Edmund's bottle of aftershave, leapt splashing out, snatched the bottle, threw open the window, cast the bottle out, heard it crash distantly in the street and a man shout, 'Oi!'

Back in the bath she dipped back so that her head too went under the water and all of Edmund in the flesh in the flat was washed away. But she knew as she dried her body and rubbed her hair dry that it was not so easy. Her eyes were used to the sight of Edmund, her ears attuned to his voice, her body habituated to fit with his.

The episode, she told herself, the episode with Willy was an episode, no more. Clambering into her lonely bed she felt as miserable and bereft as she had on the night that she heard that her father was dying. Halfway through the night she woke thinking she heard Willy's laughter and found some comfort in his amusement. Thinking of Willy she ached with desire. Unassuaged she lay awake until a blackbird sang in the dusty little square at the corner of the street.

45

Across the roofs the harvest moon and Orion were bright, there was a touch of frost. Poppy leant out of the window while the kettle boiled for coffee, craning to catch the first hint of sunrise.

She had slept for two hours.

Drinking her coffee she was uneasily aware of Edmund's possessions lurking on the landing as though threatening to re-enter the flat. She would not be truly rid of Edmund until she had removed his things.

Her car was in the country, parked where she had left it when Edmund had whisked her away from the wake. She must get down to Berkshire, retrieve the car, bring it to London, load it with Edmund's leavings, deliver them *chez* Venetia – hand them to the hall porter. There would be no need to meet Edmund or Venetia – and that would be that. *Finis.*

She shrank from the task.

Hungry, she searched the bread bin, finding half a loaf as hard as a brick, greening with mould. There was no butter, no milk, no sugar. She poured herself more coffee, drinking it bitter and black and thought what she must do. She needed a tonic.

In childhood should she sniff or grizzle or pretend illness when confronted by boredom, when she exaggerated the pains and inconveniences of her periods, Esmé would look at her with contempt and say, 'You need a tonic.'

The tonic was never forthcoming but the word had evolved in her childish mind something other, indeed the opposite of Esmé who damped the spirit. Esmé was not capable of producing a tonic for a tonic meant pleasure.

Dad's rare company exuded pleasure; it angered and frustrated Esmé. Since he was so rarely at home the benefit was presumably shared with his friends on the race course, with Life's Dividends, after she had left home to live with Edmund, in that remarkably comfortable and luxurious bed in the visitors' room. Poppy thought about the bed and smiled.

I need pleasure, she thought. A meal of pleasure, a creative bout, a crash course. There had been precious little pleasure of late with Edmund. If she admitted the truth it had always been a bit rare and if there was any going Edmund scoffed it.

The need was urgent. Drinking her bitter coffee, Poppy composed the prescription for the tonic. Agreeable company, laughter, frivolity, physical pleasure. A light diet and no commitment. A diet I can take for once without giving.

'I am sick of this eternal giving,' she said out loud, pushing the intrusive vision of Willy to the back of her mind. 'I want some fun, I want to laugh, I've had enough of love.'

She smacked the coffee cup down on the table, the bitter coffee jumped and spilled. She picked up the coffee pot and, opening the flat door, poured the gritty grounds over Edmund's things.

Inspiration brought her to the telephone. She looked Victor up in the book, discovering him among the many other Lucases hopefully awaiting her call. She dialled the number, promptly Victor answered. 'Hullo?'

'Victor? It's Poppy Carew, d'you remember me?'

'Of course.' He sounded drowsy. 'How are you?' Less enthusiastic than she expected.

'I'm fine. Sorry if it's too early, I've no idea of the time, I should have—' Disappointment in her voice.

'What is it? What can I – of course it's not too early, tell me—' He sounded now as she remembered him, kind, intelligent, caring.

'I'm interrupting your work.' (All writers work in the early morning, I've put my foot in it.)

'No, no, no I wasn't working.' He laughed. 'What's up? What can I do for you?'

She explained her predicament, wondered whether he was free, was doing nothing else, would he drive her to Berkshire to retrieve her car. She had this load of a 'friend's' things cluttering up the landing – actually blocking – she needed the car to transport them,

221

move them away. In spite of herself urgency crept into her voice, in a minute she would be whining.

'Why don't we load them into *my* car, drop them round at whoever's, then we'll go down and fetch *yours*. How would that be?' Victor suggested. 'Make a day of it, lunch in the country?'

'It's such a bore for you—' she demurred.

'Not at all, be round in a flash, 'bye.' He rang off, cutting short her thanks.

Poppy's stomach rumbled with hunger, her insides felt full of gas. She pulled on a sweater, took the few pounds she had left from her bag and ran downstairs. If quick she could run to the corner shop which would be opening at this hour to cherish local Indian and Pakistani neighbours on their way to work or coming off the night shifts, buy milk, bread, fresh coffee, sugar and butter and thus be able, when he arrived, to offer Victor breakfast, repay a little of his kindness in advance, staunch the aching void in her gut. It seemed a good idea. Who knows, she thought as she hurried along, it might be fun to have a whirl with Victor, see whether he lived up to the kiss he had planted at the wake. He might, she thought cheerfully, be even more skilled, more wonderful than Willy. She whistled as she walked in anticipation of Victor. Nice girls don't think these thoughts. She remembered the days of Esmé, mentally mimicked her. If so what else do they think about?

She was greeted by the shopkeepers, a Bengali family. Where had she been? Away on holiday? Ill?

'A Moslem country.'

'They did not treat you well.' Tender glances from under long lashes.

She made her purchases, paid Mr Bengali while Mrs Bengali packed them with delicate fingers into a carrier bag. Mr Bengali bewailed the passing of the rival shop into the hands of a chain of bookmakers. 'Temptation, temptation.' He rolled his eyes. 'Our savings will be tempted.' Poppy loved to hear about the savings which mounted with steady persistence, an example to all frugal, hardworking families.

'My father made his fortune on the horses. Don't worry, Mr Bengali, you will not be tempted.' She counted her change. Mr Bengali liked his customers to count their change. 'I must fly, see you tomorrow.' She set off, hurrying up the street. Often and often in the years of jogging with Edmund they had stopped at the shop to buy little cartons of orange juice to sip through straws as they walked the last hundred yards home.

Oh, Edmund!

She waited for the familiar pang, took note that it was faint and frail.

Getting better, nearly well.

As she reached her door Victor arrived in a smart car, stepped out smiling.

'You have a new car. Your literary success! Congratulations.' Poppy was delighted to see Victor, it had been an inspiration to phone him.

'It's mine. He's still got his old banger, we are going to sell it.' Penelope eased herself on to the pavement, careful still of her strapped ankle.

Poppy tried not to gape. What a turn up for the book.

'You haven't met my wife Penelope.' Victor happy, smiling.

'His ex-wife. He's writing a novel about how he murdered me.' Penelope beaming.

'What have you done to your foot?' I must say something. Poppy eased her Achilles tendon, still, now she thought of it, rather sore where the man at the hanging had trodden on it. Mercifully the black eye had quite faded.

'Sprained it. This the way up?' Penelope, using a stick, started up the steps. Even limping she was graceful, no wonder Victor—

'Where's all the stuff you have to move then?' Victor, proud of Penelope, bright eyes looking down at Poppy, friendly, brotherly, taking her parcels from her.

'The top floor, I'm afraid. Can you manage or would you like to wait here? I was going to offer you breakfast.'

'We've had ours, thanks. I can manage, it's nothing. Hurt like hell at the time but Victor rescued me, didn't you, darling?'

Penelope and Victor climbed the stairs following Poppy. She's got a neat little bum, thought Victor, but Penelope's has got more swing to it.

'We live on the top floor, too,' said Victor. 'Have you not had breakfast?'

'I can't remember when I ate last, on the plane, I suppose. I'm starving.'

'Where have you been? Nice holiday?' Penelope was untroubled by the stairs.

'North Africa. Not exactly a holiday.' What then? An experience, a nightmare? What?

'Oh.'

'Here we are, top floor at last.' Poppy found she was breathless, rather weak.

'Is this the stuff you have to move? All this?' Penelope poked with her stick.

'Er – yes.'

'You are throwing a lover out lock, stock—' Penelope approved.

'Er – just a minute, I'll let us into the flat – Oh God! I've locked myself out. Oh Christ, what a fool I am. The key is in my bag.' She felt she might panic, cry or something. She kicked the door.

'And the bag's inside the flat?'

'Yes. Oh bugger, my keys, the car keys, my cheque book.'

Penelope sat on the top step and laughed. Victor laughed too, then controlling himself said, 'It's not funny. She's hungry, poor little thing. I bet she's not properly up, has yet to clean her teeth and go to the lavatory. We shouldn't laugh. Who has a spare key?' he asked.

'Edmund.'

'The owner of all this?' Victor prodded a sheeted bundle with his toe.

'Yes.'

'Where does he live?'

'With Venetia Colyer.'

'Venetia!' Penelope stopped laughing. 'Good old Venetia, I know Venetia.' She did not speak particularly kindly. 'It's good riddance for you,' she said ambiguously. 'It is, I'm serious. It's another of Venetia's good turns.' Victor, grasping the situation, looked down his nose.

'Victor shall fetch the key, won't you, darling? Now what's the address, let me think.'

'Really I don't know – I can't – I don't think—'

'I remember where she lives, that posh block where somebody got raped.' Penelope told Victor the address. 'We will wait here, won't we, Poppy? Buck up love, rush. He might be out.'

Victor disappeared down the stairs. They heard the door slam and the car start up in the street.

'Don't look so miserable, this is fun,' said Penelope cheerfully.

'Not for me.' (Bang goes that tonic.)

'Serve them bloody right if Victor wakes them up.' Penelope was enjoying herself.

'He is probably jogging in the park, we always did.' Poppy momentarily forgot the broken leg.

'That's one thing you're spared. Don't be so woeful.'

'It's so stupid of me.'

'I think it's quite funny.'

'I don't.' Poppy sat beside Penelope on the top step. 'Do you mind if I drink some milk, I'm so empty.'

'Feel free. We had breakfast early. Funny that, usually I sleep late but these last few days, since Victor and I got back together, we've worked up such an appetite we wake starving. We get up, get breakfast then most times we climb straight back into bed, have a fuck and sleep again. It's making me feel so healthy!'

'Oh.' Poppy erased any tentative vision of a whirl with Victor.

'This morning,' said Penelope, 'you telephoned at the exact moment. We'd finished eating and not started again.'

Not finding a suitable reply Poppy opened her carton of milk, drank from it, wolfed some fresh bread.

'That better?' Penelope watched.

'Yes, thanks.' Poppy munched. There are lots of other fish, she told herself, the world is full of them; anyway Victor isn't all that terrific, he's too thin.

'If we want to pee we can pee on your sod's things,' suggested Penelope. 'I take it he is a sod?'

'I suppose he is – yes, on the whole – I hope it won't come to that.' Poppy thought Penelope looked able, indeed capable of carrying out her threat, that she would enjoy— 'How is Victor's trout?' she asked.

'You know Victor's trout?' Penelope was intrigued. 'It's very well, even I have been to see it.' Penelope minimised the first person, maximised her position as Victor's girl, his ex- (ludicrous to think of it) wife. 'Fancy you hearing about Victor's trout,' she said.

'I was there making arrangements for my father's funeral just after Victor had brought it down from London. Fergus and Victor had put it in the stream.'

'It's thanks to that fish we are together again. Really, to give her her due, it's thanks to Venetia.'

'How come?' How could anyone be grateful to Venetia? She was not the kind to inspire gratitude.

'Venetia and I met in the food hall at Harrods. She didn't mean to do me a good turn, quite the reverse—' Penelope, with many sidesteps and embellishments regaled Poppy with the *histoire* fish. She was still talking when the street door opened and they heard men's voices. Poppy jumped up. 'I wish I could disappear.' She was near panic.

'Don't be silly. You are throwing him out, aren't you?'

'Yes, but I—'

'He won't be drunk at this hour.'

'How d'you—'

'I've seen him about with you. Sticks out his lip. Warning signal. Venetia will limit his intake, she's a strong-minded lady. What's going on, why are they so slow?' Penelope leaned over the banister, peering down, her dark hair swinging down like seaweed in an ebb tide.

'Edmund has a broken tibia.' Remembering the circumstances of the break, Poppy broke into a nervous sweat and backed against the door of her flat.

'Here they come. He's got lovely hair, your discard.' Penelope looked down. 'He's tremendously good-looking, a bit passé perhaps. Struggling up with his crutches. One might get a bit tired of him. Okay, Victor?' she called.

'We're on our way,' shouted Victor from below. 'We have the key.'

'Why don't you bring the key up, then Edmund needn't bother. Poppy says he has a broken tibia.'

'Determined to deliver it himself.' Victor sounded not far off laughter.

'Oh.' Penelope drew back from the banister and looked at Poppy. 'Are you afraid of him?'

'Of course not,' lied Poppy.

Disbelieving, Penelope sniffed and went back to watching the slow progress below. 'One could spit on his head. Stump – hop – stump – hop – there's no need to make such heavy weather,' she jeered. 'I made it with my poor ankle.'

Edmund's head came into view as he climbed the last flight, putting his weight on his good leg, clutching the banister with his left hand, hopping with the crutch under his right arm, hopping one step at a time; Victor, following, carried the second crutch. Edmund's face was flushed with effort, his lower lip thrust out. He reached the landing, stood looking down at Poppy.

'Thanks.' There was a cold stone in her midriff.

'Here it is,' said Edmund out of breath.

Poppy took the key. 'It's fortunate Venetia has a lift.' Don't soften, don't look at him.

'Don't sneer.'

'I'm not sneering, just stating facts.' Stating facts was a favourite expression of Edmund's cast in her teeth over the years. Why am I being so utterly horrible? 'All this stuff is yours, I want to be rid of it.'

'You could have thrown it away, I don't need it,' said Edmund offhandedly.

'If I had thrown it away you would have wanted it. I foresaw weeks, months, years when you would come round to fetch it, one bit at a time.' Why be so bitchy? Edmund flushed angrily.

'Attaboy. Doesn't she know him well?' said Penelope in admiration, grinning at Victor.

'Don't be so militant feminist,' said Victor good-naturedly. 'We'd better start carrying it down, come on, darling.' He hoped to stop Penelope's mischievous trend, there was no necessity for more trouble. Poppy looked as if she might fall apart.

'Yes, you two do that,' said Edmund not taking his eyes off Poppy. 'I have to talk to Poppy.'

'But I don't want to talk.' Using the key, Poppy opened the flat door and tried to nip inside.

Before she could close the door Edmund stuck his plastered leg in it.

Penelope drew in her breath admiringly. Quite a fellow, clever blackmailer, to use the leg, a crutch, though safer, would not have had the same impact.

'Just a word,' said Edmund standing on his good leg, 'it won't take long.'

'Why doesn't she kick it?' Penelope whispered to Victor.

'Come on,' said Victor picking up the suitcases, 'come on, Penelope, help.' He started down the stairs.

Penelope looked at Poppy at bay in the doorway. 'You all right?'

'Yes.' Poppy stood keeping Edmund out, her face very white. She wished the door had a chain.

Edmund leaned against the door jamb, managing to keep his plastered leg in position.

Penelope shrugged, heaved up one of the sheeted bundles and

dropped it down the stairwell, listening until it plopped in the hall below. So successful was this manoeuvre that she repeated it until the landing was almost clear, Victor arriving back just in time to grab the radio and the last suitcase. 'Come down and help me load the car,' he said. 'You've broken quite enough.'

'Should I?' Penelope looked at Edmund and Poppy shadowed in the doorway.

'Yes, come on.' Victor pulled her away. 'Let them get it over with, it's best.'

With a last look at Poppy Penelope leaned her stomach across the banister, pushed off and slid away down out of sight. 'Whoopsie, here I come.'

'Mind your ankle,' Victor yelled, anxious, but admiring her juvenile behaviour. He hurried after her, jumping down three steps at a time, endangering his spidery legs.

'Poppy.' Edmund tried to reach her hand. 'Darling.'

'No.'

'Venetia's gobbling me up, Poppy.'

'Good.'

'It's not good. Save me. I want to come back, it was a terrible mistake.'

'I don't want you.'

'I love you.' (I really love her, I love her, I love her.)

'Nonsense,' said Poppy, trying to sound robust.

'I didn't mean to hurt you, I didn't know what I was doing—'

'And I did not mean to break your leg. I'm glad it's better. I apologise. Now please go, Edmund. Down the stairs.'

'You know you love me. You are naturally jealous of Venetia—'

'I'm not actually, that's all over. I wish her joy. I am grateful to her.'

'I want to marry you. I told you on the plane. You agreed.' Edmund reached out. Poppy drew back. 'You must remember.'

'I did *not* agree. Stupidly I tried not to be unkind. You wanted to marry me and call yourself Carew-Platt. Nastily I thought you wanted my money. Venetia has a lot more than me, Edmund, mine's peanuts compared to hers. Her father made washbasins and loos. With all the guilt in the world people wash more than ever. My father was a gambler who backed outsiders and doubles whatever that means—' Nervously Poppy gabbled, straining to be eloquent, to get through to Edmund once and for all. 'Why don't you marry

228

Venetia, keep a girlfriend round the corner? No, no, *not* me, not *me*, call yourself Colyer-Platt, that's what you'd like, it's much smarter.' Edmund winced. 'It's not on, Edmund, there's nothing doing. Nothing. Please go away.' (This is not frivolous. This isn't fun.)

'My darling—'

'I am not your darling. Go away, go back to Venetia, take all the mess you left here.' Poppy felt rising hysteria, she began to cry. 'I hope Venetia teaches you how to make love.'

'What did you say?' Edmund rocked forward glowering, managed to catch her arm as she put up a hand to wipe her tears.

'Stop, Edmund, you are hurting me.'

Edmund shook her, swinging her round by the arm, pulling her out on to the landing.

'I said – I hope – Venetia – teaches you – how to fuck. Ah!' Poppy yelled 'Ah! Ow!'

'That's quite enough of that.' Victor, reappearing, caught hold of Edmund and pulled him away from Poppy.

Losing his precarious balance Edmund swung round cracking the back of his hand against the door. 'Ouch!'

'Come away now. Downstairs,' said Victor placid but firm. 'Down we go.'

'I'm coming up,' shouted Penelope bounding up the stairs, forgetting her injured ankle. 'I'll stay with Poppy while you drive Edmund and his rubbish back to Venetia.'

'Okay,' said Victor leading Edmund down. They met on the landing. 'I'm afraid some of the things in the bundles are broken,' said Penelope to Edmund. 'There's a terrible mixed smell of after-shave and cheese.'

Clutching his shredded dignity, Edmund managed to ignore her.

46

Victor drove Penelope's car with Penelope beside him. Poppy sat in the back listening to the loverly chatter in the front seat. This was an altogether different Victor to the solitary loose-ended man she had first met, who had eyed her with appreciation and kissed her with lust. Reunited with Penelope he was more stable, less attractive.

If she had had any mind picture of Penelope before meeting her it would have been of an uncaring bitch whom Victor had quite rightly almost murdered. The Penelope who had helped in the ousting of Edmund was a girl she could be friends with, an ally.

Even when Penelope exclaimed, 'Watch out, you idiot, you are driving my car not your old banger,' when Victor tried to overtake a juggernaut on a bend, and Victor answered 'I'll murder you yet, just you wait', she gave the impression of affectionate marital give and take and clearly Victor's joke was not vindictive.

They were on their way to the country, Victor and Penelope to retrieve Victor's car and, as Penelope put it, take it to the knackers, and at the same time visit the now famous trout. They lightly toyed with the idea of buying another from a hatchery to keep it company.

Poppy was to visit her father's house and belatedly attend to dull business matters such as the lease and her inheritance. At Penelope's instigation she had packed an overnight bag and telephoned Fergus to apprise him of her plan. Mary, answering the phone, had said that Fergus was away on a job but why not stay the night? Poppy, demurring, ready to stay in the pub, had been overruled. 'Stay here.' Mary had been firm. 'Mrs Edwardes keeps the visitors' room ready for you, she says that's what you wanted.'

Shattered by the scene with Edmund, Poppy let her day be organised by others, allowed herself to drift. She would visit Anthony Green, find out what he had done about her father's house, get him to sell her flat, spare her the business details. Temporarily cocooned on the back seat of Penelope's car she put off decisions, let her mind wander. Watching the back of Victor's thin neck she tried to remember the spasm of attraction she had felt for him, looked forward to the rediscovery of Fergus, whose kiss at the wake had been if anything more ardent than Victor's, more demanding, more – she toyed with words to describe Fergus – masculine? macho? lusty? Sitting in Penelope's car, driving down the English motorway she blotted out the period with Willy. What had happened in Algiers seemed strangely improbable, so remote that it was as though it had not happened. I am frail, she thought wryly, I need a tonic; how grey the sky is compared to North Africa.

Victor, startled by the suggestion of an unpleasant death as presented by the juggernaut, drove with more circumspection. 'I was not showing off.' He squeezed Penelope's hand in her lap. 'A few weeks ago I wouldn't have minded dying. Now it seems crazy.'

'Sean Connor liked your book, that gave you hope.'

'What's the use of hope on your own?'

'I bet you were thrilled. I bet you went to bed with Julia. Do you know she jokes about my name, calls me Antelope?'

'Not exactly. I didn't go to bed with her, she only rhymes it with—'

'Only because she's fixed up with Sean. You did at one time, at least once. Confess.'

'What's once? All that's long ago. She gave me a cook book, that's all. Pretty innocent, it wasn't much.'

'I noticed the cook book,' said Penelope. 'I rather wondered about that. Who else,' she asked, her latent jealousy reviving, 'who else has there been while we've been apart. What other girls? What about Mary, she's bloody attractive, have you been making passes at her?'

'Don't be ridiculous,' Victor laughed, relieved that Penelope was not aware of his fleeting interest in Poppy Carew now sitting neutrally on the back seat. 'Mary was Fergus's province, she's never been known to look at anyone else. She doesn't seem to be attracted to anyone or anything other than the job nowadays.'

'What about the baby? What about that?'

'I can't say I'm much interested; it's said she went off to Spain and had a child by a wog. I dare say there's a story there if one grubbed about a bit.'

'Your journalistic mind,' she said. 'One notices the lack of interest.'

Victor did not like the tone in which Penelope said this nor the way she went on laughing. Uneasily he was reminded of the laughter in the bathroom above the kitchen that he and Fergus had listened to on the day he had found his darling caked in mud, her ankle sprained, having failed to catch Bolivar. Penelope and Mary had found something very comical to laugh about while Mary strapped up Penelope's injury.

'I don't ask who you have been having affairs with,' he said (I could not bear to know, I could not bear it). 'If we travel that road,' he said, 'we will only get hurt. Let's leave it, shall we?'

'Glad to.' Penelope drew the line on post mortems, perilous quagmires.

'That poor man.' In his happiness Victor was charitable. 'That poor Edmund of yours. He loves you still, Poppy,' he called over his shoulder.

Poppy on the back seat said 'Oh' doubtfully.

'He said Venetia's got cold feet,' said Victor, with Edmund's grumblings and moanings during the trip to Venetia's flat in mind.

'What does she have to be afraid of? She's got the bastard now and Poppy doesn't want him.' Penelope had little kindness to spare for Venetia.

'Not that kind. Apparently her feet are froggy, physically so.'

'Damp?'

'He said that in bed her feet are cold. He compared their temperature unfavourably with Poppy's. Her bottom too does not compare well.'

'Do you hear that, Poppy?' Penelope looked back, laughing.

'It seems Venetia is not nearly as snug to cuddle as Poppy.' Victor, disloyal to his own sex, elaborated. 'And she cries.'

'What has she to cry about?' asked Penelope.

'God knows, but it gets on his nerves. Sudden gushing tears. He says it's unnerving.'

'You got pretty pally in that short time.'

'A form of research. He chucks Poppy, saying he still loves her, and moves over to Venetia. It's of literary interest, but why?'

'Money,' Penelope suggested. 'Good old LSD?'

'Maybe. Useful for my novel anyway. I can give one of my less lovely characters chilled feet.' Victor and Penelope giggled. They forgot Poppy on the back seat and discussed Victor's book and their joint future for forty miles, arguing as to whether the character based on Penelope who was to get murdered should have cold feet or whether he might not create another girl altogether based on Venetia. 'And then, of course,' said Victor in full creative flow, 'there's the rabbit, I must not forget the rabbit.'

'What rabbit?'

'Don't you remember? You wrung that poor little inoffensive animal's neck.'

'Oh God, I remember. We had just got engaged, begun our romance.'

'I nearly broke it off. I was horrified.'

'I was showing off. I thought you wanted me to be a tough, hunting, shooting, fishing girl. It wasn't me—'

'You certainly are a nicer girl since living with me.'

'Idiot.'

'Much nicer,' insisted Victor.

'I am the same old Penelope, it's you who have improved. I love rabbits.'

'You do not wring the neck of the thing you love,' said Victor dryly.

'You are murdering me in your novel.'

'We seem to be getting into deep water.'

'Right, let's change the subject.'

Listening to them Poppy realised that their happiness was fragile, that both Victor and Penelope cared for it enough to defend it from themselves.

'When we get to the turning to the village,' she said, 'drop me off. I'd like to walk.'

'Sure?' Victor slowed the car.

'Absolutely. I'll walk across the fields.'

'Your bag?'

'It's light. I'll carry it.'

'Tell me when to stop.'

'At the next turning.'

Victor stopped the car. Poppy got out. 'Thank you for everything.' She kissed Victor's cheek. Penelope hugged her. 'Take care of yourself.'

'And you both.'

She watched them go for a moment then climbed a gate and started walking across a field full of cows.

It seemed an enormously long time since she had walked these fields as a child. It seemed an even longer time since her father's funeral. The path she was following led across the fields to the church whose tower she could see in the distance and through the churchyard into the village street. She would pass the grave where Bob Carew had recently taken up his tenancy.

Strolling slowly Poppy enjoyed the silence of the country which is not silent. Her ears attuned to the roar of the motorway took slow minutes to hear the brushing of her feet through the grass, the munch of grazing cows, their heavy breathing, the caw of rooks in lazy flight, the autumn song of a robin in the hedge, the sound of a tractor ploughing over the hill. She stopped as she walked under a row of telephone wires, looked up and listened for the twitter of swallows but they had gone to winter in Africa, last seen flighting in across the sea from Europe on the days she had witnessed the mob, the hanging, had the drama with Edmund. She walked on.

The day which had begun cold held the warmth of the October sun in the churchyard and butterflies crowded a buddleia, flies and bees worked in the long grass. She left the path and approached her father's grave.

He lay near the boundary wall. The flowers and wreaths had been removed, somebody had turfed it over, all that was left of the mound of flowers was the laurel wreath still fresh at the head of the grave.

Poppy squatted beside the grave, idly brushing grass pollen from her legs. It was peaceful. Jackdaws clacked about the church tower, she could hear the clock tocking. She stretched her legs and, sitting propped against the churchyard wall, tried to think of her father.

She was too young to know that memories do not come leaping to order, it would take her years to discover that they are evoked by a smell, a glimpse of colour, a tone of voice, a note of music. She fell asleep, her head against the wall, her feet towards the grave.

The clop of horses' hooves woke her. She sat up. The horses stopped.

'Hullo,' said Mary, high on a Dow Jones. 'I saw you from up here. How are you?'

'I fell asleep.'

'Why not? Nice day.' Mary sat the horse easily, one hand round Barnaby who perched in front of her. The other held the reins and a leading rein attached to a second horse. 'I was giving these two a little exercise, the others are away working. Coming up to the house?'

'I was on my way. Just thought I'd—'

'See your pa. Is he there?'

'No, no he's not—' Perhaps that accounted for not being able to conjure him up.

'He's at some heavenly race track. Like to ride up to the house? Can you ride?' asked Mary.

'Yes. Thanks.' Poppy climbed on to the low wall and dropped down bareback on to the spare horse and rode through the village to her father's house, her house now. Barnaby, perched in front of Mary, kicked his legs out and chuckled as they went along.

Dismounted in the yard Poppy watched Mary put the horses away. Just as Victor had changed so indefinably had Mary. She was prettier, thinner, her hair was not dyed, she looked even more withdrawn. 'How is Fergus?' Poppy asked.

'Just the same,' said Mary. 'Just the same,' she repeated, shutting a horse-box door. 'Come into the house.' She led the way in through the kitchen. 'I hope you won't find we've changed your house too much, your room is untouched.'

'It was never my room.'

'Ah.' Mary looked her up and down. 'You have changed,' she said, 'you look different.'

'I'm free. Perhaps that's it. I'm free.'

'Is that so?' Mary smiled. 'It must be nice.'

'It's *super*.' Poppy watched Mary pull off Barnaby's jersey, put him down on the floor, give him a raw carrot to gnaw.

'He's on solids now.' Mary looked down at her child. 'Got several teeth, haven't you?' She poked Barnaby's stomach gently with her toe. Barnaby looked up smiling enormously, rolling his bull's-eye eyes.

In spite of her brave words Poppy, watching Mary, suspected that the state of not being in love might wear thin when the novelty wore off. How did Mary manage? She found herself looking forward to the return of Fergus.

'Shall we see whether your room's all right?' Mary led the way upstairs. 'How is your Lochinvar?' she asked, pausing on the stair where she had sat nursing Barnaby at the funeral party. 'It caused quite a commotion when he swept you off in Venetia's car.'

'I have disposed of him,' said Poppy coolly, resenting Mary's mocking tone.

'Aha! Thinking for ourselves now, are we?' Mary laughed outright. 'Well, here's your room, nothing's changed.'

But everything's changed, thought Poppy. The room, the house may look the same, but Dad's gone. Mary, for she blamed Mary, has altered the atmosphere. There's a dangerous sparkle about her, she's some sort of volcano.

When Mary left she paced the room, went into the bathroom, touched the bath towels, the soaps and bath essence, ventured across the landing to her father's room. Mrs Edwardes had tidied and cleaned it, the bed was unmade, the furniture covered in dust sheets, no trace of Dad remained. Poppy closed the door, went back to the visitors' room where Life's Dividends had reposed in the ample bed. She unpacked her overnight bag, put her sponge and toothbrush in the bathroom, opened the windows.

It will be much better when Fergus comes in, she thought,

remembering his kiss, his tongue thrust urgently into her mouth. A whirl with Fergus would do no harm. Dad would have liked Fergus, she thought, more perhaps than Victor, been delighted at the disposal of Edmund, approved of the final parting. She stood at the window looking out at the road, trying to come to terms with Dad's absence, the change in the house's atmosphere.

After a while she left the room and explored, peeping in at bedroom doors. Girls' clothes, shoes, tights in the room that had been hers, posters of pop stars bluetacked to the wall, alien paperbacks on the floor. In the bathroom strange toothbrushes, shampoos, coloured towels. In another room a child's cot, a potty. No trace in any of these rooms of Fergus. Where did Fergus sleep?

'Fergus has taken over the top floor.' Mary had come up, silent, barefoot, carrying Barnaby. 'He's due for his afternoon sleep,' she said, laying the child in his cot.

Poppy, caught snooping, flushed. 'Are you all quite comfortable?' she asked, to fill an awkward gap.

'Sure,' said Mary. She drew the curtains, darkening the room. 'Go to sleep,' she said to the child, 'close your eyes.'

Barnaby closed his eyes and opened them again immediately.

Poppy moved back on to the landing.

'There's Bolivar,' said Mary, looking out of the landing window. 'See? There he is sitting in the road. He knows Fergus is on his way home. Hey, Bolivar,' she shouted. The cat neither twitched nor looked up. 'Fergus will be back soon. I take it you've come to see him,' said Mary obliquely.

Poppy did not answer. She looked forward to Fergus's return, he would lighten the atmosphere, put a stop to this lonely feeling, the sense of something lying in wait. She remembered him large, capable, kindly, above all, cheerful. Feeling curiously endangered by Mary she decided to rest on the Life's Dividends bed until Fergus's return.

'I think I'll have a nap like Barnaby,' she said.

Mary went away.

47

Poppy rested on the visitors' bed, she listened to the house, her childhood home, her father's house. Below the visitors' room where she lay on the bed was the room that had been Dad's study. It was silent. No occasional cough, no scrape of chair pushed back from the desk, no sound of his voice telephoning, no voice calling out as it had in her childhood to Esmé and latterly to Jane Edwardes, 'Is my tea ready?' What silly little things she remembered.

How had he appeared to the ladies who had lain in this bed? As friend? Lover? Companion? What were they like? Were they old? Arthritic? Horsey women with tinted hair and windblown complexions? Had they and Dad lain here? There was no echo of their voices, she would never know them.

She got off the bed and prowled the room. The cupboards were empty, the chest of drawers also. Life's Dividends had left no trace.

Her overnight bag looked out of place, ready to take off elsewhere.

If Life's Dividends were not here, nor was Dad, it was too late now to give him joy, she must get used to permanent regret.

Another regret, not, she told herself, of much importance, was Victor – re-absorbed by Penelope – who might, if she had handled their first meeting differently, have been more than a friend. He had certainly given that impression. But that opportunity, if opportunity it was, was past. Penelope had him back, would keep him.

I would have liked to have slept with Victor, it would have been an experience, thought Poppy, even though he is too thin, not exactly my type. But there is still Fergus, Fergus would be good for a gallop. Wasn't that one of Dad's expressions? So-and-so and so-and-so had 'a gallop' or, if the affair had been on the mild side, 'a canter'. There would always be echoes of Dad in her mind even if he had vacated the house. Sleepily considering the prospect of a gallop, canter or even a trot with Fergus, she decided that presently she would bath and change, go down looking her best to dally with him. His

237

invitation at the wake had been extremely plain, plainer, she persuaded herself, than Victor's.

Amused by the prospect, Poppy listened drowsily to the new sounds which had taken over the house; Mary singing to her child, Barnaby answering with sharp chortling shouts, the back door opening, Mary calling 'Bolivar, come boy, dinner', answered by a growling miauling; the neigh of a horse, a hoof stamped in the stables.

Only the sparrows chirping in the eaves and the jackdaws clacking were familiar. During her absence the house had changed gear; it answered now to Mary who sang in the kitchen. She would decide what windows would open, what doors close, what cooking smells would pervade the house, she was the mistress now. I am on holiday, Poppy decided sleepily, on holiday after the trauma of Edmund, I deserve a holiday, a respite.

She woke to the sound of engines, Fergus's voice answered by Annie and Frances, the sound of ramps crashing down from horseboxes, the clatter of hooves on wood, then hooves on the road passing the house, the rumble of the hearse manhandled off its lorry, shouts of 'Mind the gate, keep to your left, steady' as it was wheeled to the coach house. Fergus calling to the girls, their high voices answering, fading away round the house, then footsteps returning, the starting up of the lorry and the Land Rovers towing the horseboxes to move them away out of earshot.

There was a harsh note to Fergus's voice, a lack of cheer, which made her unwilling to hurry down and present himself. The jokes, the atmosphere of frivolity and hairwashing which she remembered when she had visited Furnival's Fine Funerals that first time was noticeable by its absence. They must all be tired to be so cheerless, perhaps the funeral had gone off badly, leaving unsatisfied customers. Funerals could not all reach the high standard of Dad's.

She heard the back door slam, Fergus's voice ordering abruptly, 'See they put them all away okay. Right? I'm going to have a bath.'

Mary made an inaudible reply.

Fergus's tread on the stairs, pausing on the landing, an aggressive shout, 'Have you fed Bolivar?'

'Yes.' Mary exasperated.

'He says *not*.' Fergus's footsteps moving up the next flight. 'Come on, my puss.' A throaty yowl, footsteps diminishing, the sound of taps being turned on in the bathroom, rushing water.

Remembering the capacity of her father's hot water tank, Poppy hopped off the bed and turned on the hot tap in the visitors' bathroom, immediately decreasing the flow into the bath above.

Fergus swore as the hot water diminished. 'Who the hell is taking all my hot water? It will run cold, blast you. Have you been washing your hair?' he shouted down the stairs.

'I told you, you have a visitor.' Mary, irritatingly patient, called up from the hall.

Poppy, aware of the exact capacity of the tank, turned off her hot tap, added cold, stepped into the bath. (Fergus sounded just as selfish as Edmund.)

Whether to instal a larger hot water tank or manage with what there was had been a question which Dad had debated with monotonous regularity over the years. Now that she was Fergus's landlord it behoved her to consider the problem, it was no longer academic. Washing her ears, she decided to discuss the matter with Anthony Green. 'A larger tank would ultimately add to the value of the house,' she would say. Anthony would prevaricate, she visualised herself quashing his objections, he would be sure to object to her spending the money. That was what solicitors were for.

Poppy got out of the bath and dressed.

Someone, Penelope perhaps, had put the multicoloured dress into her bag. She put it aside and dressed in clean jeans and shirt. The dress held too many associations. She thrust it back in the bag feeling, as she did so, that it was not the dress she was pushing out of sight, not her father, not even Edmund, but Willy and she did not propose to think of Willy now, she was going downstairs to meet Fergus.

She zipped up the bag, pushed it out of sight under the bed and left the room.

Downstairs Annie was laying the table, clattering knives, forks, spoons into careless position. Mary stood by the stove.

'Do you mind eating in the kitchen?'

'Of course not. What's for supper? Smells great.'

There was an atmosphere of constraint. Poppy wondered whether she was unwelcome among the girls, tried to appear natural and friendly. 'How have you all settled in?' she asked.

'Oh fine, fine. We love it here, it's brilliant.' Annie glanced up as Frances came into the room. 'Shall we get some booze from the pub?' she asked Mary. 'Got any money?'

'There's plenty here, Dad had quite a good cellar, I'll go and get a bottle or two.' Glad of something to do, Poppy left the room. It would be a friendly act, soften the stiff atmosphere if she contributed wine to the meal.

Coming up from the cellar carrying bottles, she met Fergus.

'Hullo, Fergus.'

'Hullo. Nice to see you. Hope you are comfortable. That for us? It's very kind of you—' His voice had changed, he sounded older, he did not seem particularly pleased to see her, there was no trace of the letching look in the eye she remembered.

'I hope I am not a nuisance. I won't stay long. It's just that I have to discuss a few things with Anthony Green. I hope he hasn't bothered you.'

'He's been very helpful, actually, thinks my stepfather's reference makes me respectable.'

'I could easily have stayed in the pub.' Poppy excused her presence, embarrassed by she knew not what.

'Don't be silly, it's your house.' Fergus frowned and glanced across the kitchen at Mary, who stood at the stove stirring something which smelt delicious with a long spoon.

Mary lifted one shoulder in a curiously defensive gesture.

'You people ready to eat?' she asked. 'Find a corkscrew, Frances, give it to Fergus.' She pointed at the bottles with her chin as Poppy put them on the table.

'Right.' Fergus took the corkscrew handed him by Frances and drew the corks. 'This is very good of you.' He poured the wine.

Mary dished up, heaping rice on to plates, adding generous portions of chicken.

'What's this, Coq Au Vin?'

'Cock.' Mary helped herself last, sat beside Poppy. 'There were some telephone calls for you,' she said to Fergus. 'I wrote them down, they are on your desk.'

Dad's desk—

'Thanks. Any orders?'

'Two definite funerals for next week, various queries. I said you'd ring tomorrow early.'

'Thanks.' Fergus ate hungrily. 'Any callers?'

'What?'

'Anybody come to the house?'

'No.'

'Where's Barnaby?'

'Asleep.'

'Oh. He all right?'

'Yes.'

'Oh.' Fergus turned to Poppy and began talking to her, enquiring where she had been, had she enjoyed herself, was it a good trip, what was North Africa like, spacing his questions between mouthfuls of food, barely listening to her replies.

Nettled, Poppy said, 'We spent a few days in Purgatory.'

'Oh,' said Fergus swallowing some wine. 'What was the food like?'

Annie and Frances smirked.

Mary laughed outright. 'Haha! Hoho!'

Fergus looked round the table, surprised.

'Did I say something amusing?'

'Oh no,' said Mary, 'not at all, of course not.'

They fell silent, looked at their plates.

Outside a robin started singing in a lilac bush. Bolivar jumped up to the windowsill and out in a long flowing movement.

'Well.' Fergus finished his meal, pushed his plate aside. 'You two girls coming to the pub with me?'

'Well,' Frances hesitated.

'Well,' said Annie, also hesitant.

'Come on, then.' Fergus pushed back his chair and stood up. 'I expect you are tired,' he said to Poppy.

'I will help Mary clear the table,' said Poppy.

'Sure you won't come?' asked Fergus, as though he had invited her.

'Yes,' said Poppy, already gathering plates. 'I must get you a new dishwasher,' she said to Mary, 'and another thing, I think you need a larger hot water supply. My father had been thinking of it for years, it just never got done.'

'Too busy picking the winners. Don't bother for my sake,' said Mary vaguely as she watched Fergus go out, followed by Annie and Frances.

'What's the matter with him?' asked Poppy, unable to stop herself.

'Just a mood.' Mary sounded unconvincing. 'I have put a lot of things away,' she said, 'things that might get broken. Some of your parents' things.'

'Oh, thank you. I should have done it myself.' (There had been no time.)

'Your solicitor thought it would be a good thing, he sent a man to make an inventory.'

'That wasn't necessary.' Poppy flushed.

'I asked him to,' said Mary. 'We have so much clutter, hats, boots, bits of harness, Fergus's gun,' she glanced up at the chimney breast, 'books, cat basket, dogs. The girls make a lot of mess, too.'

Poppy helped Mary tidy the kitchen then, excusing herself, went to her father's study, sat at his desk to make a list of matters she must discuss with Anthony. It was high time she showed herself more capable than scatterbrained. She felt the need to do something practical to dispel the shock of Fergus's snub, for what was it if not a snub?

Her fantasy of a gallop, canter or trot with Fergus was as much pie in the sky as her whirl with Victor.

She could hear Mary moving about the house, answering the telephone, talking to Barnaby in the bedroom upstairs, singing a lullaby as she put him to bed, then talking to the old dog and to Bolivar. She watched her walk past the window to pick flowers in the garden, her pale hair in sharp contrast to the brilliant zinnias she gathered. Dad had always grown these flowers, admiring their vigour and vulgarity. Mary, thought Poppy, watching her, belonged to the house and the house knew it.

When the telephone started to ring she jumped up and left the house. She needed to walk and sort her thoughts. There was the risk that the caller might be Willy Guthrie; she could not bring herself to talk to him. She crossed the field behind the house. The cat Bolivar kept her company for fifty yards before disappearing under a gate.

She had begun the day believing she could use Victor and Fergus as buffers between herself and Willy, it was plain now that she was bufferless. They would have worked too as a salve to cure the wound left by Edmund.

Taking the route she had always taken with her father she set to walk off her resentment. She climbed up behind the house to the stand of beech and on on to the downs to turn, catch her breath and look down on the village snaking along the chalk stream, the village hall, the pub, the church, the garage, her father's house, the post office.

The church clock struck the hour; the pub would soon close, spilling out Fergus and the girls. She had no wish to meet Fergus again that night, having so nearly made a fool of herself. She broke into a trot.

Trot, she thought as she jogged down the hill, any trotting must be done alone.

A hundred yards from the house she heard Fergus's voice. He was shouting. She slowed to a walk and approached the house cautiously.

In the kitchen Mary stood with her back to the stove. Annie and Frances stood on either side of the table, Fergus was in the doorway from the hall. The kitchen was brightly lit and the door open into the yard.

Poppy, fascinated, watched unseen. There was no problem about hearing, both Fergus shouting and Mary speaking quietly enunciated clearly.

The row was in full swing.

'Deceitful, sly, crafty, selfish, abominable. No man in his senses would endure such a trick.'

Mary, very quiet and cold, 'Who told you?'

'My mother, no less. I have to have my nose rubbed in it by an interfering parent whom I have hitherto loved, trusted and respected. I didn't believe her, of course, what she said was too utterly preposterous.'

'Yes.'

'Yes? It's not *yes*. It's true! What my mother says is true. I thought it was her wishful thinking, her imagination.' Fergus gasped for breath. 'She's always wanted me to have—'

Frances caught Annie's eye and jerked her head, indicating 'Let's get out of this.'

'You stay where you are,' shouted Fergus, 'you are my witnesses, don't you dare move,' he threatened.

Frances and Annie froze.

'Oh,' said Mary, cool but whitefaced. 'So?'

'So she cast my genes in my teeth.'

'Who? What?'

'My bloody mother. I told you. My genes.'

'Genes?'

'Yes, genes, fucking genes. She said it looked exactly like—'

'*He.*'

'Okay. *He* looked exactly like me as a baby and even worse my bloody filthy-tempered father. Genes, she said, don't lie.'

243

'No.'

'So I have my witnesses. I take them out to the pub, ply them with drink several boring nights running, quiz them about the holiday you spent in Spain after leaving me, ask crafty questions about your boyfriend, Joseph the father, we are led to suppose – who telephones constantly we are led to believe. Funny that it's always you who answers the telephone – Where was I? I've lost the thread. Oh, got it. This boyfriend Joseph who is the father of infant Jesus—'

'Barnaby.'

'Oh-bloody-kay, Barnaby, and I am not even consulted about his name.' Fergus yelling now.

'What's his name got to do with it?'

'Nothing,' Fergus screamed. 'Call the little bastard anything you like.'

'Thanks.'

'So I make them drunk, don't I? Out pop the indiscretions. I make a few simple passes at these nitwits – thrilled, they were. Oh, yes you were. A grown man at last not a boy from the disco. They regale me with the goings-on on the Costa where they met you. *There were no goings-on!* Saint Joseph, it turns out, is no beautiful Spanish fisher lad, he's a rather old, very fat, heavily married Swede, with a wife he adores and a grown-up family, the manager and owner of the hotel. Don't laugh!'

'I am not laughing.'

'And this Saint Joseph, this Swedish gent is fair, has almost white hair and so have all his sons and daughters and grandchildren. Grandchildren!'

'And?'

'And so have *you*. Very fair hair. You used to wear it long in a pigtail like a bellrope. Why did you cut it off?'

'So?'

'So this is where the genes come in, where you slip up in your evil deception. It's not possible for two very fair people to have a very dark baby.'

'No.'

'So *I* am very dark, my father was very dark. My mother meets Barnaby, puts two and two together and tells me I am his father.' Fergus loomed over Mary standing backed against the stove with her hands gripping the stove rail. She pushed herself away from it.

'It will not take me long to pack.' She walked past Fergus and left the room. They heard her run lightly up the stairs.

Fergus slumped down on a chair by the table.

Frances and Annie edged towards the door. Poppy, ashamed of greedily listening, came forward into the light.

Nobody spoke.

After a few minutes Mary appeared carrying Barnaby wrapped sleepy in a shawl. She walked past Fergus without looking at him, snatched a bunch of car keys from the dresser and walked on through the house and out.

Poppy, Annie and Frances followed her on to the porch.

'She can't,' said Annie.

'She will,' said Frances.

Mary settled Barnaby in a basket cot on the back seat, got in behind the wheel and started the car. She was turning it in the road when Fergus pushed the girls roughly aside and shouted, 'Don't!'

Mary paid no attention.

Fergus rushed back into the house.

'Is he drunk?' asked Annie.

'No,' said Frances, 'he didn't drink a thing, it was we who were drinking.'

'Oh God,' said Annie, 'Oh God.' she moaned. Both girls were crying.

Mary was finishing a three-point turn and putting the car into gear when Fergus reappeared with his gun.

Annie and Frances shrieked.

Fergus fired.

Mary's car slewed sideways into a flowerbed.

Fergus fired again. The car stopped.

In the ensuing pause Mary said, 'Damn you.'

Fergus dropped the gun on Poppy's foot.

Poppy yelped.

Fergus shouted, 'I love you, you FOOL!' and rushed down the steps to the car.

'And now he'll wake the baby,' said Willy, coming into the bright glare of the porch. 'Why the hell didn't you answer when I telephoned?'

48

Barnaby, waked by the shots, filled his lungs and began to scream like a steam kettle on a high-pitched, ear-piercing, bat-deafening note which terrified Poppy who was unversed in babies and paralysed Frances and Annie with fright.

Fergus, reaching into the back of Mary's car, took the baby out as Mary leapt furiously from the driving seat.

'Gosh, what lungs,' exclaimed Willy. 'The child is perfectly all right, leave them.' His urgent voice carried conviction. 'For Christ's sake, leave them alone. Here,' he said, picking up the gun from where Fergus had dropped it, 'put this back where it belongs.' He thrust the gun into Frances's hands. 'Hurry, it won't go off, he fired both barrels.'

Arriving fortuitously to lure Annie and Frances to the disco, two youths now found themselves pressganged by Willy into pushing the flat-tyred car into the yard out of sight of the road. (Fergus, being an excellent shot, had hit what he aimed for, the back tyres.)

Mesmerised by Willy's authority, the girls' escorts asked, 'What happened? What happened?' as they pushed, trying at the same time not to spoil their party clothes. 'What happened?'

'Nothing, nothing happened,' said Willy, pushing. 'A couple of blow outs, it was nothing, nothing.'

'Oh nothing, it was nothing.' Annie, taking her lead from Willy, pushed the car also.

'It was all our fault.' Frances returned from putting the gun away and stood with Poppy on the front steps. 'Fergus teased and tricked us into telling him about kind old Mr Joseph who gave Mary a job when she was pregnant. He and his wife warded off her family, they wanted to keep Barnaby, wanted to adopt him. Mary had to tear herself away from them. They still write and telephone, they've got a thing about Barnaby. Oh, poor baby.' Frances sobbed loudly.

'Shut up, stop that noise,' snapped Poppy, furious in relief, wishing she had a second pair of eyes and ears to simultaneously watch the removal of the car and the taut drama between Fergus and Mary, who now stood in the road muttering.

Each time Fergus's voice rose to audibility it was drowned by shouting from the yard: 'Put the bloody brake on, you git', and 'mind my foot', and 'watch it', as the car was pushed by willing hands to bump into a wall to the accompaniment of crunching headlights and yells of anarchic irrepressible laughter.

Fergus and Mary might have been alone on Mars for all the attention they paid to the outer world.

Mary took Barnaby from Fergus as he stopped shrieking. He leaned towards her talking and presently took the child back, muttering intensely, his voice low, grumbling like summer waves on a cobbled beach. Mary gently took the child again, holding him up near her face as she answered in a very quiet urgent voice.

The two were so preoccupied Poppy wondered whether they were aware of what they did as turn and turn about they took the child from each other with reassuring ritualistic movements. Fergus's voice, still inaudible, rumbled and fell lower. Mary spoke less and less. From time to time Barnaby crowed as he was handed from one to the other, staking his part in the game. He had reverted after his shocked surprise to his habitual humorous self.

'Amazing,' said Frances, standing watching with Poppy. 'Incredible,' she sniffed, wiping her tears with the back of her hand.

'Did I hear a gun go off? Thought I heard shots.' Jane Edwardes came up the road. 'We thought we heard a gun.'

'Oh, hullo Mrs Edwardes.' Willy came through from the back of the house. 'Do you remember me? I helped you clean up the golden syrup.'

'Oh yes, so you did,' said Mrs Edwardes. 'Honey too, such waste. We were watching TV and thought we heard a gun. Boring programme, silly old Party Conference. I told my husband I'd come and look, he's interested in politics, I'm not. Did you hear about the golden syrup, Poppy? Mr – er – helped me clean it up.'

'What?' said Poppy, still watching the two figures with the child. 'He's called Willy Guthrie.'

'Yes, I know,' said Jane Edwardes.

'Did you ever find out who did it?' asked Willy.

'No,' said Mrs Edwardes, 'I did not.'

'Did *what*?' asked Poppy, irritated at not being able to hear what Fergus and Mary were saying.

'I wonder if that was a gun we heard.' Mrs Edwardes reverted to the cause of her call.

'Why don't we go into the kitchen and make some coffee,' suggested Willy, edging Jane Edwardes and Poppy into the house. 'We can tell Poppy about the drama of the treacle,' he said as they moved indoors. 'And you,' he turned to Frances, 'are off to the disco, I gather.'

'Oh, are we?' said Frances, latching on. 'I'd better be off, then. Bye,' she called as she ran off to join Annie and the boys. 'I'd been going to wash my hair.' They heard her voice diminish, the visiting car start up and mixed-sex laughter as it drove away.

In the kitchen Bolivar lay on his back in front of the stove exposing his gingery stomach to the warmth, his hind legs splaying out from his furry balls, eyes closed, front paws dangling across his chest.

'If anyone had fired a gun that cat would have been up and away,' said Mrs Edwardes, moving the kettle across to the hotplate.

Willy grinned at Poppy.

'I hope no nosey-parker has telephoned the police,' said Mrs Edwardes, spooning Nescafé into mugs. 'Reach me the milk, dear, from the fridge. Thank you. I heard their sirens as I came along.'

'There's been a pile-up on the motorway, I had difficulty in getting past on my way over,' said Willy. 'I expect the police are all busy with that.'

'That's all right, then,' said Mrs Edwardes, pouring boiling water into the mugs. 'Can't be everywhere, can they? Milk? Sugar?'

'Both, please,' said Willy.

'I know how you like yours,' Jane Edwardes said to Poppy.

'Thank you,' said Poppy, 'so you should.'

'Thank you,' said Willy.

They took their mugs, stood grouped by the stove. Willy caressed Bolivar's stomach delicately with his toe. Bolivar yawned, sneezed, went on snoozing.

'All the same,' said Jane Edwardes, 'it would be a sensible thing if he cleaned his gun when he stops being so busy.' She jerked her chin slightly towards the road.

Willy laughed. 'I'll do it now,' he said. 'He may be busy for quite a while.'

'Got a lot to say to each other, no doubt,' said Mrs Edwardes. 'He keeps the cleaning things in that drawer,' she pointed, 'the one on the left.'

'Thanks.' Willy put down his mug.

Poppy watched him clean the gun and return it to its place.

'That's all right, then,' said Mrs Edwardes, satisfied. 'Didn't take care of your father all those years without learning a thing or two. I'll be off now, Poppy. I'll send young Bill up to change those tyres in the morning first thing.'

'Oh,' said Poppy, 'you were watching.'

'I wouldn't say that,' said Jane Edwardes, 'not exactly. I'll be getting along. They'll take some time getting it all said, I dare say. Well, good night, I'll be missing the news if I hang about.' She kissed Poppy.

Willy went with Mrs Edwardes to the front door. Coming back he said, 'And I have a lot to say to you.'

Poppy said quickly, 'Are they all right, Fergus and Mary?'

'Looks like it. They seem to have taken root in the road.'

'What do you know?'

'Fergus's mother came and moaned it all out to my aunt when she rumbled the situation.'

'Oh.'

'They share the child.'

'How?'

'As people do, the accident of procreation.' It's different, thought Willy, with my pigs. *There*'s family planning for you.

'Accident! Good God!' said Poppy.

Willy looked at her with careful eyes. Poppy flushed.

'Or,' said Willy, 'it was some convoluted form of love and Mary's pride got in the way.'

'I admire and like Mary,' said Poppy stoutly.

'So do I, so do I,' said Willy. (Curious this little trick he has of repeating himself, said a little nerve in Poppy's head.)

'Where's your bag?' Willy was saying. 'I am taking you home.'

'Supposing I don't want to come?' she prevaricated.

'Not that again,' said Willy. 'Let's get cracking.'

49

Willy holding Poppy by the hand pulled her towards his car.

As they passed Fergus and Mary he squeezed her hand but got no response. If Poppy was not exactly holding back physically she was confused and recalcitrant.

Fergus's dogs, crouching in the vicinity of their master, uncertain of what was going on, jerked hurriedly aside, jumping to their feet to let Willy and Poppy pass. The oldest dog, who did not normally concern himself with anything much, gave the whisper of a growl. None of the dogs had barked when Fergus loosed off his gun; two of them had run to Mary, the third, who now growled, had stood looking from Fergus to Mary, a prey to indecision.

Passing by the silent pair Poppy wondered how long they would stand bemused, whether Barnaby would catch cold in the night air, whether she wanted to stay and watch the upshot of this curious scene, whether she ought to stay or would it be better to allow Willy to take her away as he was now doing.

Possibly she had counted on another night in the Dividend bed. As she thought of this it became almost certain that this was what she wanted and Willy was depriving her of it.

As they pushed past Fergus he took Mary's head between both hands and, leaning to kiss her, said, 'Promise you will let it grow?'

Mary said, 'All right, I will,' laughing, putting the arm not holding Barnaby round Fergus's neck, returning his kiss. 'You shall have your bellrope.'

'Then let's go back and start.' Fergus turned Mary towards the house.

Overhearing this exchange, allowing herself to be pushed into Willy's car, Poppy craned back to watch as Willy pulled the safety belt across to fasten her in.

'He wants her to grow her hair,' she said. 'That's what he means.'

'And to let l-o-v-e grow too.' Willy slammed the car door, irritated with his darling.

Poppy wound the window down the better to watch Fergus and Mary disappear into the house.

'I bet they sleep in the Dividend bed tonight,' she said.

'The what bed?'

'It's neutral ground. My bed. Well, Dad's visitors' bed. Some day I'll tell you—'

Some day, thought Willy, starting the car, engaging the gears, some day I shall have learned much about her but never the whole of it. There is no way that two people can know each other wholly, nor do I want that. He switched on the headlights, accelerated.

Some day I shall persuade Jane Edwardes to tell me all she knows about Life's Dividends, thought Poppy, regretting the so comfortable bed, or would it be wiser not to ask, just be grateful to them for their money?

Edmund would search around, poke and pry into Dad's past, suggest Life's Dividends could be better invested, know better, interfere. Thank God that is not Willy's style. But, she thought, amused as Willy swung the car too fast out of the village, I am not sure Edmund is not the better driver. Willy is a bit erratic.

'The last time I was driven away from Dad's house without prior consultation or consent was by Edmund,' she said. 'I have a distinct feel of déjà vu.'

'I am not interested in Edmund,' said Willy, keeping his eyes on the road, 'until I have a spare moment and can take time off to murder him.'

'Oh my!' exclaimed Poppy mockingly. Willy, not keen on Poppy's mood, drove on in silence.

He is assuming possession, thought Poppy. He has not asked whether I *want* to come with him. I have not been *asked* what I want. Yesterday I wanted a bit of experimental fun with Victor and lo he was snitched back into Penelope's marital orbit. Today I had promised myself a trot, canter or gallop with Fergus and now it's clear that he and Mary love each other and have even gone so far as to have a ready-made child. As far as my love life goes those two men are non-starters. She resigned herself to Willy. Just for a while, she assured herself, it's purely temporary of course.

'Do you think it possible,' she asked presently, 'that Fergus really did not know Mary's baby was his?'

'Perfectly possible,' said Willy. 'I know other people who can't recognise what's going on under their noses.'

'Such as?' Poppy resented Willy's tone which was sarcastic.

'Such as you,' said Willy on the same note.

'In what context?' she asked sharply.

'In the context of love,' said Willy. 'You busily pretend that you do not know that I love you. I should have thought by now you would be fully aware of it. Cognisant, if we are being pompous.'

'I resent – busily.'

'Hah!'

'I haven't had time to think about it. I am still bruised and battered by Edmund—' (This whining is ridiculous and also false.)

'Come off it.'

'I want time to think,' she complained.

'You are not slow witted. You've had time.'

'No, I haven't. When Edmund and I parted—'

'He left you.'

'Agreed. But he came back—'

'You wanted to annoy Venetia. You told me.'

'So I did – and I did.' Poppy relished the memory of an unsurpassed act of annoyance.

'Well then,' said Willy, his eyes on the road.

'Well then, when we'd parted, split up, finished, when Dad had died, I was deciding what to do with myself, sorting myself out, taking my time.'

'I came along,' said Willy cheerfully.

'That didn't settle anything, Willy.'

'It did for me.'

'But not me. I was thinking of selling my flat and buying a little house in London, starting all over—'

'That's what you are doing now, starting afresh with me.'

'No.'

'I am taking you home.'

Home, thought Poppy, what is home? My flat, with its connotations of Edmund, is impossible, even though I have thrown out all his things, he will still be in the air I breathe. Dad's house, my early home, it's now, thanks to my own bright idea, Mary and Fergus's. Would a little house in London, always supposing I found one, be a better deal? To be honest, until a moment ago, when Willy acted so sure of himself, I had forgotten that slight conversation with boring Les Poole at the bank. I am not being honest with Willy but no need to let on just yet.

There is always the possibility of nothing, doing nothing, nothing happening. One night or three in the Dividend bed is fine, but what about longer? What about it?

There is no way I can start afresh, thought Willy. I have been clumsy. I was so sure of my own love I didn't take hers into account. Does it exist? Am I rushing her too fast? With other girls I have sailed ahead not really caring, felt so confident, so carefree. This is absolutely bloody. Surely that was love as well as enjoyment we had in Algiers? Is it possible she was fucking for fucking's sake when she laughed and cried out for more? Is it possible it all means nothing to her? Am I making the most awful fool of myself? What does she think I mean when I say I am taking her home. If I told her her home is my heart she would call me a sloppy romantic and I am one, unashamedly, hopelessly so where she is concerned.

Willy began to sweat. He had wanted to surprise and delight her with the charms of his farm, see her fall in love with it, fit into it, love it as he did.

'Perhaps I had better tell you where I am taking you,' he said tentatively. 'My farm.'

'You were keeping it as a surprise.'

'I was.'

'Tell me now then.'

She had seen a pig farm once. Long concrete buildings with hard concrete floors crowded with pigs penned in cramped partitions, fed in long communal troughs, no peace, no room to move, no privacy, no dignity. She had been aghast, repelled by the questing snouts, the hot atmosphere, the squeals and grunts, the slopping sound as they souped up their food, hastening to grow to the correct weight for the bacon factory.

Edmund, having taken her (it was in his house agent days) to view a house near the farm, had reacted quite otherwise, approving of the use of minimal space, the speed of growth, the financial turnover achieved by modern farming techniques. For her part she had been so shocked by the sight of the degraded pigs that she gave up eating bacon for at least a month. (If I were honest I would remember it was only a week.) I must be deranged, thought Poppy, sitting here letting Willy take me to a place like that, out of my tiny mind.

But Willy was talking.

'There was this group of farm buildings, my uncle restored them in his day. When I took over I did a lot more. The buildings are rather

253

lovely pink brick barns with tiled roofs. The principal ones are squared round a cobbled courtyard with a well in the middle. I keep a few bantams and ducks because I like the noise they make and they look pretty. I live in one wing I converted into a cottage. I have a very large flagged living room with an Aga at one end, an open fire at the other. I can walk out either into the yard or into a walled garden. I made the garden but it still needs a lot doing to it. There's a dovecot, one of those conical jobs with a tiled roof. No doves at present, though.' (Doves, white fantails, would be lovely, thought Poppy.) 'Above the living room I have a large bedroom with an open fire and bathroom and you can see across the fields to the wood. I use a second barn as my office and store.' (Is she listening? I am being very boring, wouldn't it have been better to wait and let her see it, judge for herself?) 'The pigs, the principal sows have the other two sides of the square, each has her own space; pigs need lots of space.'

'What?' Poppy, adjusting her thoughts, felt as though they were in a tumble-dryer.

'I said pigs need lots of space. You see them lolling together in groups of course when they are feeling sociable.'

'Go on.'

'My sows all have their separate styes. Terribly clean animals, pigs, did you know?' (What does she know? She must have some clue, she's lived in the country.)

'Not enough.'

'My breeding sows, most of them, well, all of them now, I bred myself. The principal, most important to me, are Mrs Future and her aunt. I admit that to the uninitiated they all look alike. The little pigs, when they are old enough, live in groups in deep litter.'

'Not on concrete?'

'Good God, no!' Willy exploded.

'Oh.'

'I believe you thought I was a factory farmer,' Willy accused, furious.

'No, no, of course not.' (That was it, that was what Edmund admired, a factory farm. Oh Edmund, what a lamentable mistake you have been.) 'Go on,' she said, 'please go on.'

'All the pigs are out in the fields when it's not raining, rooting about playing.'

'Playing? What?'

'Pigs are humorous animals.' Willy was quite huffy now.

254

'I had not realised.'

'I believe in my animals having happy lives.'

'And after? What about after?'

'After life is ham. I specialise in smoked ham, the trade name is Guthrie.'

'I've seen it in Fortnum's catalogue.' Poppy steadied the tumble-dryer.

'I have my own smokery.'

'Goodness.'

'They live cheerfully, die quickly without prior knowledge. They reward me with a fat profit. It's a lot neater than what happens to humans.'

'We are not eaten for breakfast.'

'You split hairs. Your father—'

Poppy remembered Dad in the hospital bed surrounded by those sad grey old men. He had not been cheerful there. True, his life had been pretty comfortable – very comfortable, if one remembered the Dividend bed – he'd obviously enjoyed himself at the races but what about all those coronaries and although laughter had killed him—

'Do they smell?' she asked, seeking something derogatory to say, trying not to surrender to the description of the farm which sounded bliss. She had always longed for a large bedroom with an open fire. 'Do they smell?' she repeated as Willy did not answer.

'About as much as Venice and not all the time. A good pig farm should not smell.' (One must be truthful, there were times the pigs smelled, times they did not.)

'Do you grow fond of them?' (Keep on doubting, do not yield to this insidious propaganda.)

'Of course I do. I am particularly partial to Mrs Future and her aunt. I love them.' Willy laughed.

'What's funny?' There was something suspicious in Willy's laughter.

'They are pigs of character.'

'Tell me about them.'

'I brought Mrs Future up on a bottle, she was a runt, she used to follow me about like a dog.'

'And her aunt?'

'She's something quite else. Once, to make it easier to care for her I moved her and her litter. She ate the lot. You remind me of her.'

'Thanks a lot,' exclaimed Poppy.

'Oh *shit.*' Willy trod hard on the brakes as the car was engulfed in sudden dense deafening fog. 'Curse it. Can you see out your side? We seem to have hit a bit of road without markings or cats' eyes. Oh bloody hell, I hate fog.'

'It's beautiful new macadam.' Poppy peered down at the road. 'So fresh I can smell it. Delicious.'

'Fuck the new macadam.' Willy reduced the car to a crawl. The car lights, drowned in the fog, came bouncing back. 'You all right?'

'Yes, I think so.'

The fog was dense and eerie. Trying to see, seeing nothing, they were quiet for a while, crawling in low gear.

'Can you see the verge?'

'Just. I'll keep my window open.' Poppy leaned sideways, watching the verge. 'It may only be a patch.'

'And it may go on for miles; this road runs along a river.'

They crawled on, nosing into the fog which fingered cold and wetly into the car. Willy switched on the wipers.

'There's a foghorn,' said Poppy.

'It's a cow, stupid. In a field somewhere near.'

'Oh.'

A motorbicycle came suddenly out of the fog, swerved to avoid them, the rider shouted something antagonistic before disappearing, its noisy engine silenced in the vaporous air.

Suddenly all around them loomed enormous shapes. Dazzled by the headlights a vast Friesian bumped into the car, lurching against it so that the chassis rocked.

Poppy gave a surprised shriek as another cow blew sweet breath in her face through the window, starting back, slipping awkwardly on the road as her nose touched Poppy's cheek, her bland eye rolling in terror.

'I can't see the verge any more,' she exclaimed.

Willy edged the car back to the side. 'See it now?'

'Yes.'

Willy switched off the engine. 'Some clot has let these cows out.' He got out of the car, cupped his hands round his mouth, shouted, 'Anybody with this lot?'

His voice echoed back, 'Islot – islot—' 'You stay there, I must get them back, find their field, otherwise there will be a smash. There will be a gate open. Sit tight.'

Willy disappeared along the road they had come, following the cows. She heard his voice 'How-how-how' and soon the cows lumbered past the car at a trot in the reverse direction. For a second she saw Willy following them. 'Whoa there, steady there, no need to rush. Stay where you are, I won't be long,' he called to her as he and the cows were swallowed into the fog.

For a few minutes the steam rising from the cows' bodies sweetened the fog, then it was back swirling cold and inimical. There was a strong smell of cowpat and silence.

Curiously afraid, Poppy undid her safety belt and scrambled out of the car. She called, 'Willy, Willy.'

The fog replied, 'Silly – silly', remote, impersonal. She strained her ears, heard nothing. It may be miles before he finds the open gate, hours before he comes back. Supposing this is it, suppose this is the nothing, supposing he is gone?

'Willy.' Poppy shouted louder now, urgently, experiencing the acute terror Nature's vagaries can engender. 'Why was I so detestable?' she cried aloud and then again, 'Willy, come back.'

'Ack,' rejoined the fog laconically. She stood straining her ears, her hand on the cold metal of the car, beaded with droplets from the fog. Should she switch off the headlights to save the battery? No, they must serve to guide Willy back.

He must come back.

She felt as though she was alone on top of a high mountain in her fear, she felt exalted. She listened so hard she was deafened by the fearful blood thumping in her ears.

The transport lorry hit the car so suddenly there was no time to jump clear. It crunched over the bonnet and straddled the chassis with its giant wheels as it shuddered, clanked, crackled to a stop. Breaking glass tinkled and chinked, there was the smell of hot oil, mingling with cowpat and spilling petrol and the blare of the car horn jammed on by the accident.

Oh God, I've peed all over myself, I am lying in a cowpat. She was flat on her back pinned down.

Slightly concussed, too frightened to lose consciousness, Poppy expected her past life to flash by. At top level her mind rummaged around to locate broken bones and torn sinews, at a deeper level it seemed imperative to recall Dad's message about, what was it, money lenders, racing tips?

She tried to move her head and yelped with pain as the hair was

257

wrenched from her scalp (I am trepanned).

She tried moving her legs but somebody had put them in a bag and bound them tightly.

Warm oil dripped on her face but she could not turn her head to escape it.

I shall drown in a sack she thought, my legs are paralysed, if I survive I shall be a paraplegic. She tried to call out 'Get me out of here' but her mouth filled with oil. She choked and gagged.

She remembered the terror and anguish of falling out of bed during nightmares as a child, all wound up in the bedclothes, and her father coming from his room across the passage to unravel her. She spat out the foul oil.

I have been run over by a lorry and am pinned underneath it.

I am soaked in oil and petrol and when it catches fire I shall fry.

I am paralysed.

I have something to say to Willy, it's important. I was forming a witty phrase when this thing hit me.

I wish someone would turn off the car horn, it is getting on my nerves.

I am too badly hurt to feel anything.

My central nervous system is gone.

I wish I could lose consciousness. I need to tell Willy I love him.

This will teach me to prevaricate and play hard to get (not that he was taking a blind bit of notice).

All I want is to be safe in his arms for ever, oh dear God, I am so cold.

Shut up, you fool, stop whingeing and whining and pitying yourself. Listen, listen to hear if there is anyone there.

There may be some sound not drowned by the car's horn. It will stop when the battery goes flat.

This lot may go up in a whoosh of flame before the horn stops.

Somebody must have been driving the lorry.

I am alone.

Somebody *must* have been driving it. There *must* be somebody there.

Nobody.

The car's horn stopped abruptly.

Running footsteps circled the wrecked vehicles, men's voices, lights.

'The driver's dead.' 'Have to cut him out.' 'Got a torch?' 'Bring it

258

here.' 'Who was in the other car?' 'They dead too?' 'It's empty, some damned fool left it parked.' 'There's a body here. Run over, looks like. Must have been standing by the car when the lorry hit.'

A torch shone in her eyes.

Willy calling, 'Poppy, Poppy. Where are you? *Answer me.*' Running, running, frantic.

Poppy spat oil, then, keeping her mouth shut, managed a sort of mooing sound, 'OOOO—'

A scrabbling behind her head, Willy's voice hoarse with anxiety. 'I'm here, darling, I'm on my way.'

'Ooooo—' She began to weep.

Willy's face upside-down, his velvet eyes close to hers beady with anxiety, the oil from the crankshaft dropping on to his head now cloying in long trails down his cheeks, his hands reaching round her, exploring her plight, his mouth kissing hers briefly.

'This is a novel sort of Soixante Neuf. Will you marry me?'

'I can't, I'm paralysed.'

'Nonsense, don't be imaginative, your hair and skirt are pinned by the wheel of the lorry.' Turning his head to one side Willy yelled, 'Someone bring me a knife.'

'A what? We're busy with the driver.'

'A knife. A fucking knife, hurry up, or scissors.'

'Okay, okay, keep your cool.'

'Better hurry, the petrol isn't safe. Here's a knife, what d'you want it for?' said a voice.

Then Willy speaking gently. 'Sorry about this, darling, I'll try not to hurt.'

Willy sawing at her hair, her head suddenly free.

'That's better, now let me get at your skirt. Keep still or I'll cut your stomach open. Right. Can you move your legs?'

'Yes.' Amazed. 'Yes, I can.'

'How d'you feel?' His voice quite wobbly.

'The fear of death has sharpened my intellect.'

'Great! Now keep still a moment then I'll haul you out.'

Willy edged backwards.

'I was so frightened I peed and worse, Willy. Ouch, what are you doing?'

'Pulling you out from under, let me get hold of your arms.' Willy heaved, Poppy kicked as she scraped along the tarmac.

'Get a blanket from the ambulance,' said a voice bossily.

'Got the stretcher here,' said another invitingly.

'Easy does it,' said a third. 'That was just in time, I'd say.'

'Where do they all come from?' Poppy staggered to her feet. The fog was clearing.

'Police and ambulances left over from the pile-up earlier tonight on the motorway.' Willy wrapped her in a blanket, kept his arms round her.

'Lie on the stretcher, love,' invited a policeman.

'No thanks, I'm perfectly—' She put her hand to her head and felt her hair gone from one side. 'Oh.'

'You can race Mary growing it.' Willy was laughing with relicf, covered in oil, his shirt torn.

'What is that?' There was an inert body on a stretcher, they were pushing it up into the ambulance, it looked very dead.

'The lorry driver,' said Willy, 'don't look.'

'Watch out!' cried a man. 'Up she goes!'

There was a thump and a whoosh of flame as the entangled machines finally caught. Willy, clutching Poppy, threw himself backwards. They toppled, staggering down a bank into a ditch. As they splashed down Poppy shouted 'What did you do that for?' indignantly.

'I don't want to marry a Roman candle.' He pulled her along the ditch away from the blaze.

In the distance a fire engine raced, its siren blaring, spreading panic.

Presently, teeth chattering, wrapped in a dry blanket, she was in a police car with Willy. Somehow blessedly he had persuaded these authoritative people that there was no need for the hospital, they could skip it and after answering questions go home.

Aeons later, awash with sweet tea, still wrapped in a blanket, she was standing beside Willy watching the police car drive away.

Last night's fog was reduced to swags of mist circling round the willows along the stream running through the meadow. A pair of mallard flew up and away with a quack. A rosy sun was swinging up the sky. A bantam cock crowed in the barn.

Calypso's dog, loosed for his morning run, ran over the grass to greet them. A faint smell of pig, sounds of rustling straw, contented grunts and chomping jaws drifted across the yard.

'We both need baths. I'll put a match to the fires.'

'Might I meet Mrs Future and her aunt first?'

'Of course.'

Willy, watching her walk barefoot across the cobbles, almost choked with emotion. She was so filthy. She looked so comical. 'Here they are.'

The giant sows were spotless, their flanks pink, their sparse hair crisp and bristly. The row of pearly piglets ranged sleepy, each snout aimed at a teat ready for the next meal.

The sow rustled the straw with her trotters as Poppy leaned over and whispered into an arum lily ear, 'Hello, there.'

'Ham for breakfast?' suggested Willy lightly.

Poppy looked up. 'I realise I should feel flattered at being compared to Mrs F's aunt,' she said. 'I had not realised it was a compliment.'

Willy stared at her.

I must get this straight, he thought. She has taken my feeble joke as an insult. She's had a knock on the head, she is probably concussed. She looks too silly for words, I've made a terrible mess of her hair. I shall cut the other side to even it up, give her breakfast and a bath, borrow some clothes from Calypso and take her home. I should never have rushed her in this way. I can't even learn to behave from a pig. I have behaved exactly like that shit Edmund. I need my head examined. Well, there will be plenty of time for that in the years ahead, he thought bitterly. I've really loused this up.

'When I saw you at your father's funeral,' he said carefully, 'I fell in love with you. As far as I was concerned that was that. I realise I have behaved selfishly in trying to force you. Of course you have your own ideas about what you want to do with your life. I suggest you have a bath. I'll borrow some of my aunt's clothes for you and drive you home in her car as mine is wrecked. I hope you will perhaps remember you felt some of your time in Algiers was quite fun.'

'What's got into you?' cried Poppy. 'I don't want to borrow your aunt's clothes. I don't want to be driven anywhere in her car. If you want to get shot of me I'll hire a taxi.' She raised her voice to a shout. 'Any feelings I had in Algiers were mere hors d'oeuvres, but oh, Willy, could I have something real to eat before we get on with dinner?'

'At once,' said Willy, not trusting himself to say more.

As they crossed the yard to his cottage he looked at her sidelong. She looked so funny holding the blanket up to cover her breasts, nearly tripping as it trailed round her feet. She looked like some strange punk with hair topped from the left side of her head.

'I trust you won't be chopping and changing your mind,' he said. 'I don't think my nerves could stand it.'

'After this I shan't be placing any more bets,' she said. 'I'm not very good at it.'

Willy bent to kiss her, pushing her hair aside, tracing the streaks of oil down her face to her neck.

'One thing we don't need is all this lubrication. Let's get ourselves a bath, see whether we can manage without drowning, then breakfast, how's that?'

Later, eating breakfast, Willy, watching Poppy dressed now in one of his sweaters, her hair still damp from the bath, was seized by a terrible twinge of fear.

'If you *don't* like it here,' he said, 'you may rather live in London, I have a small house there.' He was prepared to give everything up, to sacrifice Mrs Future if Poppy would stay with him (he would of course never forgive her). Since lunching with his old cousin he had almost forgotten the house, his mind obsessed with Poppy; now he saw its value and offered it as a forlorn alternative.

Poppy flushed. 'I don't need bribing. When I changed my mind, wouldn't come back here with you, I was under the delusion that what I wanted was a lover, a pleasure man. I thought I might try Victor or Fergus or both.' She watched Willy (if I said anything like this to Edmund he would black my eye and be off to Venetia). 'Stuck under that lorry I realised that it wasn't just pleasure I wanted, I want the lot. Right?' Have I said too much, been, as usual, a fool? She looked away, afraid of meeting Willy's eyes.

But Willy was laughing, ebullient with relief. 'I foresee lots of pleasure,' he said, 'as well as the rest. Besides,' he went on, containing his mirth, able now to tease, 'those two jokers are fully booked.'